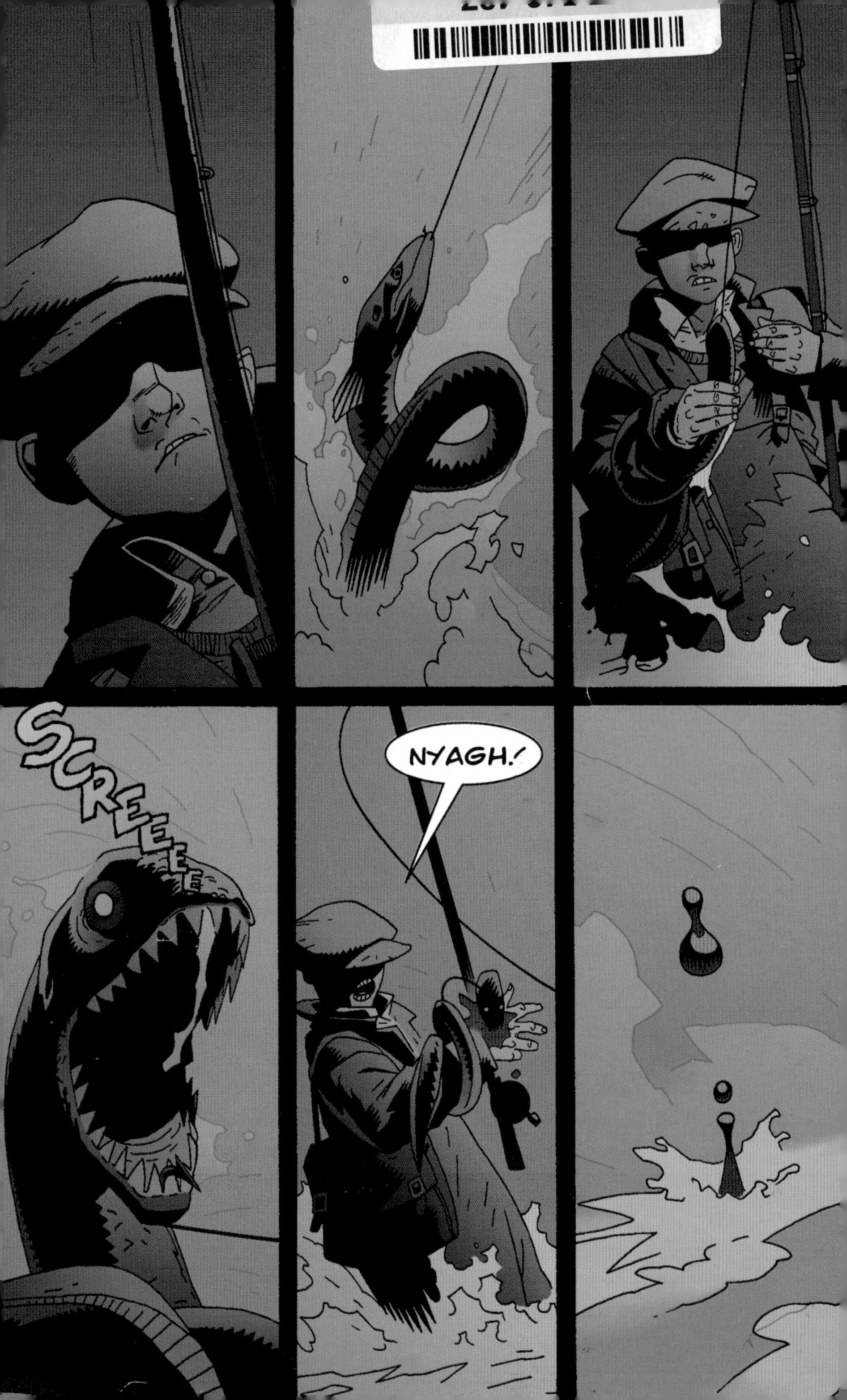
SCREEEEE
NYAGH!

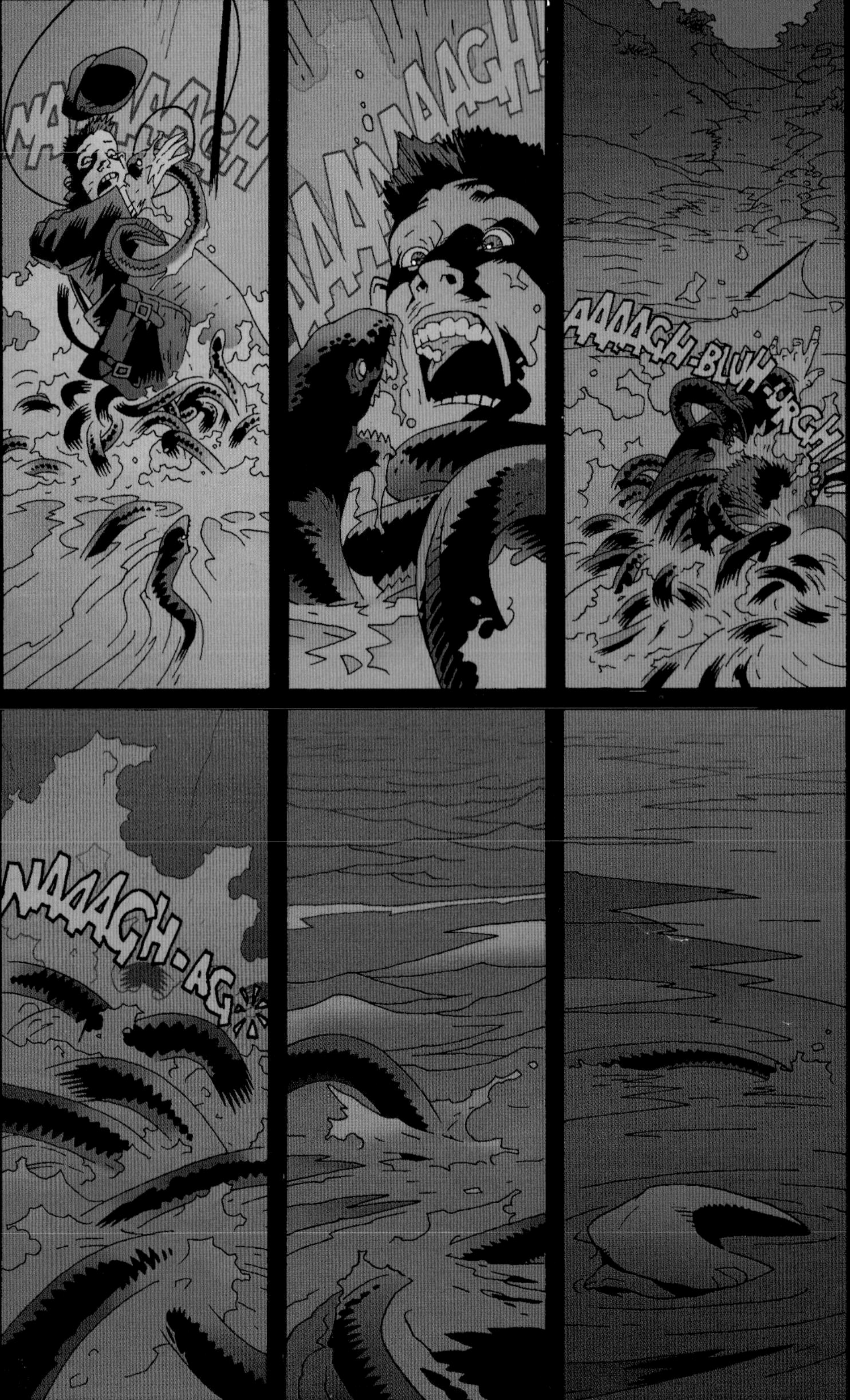
NAAAAACH
AAAAAAAAAACH!
AAAAACH-BLUH-URCH!!
NAAACH-AG

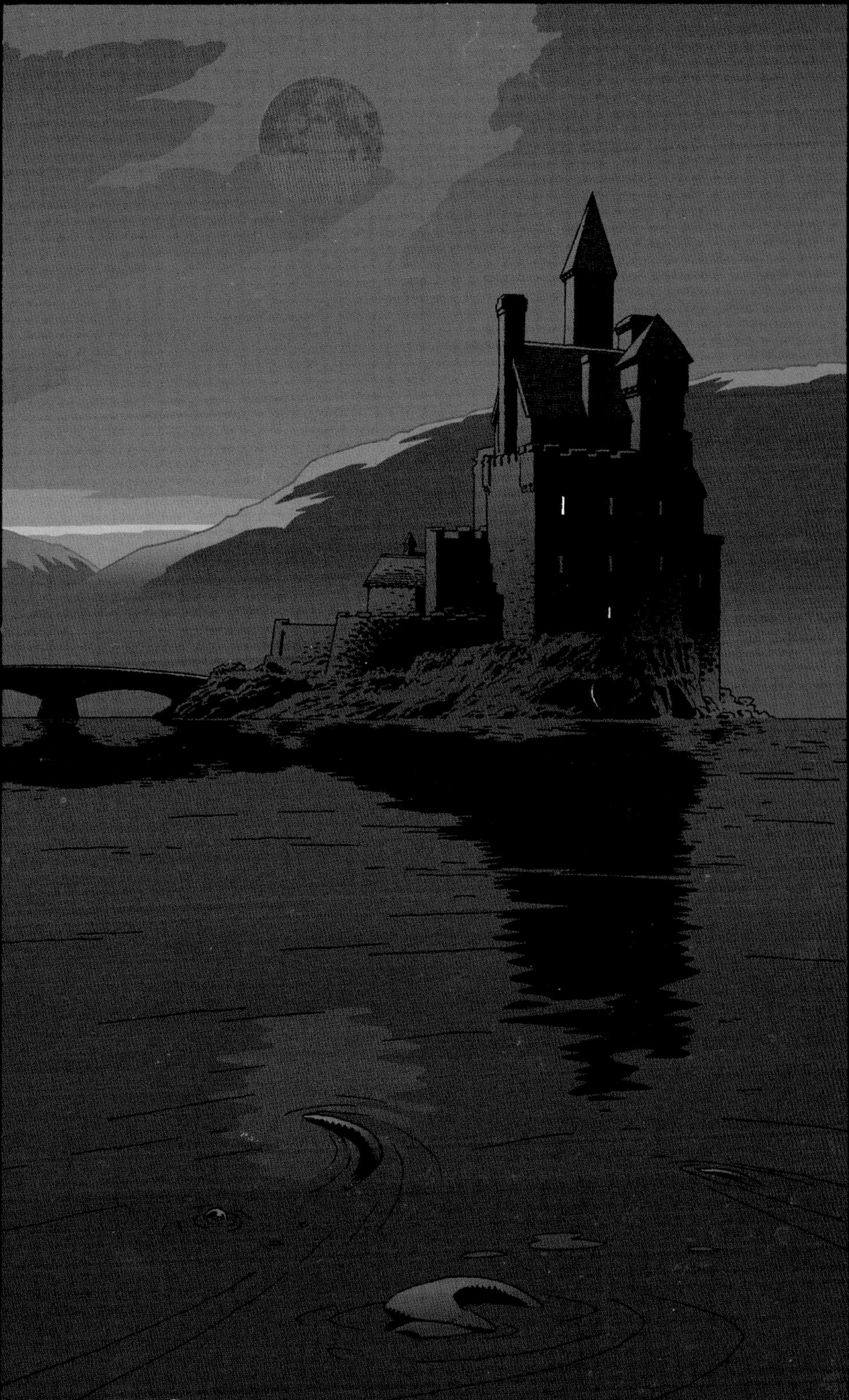

CHARLIE HIGSON & KEV WALKER

SILVERFIN

THE GRAPHIC NOVEL

PUFFIN

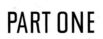

PART ONE

ETON

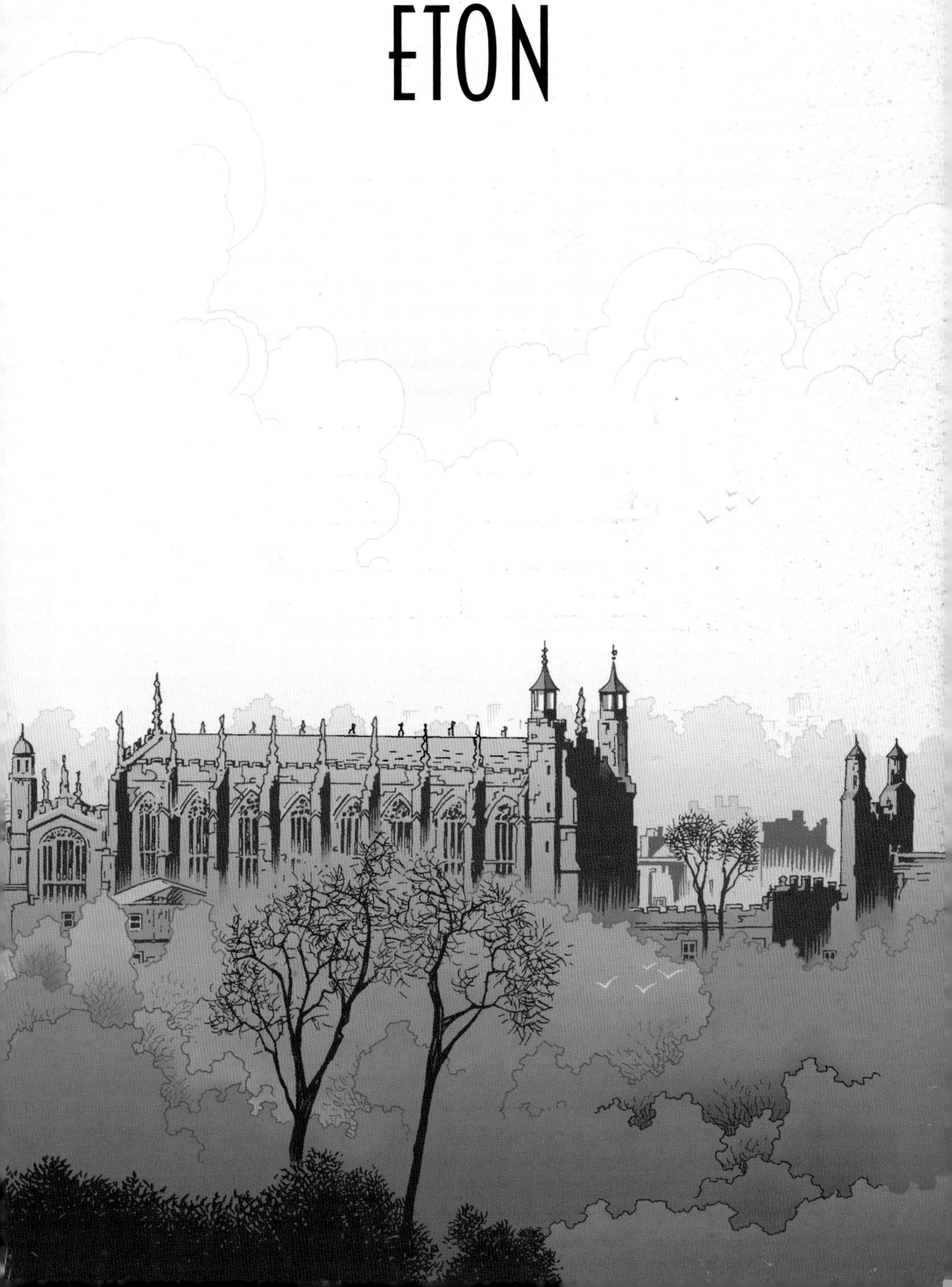

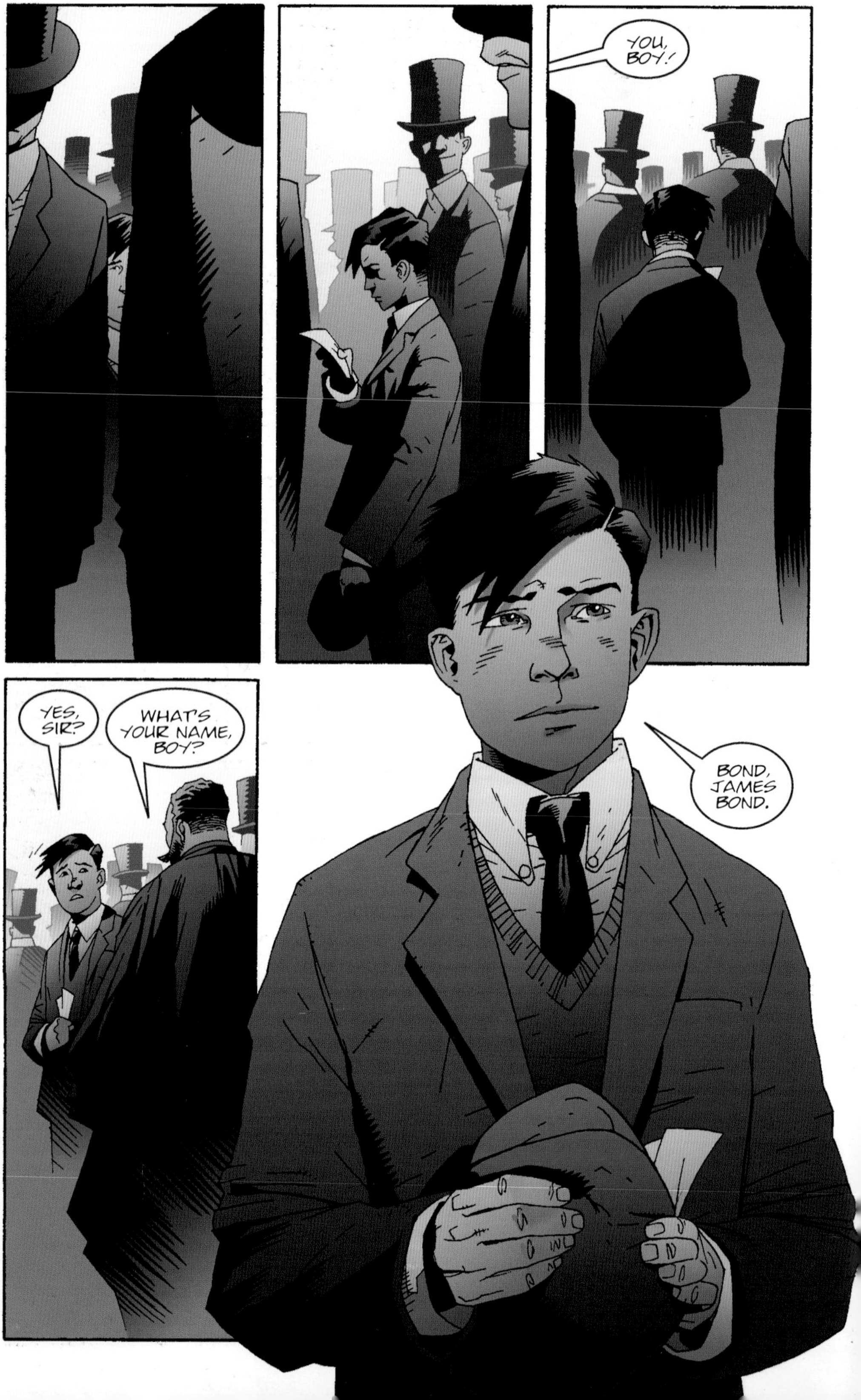
YOU, BOY!
YES, SIR?
WHAT'S YOUR NAME, BOY?
BOND, JAMES BOND.

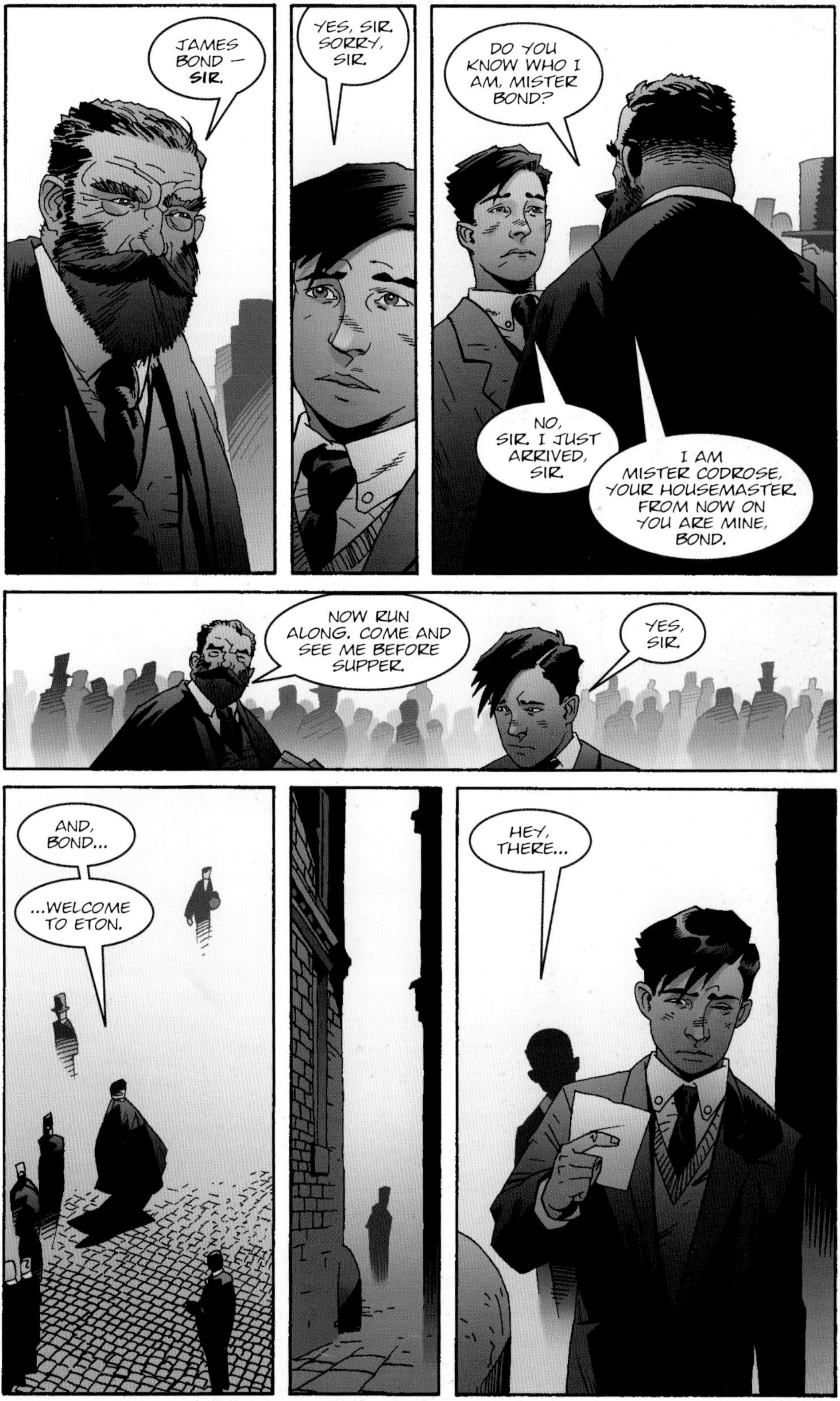
JAMES BOND — **SIR.**
YES, SIR. SORRY, SIR.
DO YOU KNOW WHO I AM, MISTER BOND?
NO, SIR. I JUST ARRIVED, SIR.
I AM MISTER CODROSE, YOUR HOUSEMASTER. FROM NOW ON YOU ARE MINE, BOND.
NOW RUN ALONG. COME AND SEE ME BEFORE SUPPER.
YES, SIR.
AND, BOND...
...WELCOME TO ETON.
HEY, THERE...

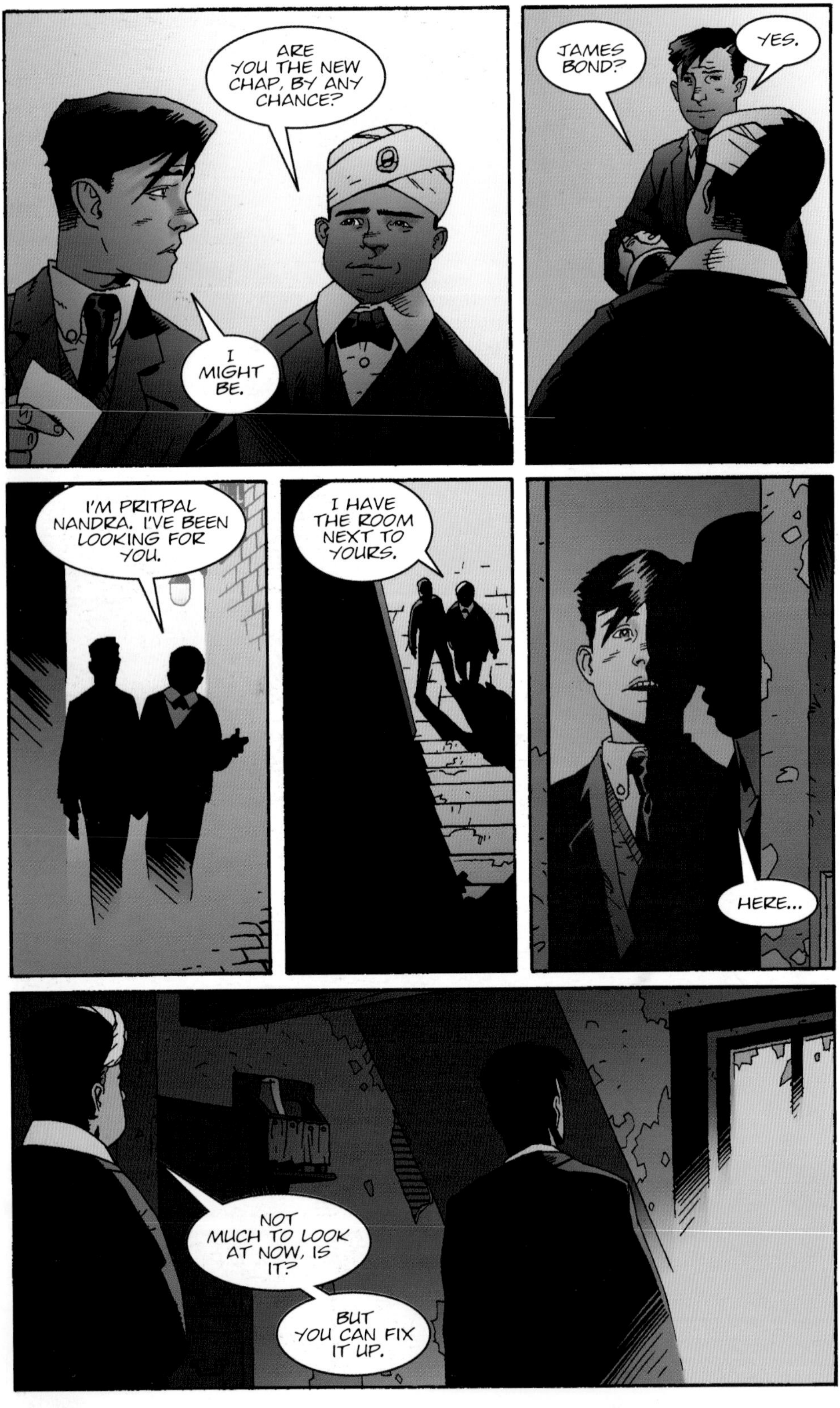
ARE YOU THE NEW CHAP, BY ANY CHANCE?
I MIGHT BE.
JAMES BOND?
YES.
I'M PRITPAL NANDRA. I'VE BEEN LOOKING FOR YOU.
I HAVE THE ROOM NEXT TO YOURS.
HERE...
NOT MUCH TO LOOK AT NOW, IS IT?
BUT YOU CAN FIX IT UP.

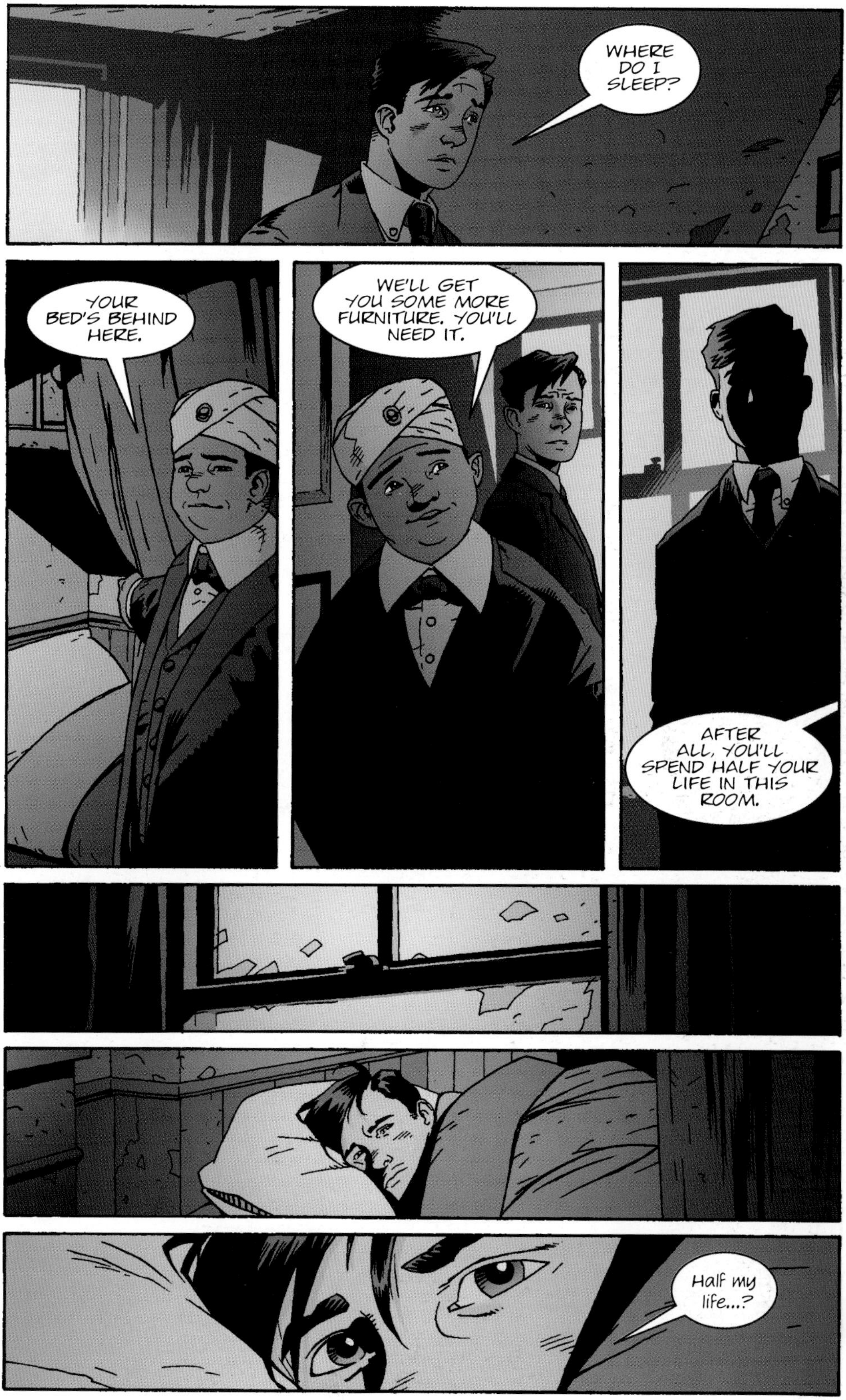
WHERE DO I SLEEP?
YOUR BED'S BEHIND HERE.
WE'LL GET YOU SOME MORE FURNITURE. YOU'LL NEED IT.
AFTER ALL, YOU'LL SPEND HALF YOUR LIFE IN THIS ROOM.
Half my life...?

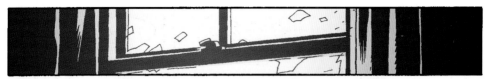

WAKEY, WAKEY. RISE AN' SHINE, YOU LAZY LUMP.

SPLASH!!

WHA....!

TIME TO GET UP, MISTER BOND.

OH...YES... RIGHT.

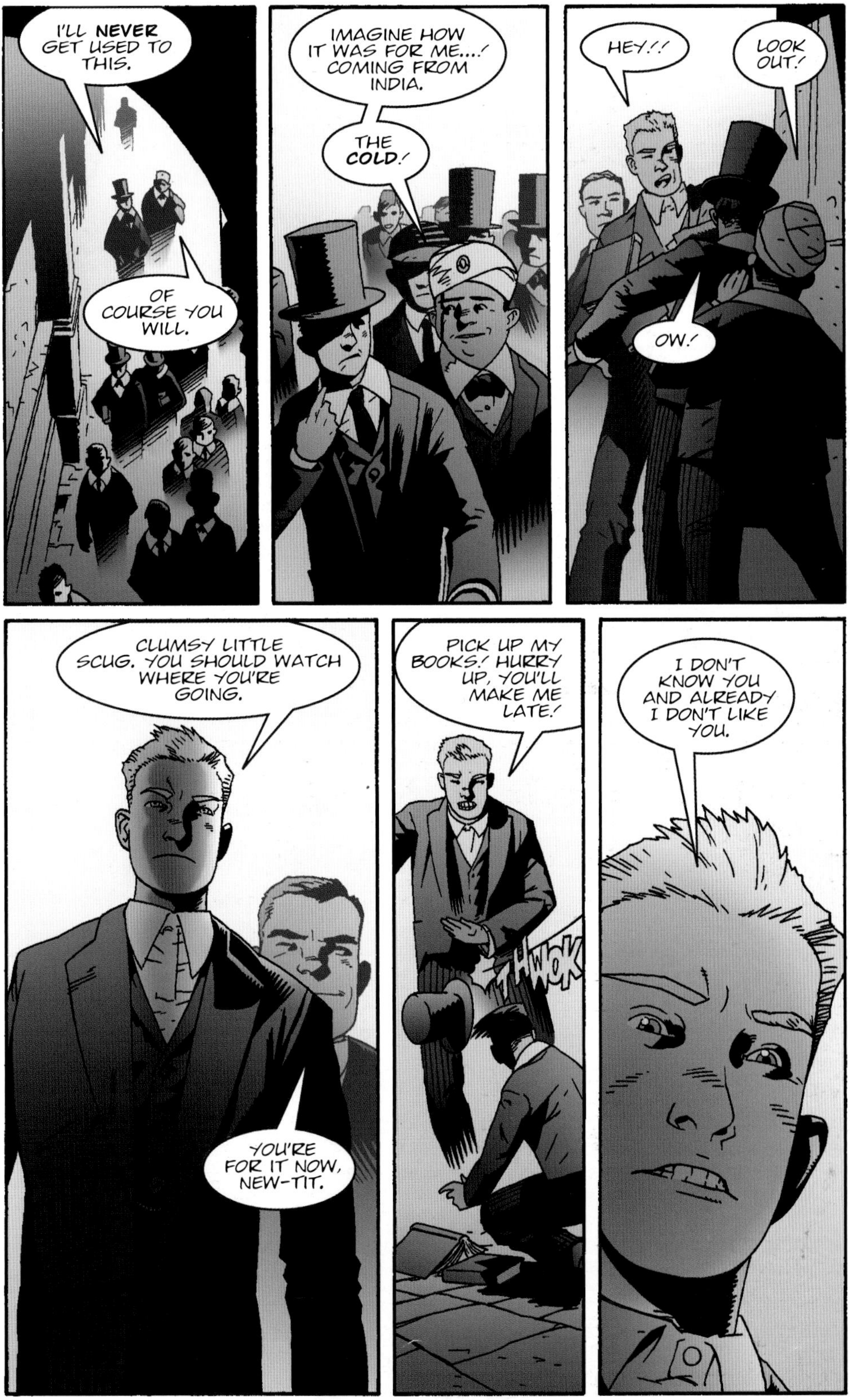
I'LL **NEVER** GET USED TO THIS.
OF COURSE YOU WILL.
IMAGINE HOW IT WAS FOR ME...! COMING FROM INDIA.
THE **COLD**!
HEY!!
LOOK OUT!
OW!
CLUMSY LITTLE SCUG. YOU SHOULD WATCH WHERE YOU'RE GOING.
YOU'RE FOR IT NOW, NEW-TIT.
PICK UP MY BOOKS! HURRY UP, YOU'LL MAKE ME LATE!
THWOK
I DON'T KNOW YOU AND ALREADY I DON'T LIKE YOU.

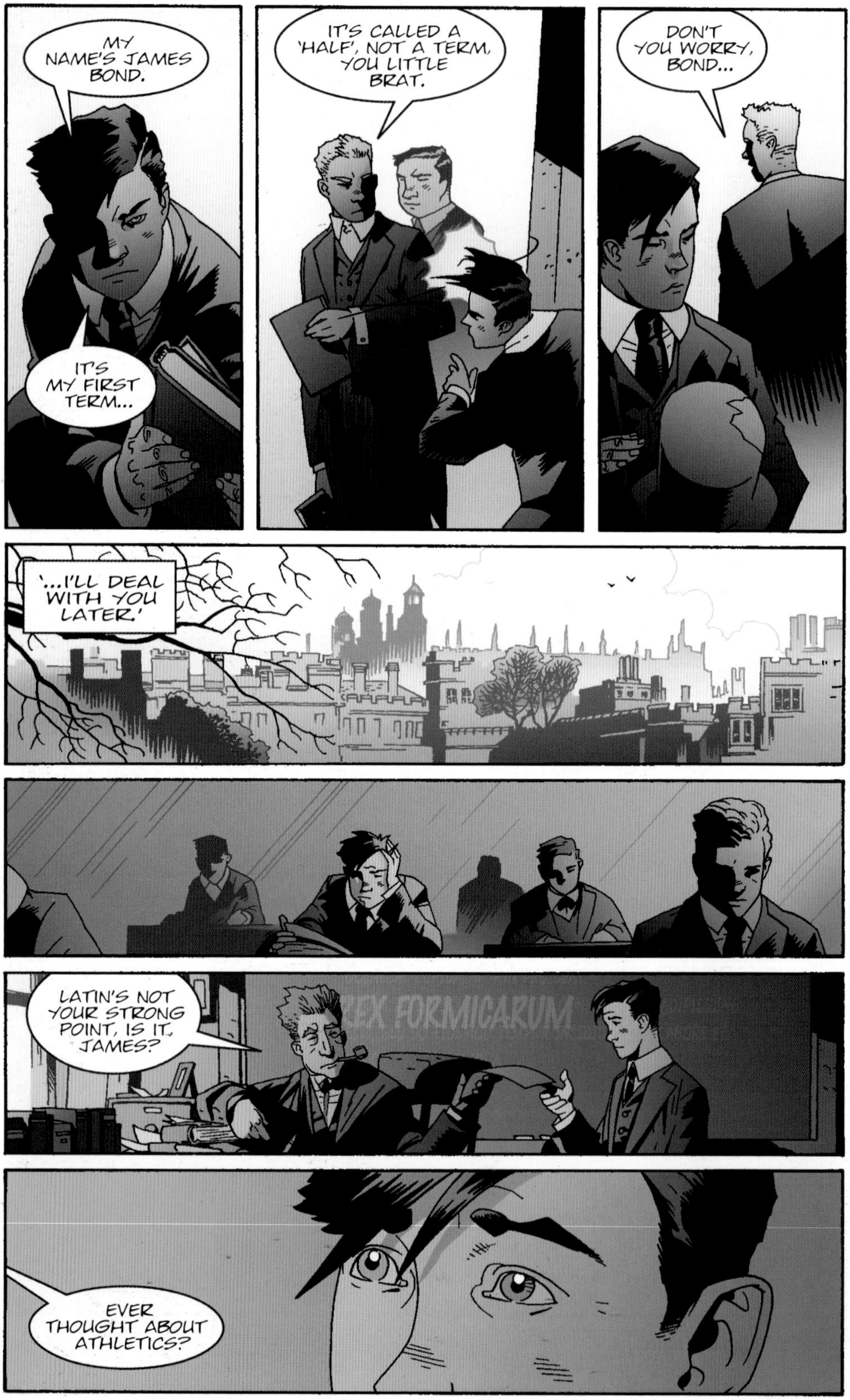
MY NAME'S JAMES BOND.
IT'S MY FIRST TERM...
IT'S CALLED A 'HALF', NOT A TERM, YOU LITTLE BRAT.
DON'T YOU WORRY, BOND...
'...I'LL DEAL WITH YOU LATER.'
LATIN'S NOT YOUR STRONG POINT, IS IT, JAMES?
REX FORMICARUM
EVER THOUGHT ABOUT ATHLETICS?

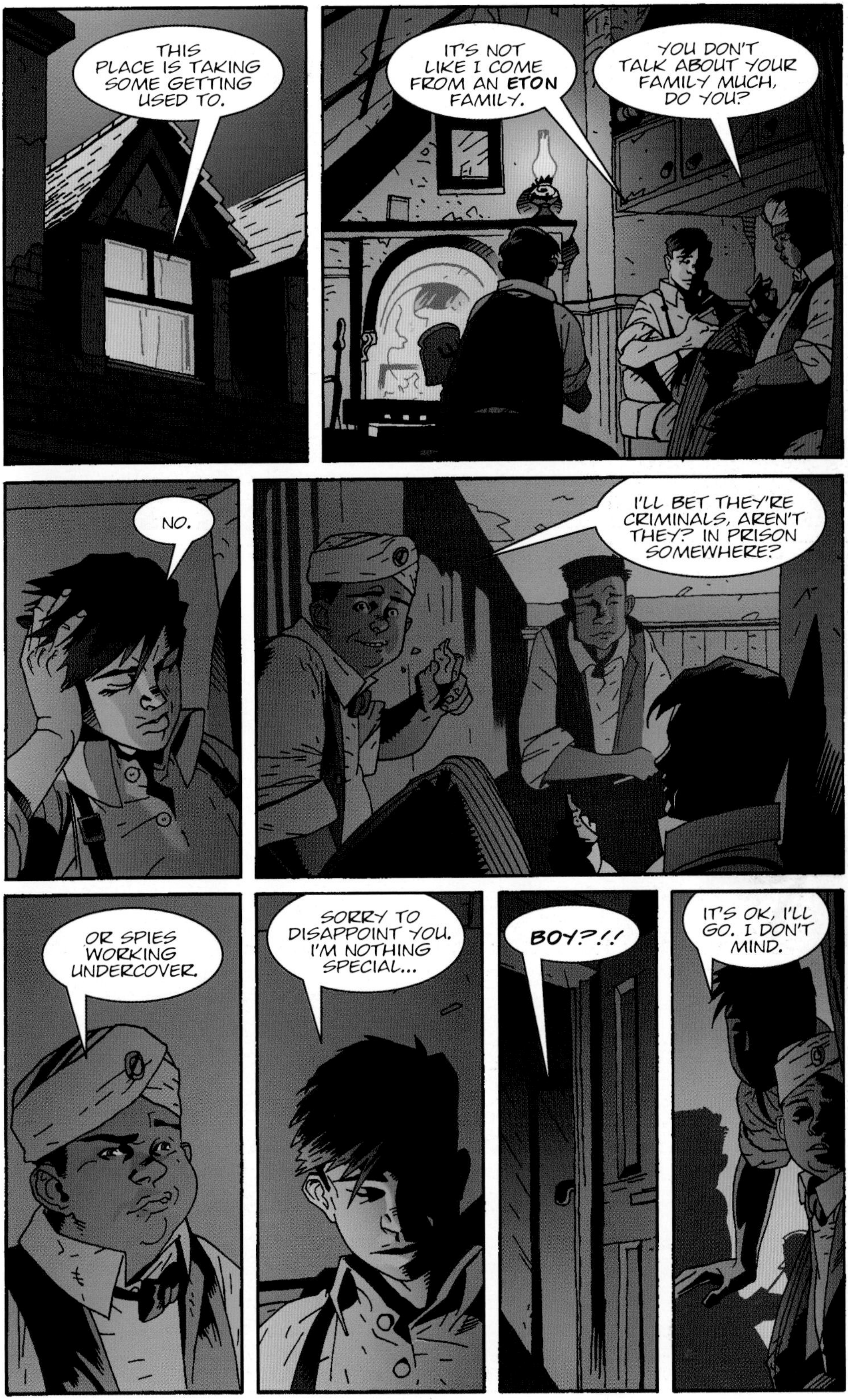
THIS PLACE IS TAKING SOME GETTING USED TO.
IT'S NOT LIKE I COME FROM AN ETON FAMILY.
YOU DON'T TALK ABOUT YOUR FAMILY MUCH, DO YOU?
NO.
I'LL BET THEY'RE CRIMINALS, AREN'T THEY? IN PRISON SOMEWHERE?
OR SPIES WORKING UNDERCOVER.
SORRY TO DISAPPOINT YOU. I'M NOTHING SPECIAL...
BOY?!!
IT'S OK, I'LL GO. I DON'T MIND.

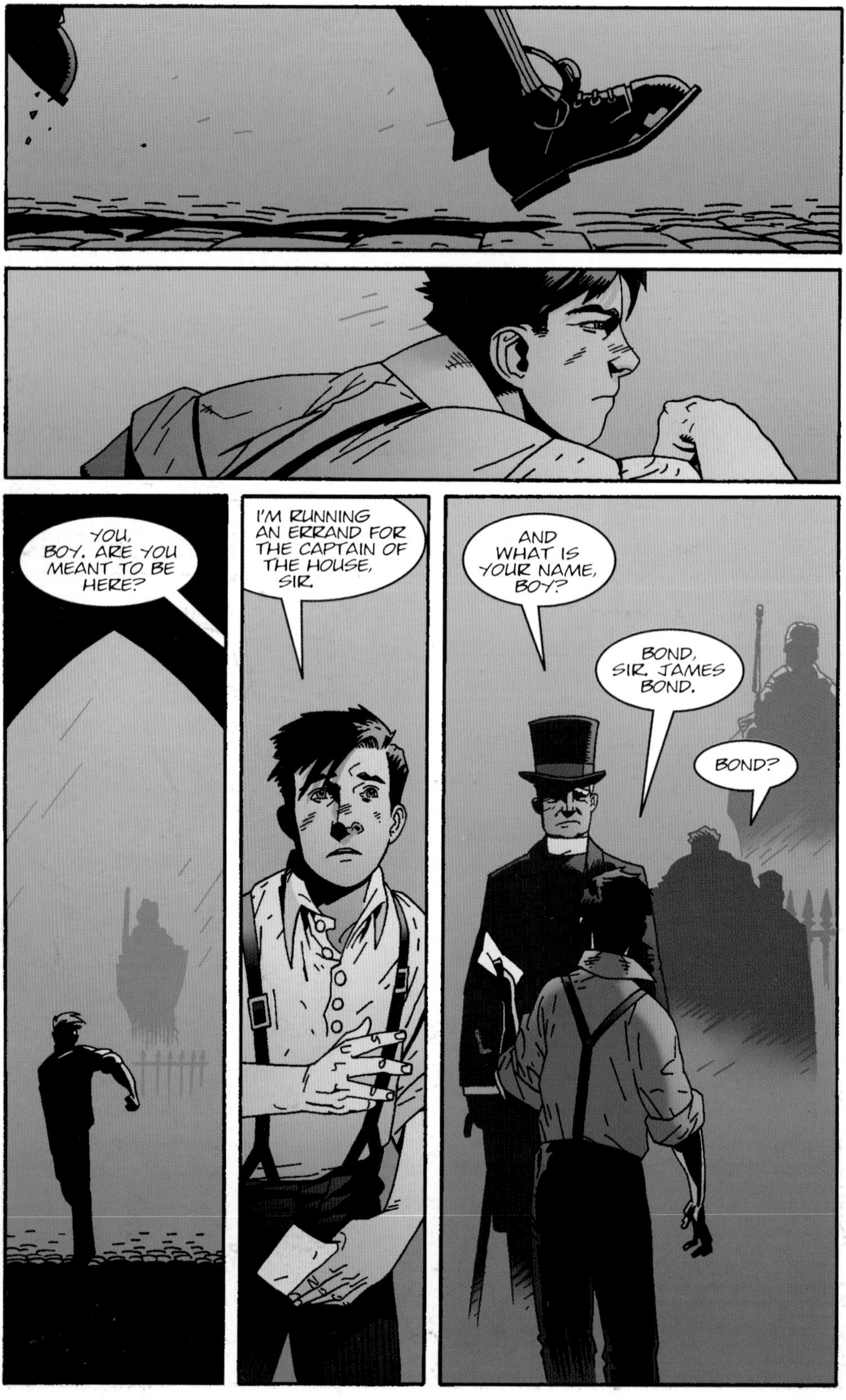
YOU, BOY. ARE YOU MEANT TO BE HERE?
I'M RUNNING AN ERRAND FOR THE CAPTAIN OF THE HOUSE, SIR.
AND WHAT IS YOUR NAME, BOY?
BOND, SIR. JAMES BOND.
BOND?

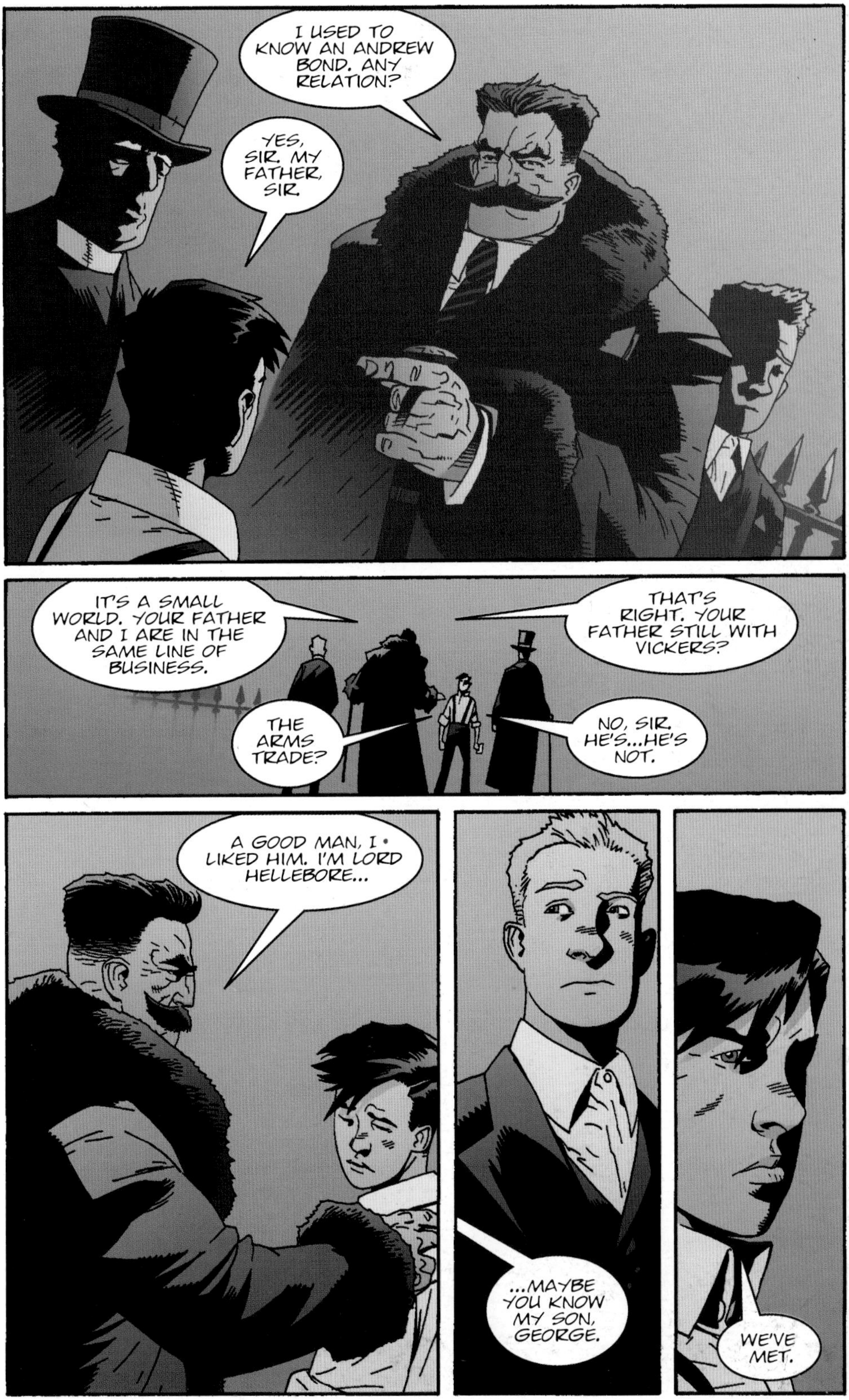
I USED TO KNOW AN ANDREW BOND. ANY RELATION?
YES, SIR. MY FATHER, SIR.
IT'S A SMALL WORLD. YOUR FATHER AND I ARE IN THE SAME LINE OF BUSINESS.
THE ARMS TRADE?
THAT'S RIGHT. YOUR FATHER STILL WITH VICKERS?
NO, SIR. HE'S...HE'S NOT.
A GOOD MAN, I LIKED HIM. I'M LORD HELLEBORE...
...MAYBE YOU KNOW MY SON, GEORGE.
WE'VE MET.

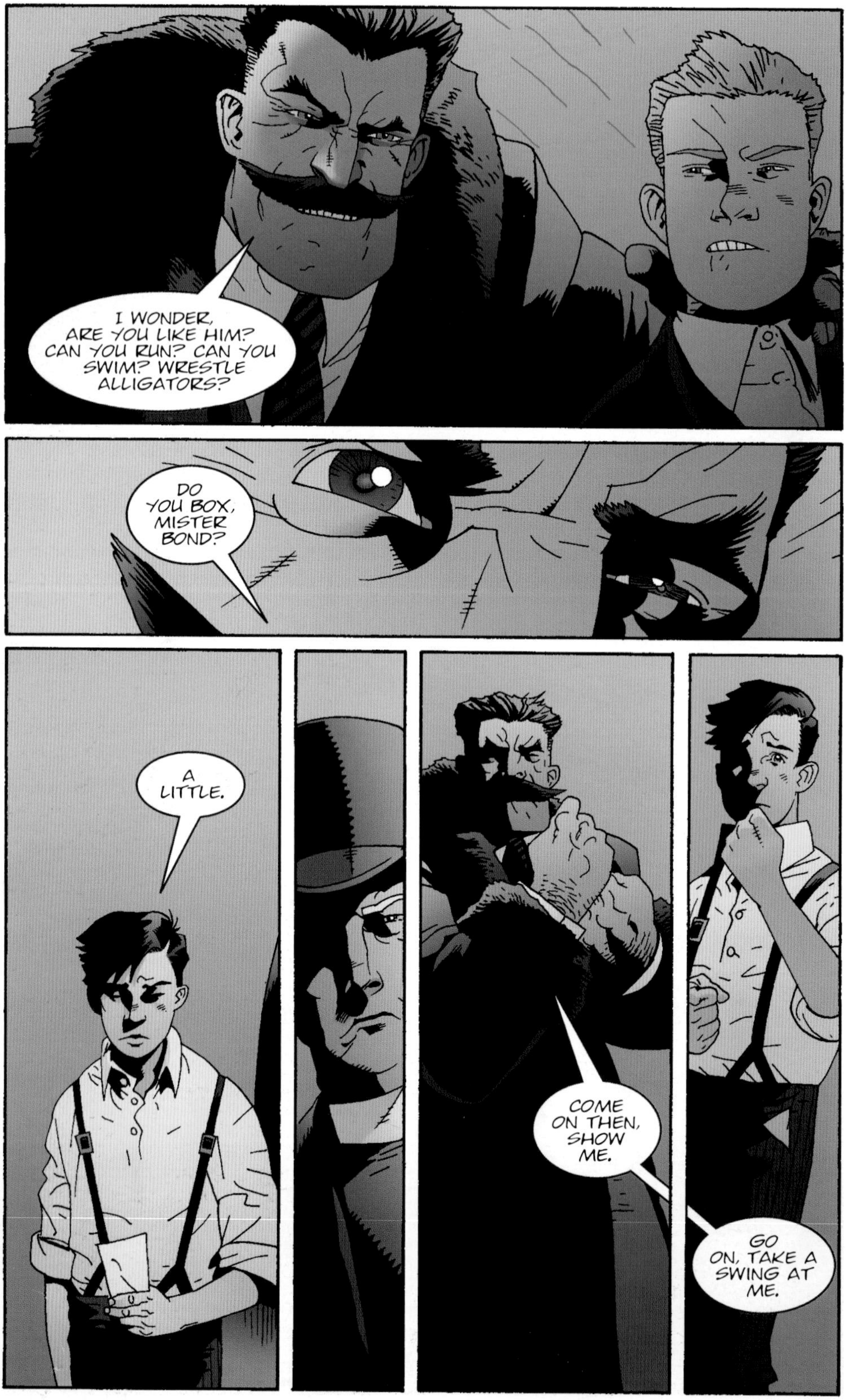
I WONDER, ARE YOU LIKE HIM? CAN YOU RUN? CAN YOU SWIM? WRESTLE ALLIGATORS?
DO YOU BOX, MISTER BOND?
A LITTLE.
COME ON THEN, SHOW ME.
GO ON, TAKE A SWING AT ME.

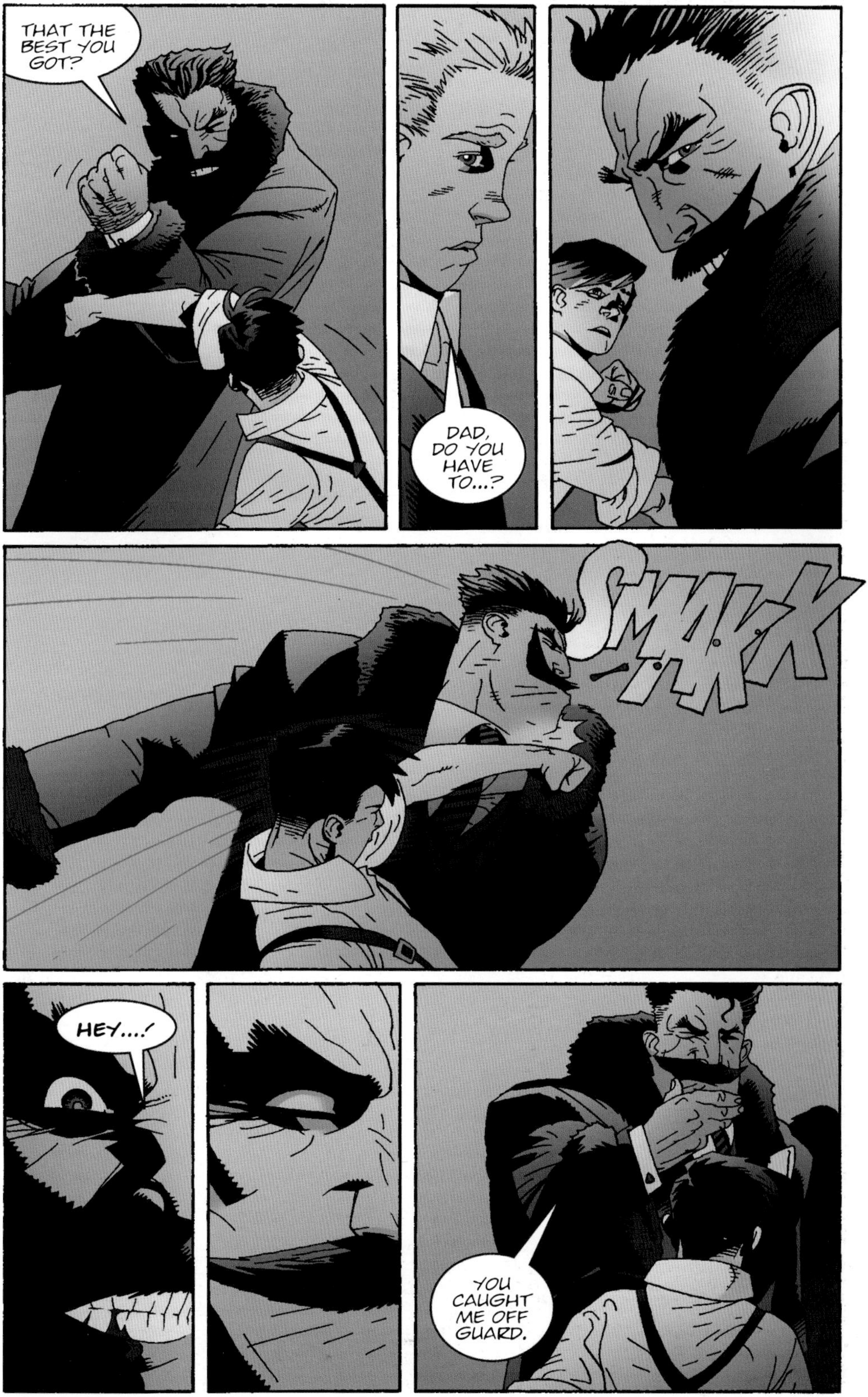
THAT THE BEST YOU GOT?
DAD, DO YOU HAVE TO...?
SMAK-K
HEY...!
YOU CAUGHT ME OFF GUARD.

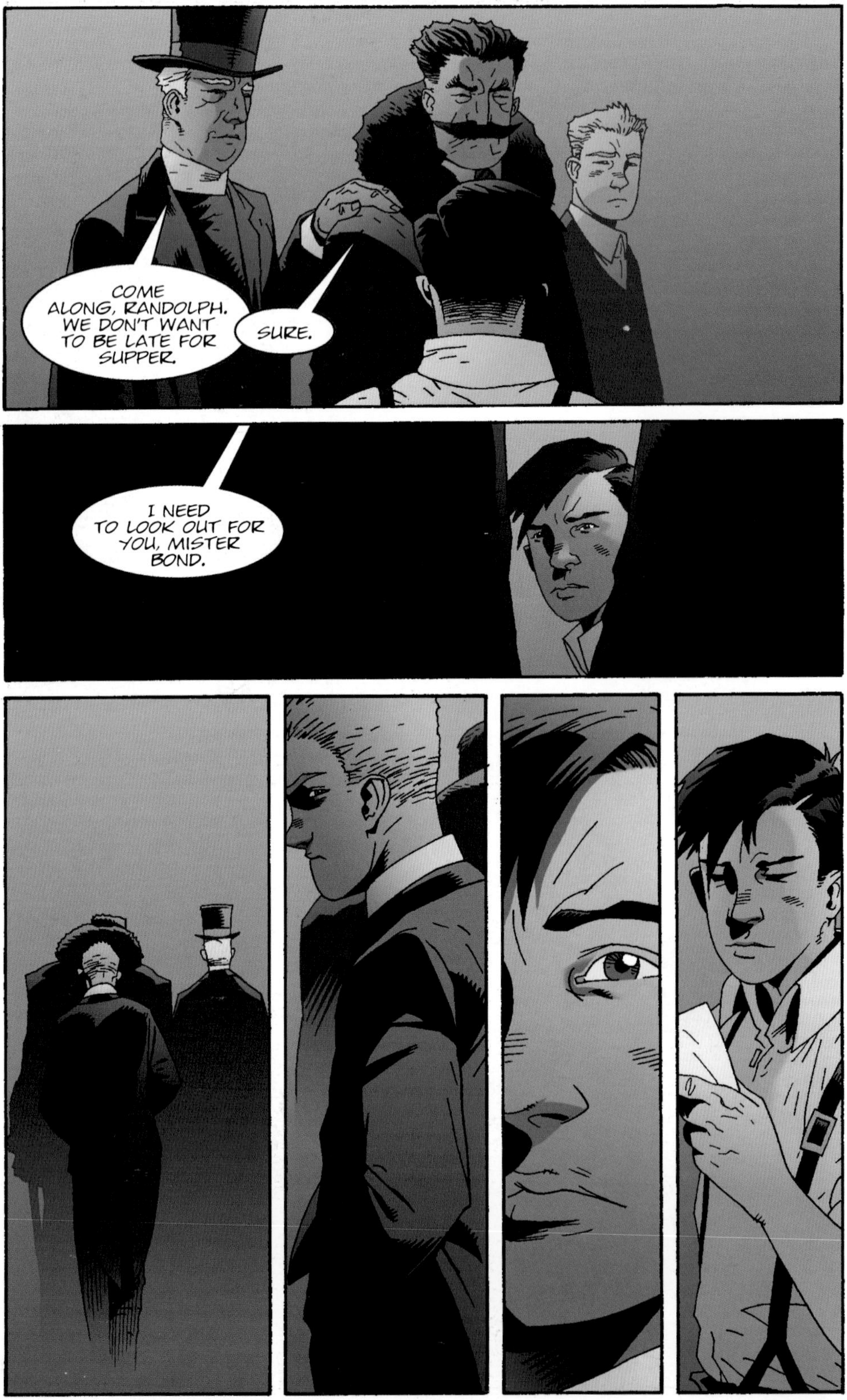
COME ALONG, RANDOLPH. WE DON'T WANT TO BE LATE FOR SUPPER.
SURE.
I NEED TO LOOK OUT FOR YOU, MISTER BOND.

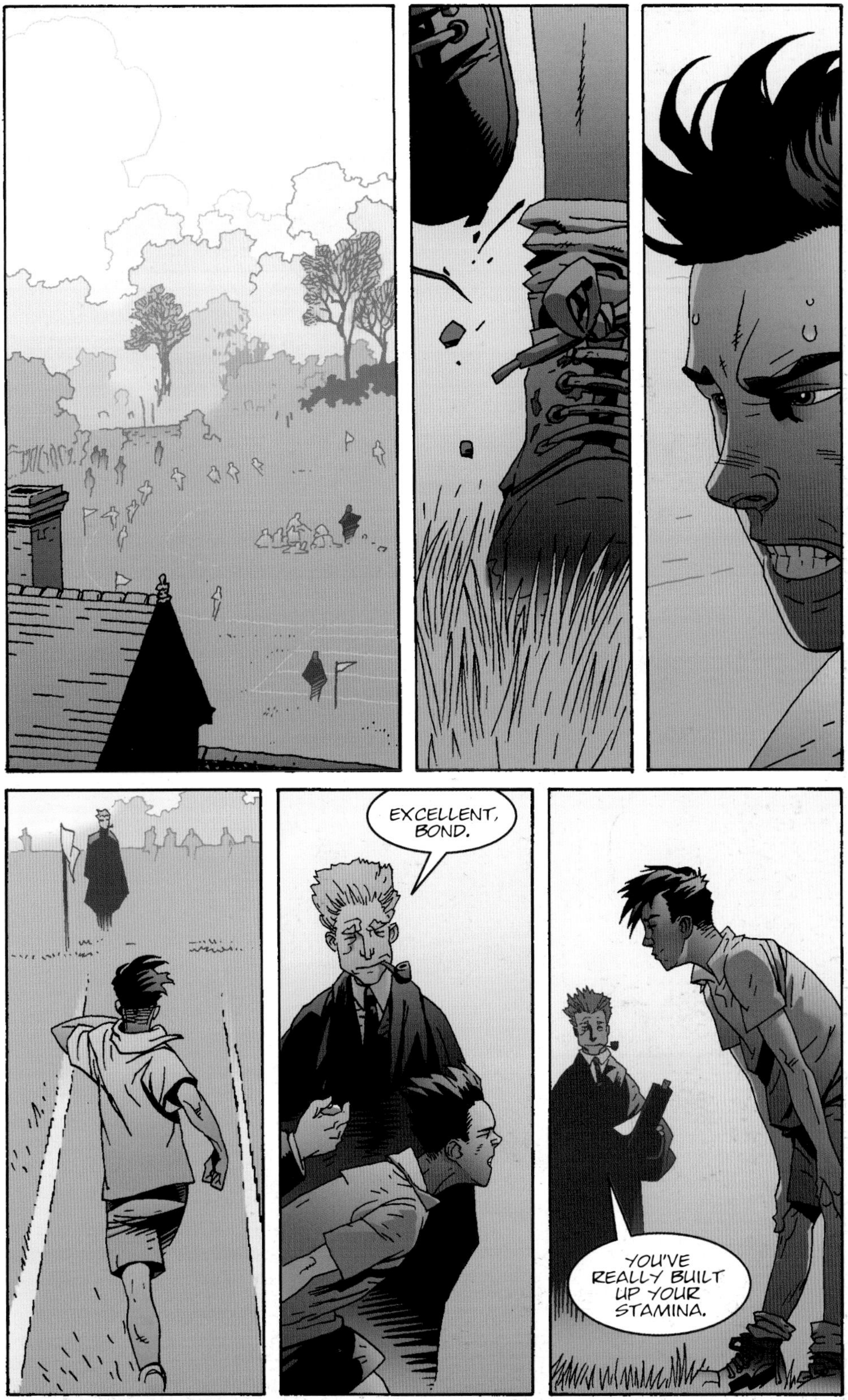
EXCELLENT, BOND.
YOU'VE REALLY BUILT UP YOUR STAMINA.

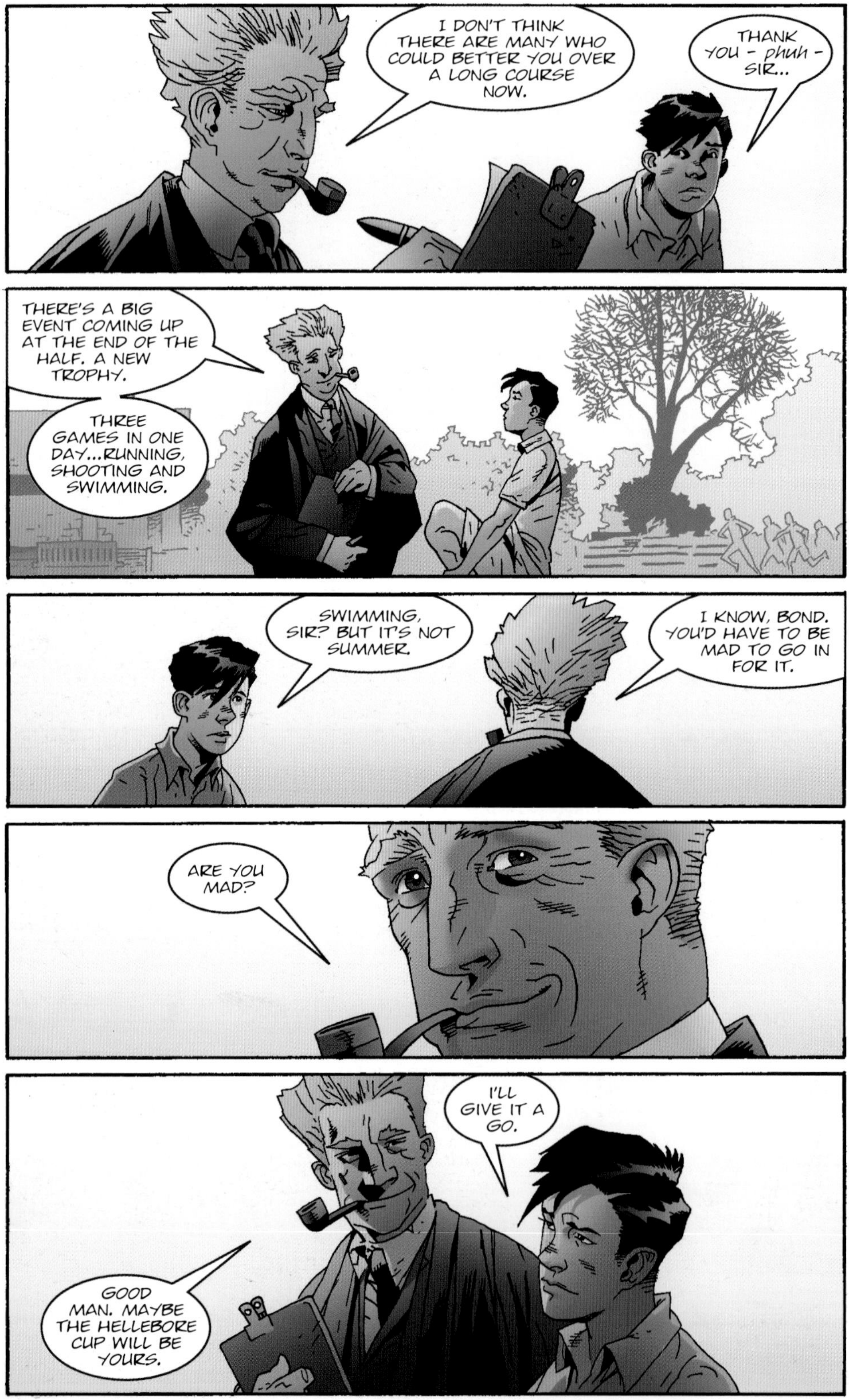
I DON'T THINK THERE ARE MANY WHO COULD BETTER YOU OVER A LONG COURSE NOW.
THANK YOU - phuh - SIR...
THERE'S A BIG EVENT COMING UP AT THE END OF THE HALF. A NEW TROPHY.
THREE GAMES IN ONE DAY...RUNNING, SHOOTING AND SWIMMING.
SWIMMING, SIR? BUT IT'S NOT SUMMER.
I KNOW, BOND. YOU'D HAVE TO BE MAD TO GO IN FOR IT.
ARE YOU MAD?
I'LL GIVE IT A GO.
GOOD MAN. MAYBE THE HELLEBORE CUP WILL BE YOURS.

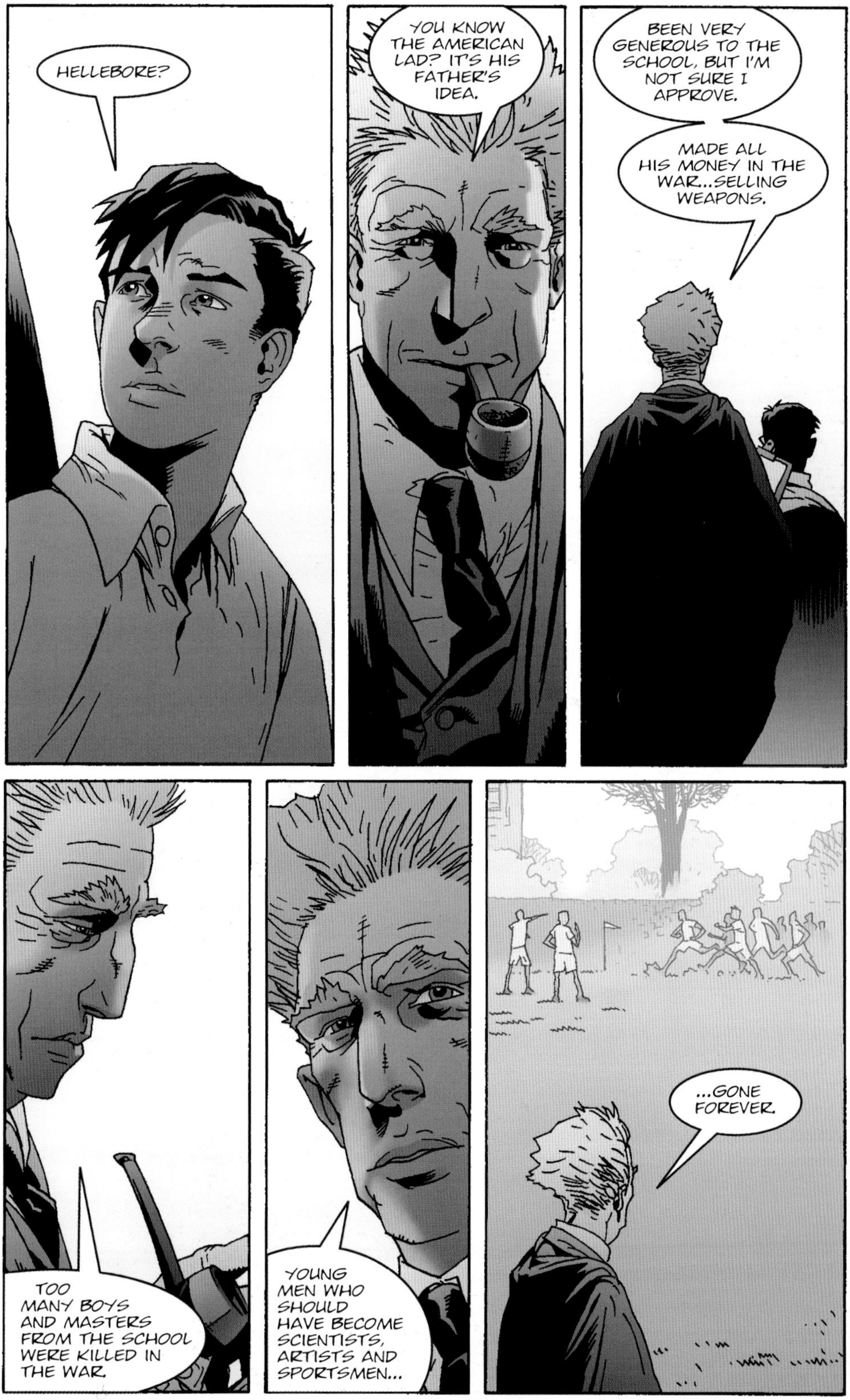
HELLEBORE?
YOU KNOW THE AMERICAN LAD? IT'S HIS FATHER'S IDEA.
BEEN VERY GENEROUS TO THE SCHOOL, BUT I'M NOT SURE I APPROVE.
MADE ALL HIS MONEY IN THE WAR...SELLING WEAPONS.
TOO MANY BOYS AND MASTERS FROM THE SCHOOL WERE KILLED IN THE WAR.
YOUNG MEN WHO SHOULD HAVE BECOME SCIENTISTS, ARTISTS AND SPORTSMEN...
...GONE FOREVER.

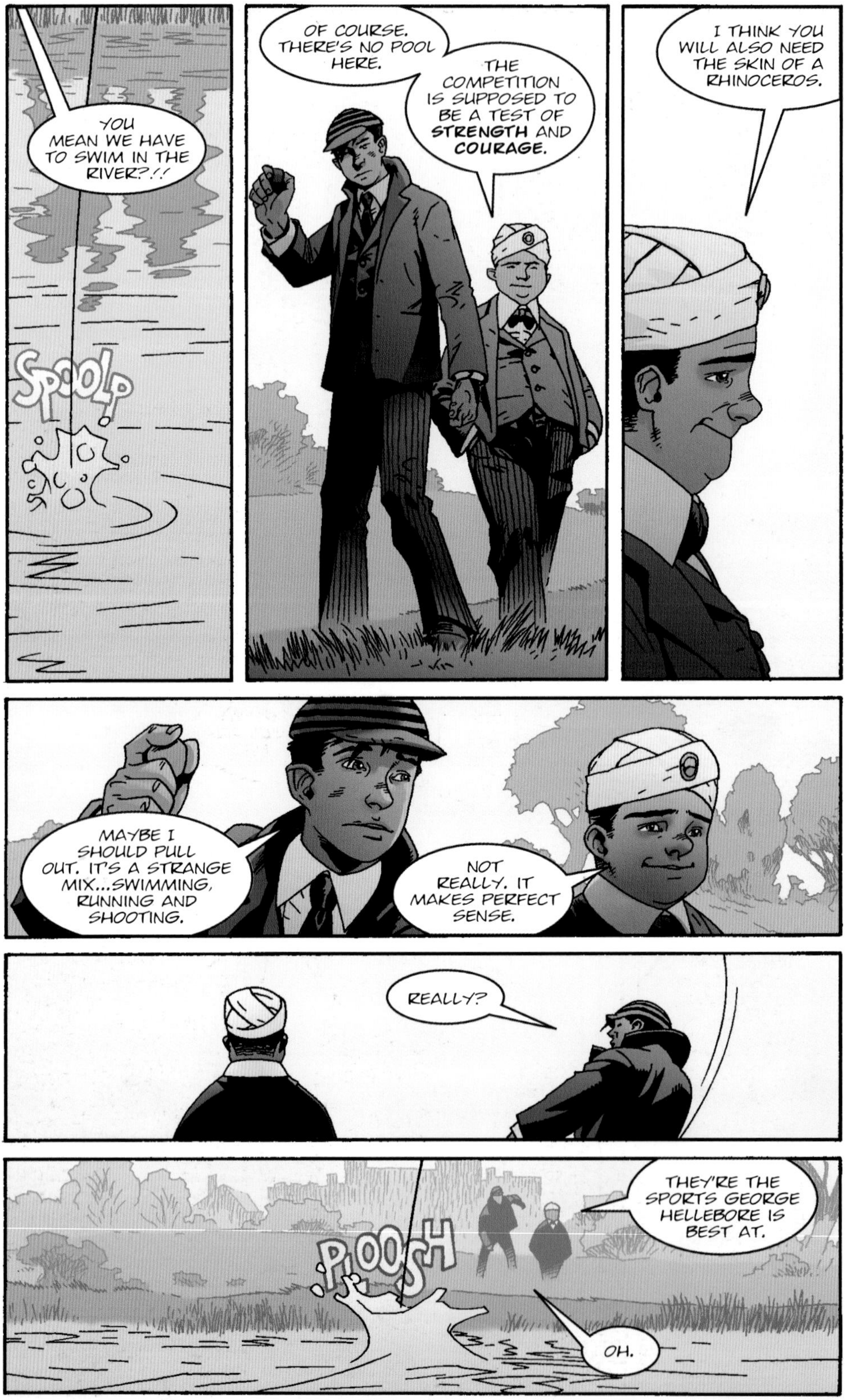
YOU MEAN WE HAVE TO SWIM IN THE RIVER?!!
SPOOLP
OF COURSE. THERE'S NO POOL HERE.
THE COMPETITION IS SUPPOSED TO BE A TEST OF STRENGTH AND COURAGE.
I THINK YOU WILL ALSO NEED THE SKIN OF A RHINOCEROS.
MAYBE I SHOULD PULL OUT. IT'S A STRANGE MIX...SWIMMING, RUNNING AND SHOOTING.
NOT REALLY. IT MAKES PERFECT SENSE.
REALLY?
THEY'RE THE SPORTS GEORGE HELLEBORE IS BEST AT.
PLOOSH
OH.

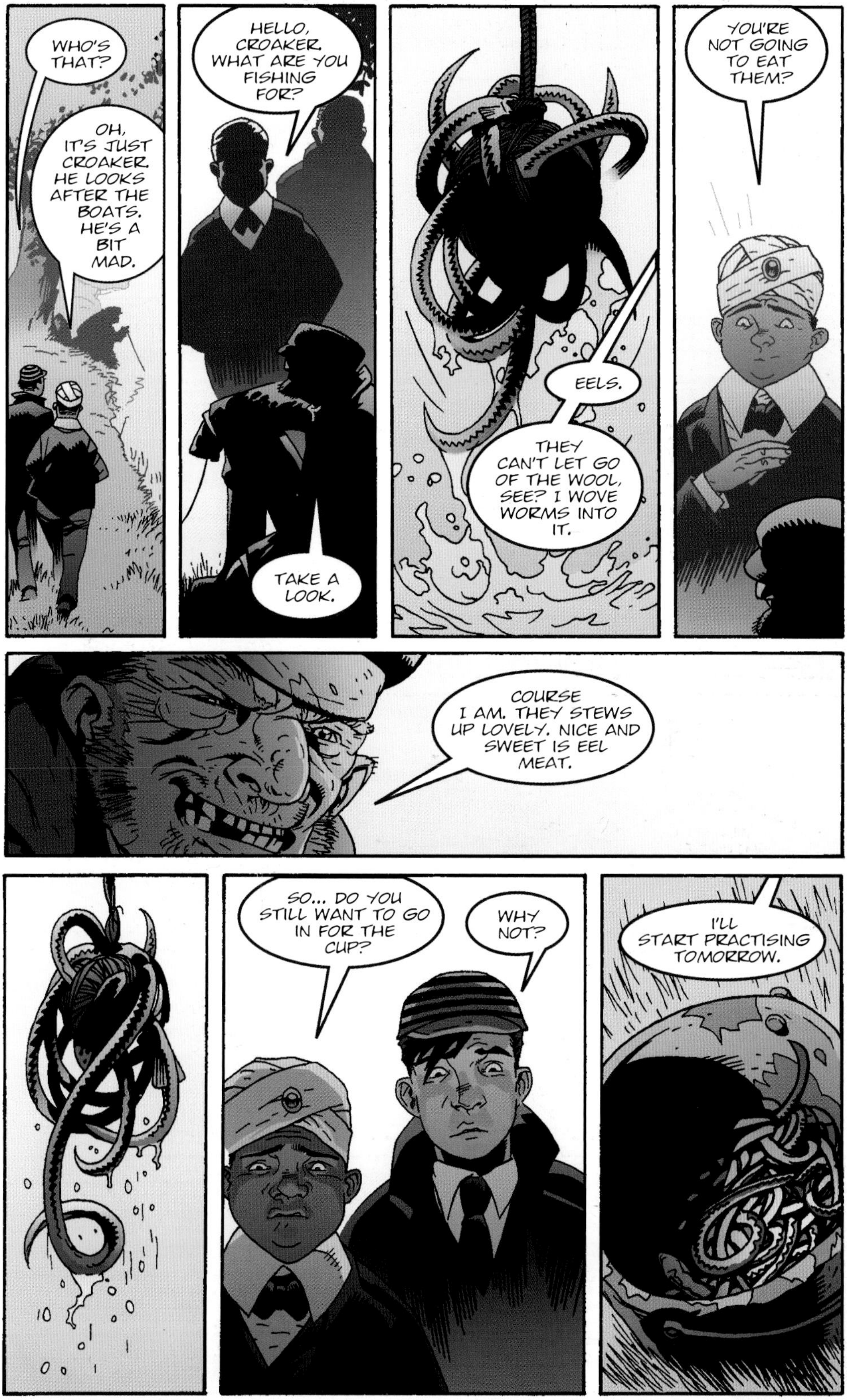
WHO'S THAT?
OH, IT'S JUST CROAKER. HE LOOKS AFTER THE BOATS. HE'S A BIT MAD.
HELLO, CROAKER. WHAT ARE YOU FISHING FOR?
TAKE A LOOK.
EELS.
THEY CAN'T LET GO OF THE WOOL, SEE? I WOVE WORMS INTO IT.
YOU'RE NOT GOING TO EAT THEM?
COURSE I AM. THEY STEWS UP LOVELY. NICE AND SWEET IS EEL MEAT.
SO... DO YOU STILL WANT TO GO IN FOR THE CUP?
WHY NOT?
I'LL START PRACTISING TOMORROW.

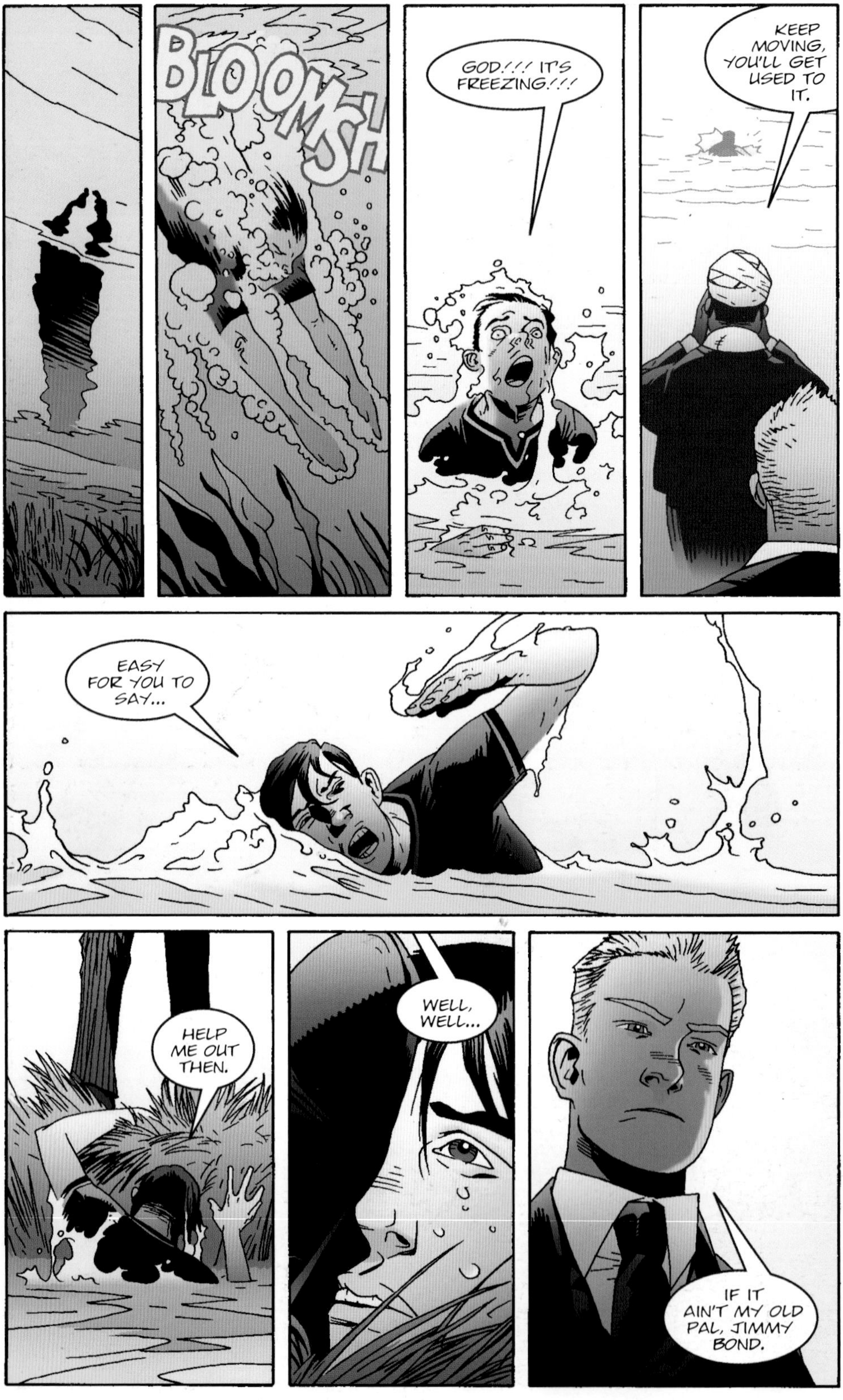
BLOOMSH
GOD!!! IT'S FREEZING!!!
KEEP MOVING, YOU'LL GET USED TO IT.
EASY FOR YOU TO SAY...
HELP ME OUT THEN.
WELL, WELL...
IF IT AIN'T MY OLD PAL, JIMMY BOND.

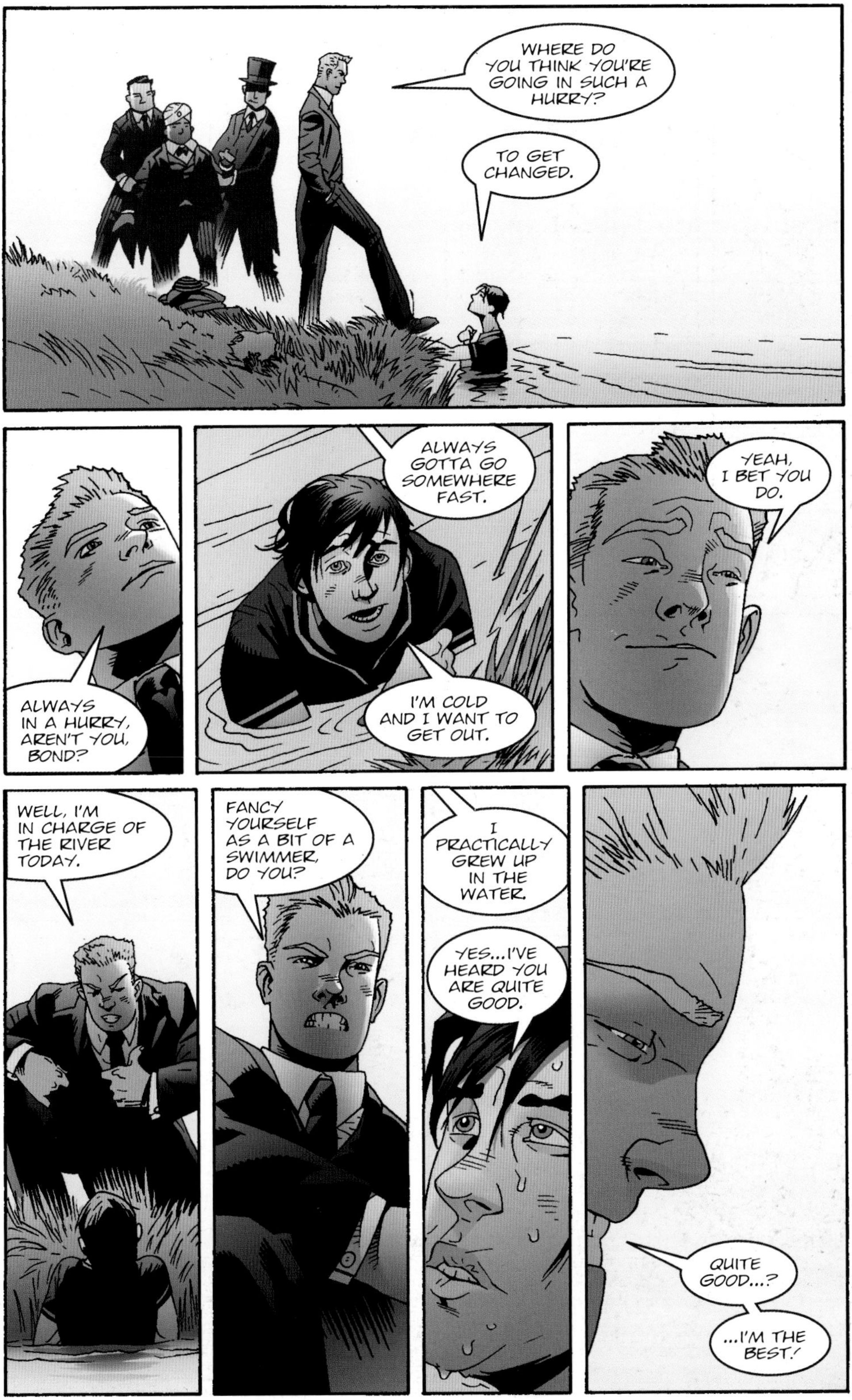
WHERE DO YOU THINK YOU'RE GOING IN SUCH A HURRY?
TO GET CHANGED.
ALWAYS IN A HURRY, AREN'T YOU, BOND?
ALWAYS GOTTA GO SOMEWHERE FAST.
I'M COLD AND I WANT TO GET OUT.
YEAH, I BET YOU DO.
WELL, I'M IN CHARGE OF THE RIVER TODAY.
FANCY YOURSELF AS A BIT OF A SWIMMER, DO YOU?
I PRACTICALLY GREW UP IN THE WATER.
YES...I'VE HEARD YOU ARE QUITE GOOD.
QUITE GOOD...?
...I'M THE BEST!

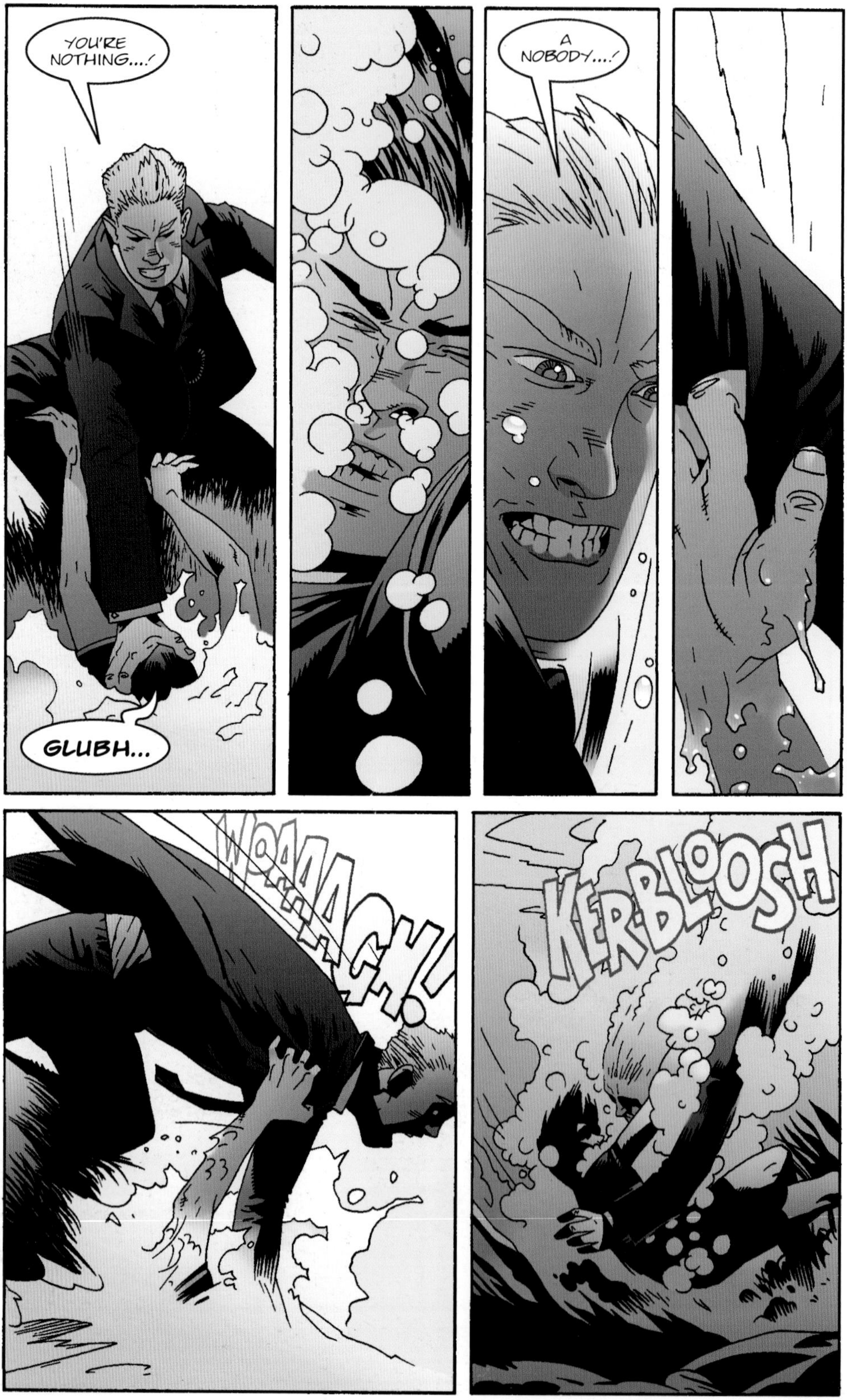
YOU'RE NOTHING....!
GLUBH...
A NOBODY....!
WOAAAACH!
KERBLOOSH

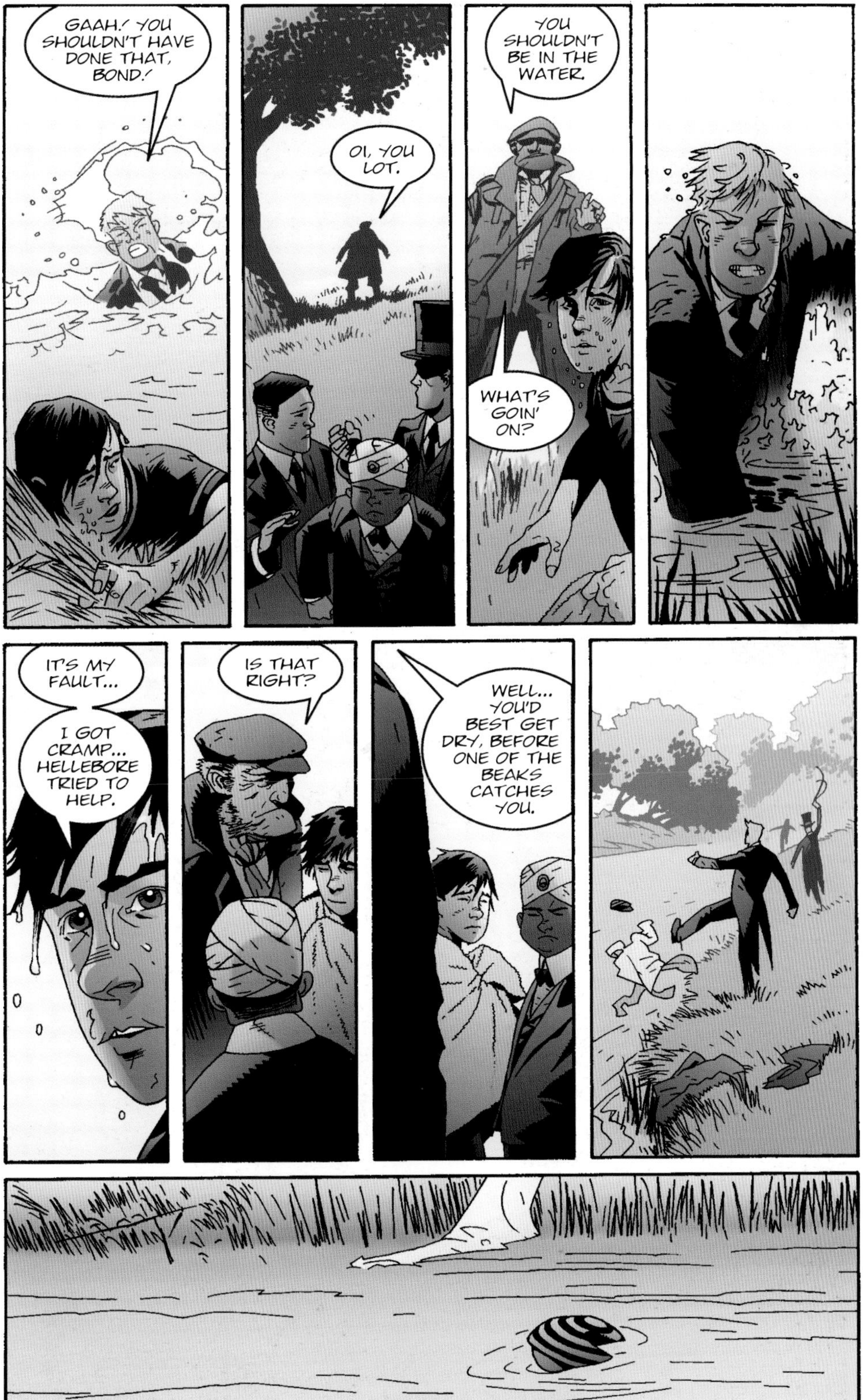
GAAH! YOU SHOULDN'T HAVE DONE THAT, BOND!
OI, YOU LOT.
YOU SHOULDN'T BE IN THE WATER.
WHAT'S GOIN' ON?
IT'S MY FAULT...
I GOT CRAMP... HELLEBORE TRIED TO HELP.
IS THAT RIGHT?
WELL... YOU'D BEST GET DRY, BEFORE ONE OF THE BEAKS CATCHES YOU.

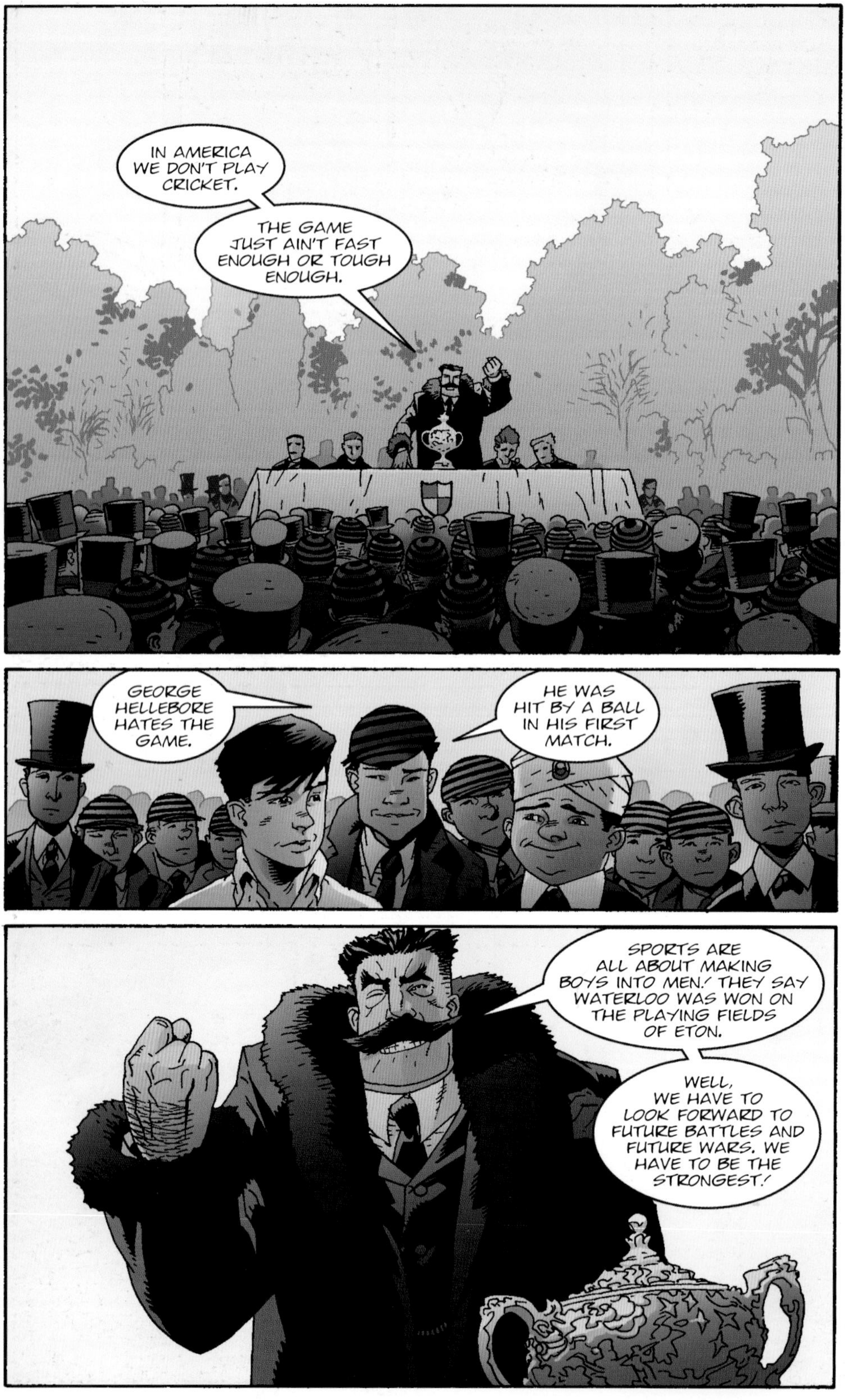
IN AMERICA WE DON'T PLAY CRICKET.
THE GAME JUST AIN'T FAST ENOUGH OR TOUGH ENOUGH.
GEORGE HELLEBORE HATES THE GAME.
HE WAS HIT BY A BALL IN HIS FIRST MATCH.
SPORTS ARE ALL ABOUT MAKING BOYS INTO MEN! THEY SAY WATERLOO WAS WON ON THE PLAYING FIELDS OF ETON.
WELL, WE HAVE TO LOOK FORWARD TO FUTURE BATTLES AND FUTURE WARS. WE HAVE TO BE THE STRONGEST!

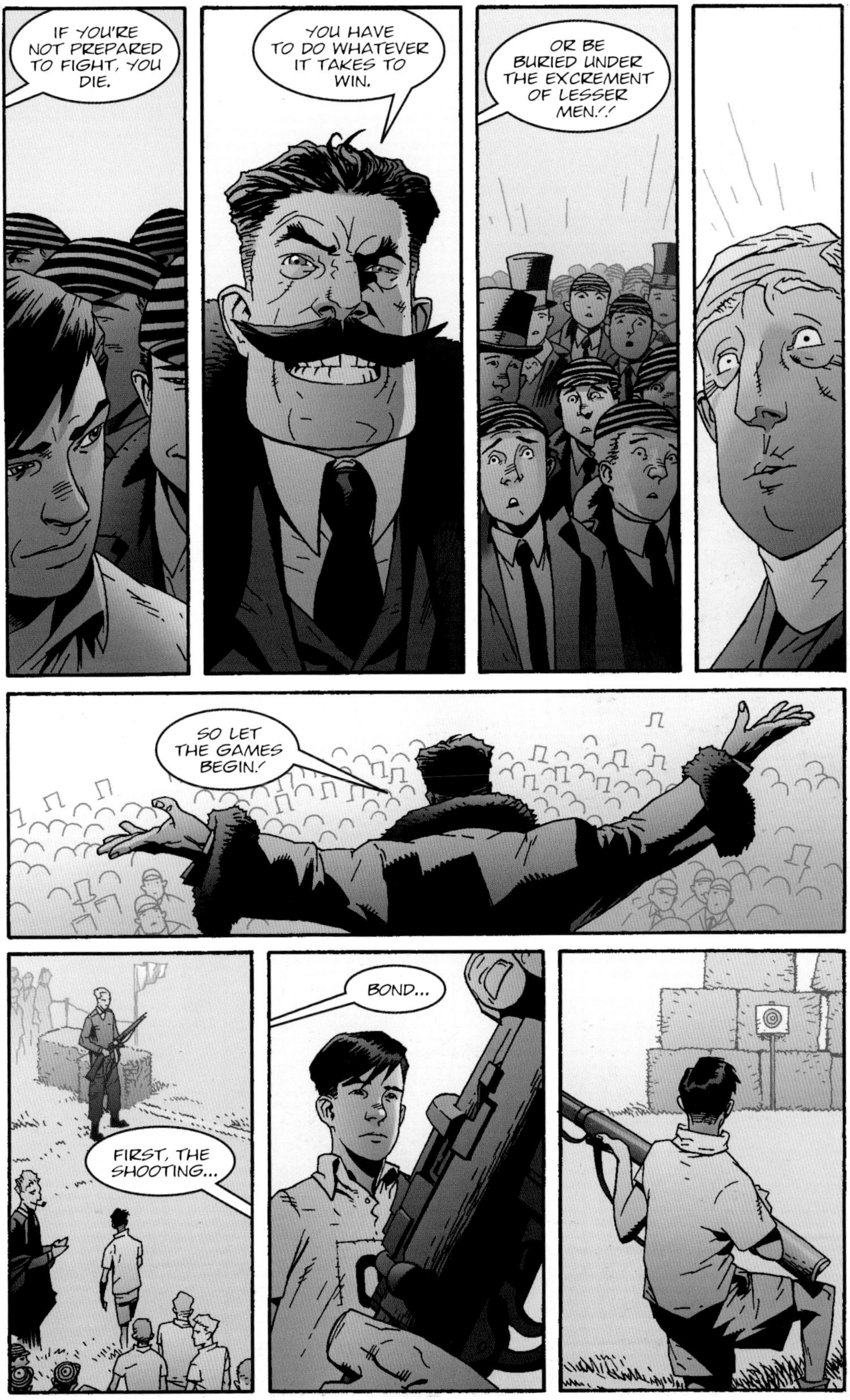
IF YOU'RE NOT PREPARED TO FIGHT, YOU DIE.
YOU HAVE TO DO WHATEVER IT TAKES TO WIN.
OR BE BURIED UNDER THE EXCREMENT OF LESSER MEN!!
SO LET THE GAMES BEGIN!
FIRST, THE SHOOTING...
BOND...

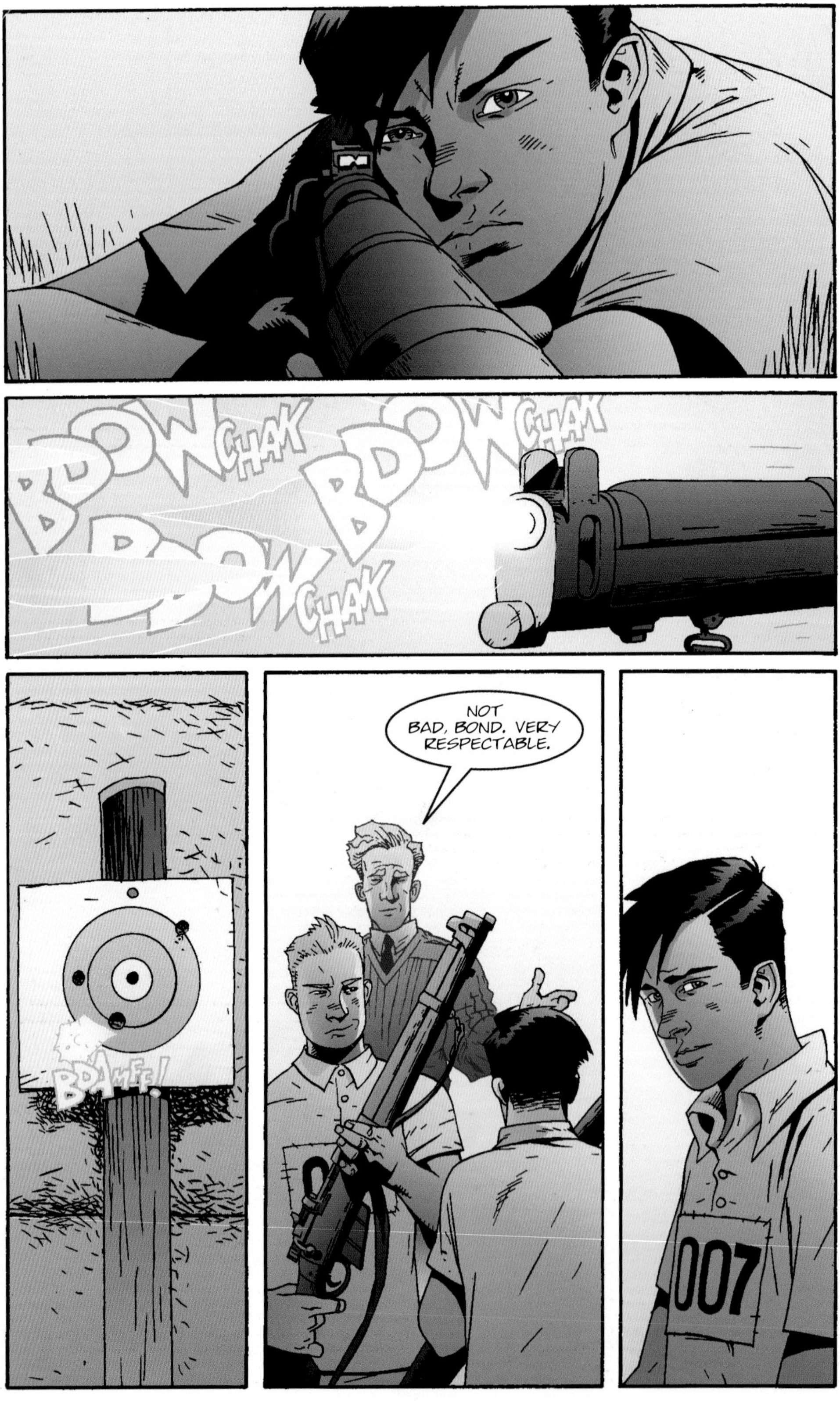
BDOW CHAK
BDOW CHAK
BDOW CHAK
BRAMFF!
NOT BAD, BOND. VERY RESPECTABLE.
007

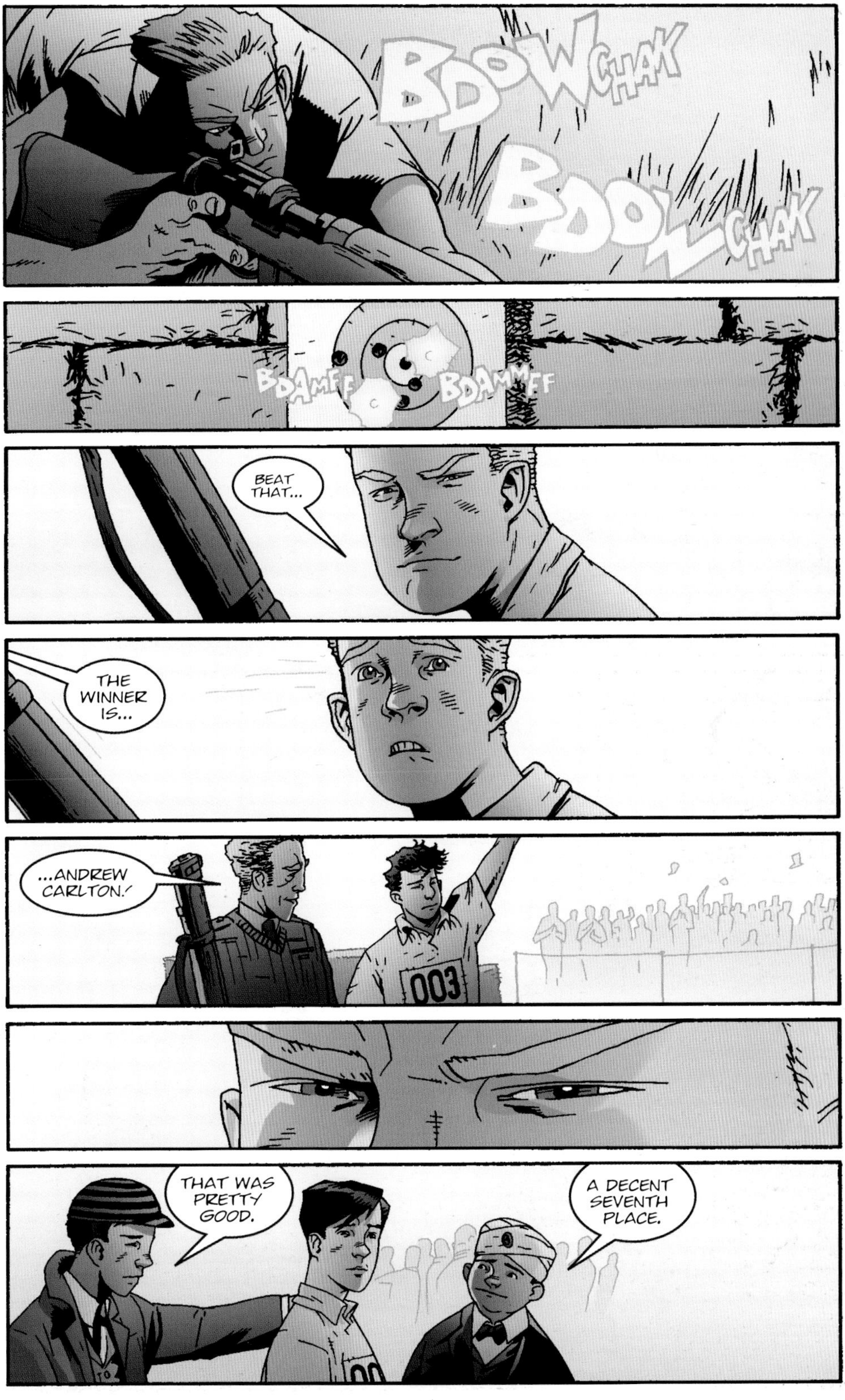
BDOW CHAK
BDOW CHAK
BDAMFF
BDAMMFF
BEAT THAT...
THE WINNER IS...
...ANDREW CARLTON!
003
THAT WAS PRETTY GOOD.
A DECENT SEVENTH PLACE.

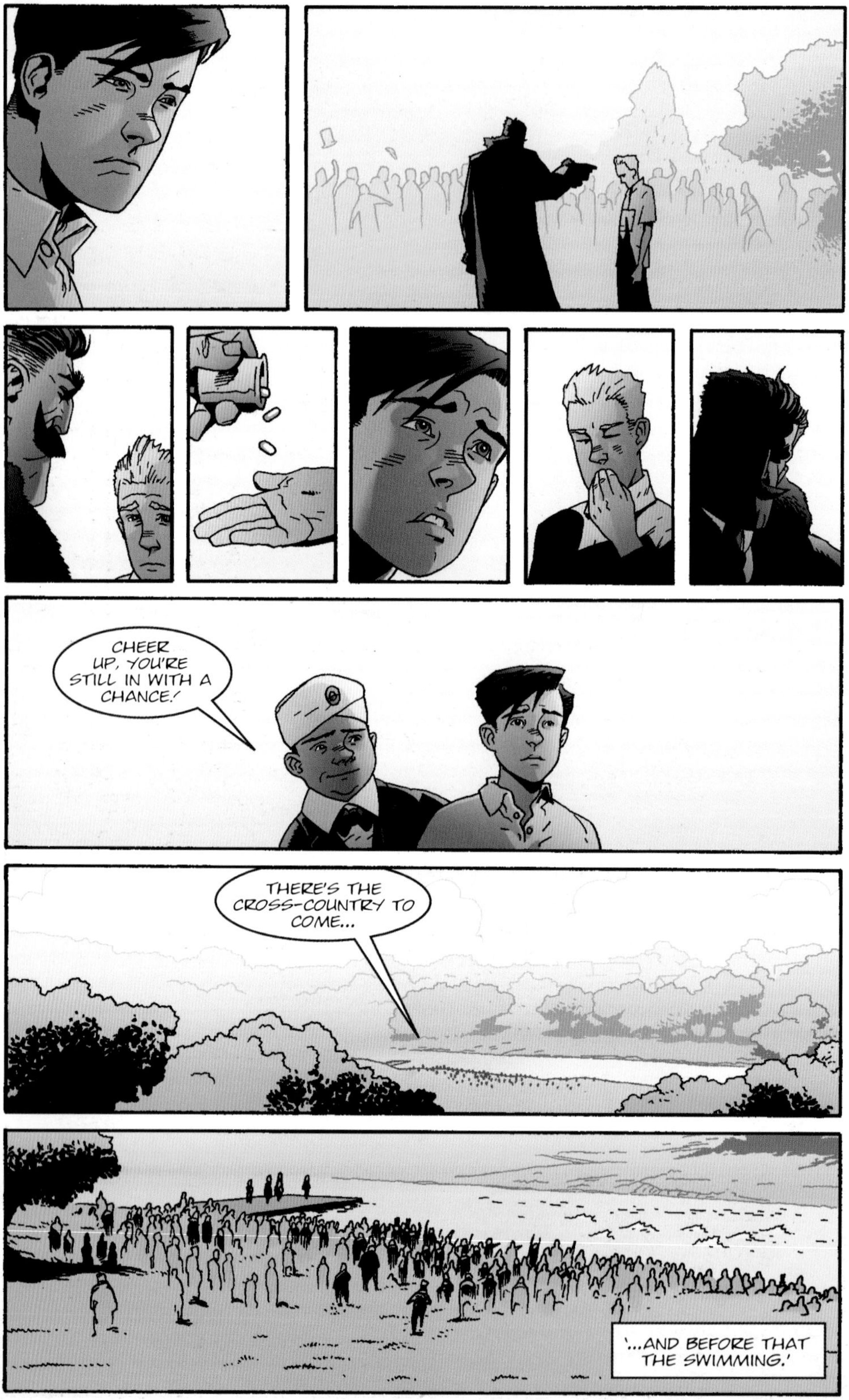
CHEER UP, YOU'RE STILL IN WITH A CHANCE!
THERE'S THE CROSS-COUNTRY TO COME...
'...AND BEFORE THAT THE SWIMMING.'

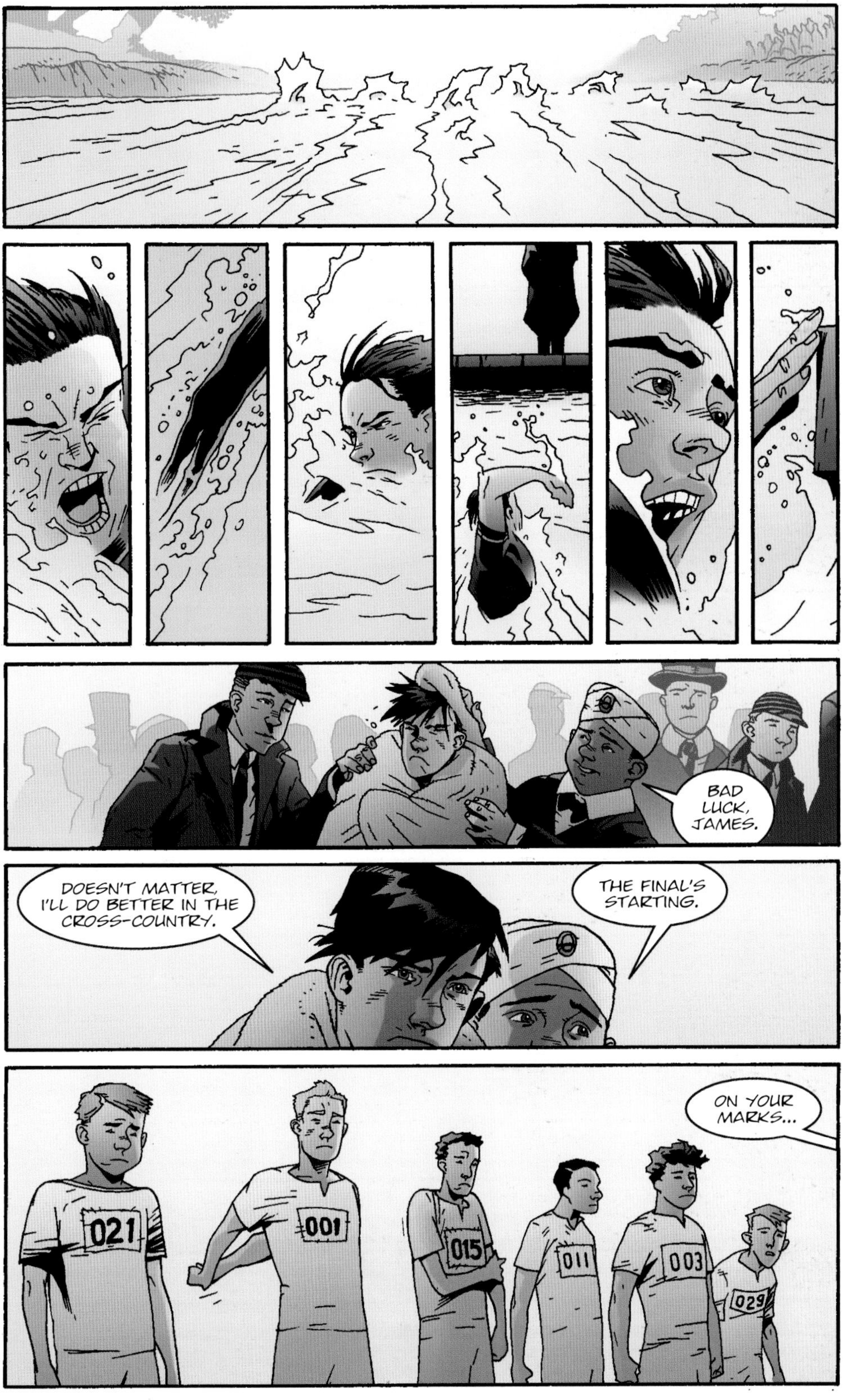
BAD LUCK, JAMES.
DOESN'T MATTER, I'LL DO BETTER IN THE CROSS-COUNTRY.
THE FINAL'S STARTING.
ON YOUR MARKS...
021
001
015
011
003
029

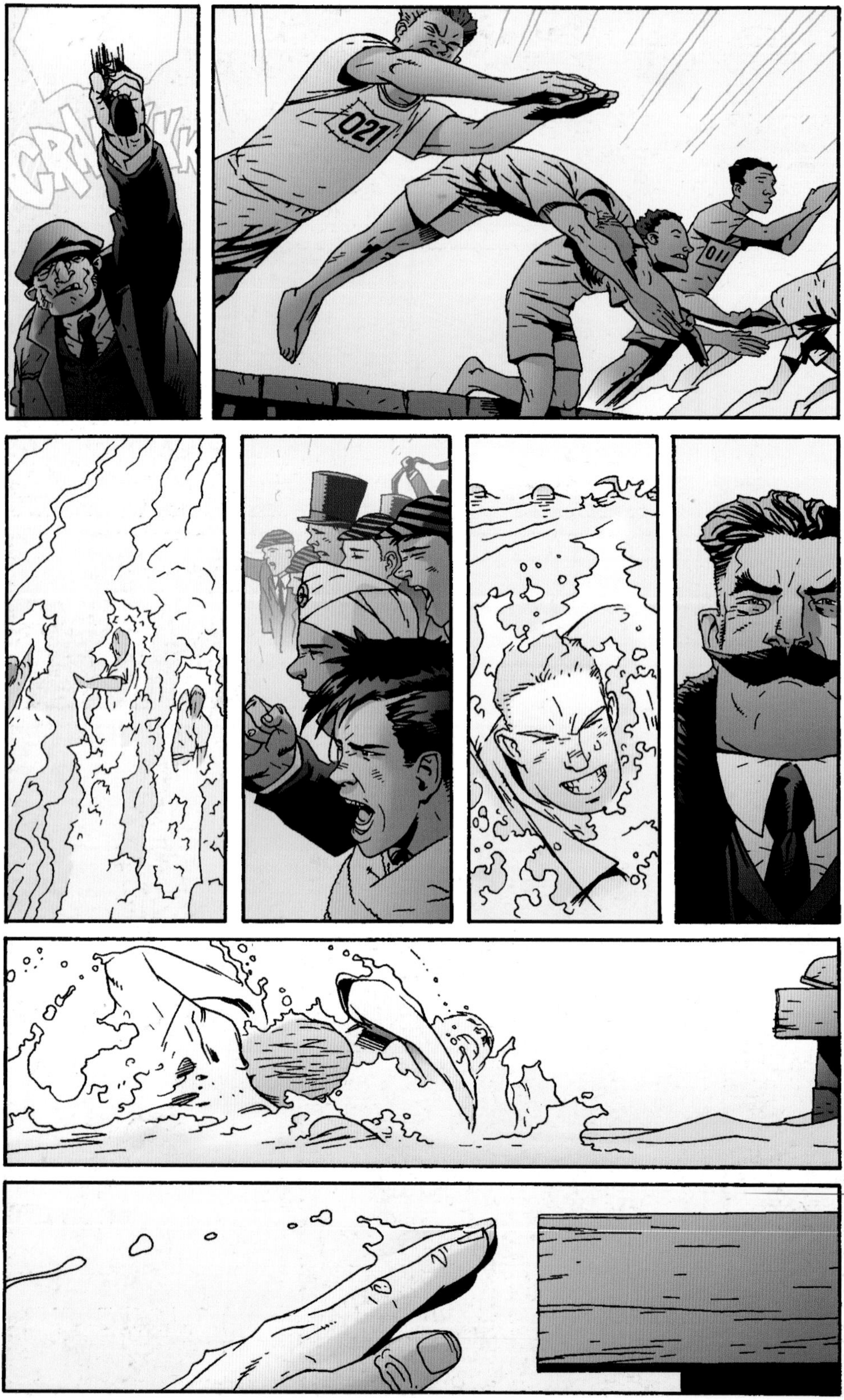
021
011

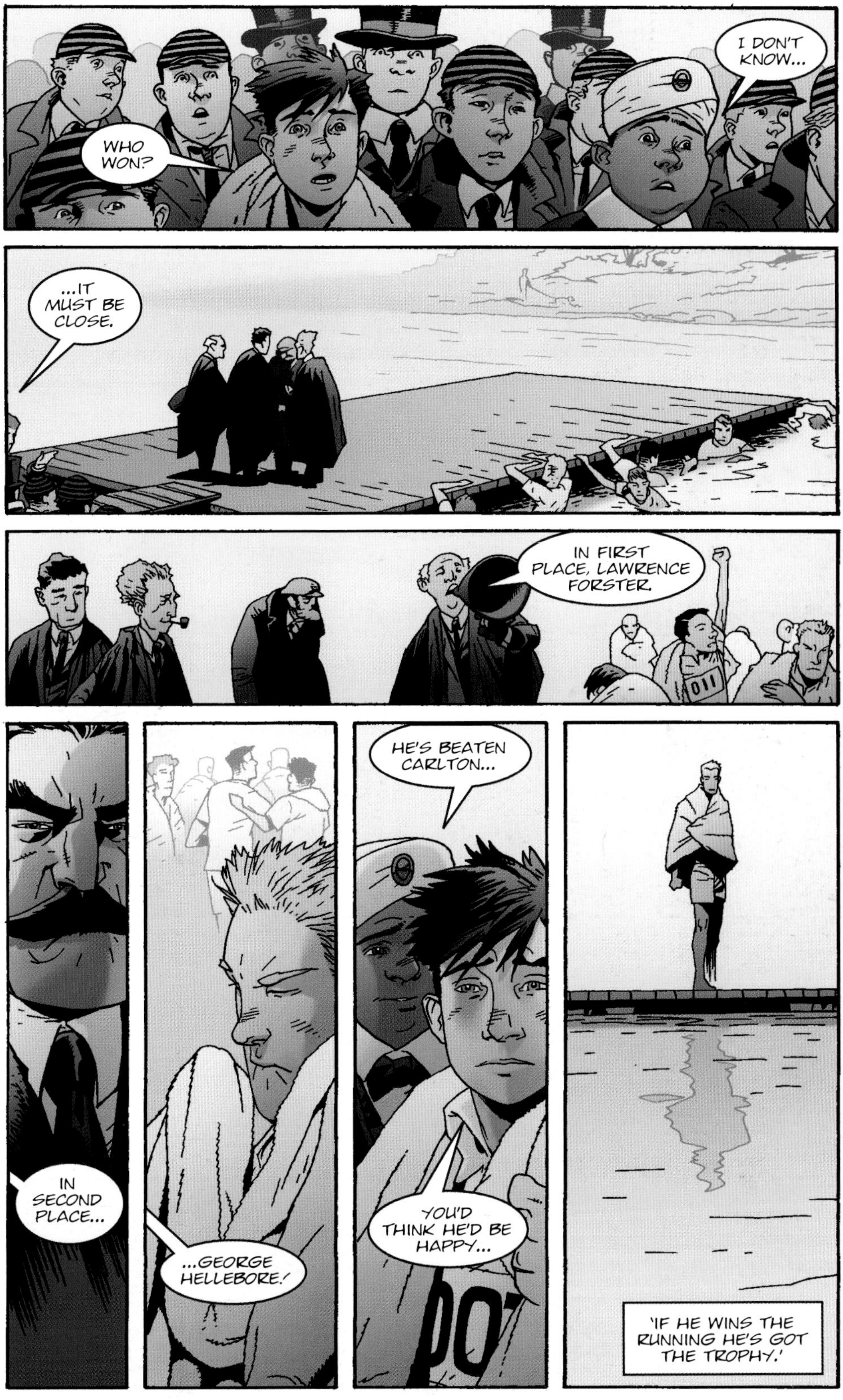
WHO WON?
I DON'T KNOW...
...IT MUST BE CLOSE.
IN FIRST PLACE, LAWRENCE FORSTER.
IN SECOND PLACE...
...GEORGE HELLEBORE!
HE'S BEATEN CARLTON...
YOU'D THINK HE'D BE HAPPY...
'IF HE WINS THE RUNNING HE'S GOT THE TROPHY.'

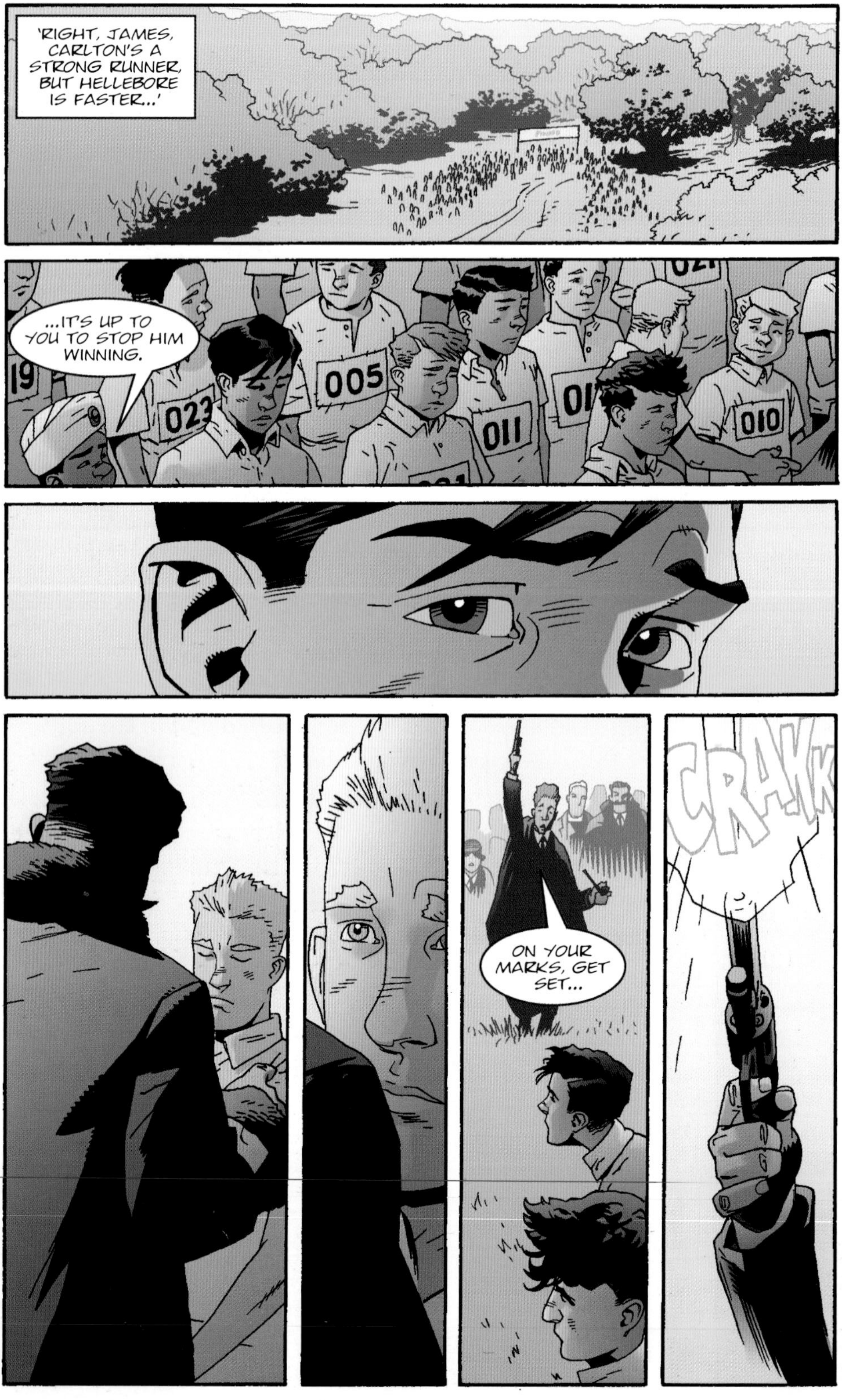
'RIGHT, JAMES, CARLTON'S A STRONG RUNNER, BUT HELLEBORE IS FASTER...'
...IT'S UP TO YOU TO STOP HIM WINNING.
ON YOUR MARKS, GET SET...
CRAKK

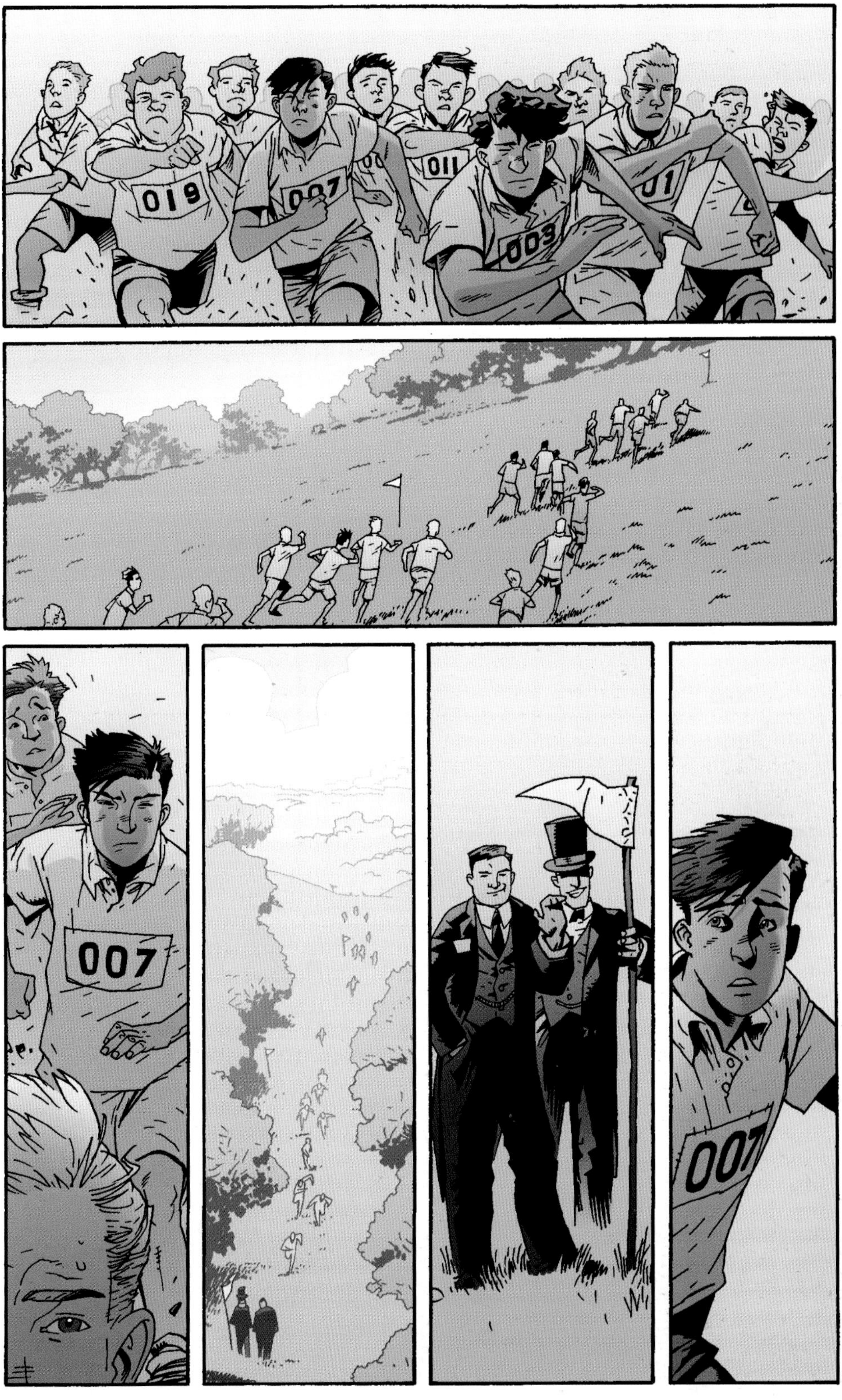
019
011
003
007

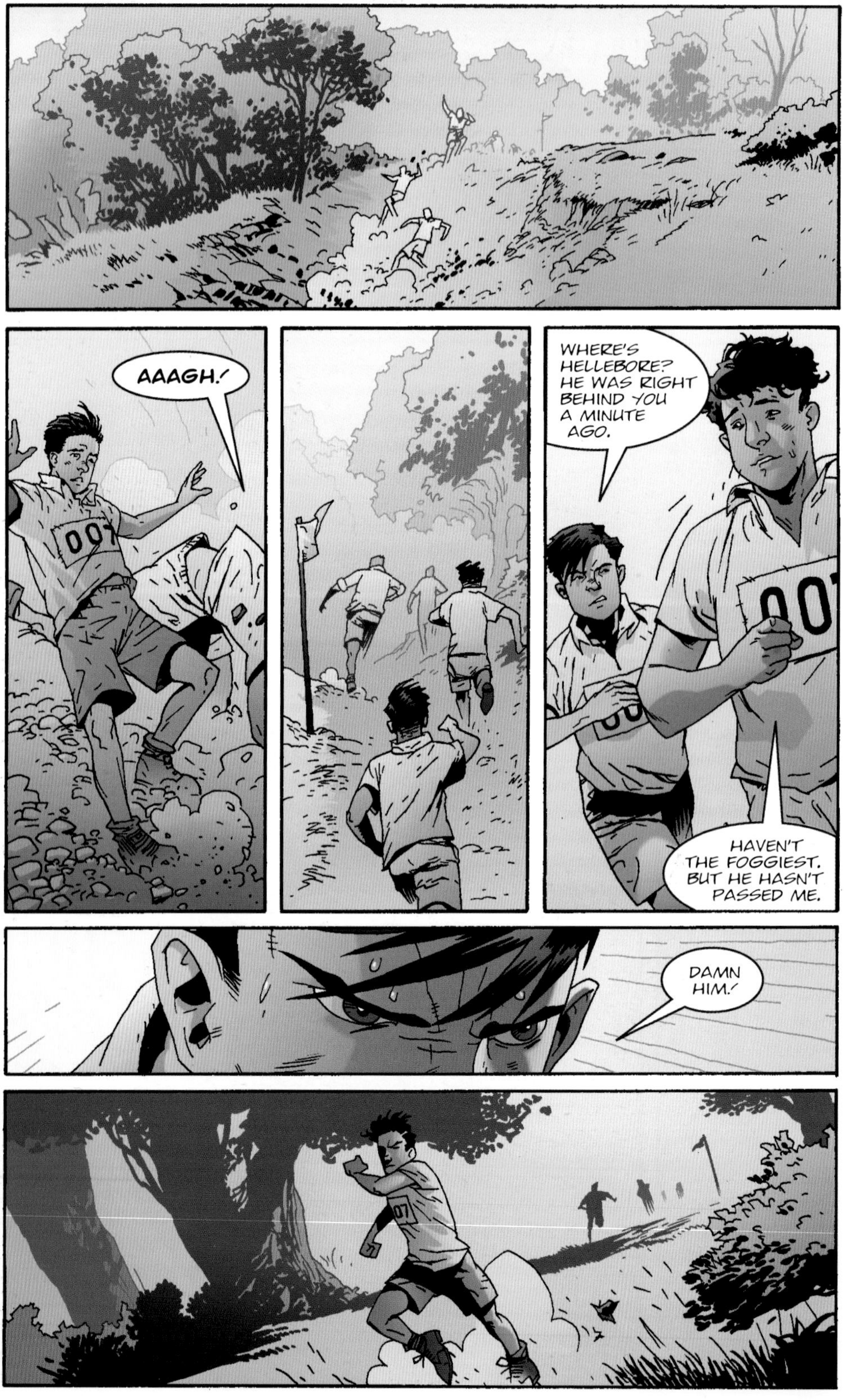
AAAGH!
WHERE'S HELLEBORE? HE WAS RIGHT BEHIND YOU A MINUTE AGO.
HAVEN'T THE FOGGIEST. BUT HE HASN'T PASSED ME.
DAMN HIM!

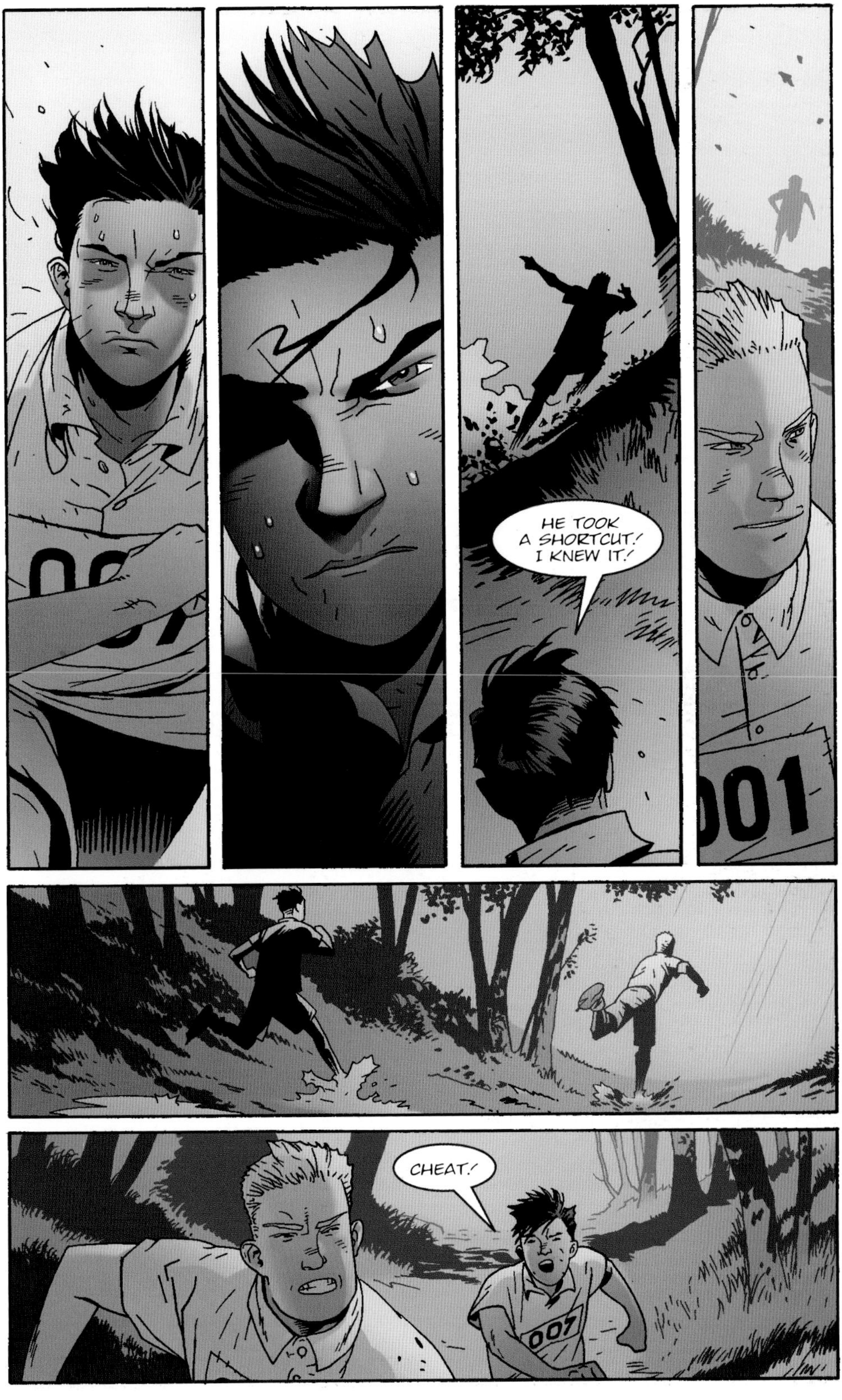
HE TOOK A SHORTCUT! I KNEW IT!
001
CHEAT!
007

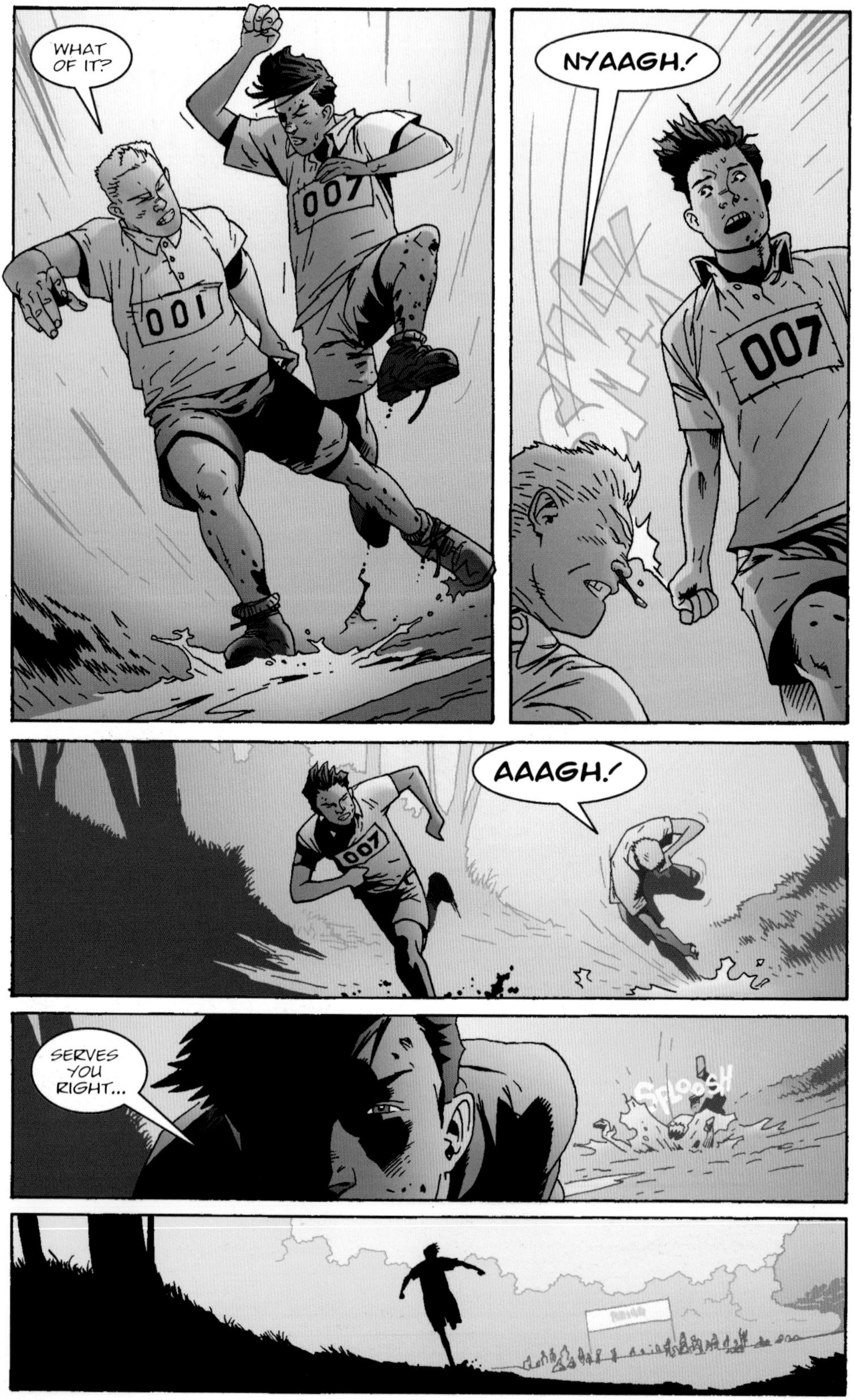
WHAT OF IT?
NYAAGH!
AAAGH!
SERVES YOU RIGHT...
SPLOOSH

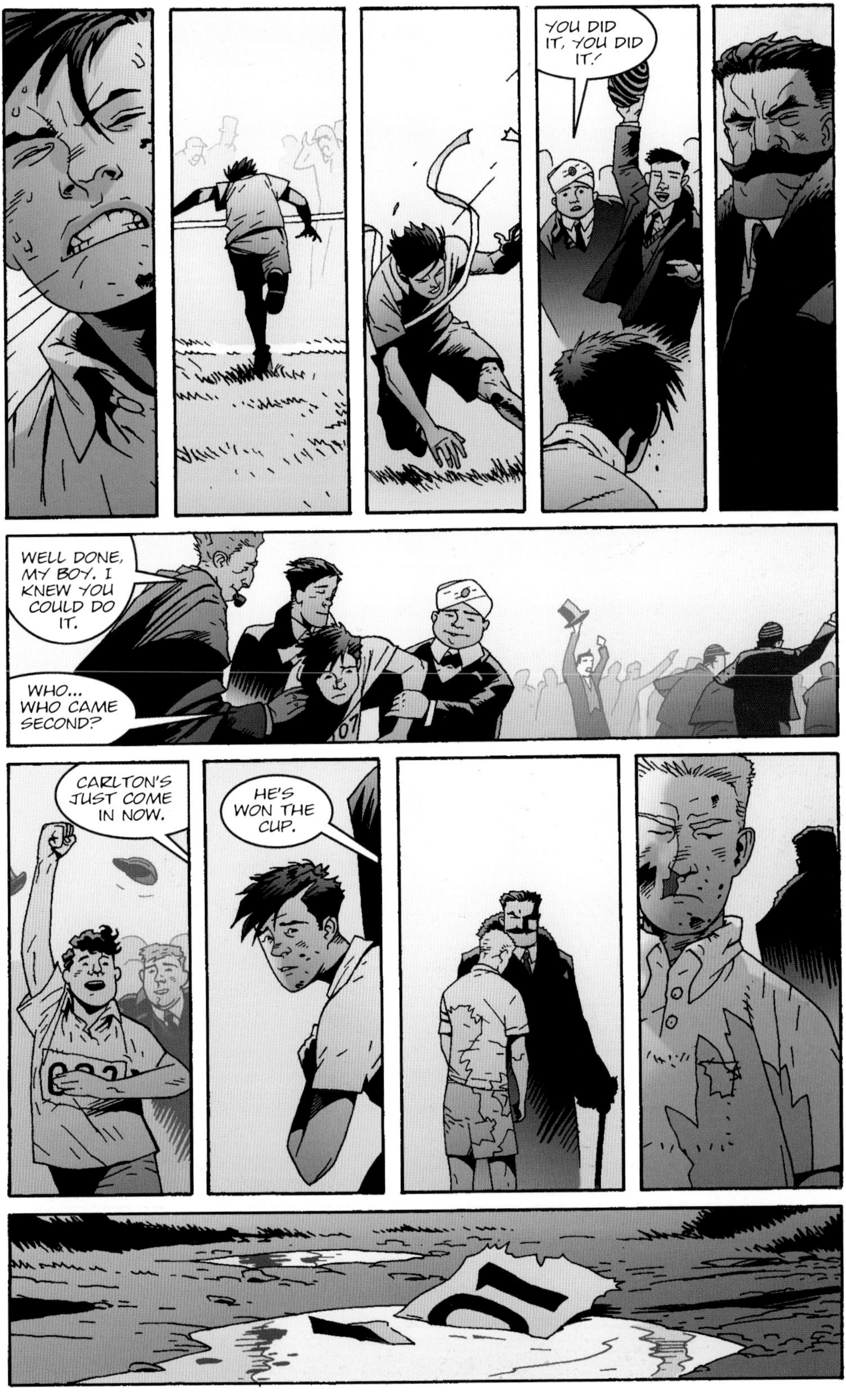
YOU DID IT, YOU DID IT!
WELL DONE, MY BOY. I KNEW YOU COULD DO IT.
WHO... WHO CAME SECOND?
CARLTON'S JUST COME IN NOW.
HE'S WON THE CUP.

PART TWO

SCOTLAND

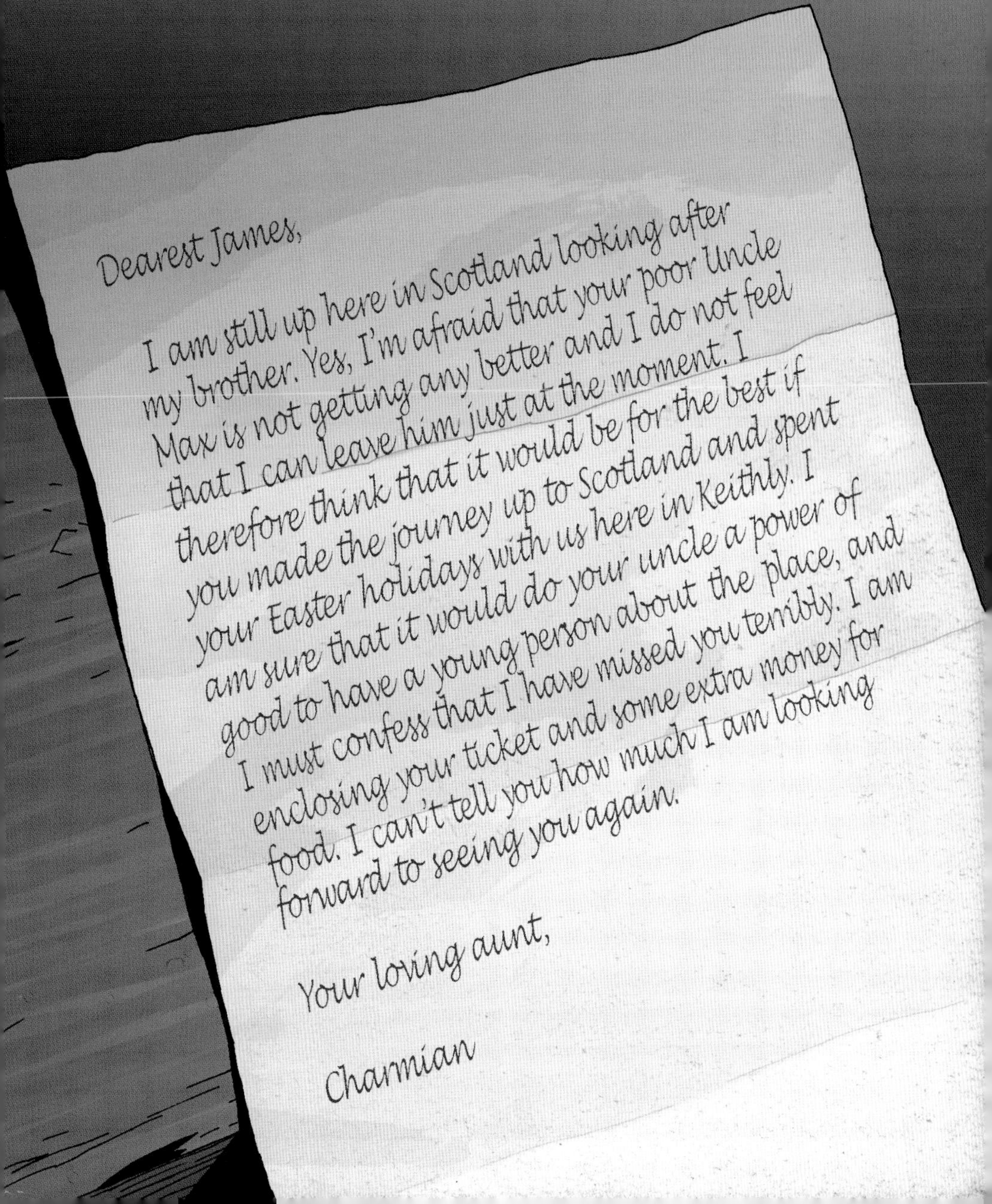

Dearest James,

I am still up here in Scotland looking after my brother. Yes, I'm afraid that your poor Uncle Max is not getting any better and I do not feel that I can leave him just at the moment. I therefore think that it would be for the best if you made the journey up to Scotland and spent your Easter holidays with us here in Keithly. I am sure that it would do your uncle a power of good to have a young person about the place, and I must confess that I have missed you terribly. I am enclosing your ticket and some extra money for food. I can't tell you how much I am looking forward to seeing you again.

Your loving aunt,

Charmian

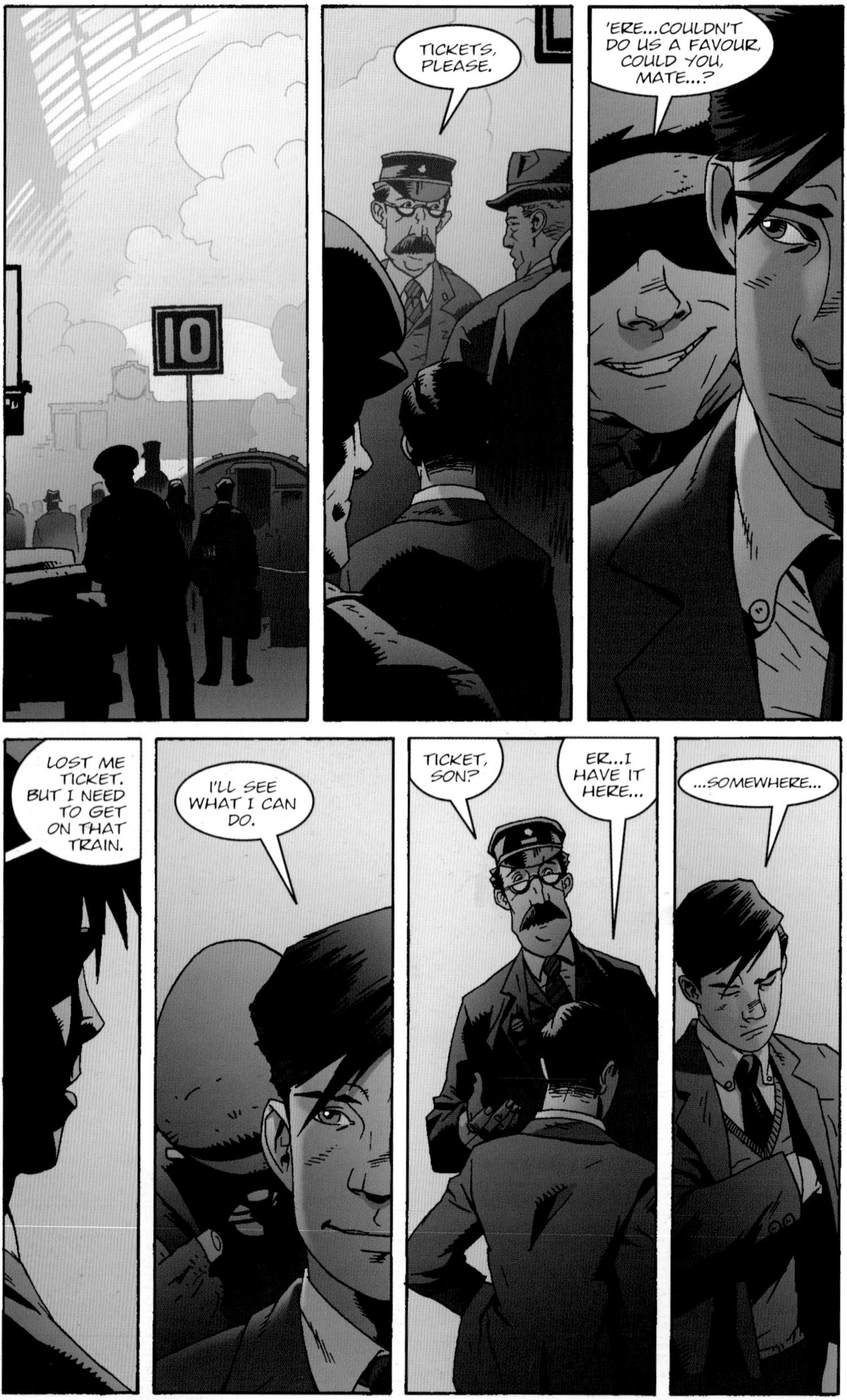
10
TICKETS, PLEASE.
'ERE...COULDN'T DO US A FAVOUR, COULD YOU, MATE...?
LOST ME TICKET. BUT I NEED TO GET ON THAT TRAIN.
I'LL SEE WHAT I CAN DO.
TICKET, SON?
ER...I HAVE IT HERE...
...SOMEWHERE...

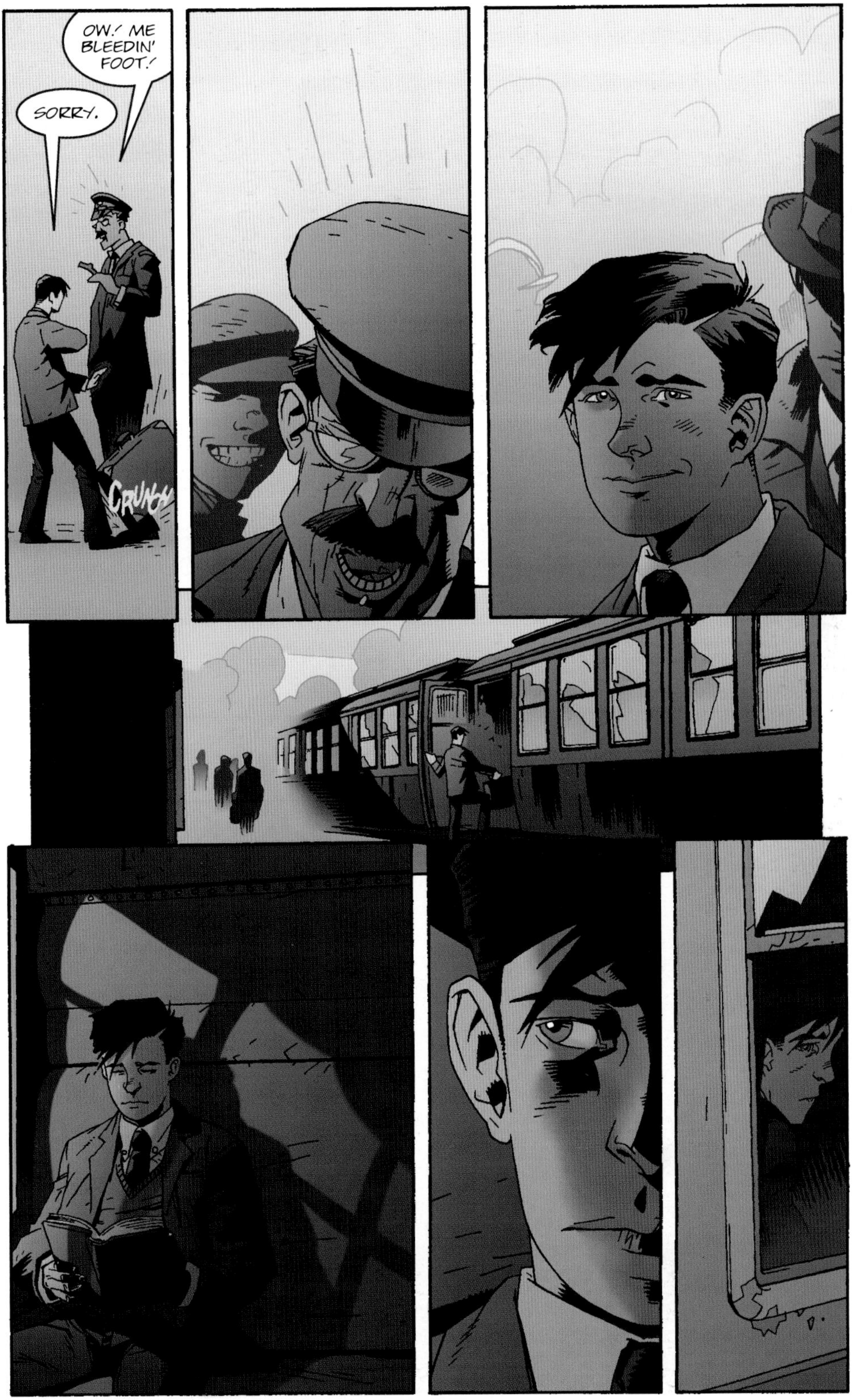
OW.! ME BLEEDIN' FOOT.!
SORRY.
CRUNCH

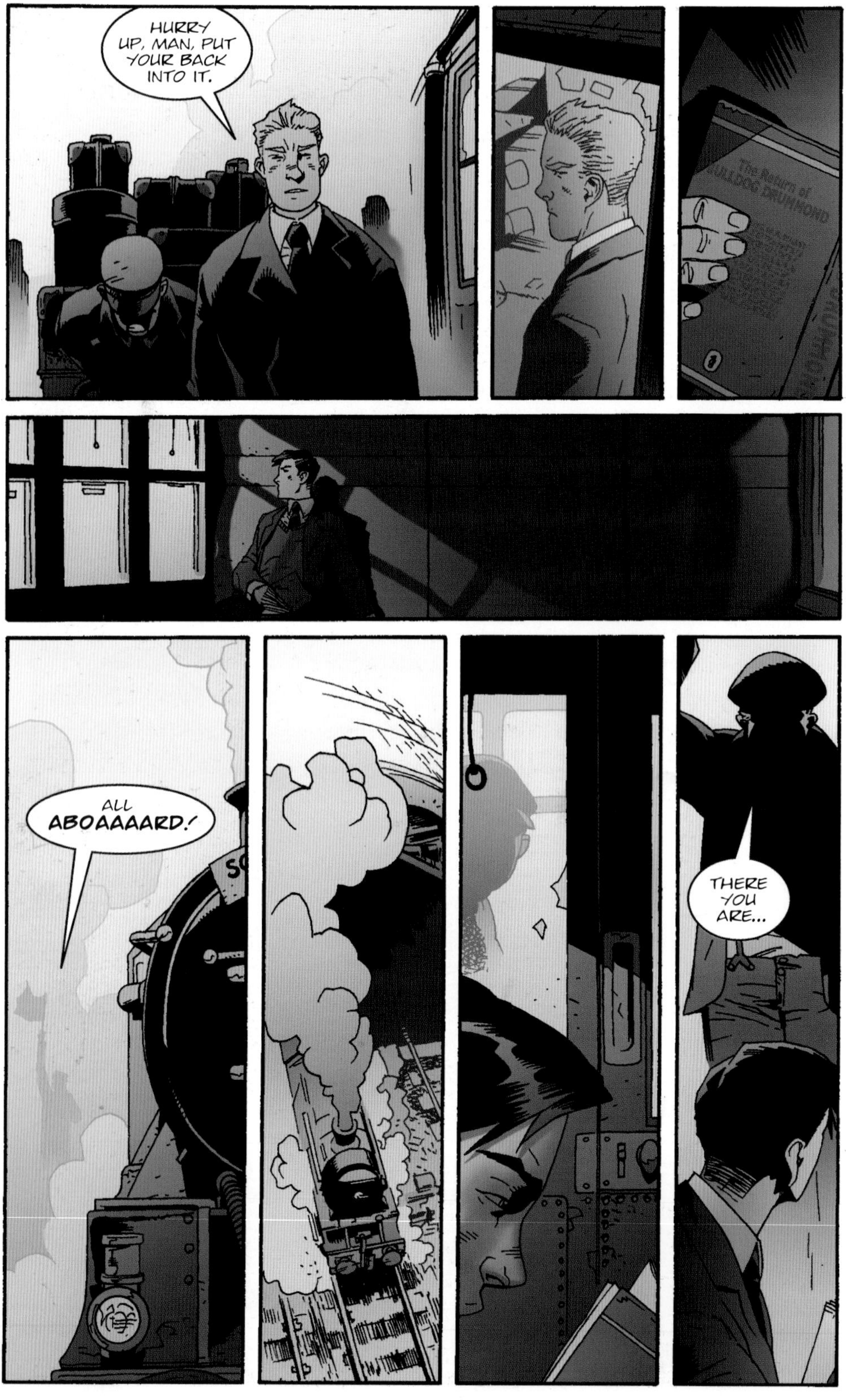
HURRY UP, MAN, PUT YOUR BACK INTO IT.
The Return of BULLDOG DRUMMOND
ALL ABOAAAARD!
THERE YOU ARE...

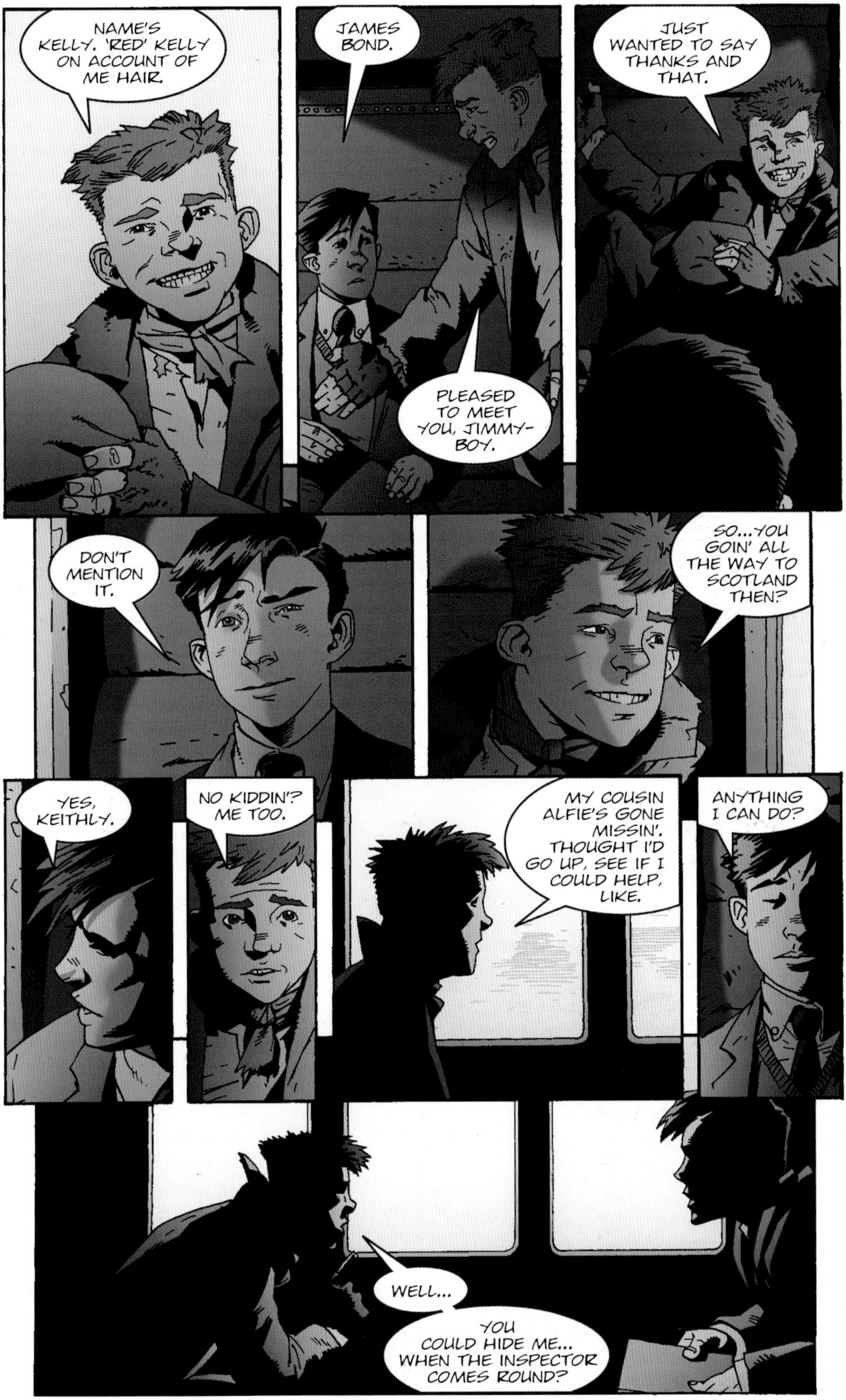
NAME'S KELLY. 'RED' KELLY ON ACCOUNT OF ME HAIR.
JAMES BOND.
PLEASED TO MEET YOU, JIMMY-BOY.
JUST WANTED TO SAY THANKS AND THAT.
DON'T MENTION IT.
SO...YOU GOIN' ALL THE WAY TO SCOTLAND THEN?
YES, KEITHLY.
NO KIDDIN'? ME TOO.
MY COUSIN ALFIE'S GONE MISSIN'. THOUGHT I'D GO UP, SEE IF I COULD HELP, LIKE.
ANYTHING I CAN DO?
WELL...
YOU COULD HIDE ME... WHEN THE INSPECTOR COMES ROUND?

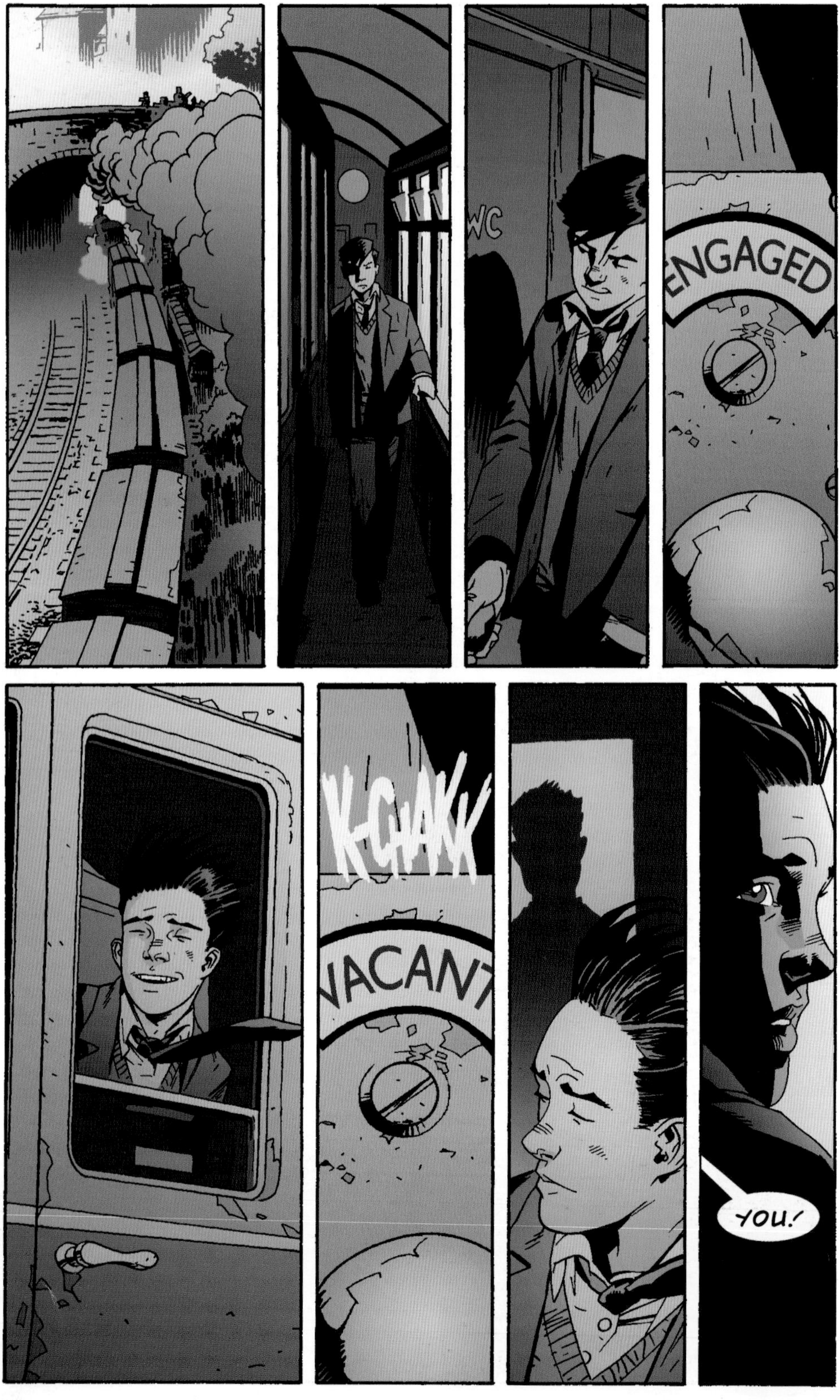
WC
ENGAGED
K-CHAKK
VACANT
YOU!

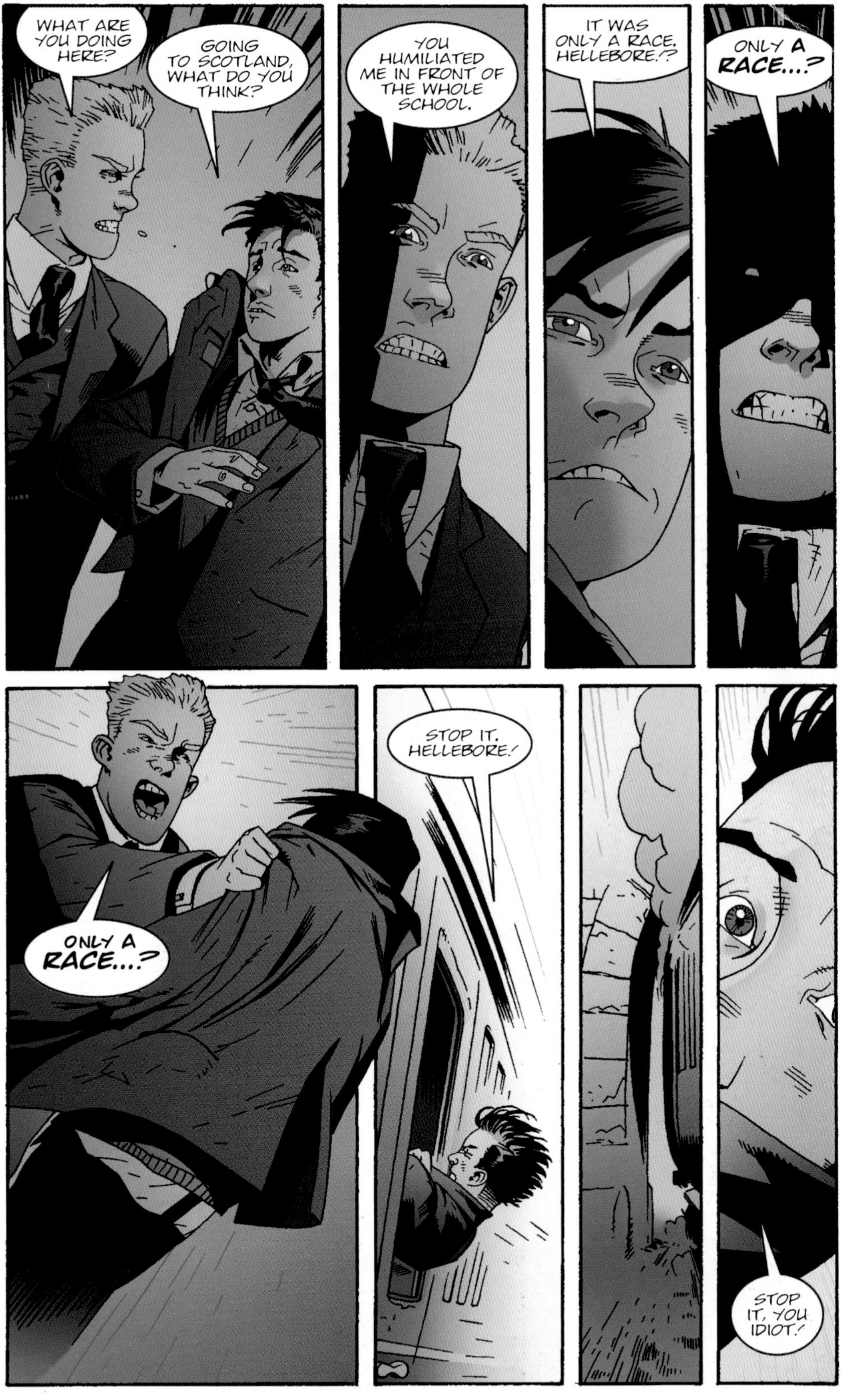
WHAT ARE YOU DOING HERE?
GOING TO SCOTLAND, WHAT DO YOU THINK?
YOU HUMILIATED ME IN FRONT OF THE WHOLE SCHOOL.
IT WAS ONLY A RACE, HELLEBORE.!?
ONLY A RACE...?
ONLY A RACE...?
STOP IT, HELLEBORE!
STOP IT, YOU IDIOT!

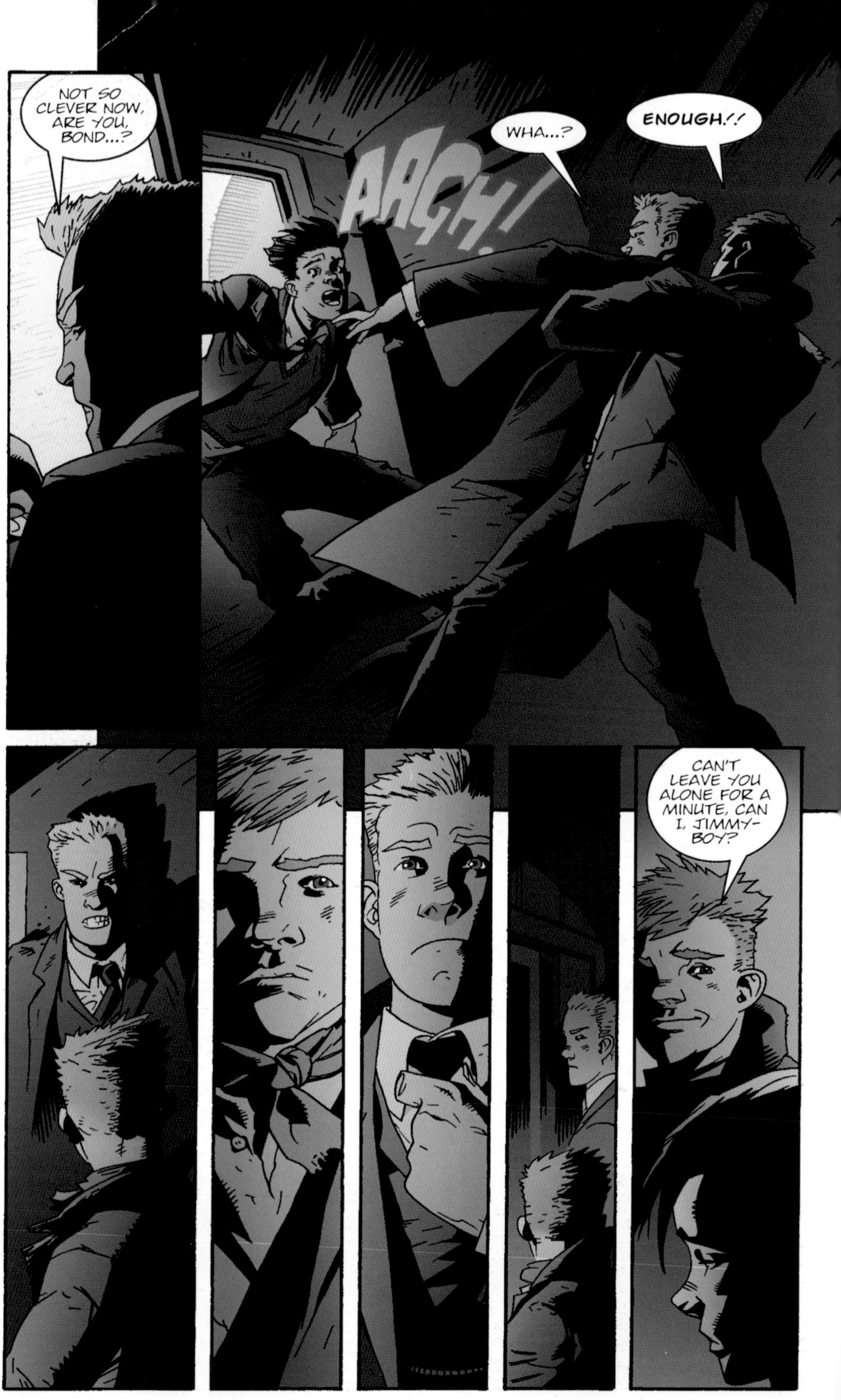
NOT SO CLEVER NOW, ARE YOU, BOND...?
AARGH!
WHA...?
ENOUGH!!
CAN'T LEAVE YOU ALONE FOR A MINUTE, CAN I, JIMMY-BOY?

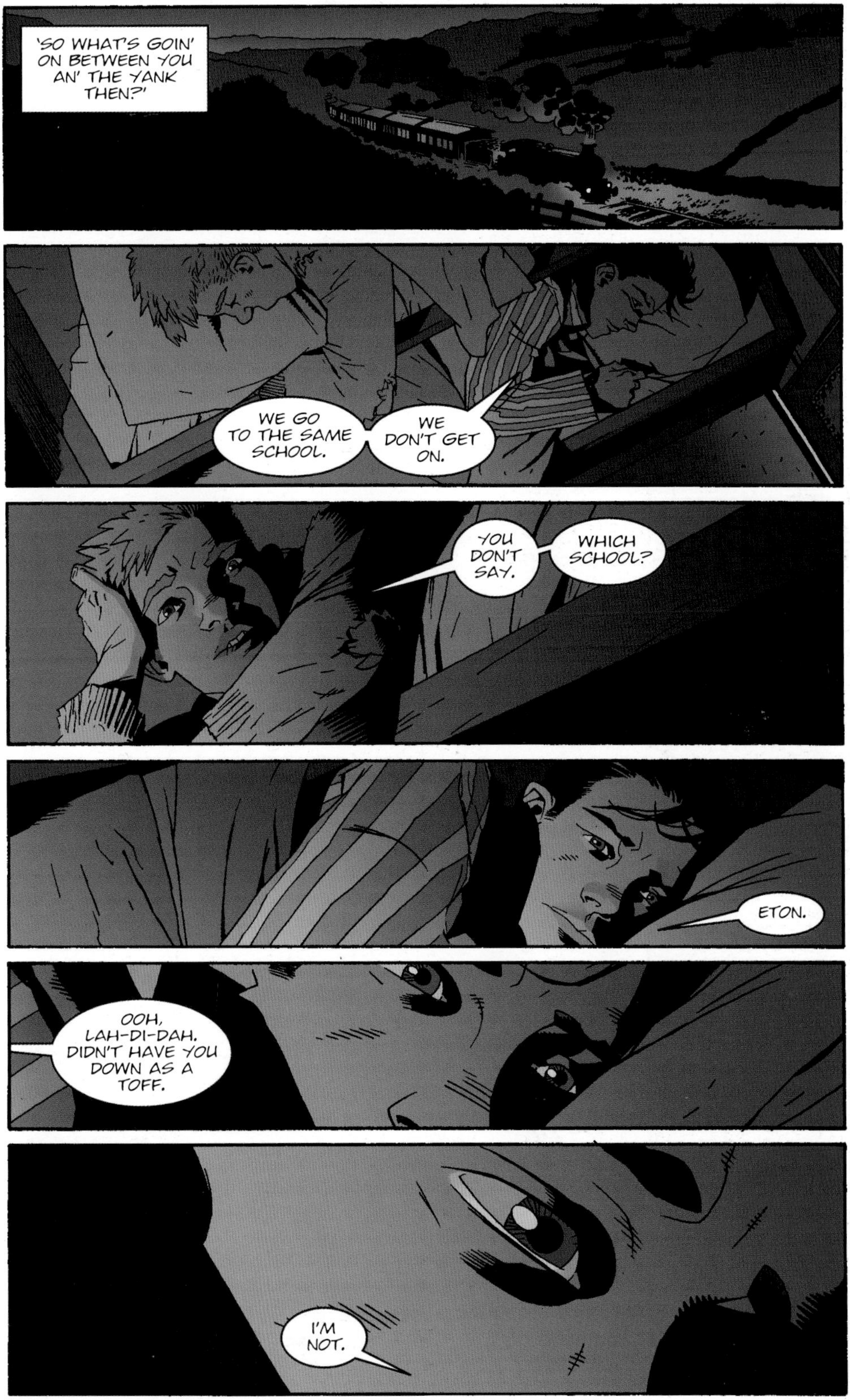
'SO WHAT'S GOIN' ON BETWEEN YOU AN' THE YANK THEN?'
WE GO TO THE SAME SCHOOL.
WE DON'T GET ON.
YOU DON'T SAY.
WHICH SCHOOL?
ETON.
OOH, LAH-DI-DAH. DIDN'T HAVE YOU DOWN AS A TOFF.
I'M NOT.

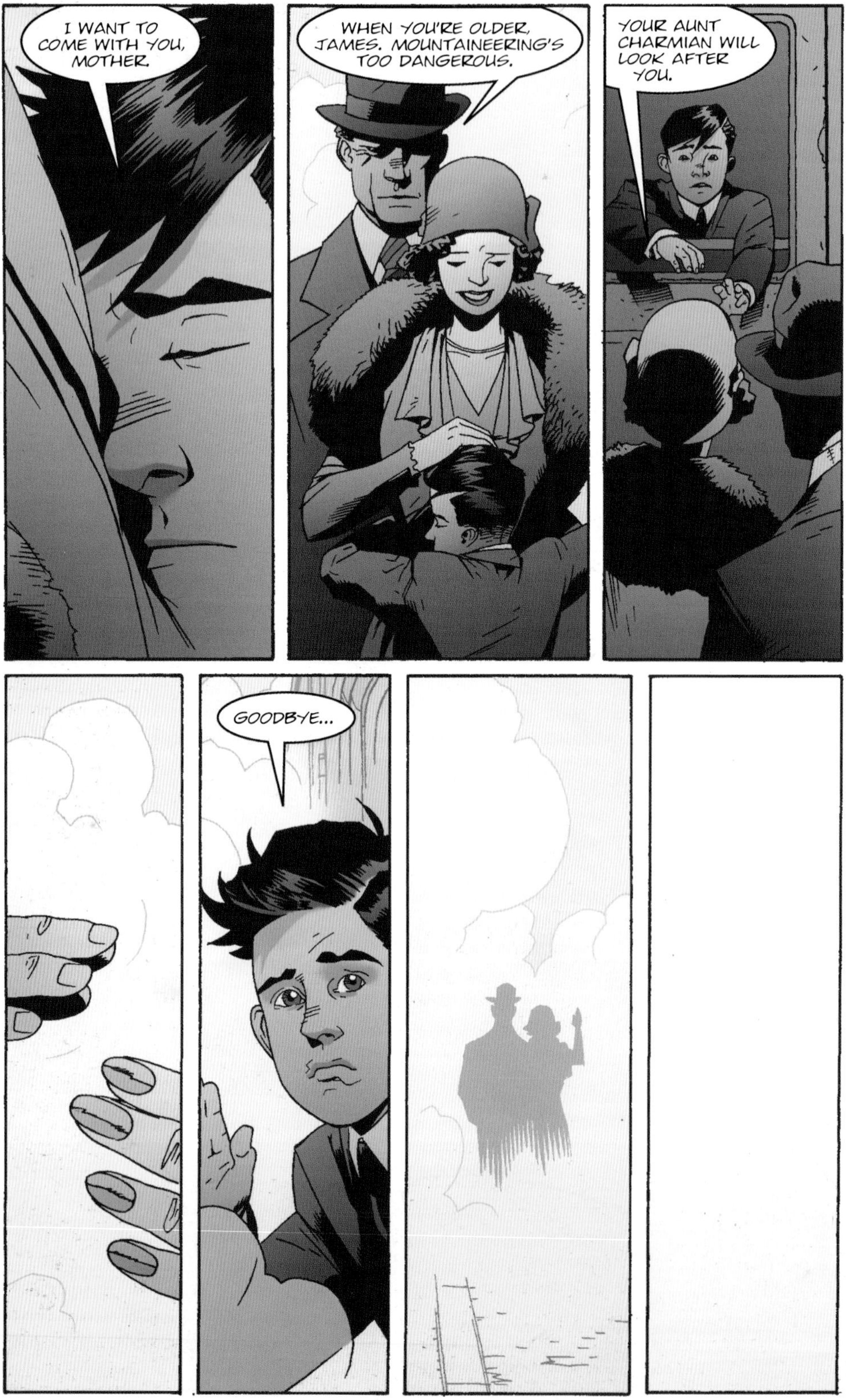
I WANT TO COME WITH YOU, MOTHER.
WHEN YOU'RE OLDER, JAMES. MOUNTAINEERING'S TOO DANGEROUS.
YOUR AUNT CHARMIAN WILL LOOK AFTER YOU.
GOODBYE...

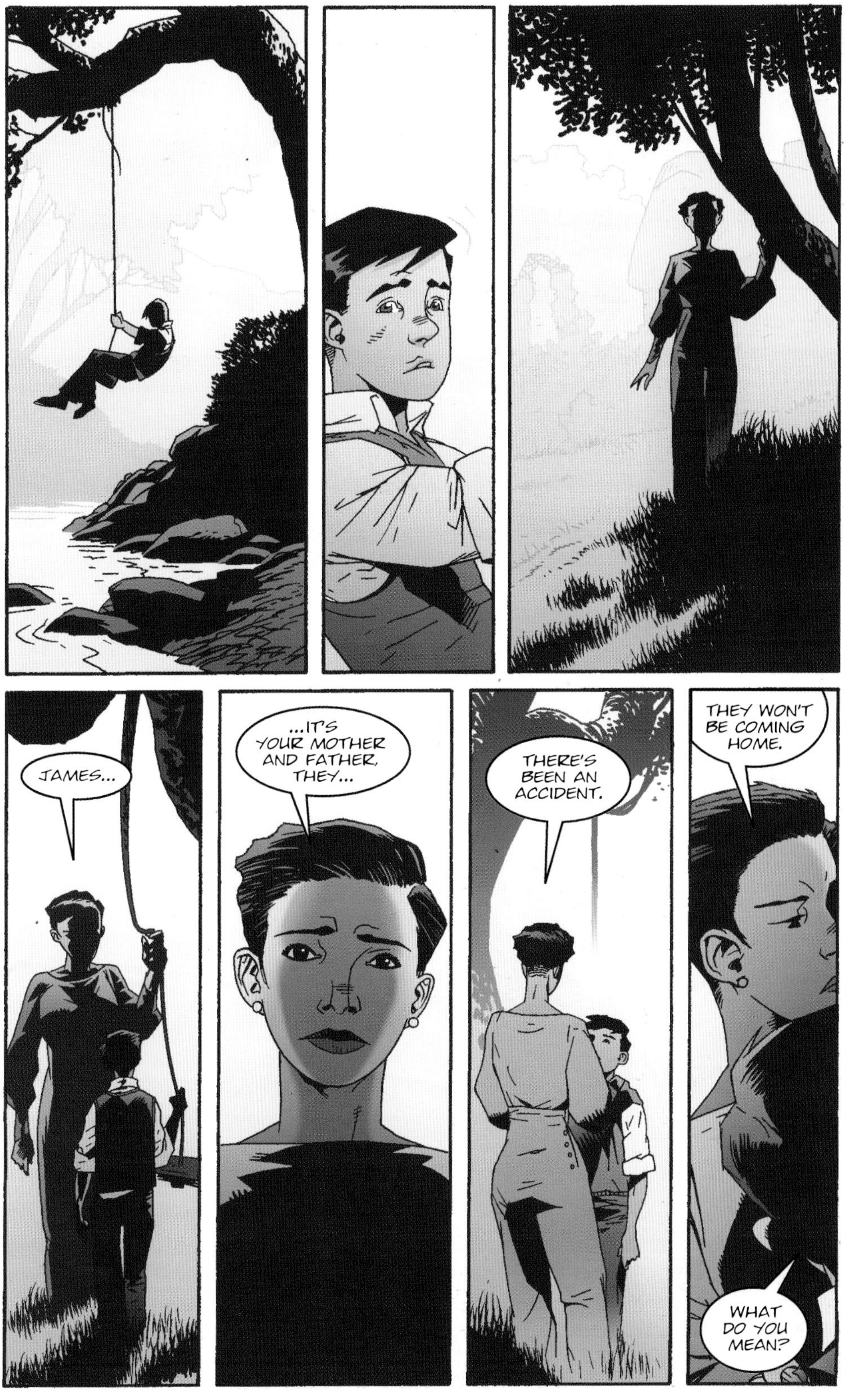
JAMES...
...IT'S YOUR MOTHER AND FATHER, THEY...
THERE'S BEEN AN ACCIDENT.
THEY WON'T BE COMING HOME.
WHAT DO YOU MEAN?

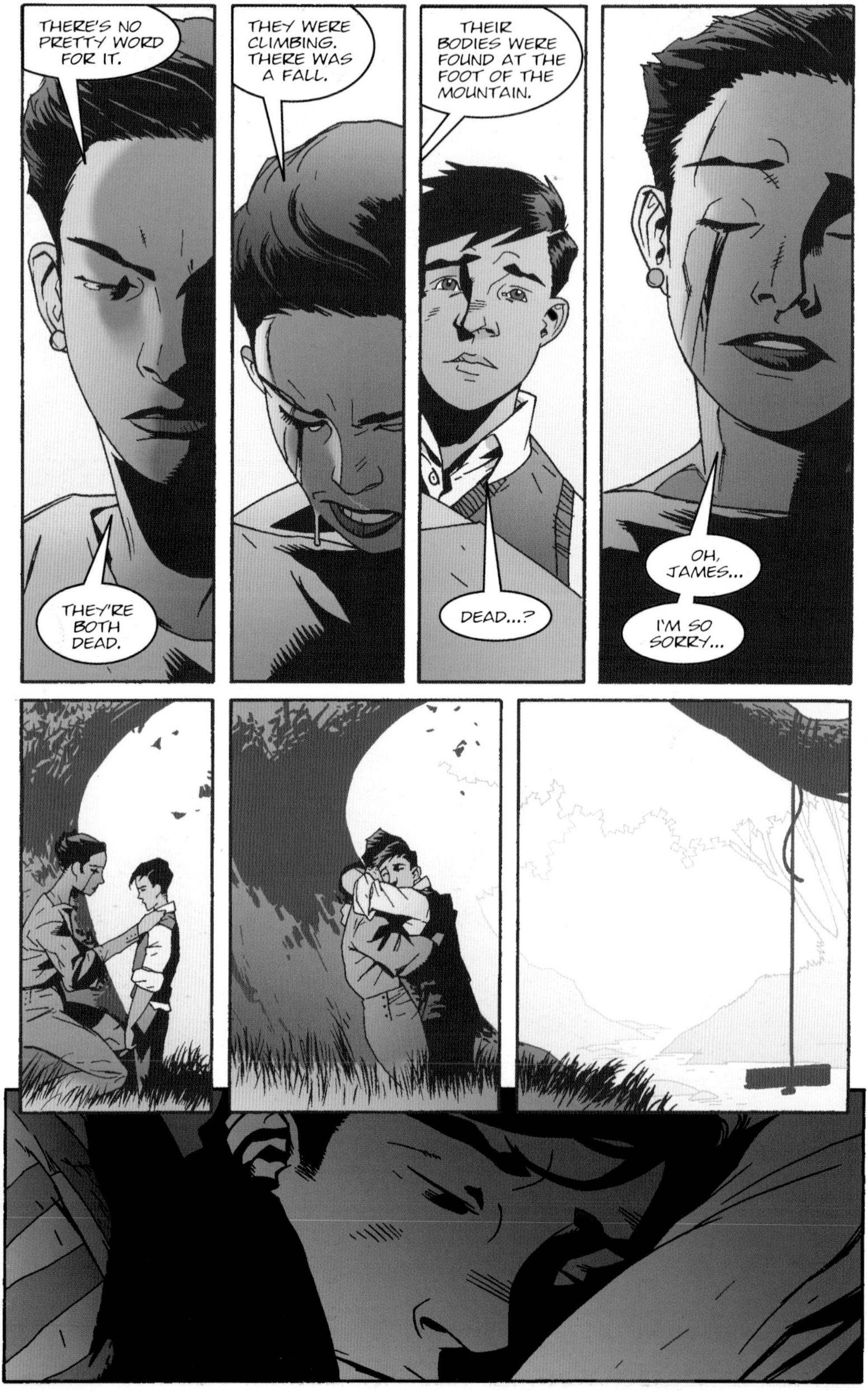
THERE'S NO PRETTY WORD FOR IT.
THEY'RE BOTH DEAD.
THEY WERE CLIMBING. THERE WAS A FALL.
THEIR BODIES WERE FOUND AT THE FOOT OF THE MOUNTAIN.
DEAD...?
OH, JAMES...
I'M SO SORRY...

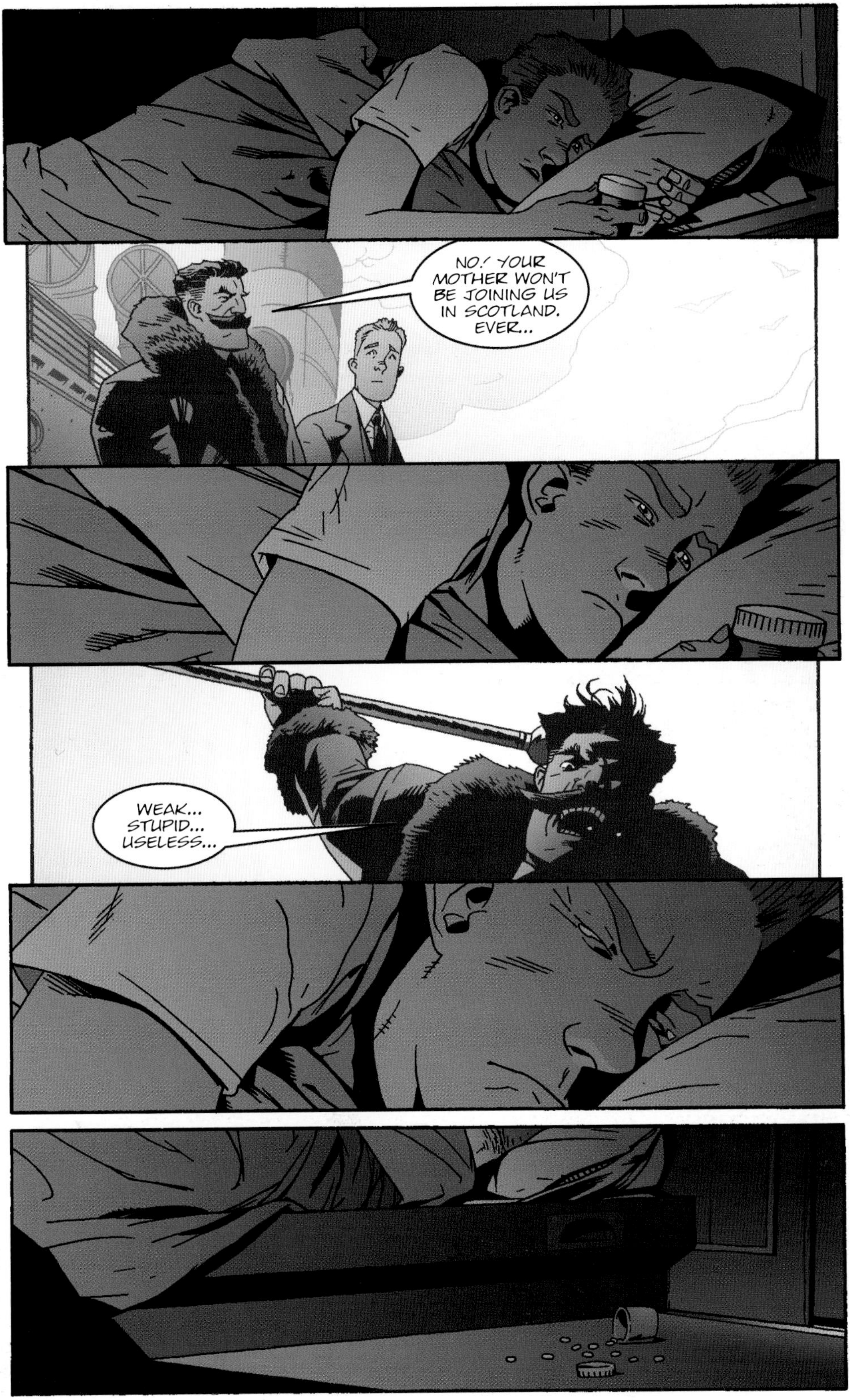
NO! YOUR MOTHER WON'T BE JOINING US IN SCOTLAND. EVER...
WEAK... STUPID... USELESS...

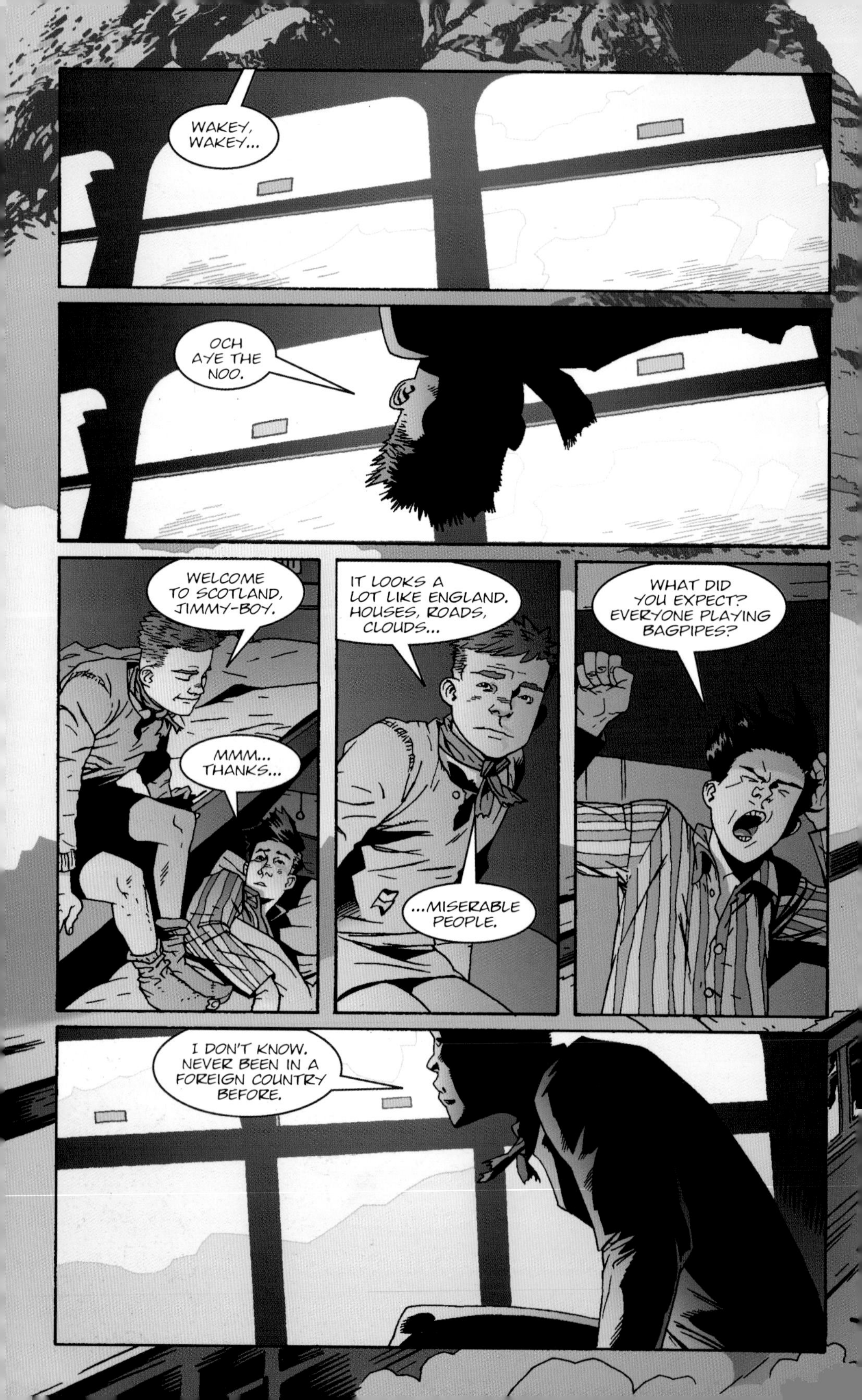
WAKEY, WAKEY...
OCH AYE THE NOO.
WELCOME TO SCOTLAND, JIMMY-BOY.
MMM... THANKS...
IT LOOKS A LOT LIKE ENGLAND. HOUSES, ROADS, CLOUDS...
...MISERABLE PEOPLE.
WHAT DID YOU EXPECT? EVERYONE PLAYING BAGPIPES?
I DON'T KNOW. NEVER BEEN IN A FOREIGN COUNTRY BEFORE.

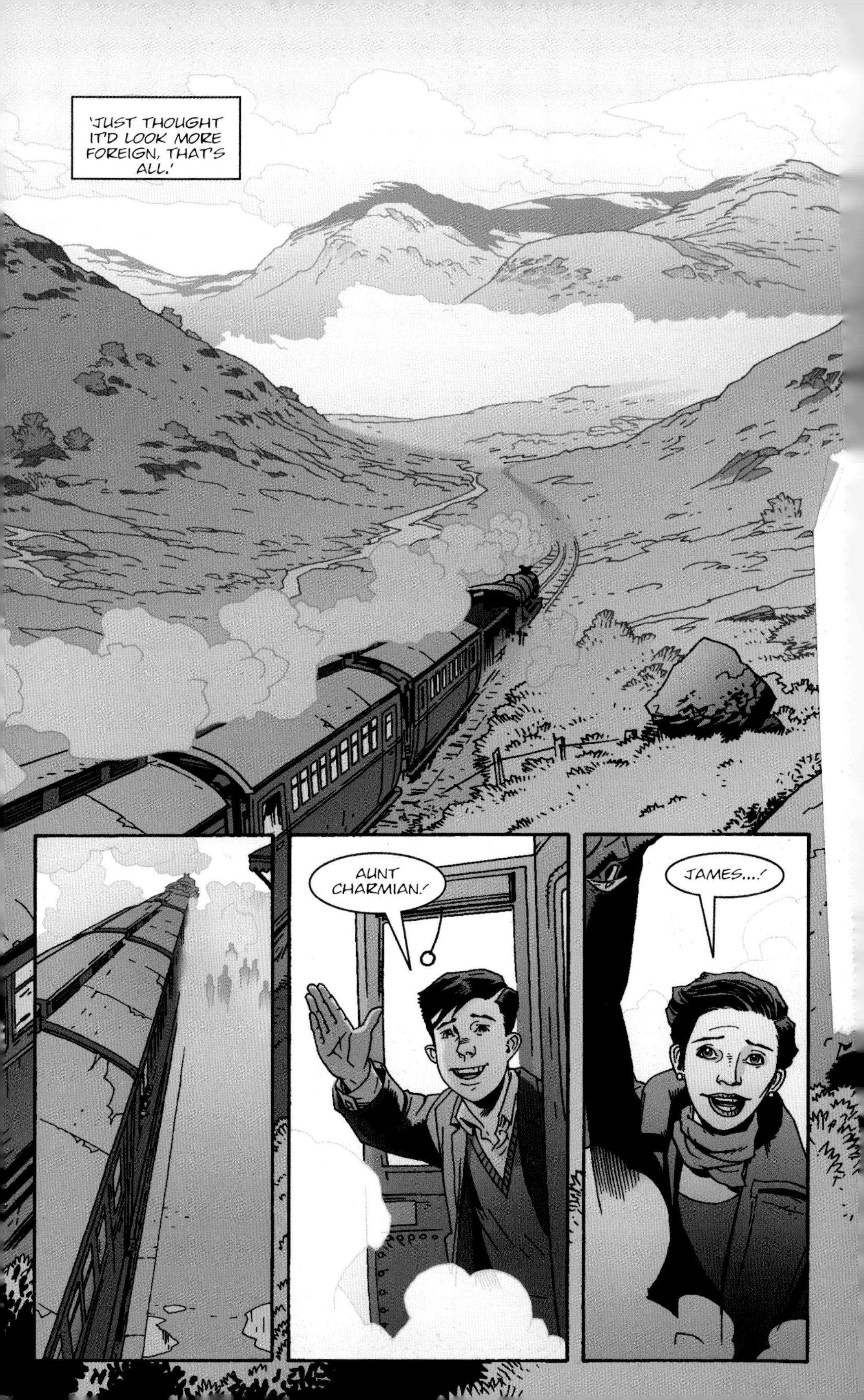
'JUST THOUGHT IT'D LOOK MORE FOREIGN, THAT'S ALL.'
AUNT CHARMIAN!
JAMES...!

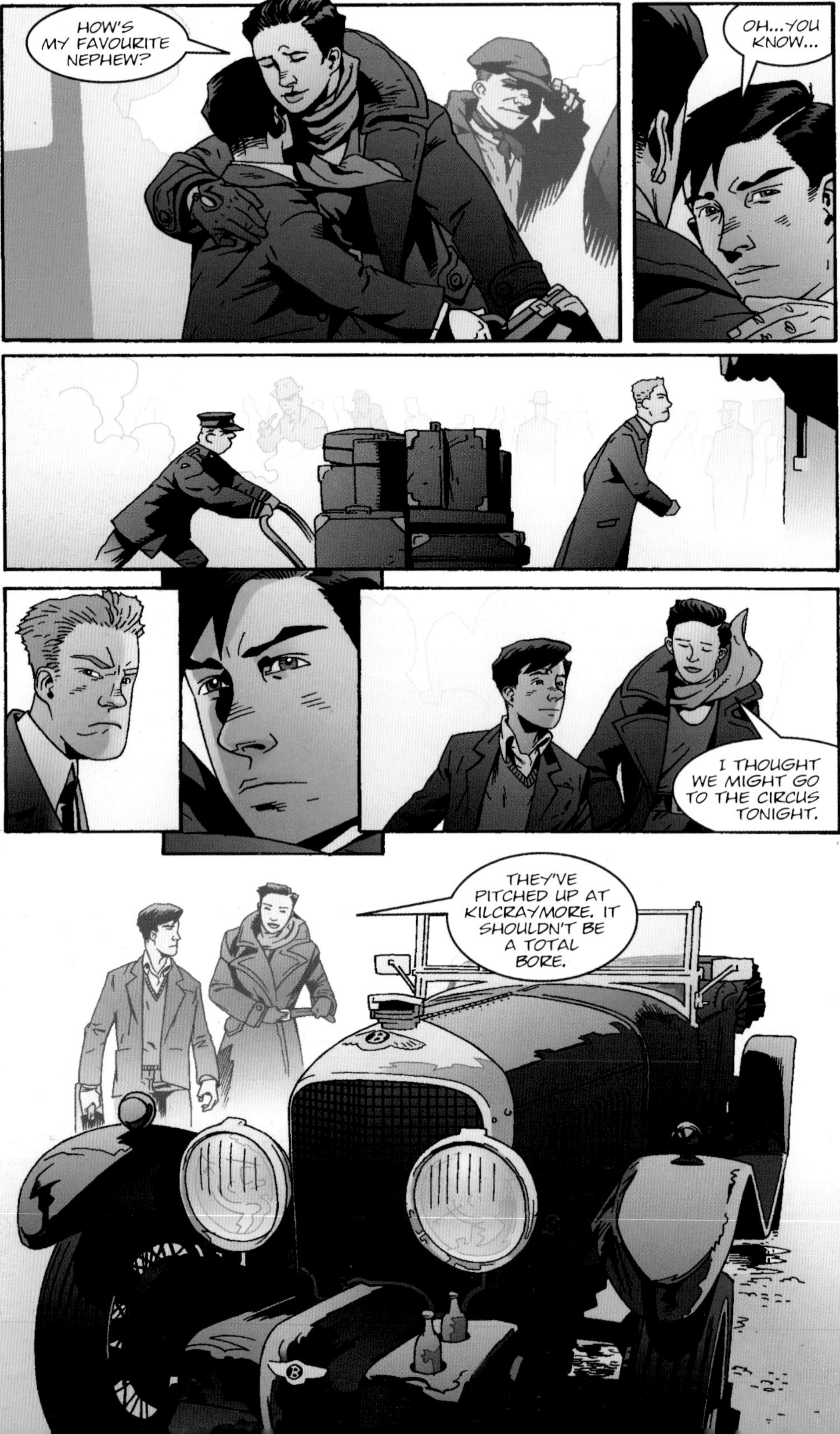
HOW'S MY FAVOURITE NEPHEW?
OH...YOU KNOW...
I THOUGHT WE MIGHT GO TO THE CIRCUS TONIGHT.
THEY'VE PITCHED UP AT KILCRAYMORE. IT SHOULDN'T BE A TOTAL BORE.

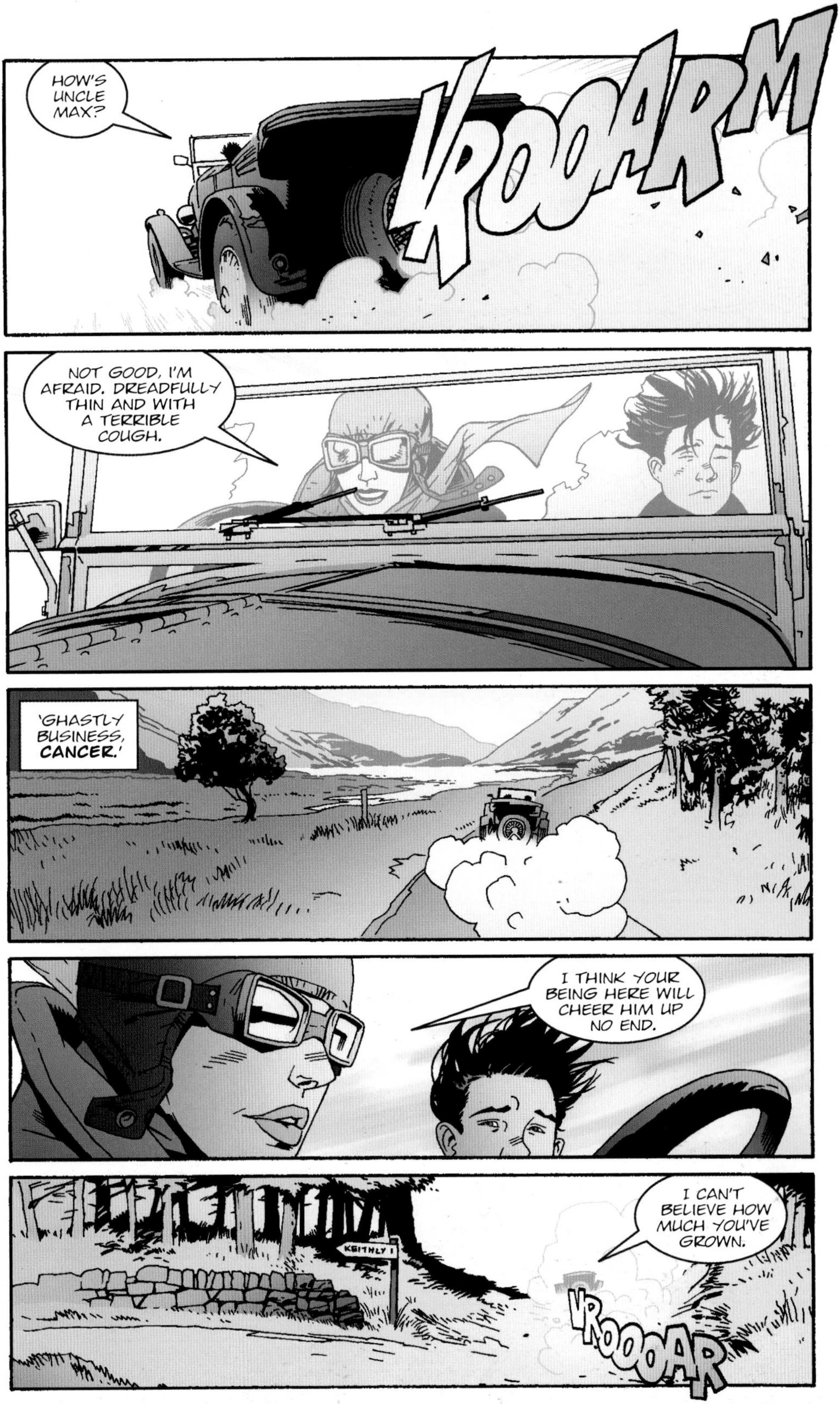
HOW'S UNCLE MAX?
VROOARM
NOT GOOD, I'M AFRAID. DREADFULLY THIN AND WITH A TERRIBLE COUGH.
'GHASTLY BUSINESS, **CANCER**.'
I THINK YOUR BEING HERE WILL CHEER HIM UP NO END.
KEITHLY 1
I CAN'T BELIEVE HOW MUCH YOU'VE GROWN.
VROOOOAR

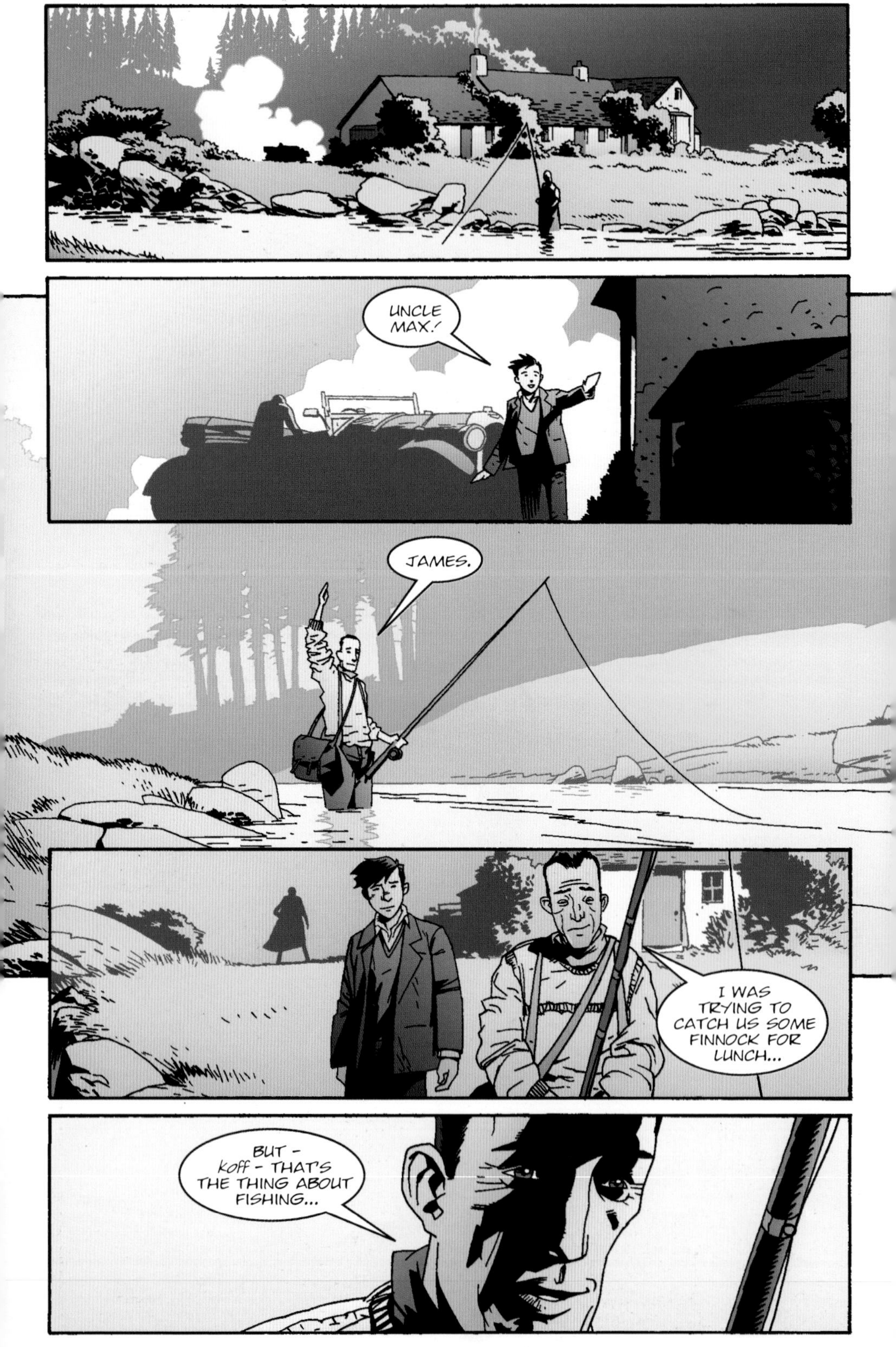
UNCLE MAX!
JAMES.
I WAS TRYING TO CATCH US SOME FINNOCK FOR LUNCH...
BUT - koff - THAT'S THE THING ABOUT FISHING...

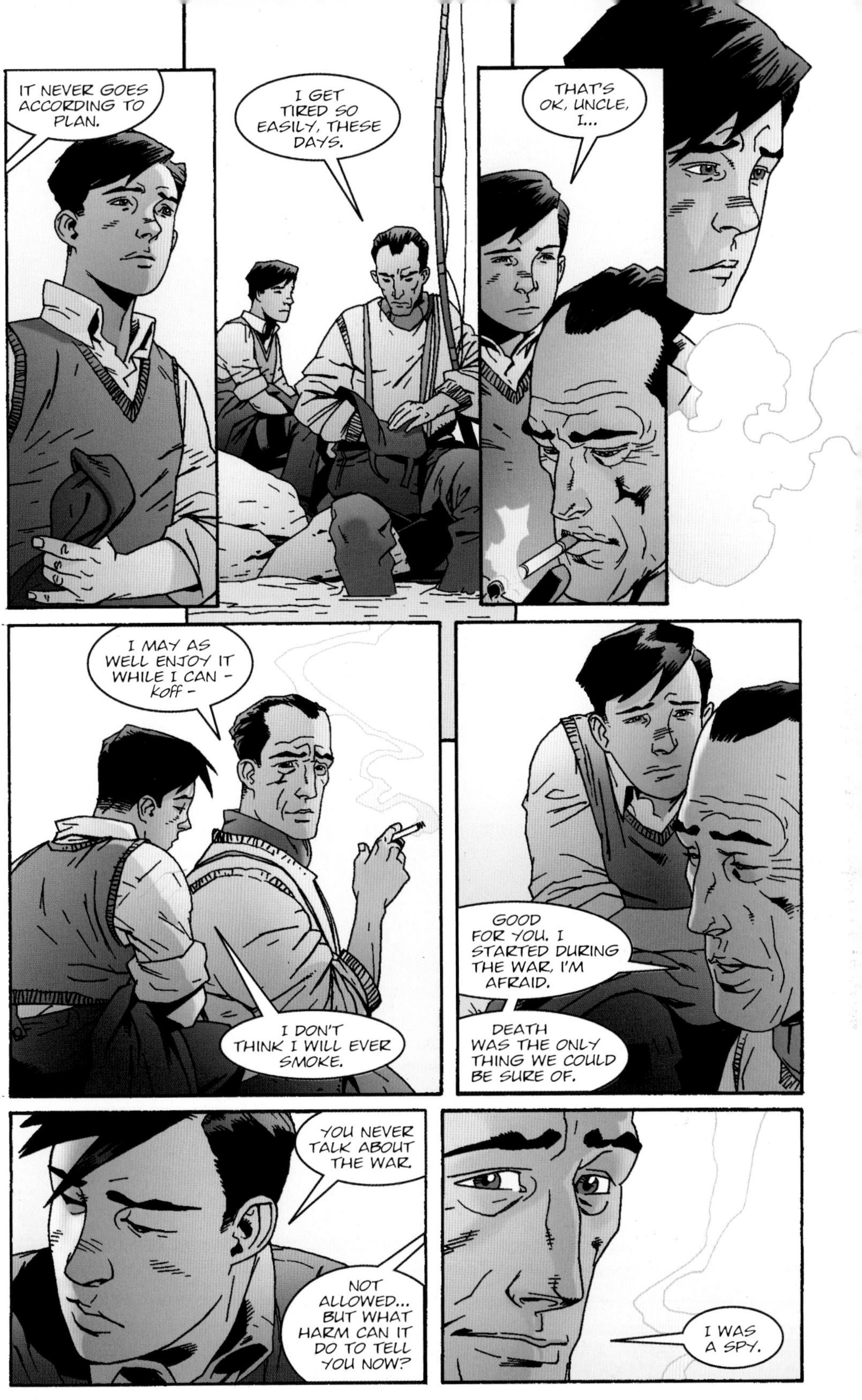
IT NEVER GOES ACCORDING TO PLAN.
I GET TIRED SO EASILY, THESE DAYS.
THAT'S OK, UNCLE, I...
I MAY AS WELL ENJOY IT WHILE I CAN - koff -
I DON'T THINK I WILL EVER SMOKE.
GOOD FOR YOU. I STARTED DURING THE WAR, I'M AFRAID.
DEATH WAS THE ONLY THING WE COULD BE SURE OF.
YOU NEVER TALK ABOUT THE WAR.
NOT ALLOWED... BUT WHAT HARM CAN IT DO TO TELL YOU NOW?
I WAS A SPY.

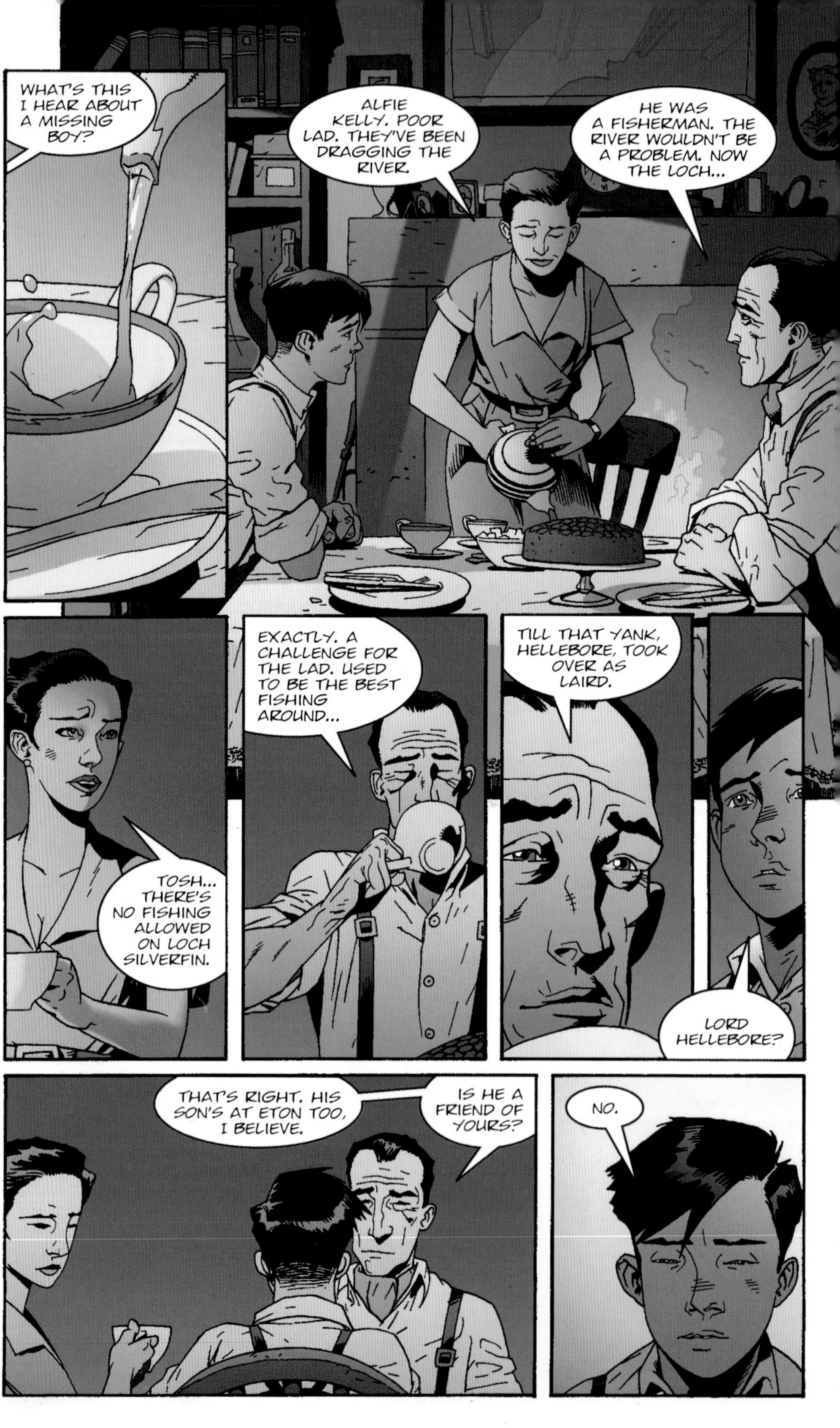
WHAT'S THIS I HEAR ABOUT A MISSING BOY?
ALFIE KELLY. POOR LAD. THEY'VE BEEN DRAGGING THE RIVER.
HE WAS A FISHERMAN. THE RIVER WOULDN'T BE A PROBLEM. NOW THE LOCH...
TOSH... THERE'S NO FISHING ALLOWED ON LOCH SILVERFIN.
EXACTLY. A CHALLENGE FOR THE LAD. USED TO BE THE BEST FISHING AROUND...
TILL THAT YANK, HELLEBORE, TOOK OVER AS LAIRD.
LORD HELLEBORE?
THAT'S RIGHT. HIS SON'S AT ETON TOO, I BELIEVE.
IS HE A FRIEND OF YOURS?
NO.

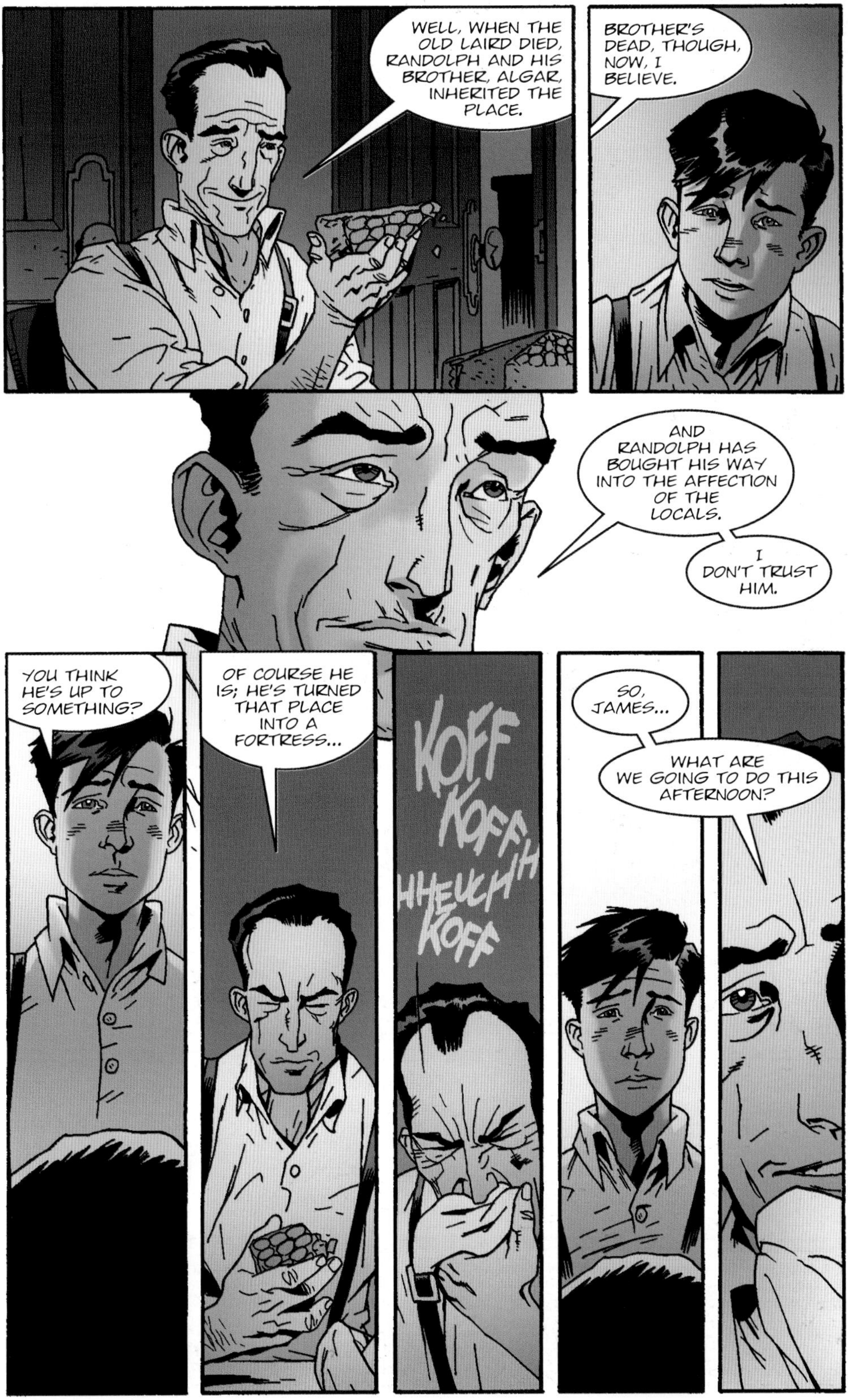
WELL, WHEN THE OLD LAIRD DIED, RANDOLPH AND HIS BROTHER, ALGAR, INHERITED THE PLACE.
BROTHER'S DEAD, THOUGH, NOW, I BELIEVE.
AND RANDOLPH HAS BOUGHT HIS WAY INTO THE AFFECTION OF THE LOCALS.
I DON'T TRUST HIM.
YOU THINK HE'S UP TO SOMETHING?
OF COURSE HE IS; HE'S TURNED THAT PLACE INTO A FORTRESS...
KOFF
KOFFHH
HHEUCH
KOFF
SO, JAMES...
WHAT ARE WE GOING TO DO THIS AFTERNOON?

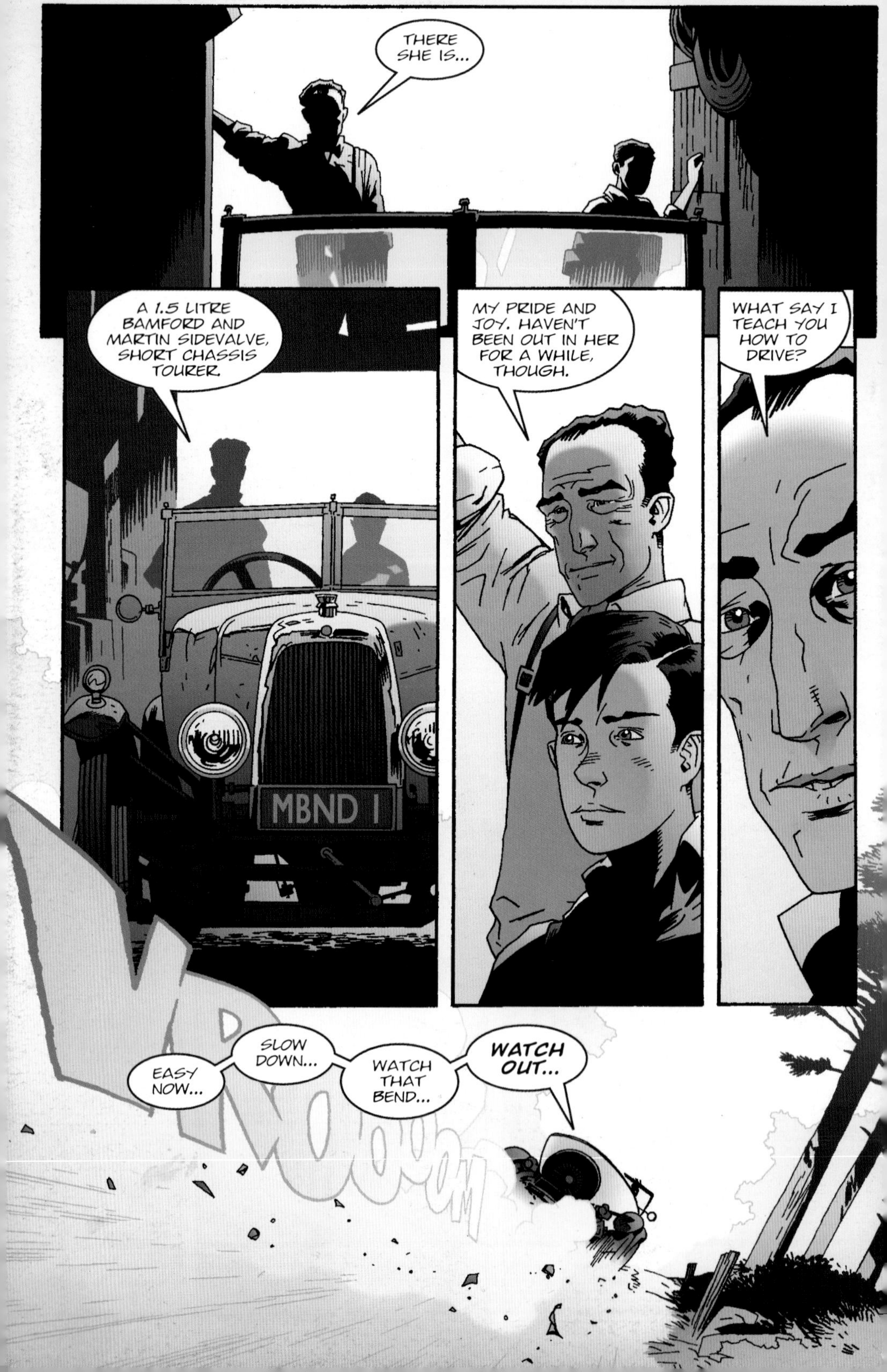
THERE SHE IS...
A 1.5 LITRE BAMFORD AND MARTIN SIDEVALVE, SHORT CHASSIS TOURER.
MBND 1
MY PRIDE AND JOY. HAVEN'T BEEN OUT IN HER FOR A WHILE, THOUGH.
WHAT SAY I TEACH YOU HOW TO DRIVE?
EASY NOW...
SLOW DOWN...
WATCH THAT BEND...
WATCH OUT...
VROOOOOM

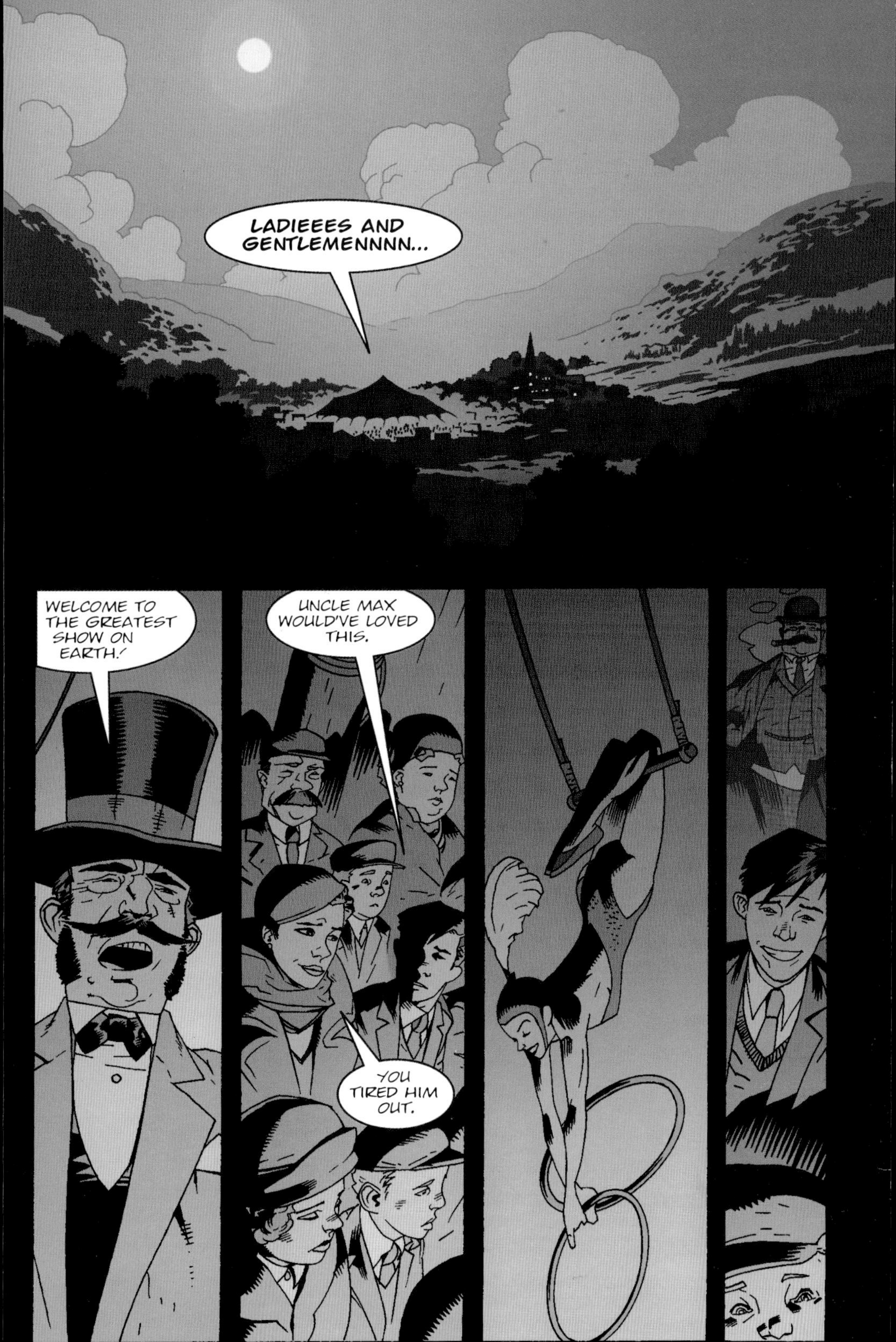

LADIEEES AND GENTLEMENNNN...
WELCOME TO THE GREATEST SHOW ON EARTH!
UNCLE MAX WOULD'VE LOVED THIS.
YOU TIRED HIM OUT.

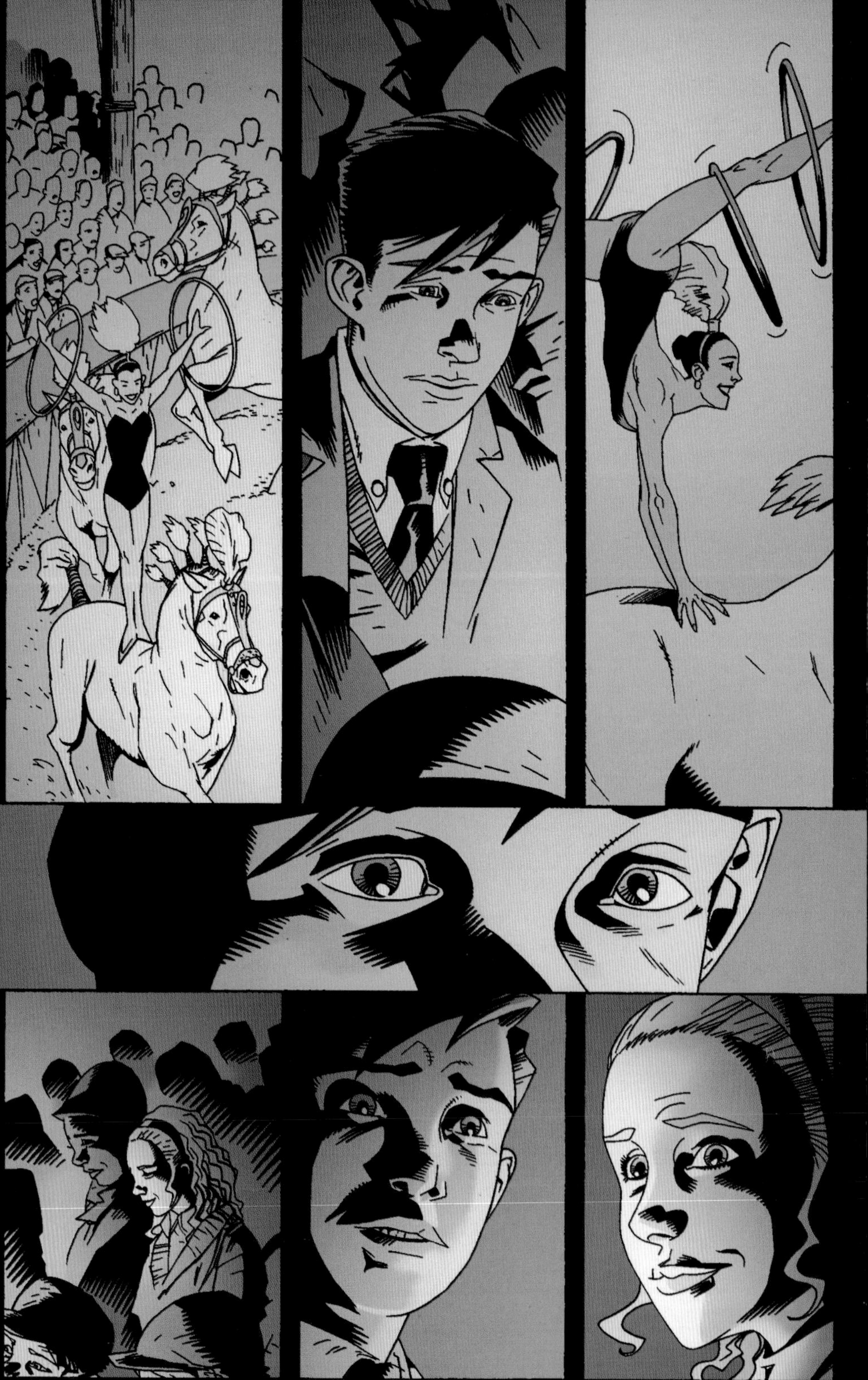

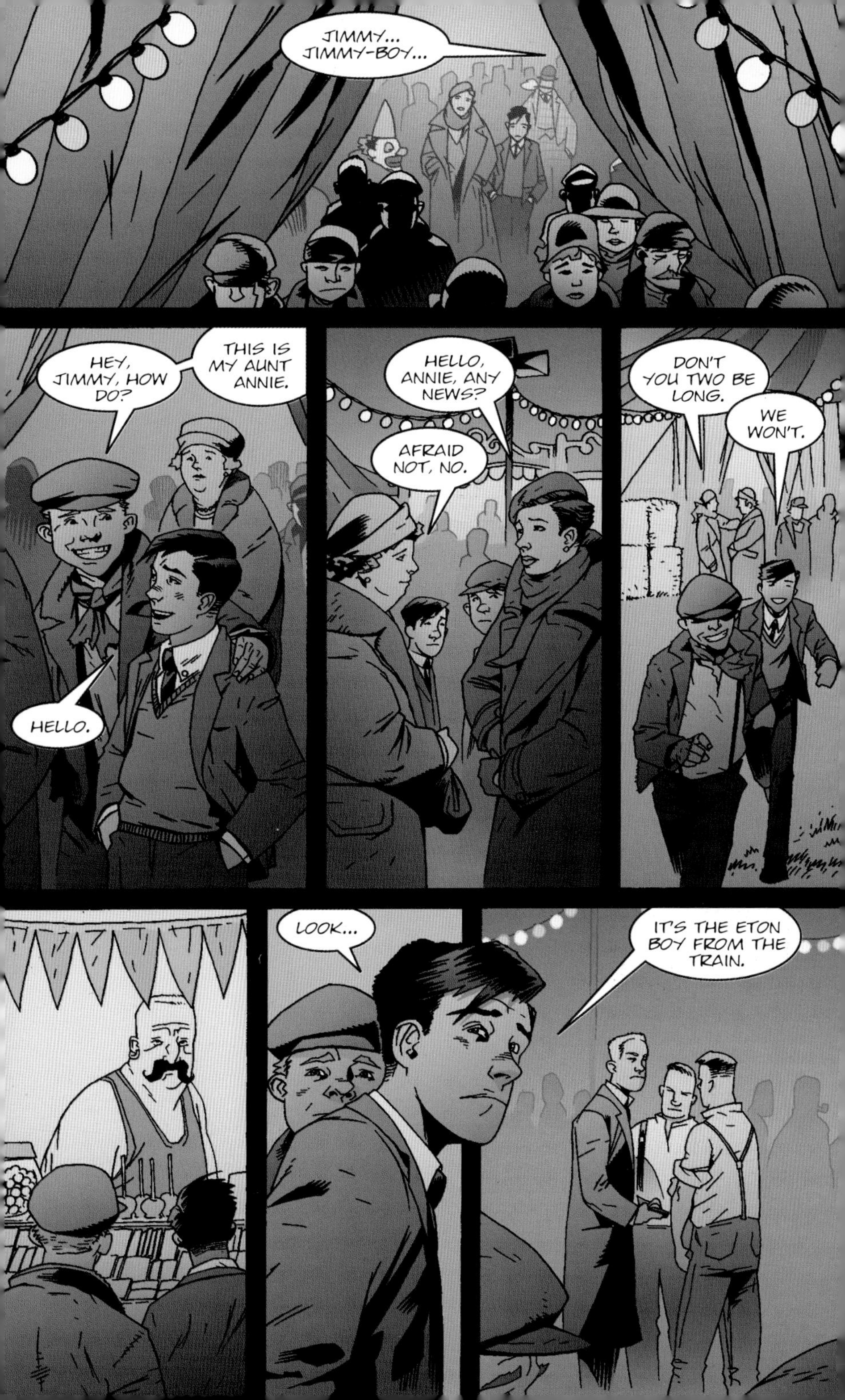
JIMMY... JIMMY-BOY...
HEY, JIMMY, HOW DO?
THIS IS MY AUNT ANNIE.
HELLO.
HELLO, ANNIE, ANY NEWS?
AFRAID NOT, NO.
DON'T YOU TWO BE LONG.
WE WON'T.
LOOK...
IT'S THE ETON BOY FROM THE TRAIN.

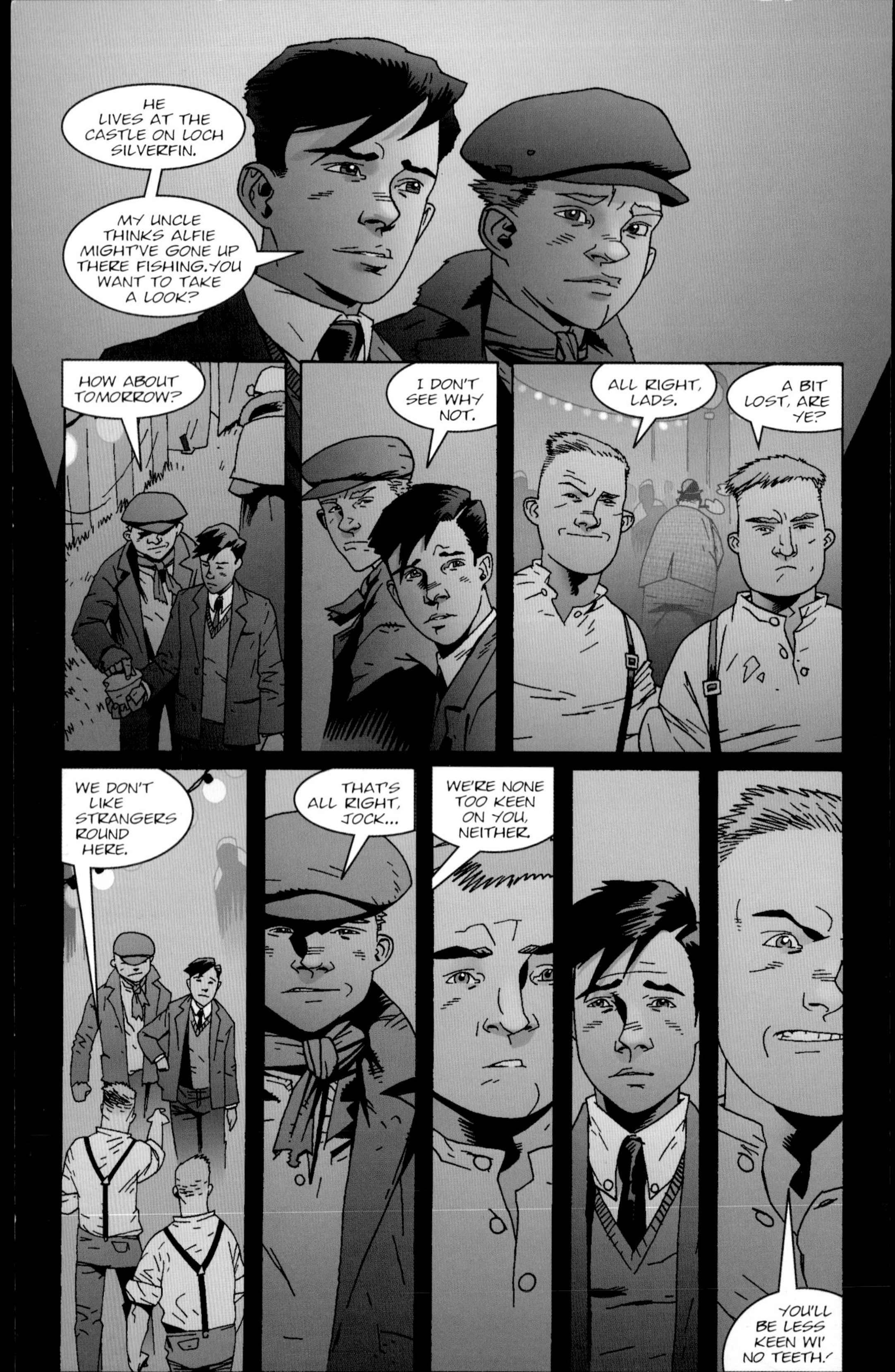
HE LIVES AT THE CASTLE ON LOCH SILVERFIN.
MY UNCLE THINKS ALFIE MIGHT'VE GONE UP THERE FISHING. YOU WANT TO TAKE A LOOK?
HOW ABOUT TOMORROW?
I DON'T SEE WHY NOT.
ALL RIGHT, LADS.
A BIT LOST, ARE YE?
WE DON'T LIKE STRANGERS ROUND HERE.
THAT'S ALL RIGHT, JOCK...
WE'RE NONE TOO KEEN ON YOU, NEITHER.
YOU'LL BE LESS KEEN WI' NO TEETH!

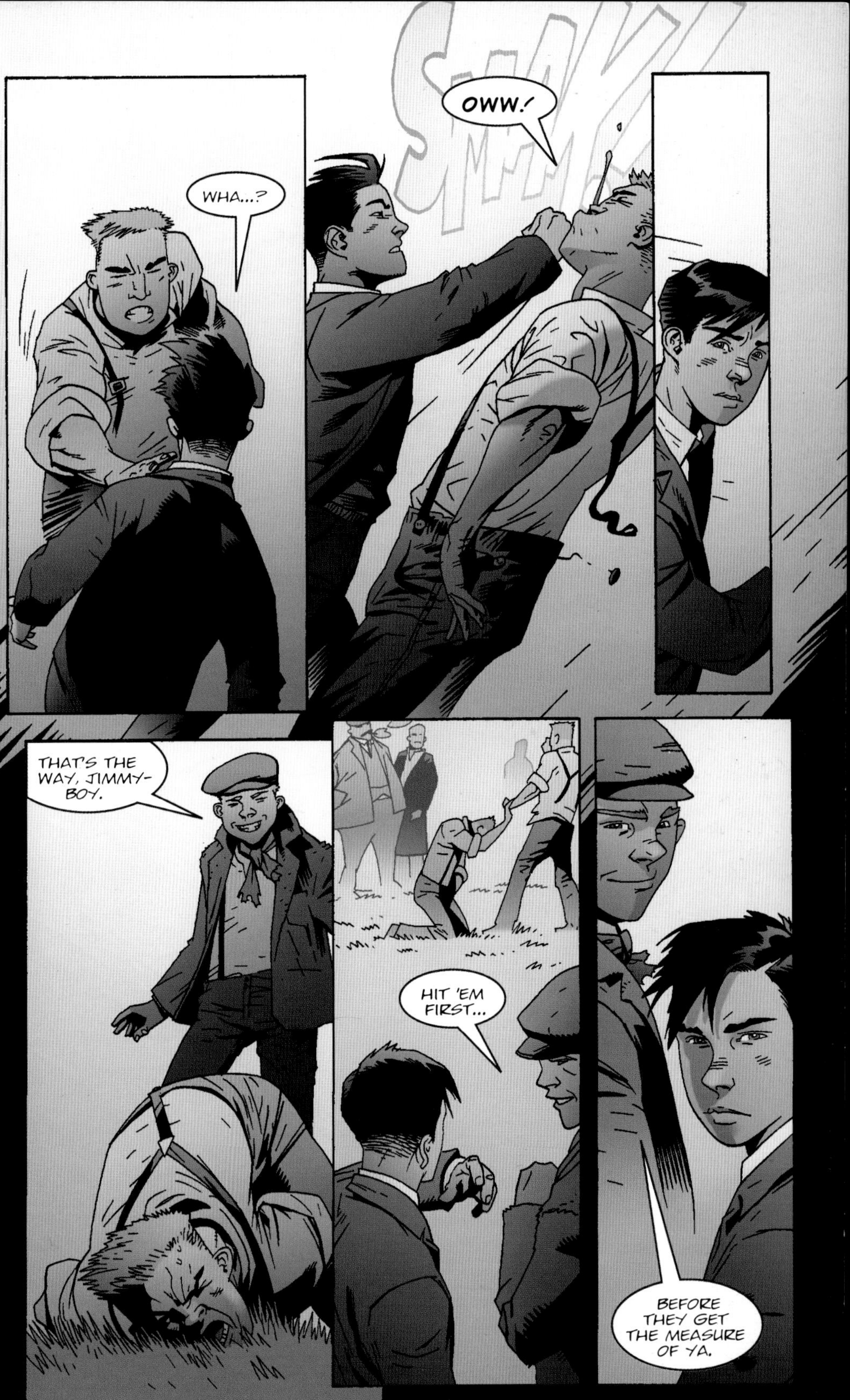
WHA...?
SMAK!
OWW!
THAT'S THE WAY, JIMMY-BOY.
HIT 'EM FIRST...
BEFORE THEY GET THE MEASURE OF YA.

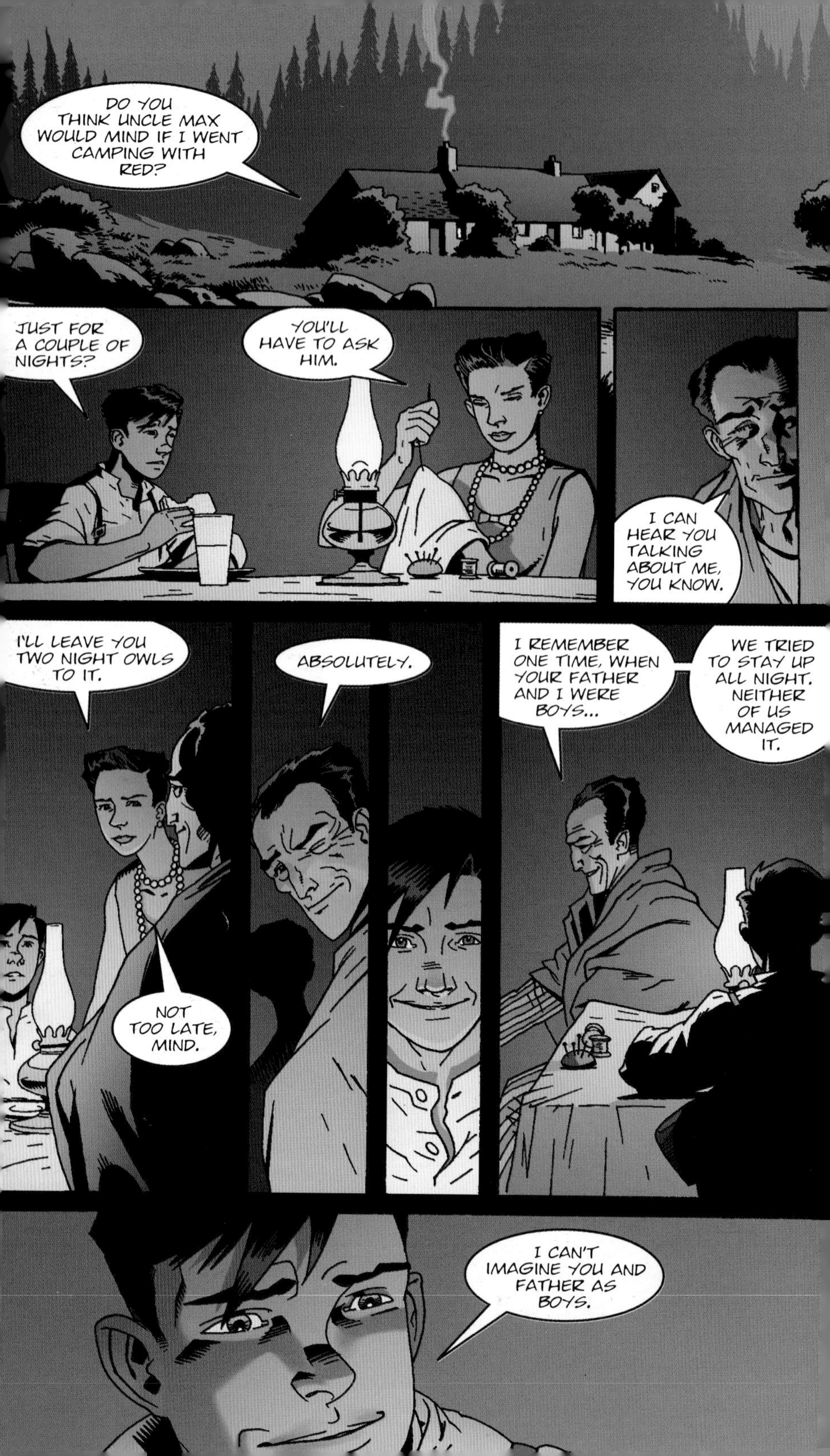
DO YOU THINK UNCLE MAX WOULD MIND IF I WENT CAMPING WITH RED?
JUST FOR A COUPLE OF NIGHTS?
YOU'LL HAVE TO ASK HIM.
I CAN HEAR YOU TALKING ABOUT ME, YOU KNOW.
I'LL LEAVE YOU TWO NIGHT OWLS TO IT.
NOT TOO LATE, MIND.
ABSOLUTELY.
I REMEMBER ONE TIME, WHEN YOUR FATHER AND I WERE BOYS...
WE TRIED TO STAY UP ALL NIGHT. NEITHER OF US MANAGED IT.
I CAN'T IMAGINE YOU AND FATHER AS BOYS.

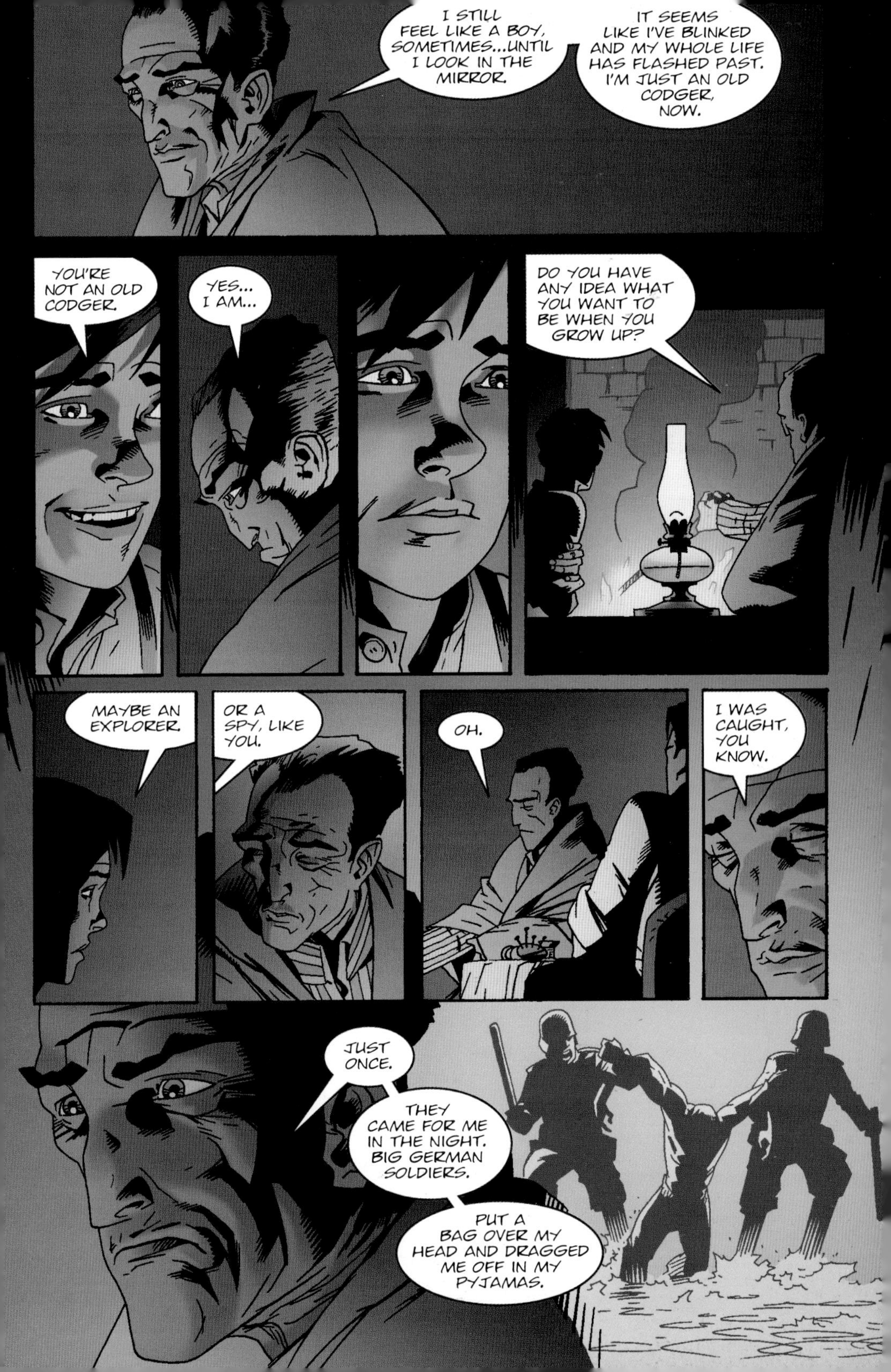
I STILL FEEL LIKE A BOY, SOMETIMES...UNTIL I LOOK IN THE MIRROR.
IT SEEMS LIKE I'VE BLINKED AND MY WHOLE LIFE HAS FLASHED PAST. I'M JUST AN OLD CODGER, NOW.
YOU'RE NOT AN OLD CODGER.
YES... I AM...
DO YOU HAVE ANY IDEA WHAT YOU WANT TO BE WHEN YOU GROW UP?
MAYBE AN EXPLORER.
OR A SPY, LIKE YOU.
OH.
I WAS CAUGHT, YOU KNOW.
JUST ONCE.
THEY CAME FOR ME IN THE NIGHT. BIG GERMAN SOLDIERS.
PUT A BAG OVER MY HEAD AND DRAGGED ME OFF IN MY PYJAMAS.

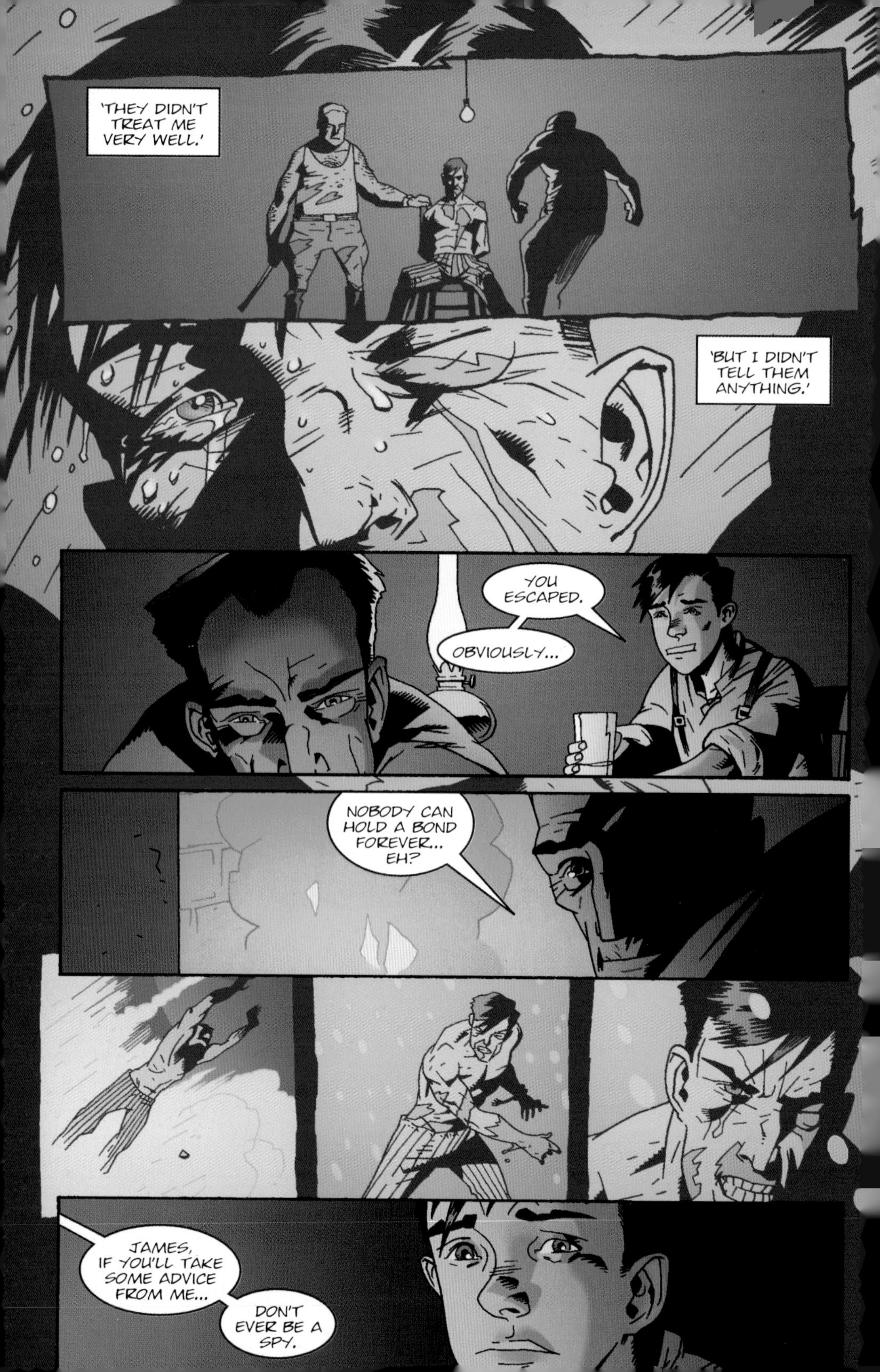
'THEY DIDN'T TREAT ME VERY WELL.'
'BUT I DIDN'T TELL THEM ANYTHING.'
YOU ESCAPED.
OBVIOUSLY...
NOBODY CAN HOLD A BOND FOREVER... EH?
JAMES, IF YOU'LL TAKE SOME ADVICE FROM ME...
DON'T EVER BE A SPY.

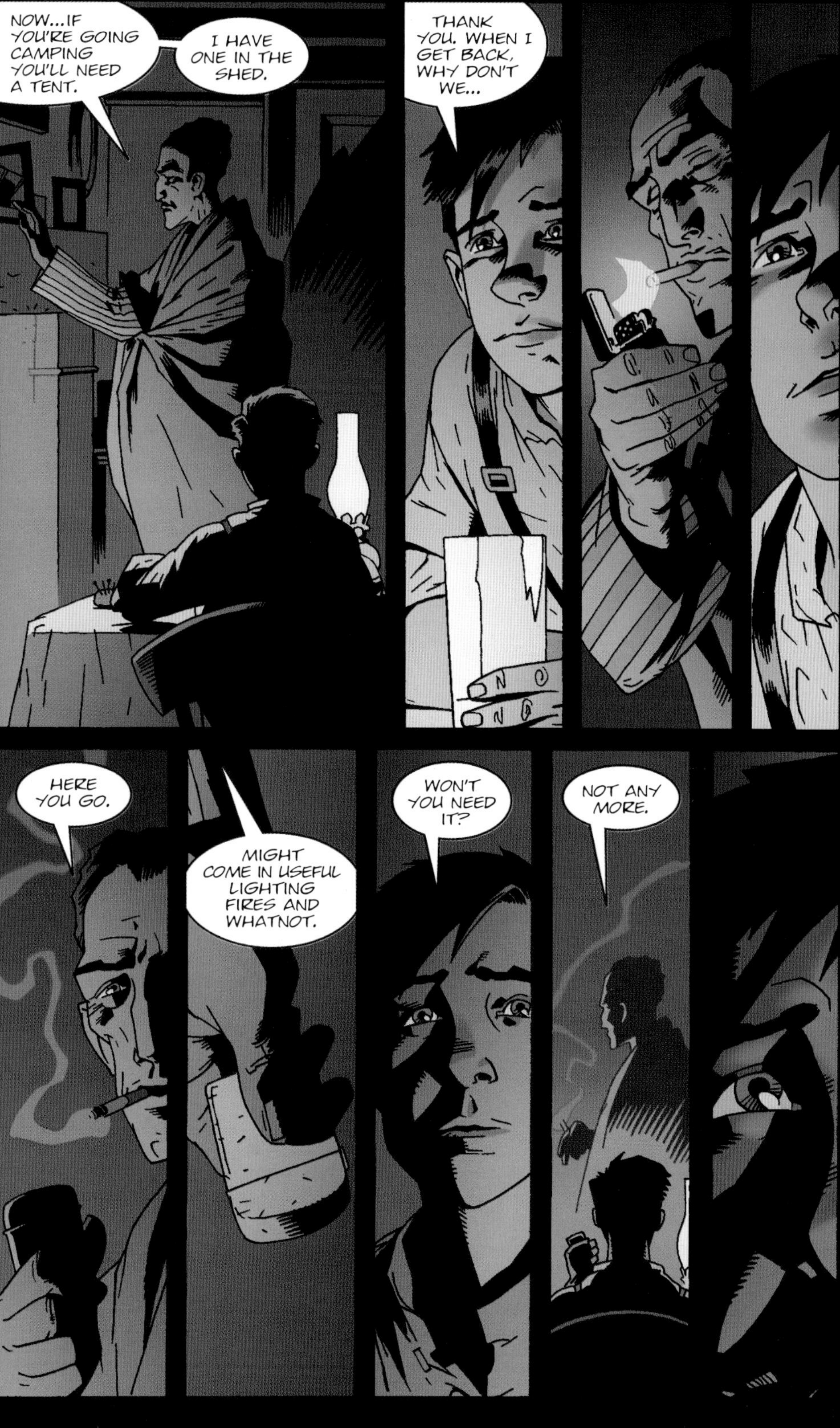
NOW...IF YOU'RE GOING CAMPING YOU'LL NEED A TENT.
I HAVE ONE IN THE SHED.
THANK YOU. WHEN I GET BACK, WHY DON'T WE...
HERE YOU GO.
MIGHT COME IN USEFUL LIGHTING FIRES AND WHATNOT.
WON'T YOU NEED IT?
NOT ANY MORE.

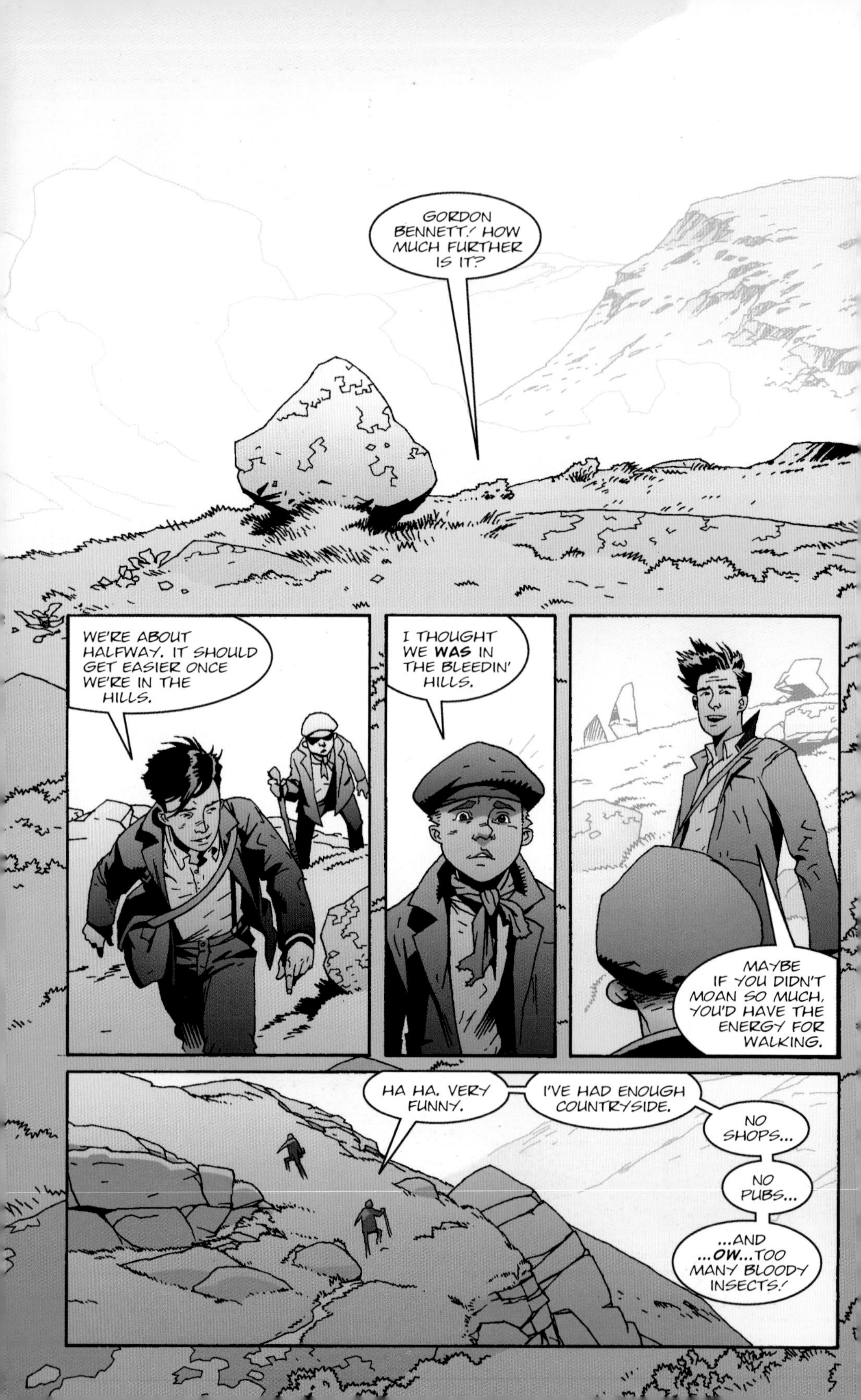
GORDON BENNETT! HOW MUCH FURTHER IS IT?
WE'RE ABOUT HALFWAY. IT SHOULD GET EASIER ONCE WE'RE IN THE HILLS.
I THOUGHT WE **WAS** IN THE BLEEDIN' HILLS.
MAYBE IF YOU DIDN'T MOAN SO MUCH, YOU'D HAVE THE ENERGY FOR WALKING.
HA HA. VERY FUNNY.
I'VE HAD ENOUGH COUNTRYSIDE.
NO SHOPS...
NO PUBS...
...AND ...**OW**...TOO MANY BLOODY INSECTS!

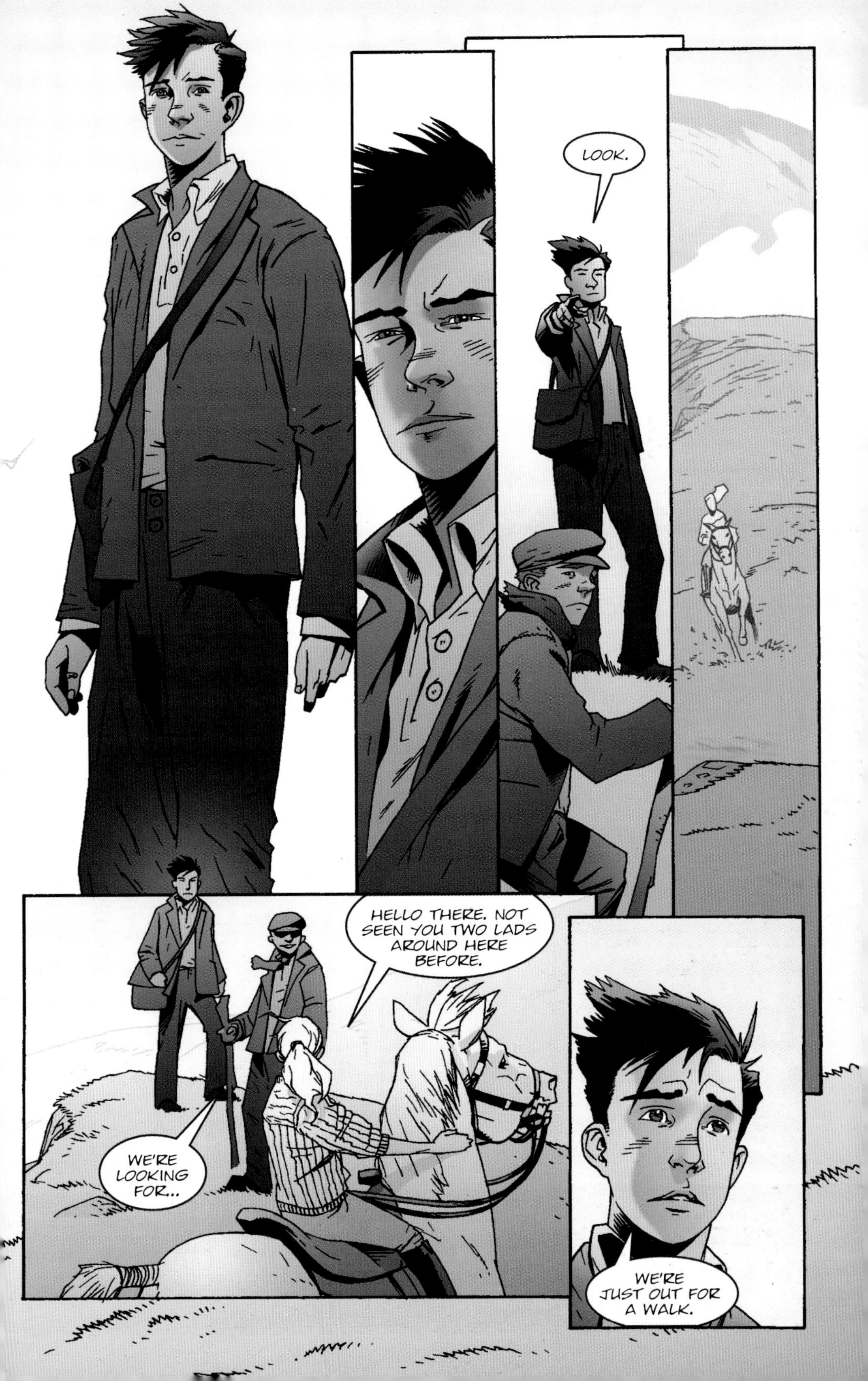
LOOK.
HELLO THERE. NOT SEEN YOU TWO LADS AROUND HERE BEFORE.
WE'RE LOOKING FOR...
WE'RE JUST OUT FOR A WALK.

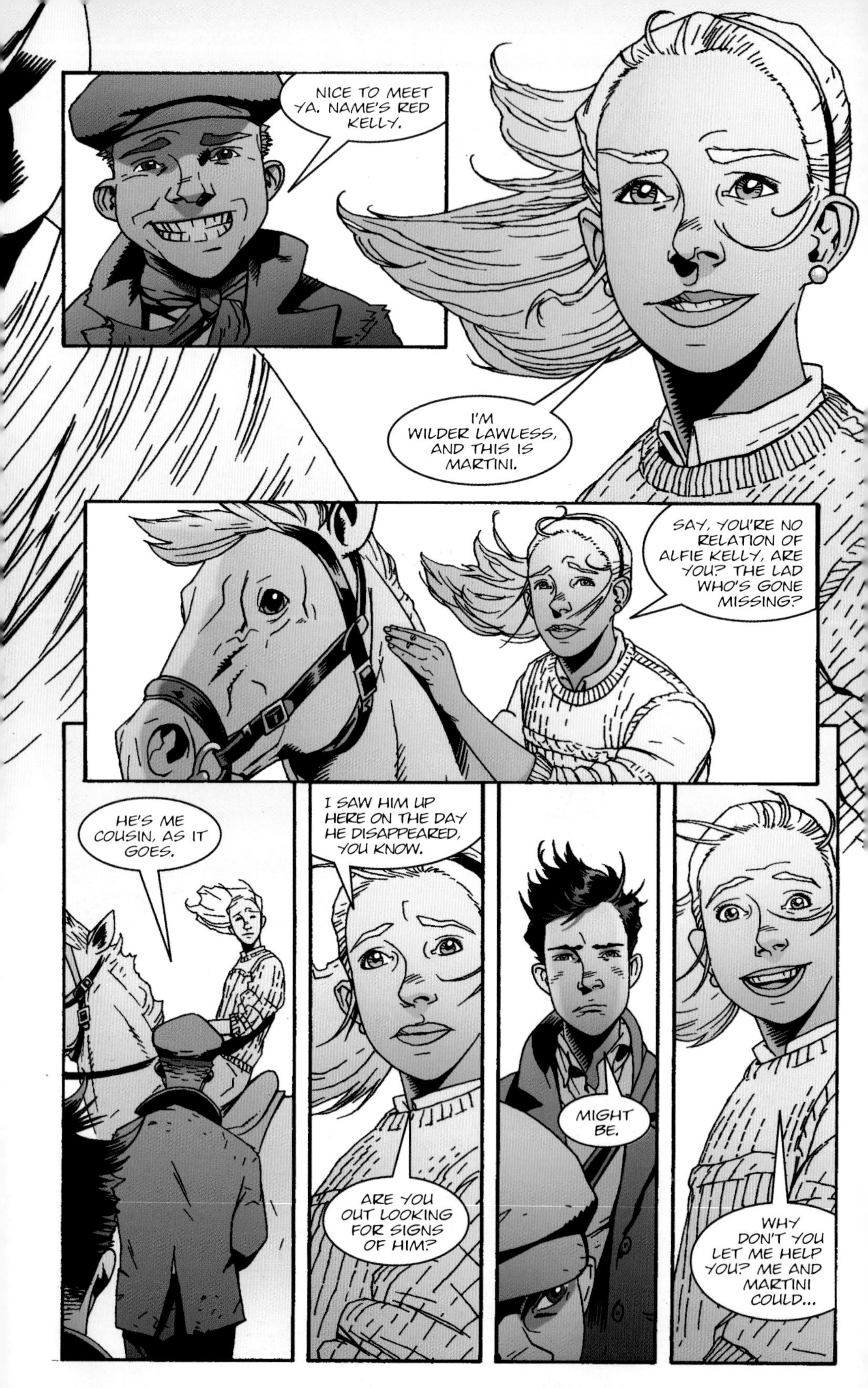
NICE TO MEET YA. NAME'S RED KELLY.
I'M WILDER LAWLESS, AND THIS IS MARTINI.
SAY, YOU'RE NO RELATION OF ALFIE KELLY, ARE YOU? THE LAD WHO'S GONE MISSING?
HE'S ME COUSIN, AS IT GOES.
I SAW HIM UP HERE ON THE DAY HE DISAPPEARED, YOU KNOW.
ARE YOU OUT LOOKING FOR SIGNS OF HIM?
MIGHT BE.
WHY DON'T YOU LET ME HELP YOU? ME AND MARTINI COULD...

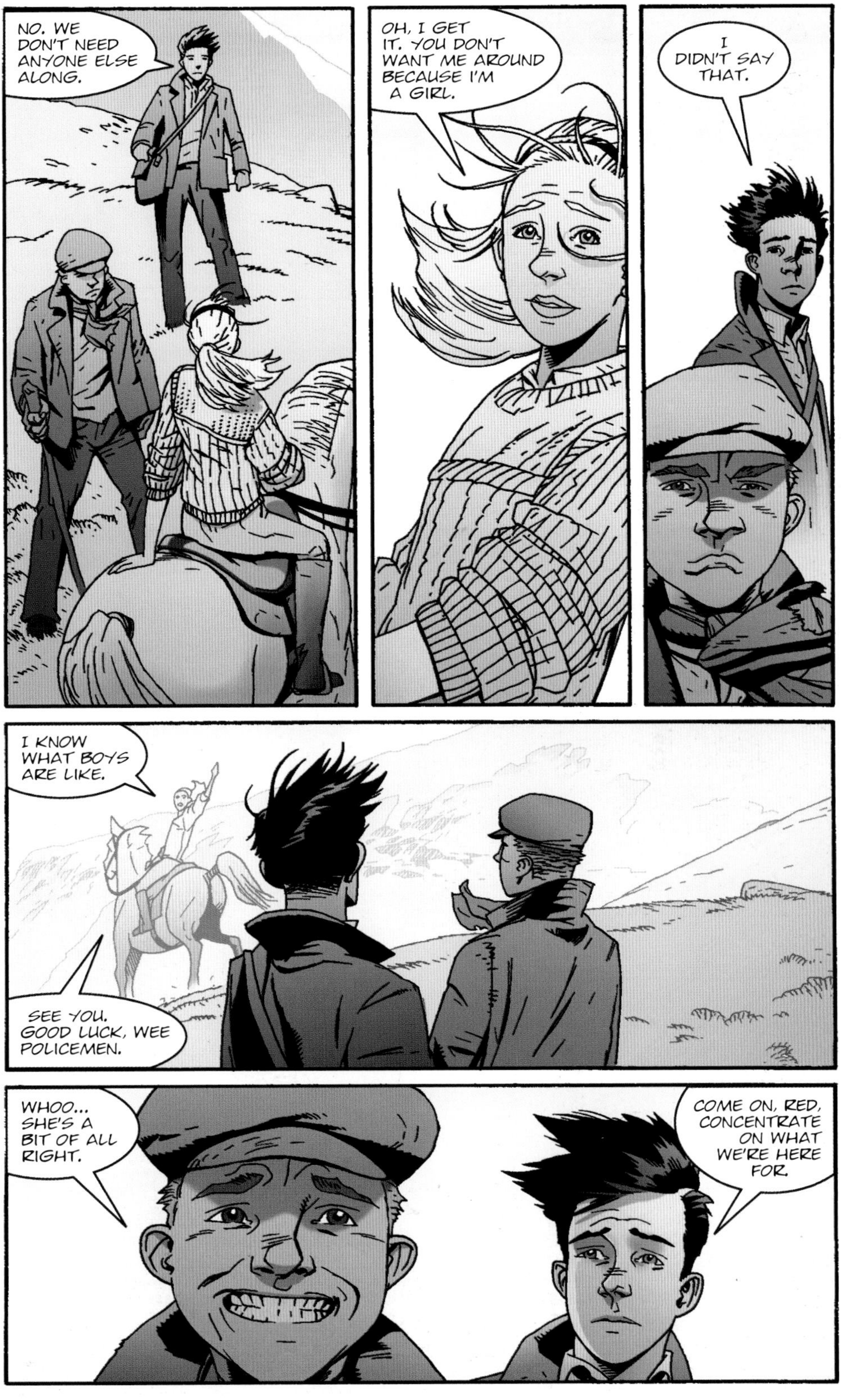
NO. WE DON'T NEED ANYONE ELSE ALONG.
OH, I GET IT. YOU DON'T WANT ME AROUND BECAUSE I'M A GIRL.
I DIDN'T SAY THAT.
I KNOW WHAT BOYS ARE LIKE.
SEE YOU. GOOD LUCK, WEE POLICEMEN.
WHOO... SHE'S A BIT OF ALL RIGHT.
COME ON, RED, CONCENTRATE ON WHAT WE'RE HERE FOR.

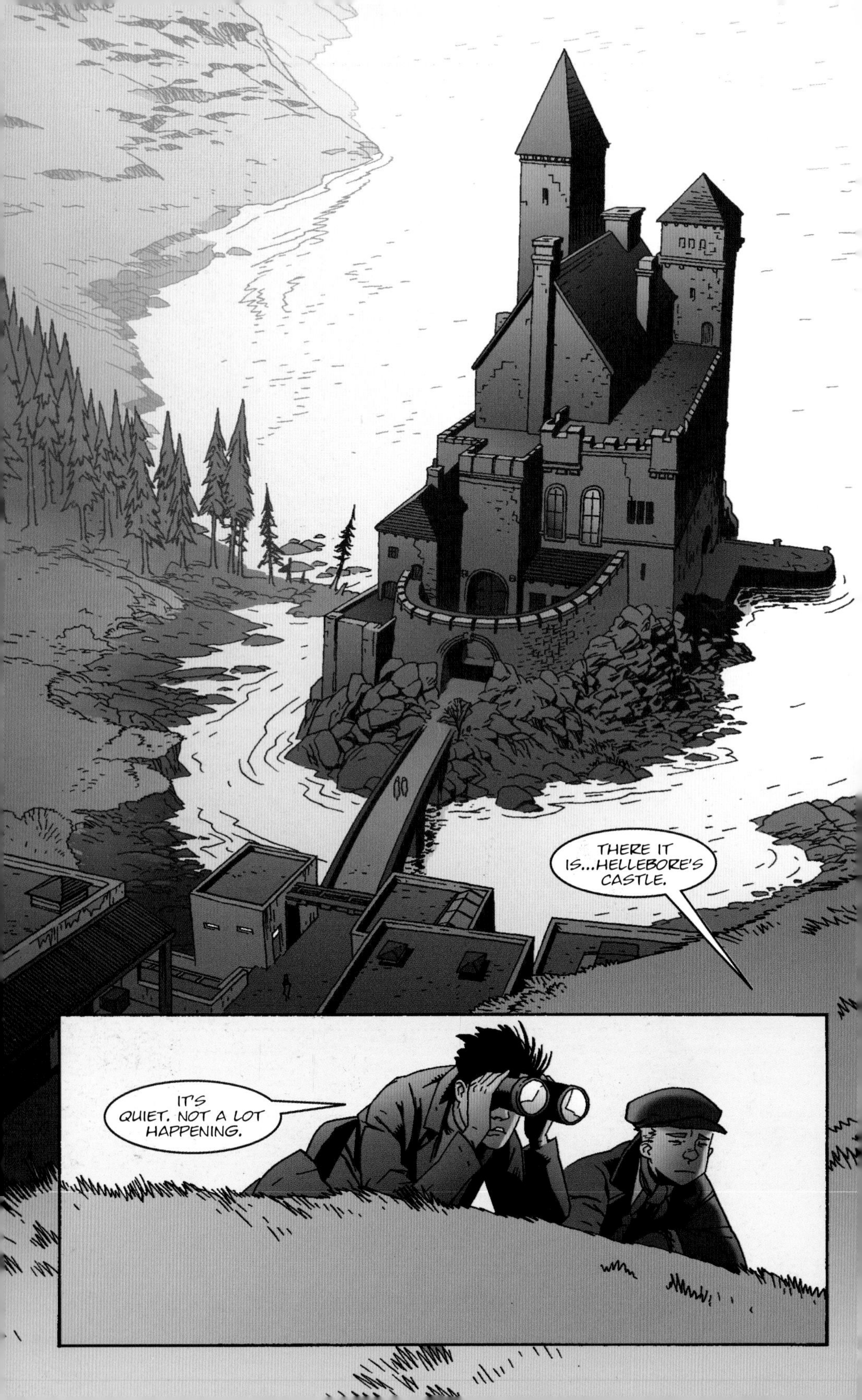
THERE IT IS...HELLEBORE'S CASTLE.
IT'S QUIET. NOT A LOT HAPPENING.

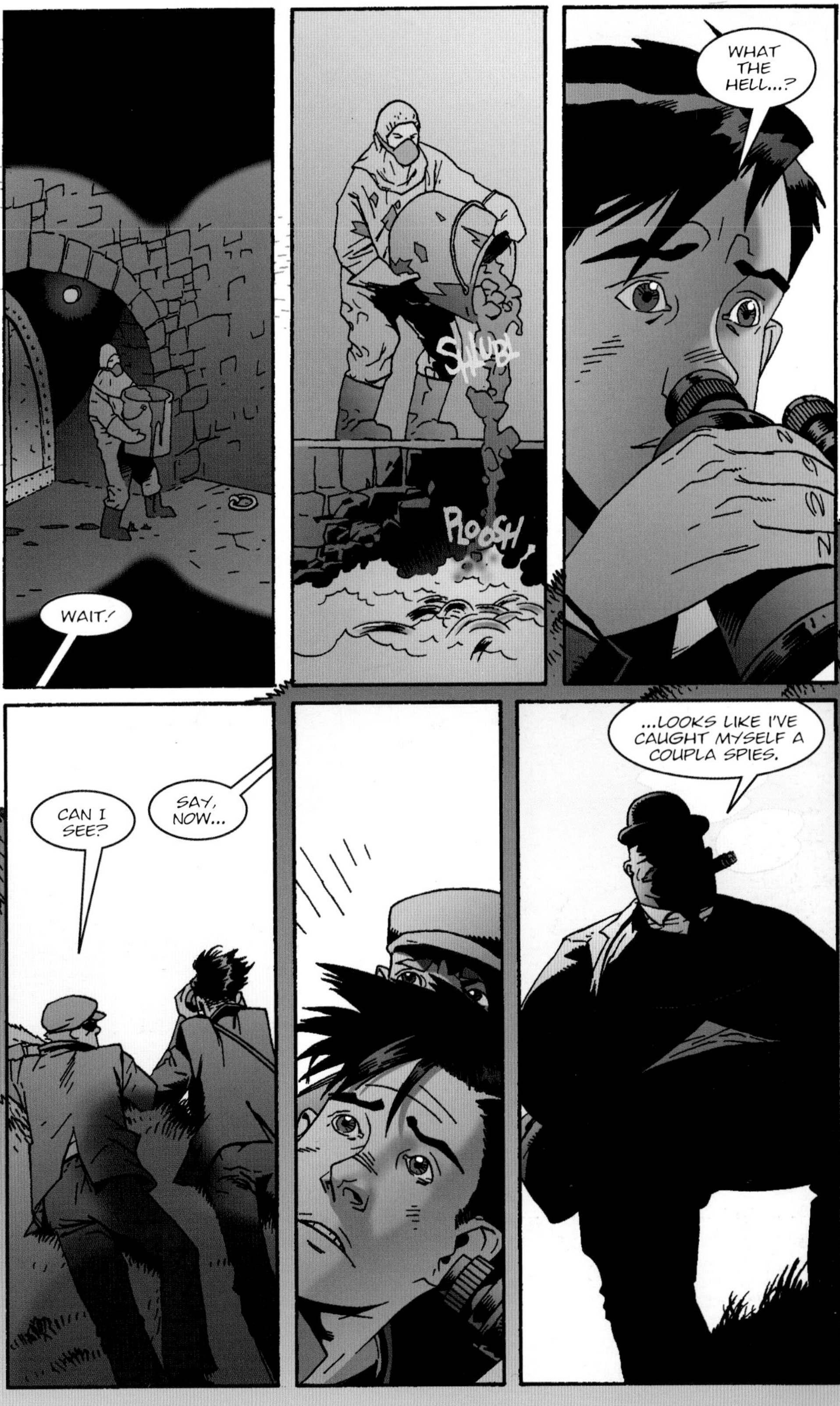
WAIT!
SHLUBL
PLOOSH
WHAT THE HELL...?
SAY, NOW...
CAN I SEE?
...LOOKS LIKE I'VE CAUGHT MYSELF A COUPLA SPIES.

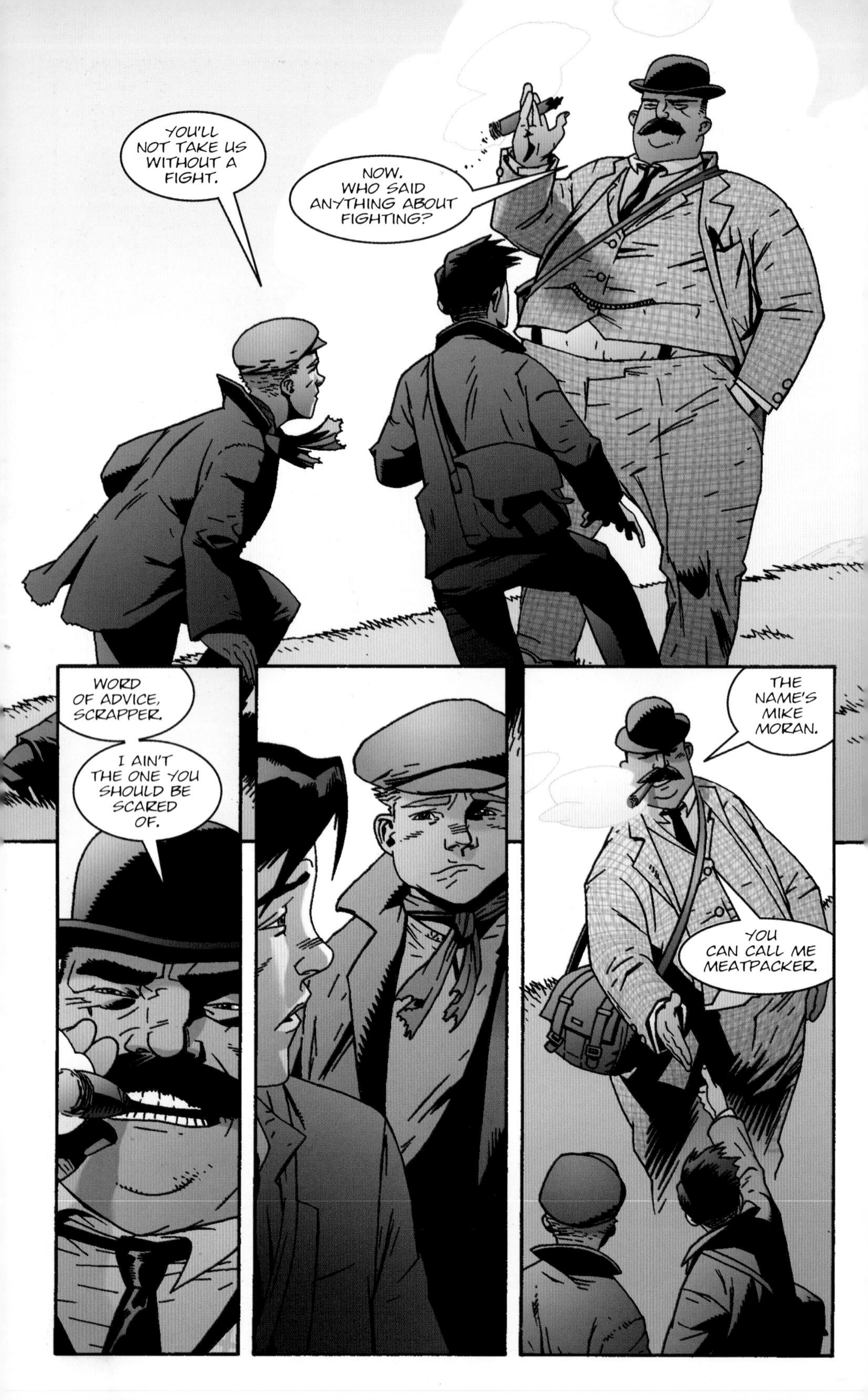
YOU'LL NOT TAKE US WITHOUT A FIGHT.
NOW. WHO SAID ANYTHING ABOUT FIGHTING?
WORD OF ADVICE, SCRAPPER.
I AIN'T THE ONE YOU SHOULD BE SCARED OF.
THE NAME'S MIKE MORAN.
YOU CAN CALL ME MEATPACKER.

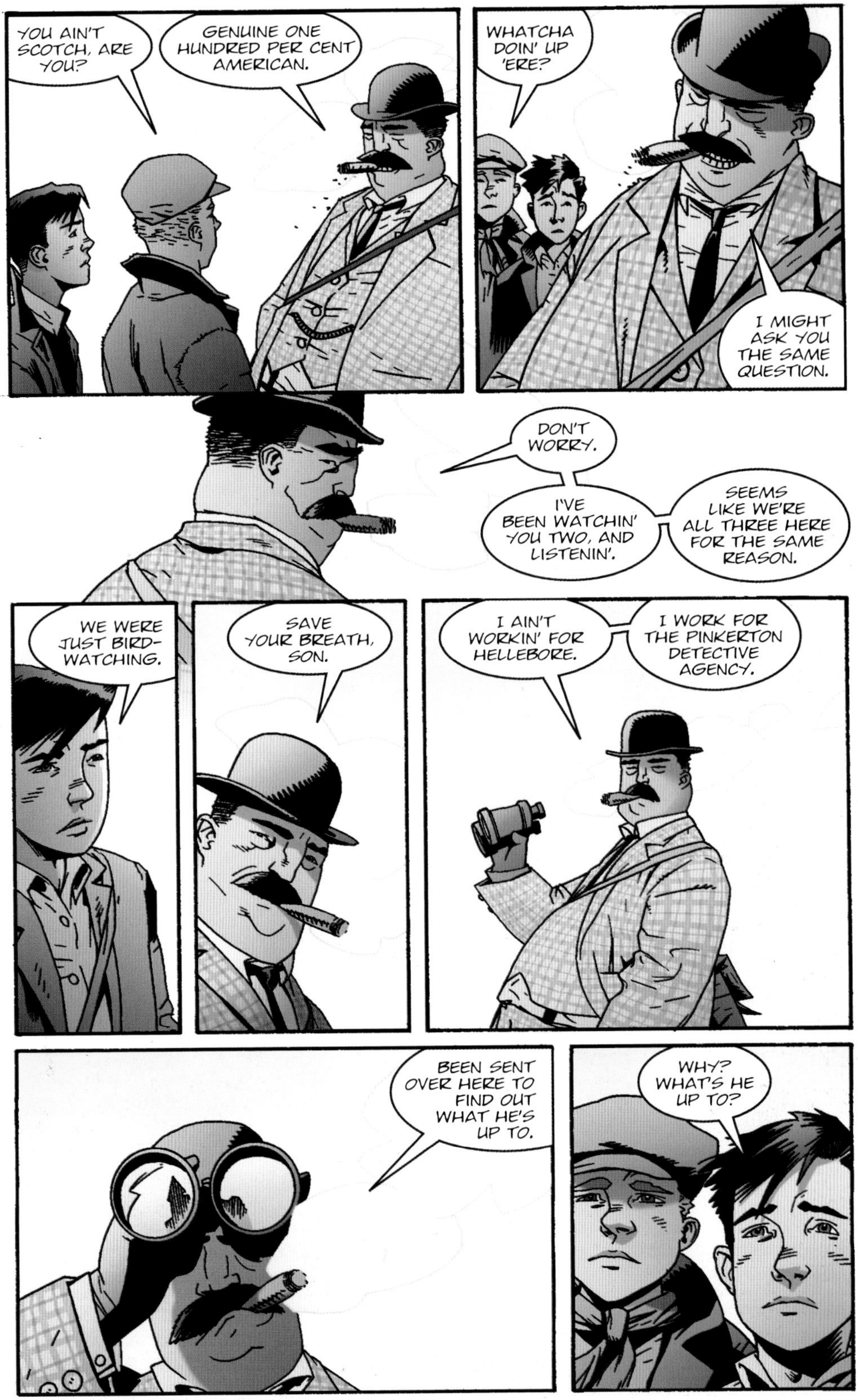
YOU AIN'T SCOTCH, ARE YOU?
GENUINE ONE HUNDRED PER CENT AMERICAN.
WHATCHA DOIN' UP 'ERE?
I MIGHT ASK YOU THE SAME QUESTION.
DON'T WORRY.
I'VE BEEN WATCHIN' YOU TWO, AND LISTENIN'.
SEEMS LIKE WE'RE ALL THREE HERE FOR THE SAME REASON.
WE WERE JUST BIRD-WATCHING.
SAVE YOUR BREATH, SON.
I AIN'T WORKIN' FOR HELLEBORE.
I WORK FOR THE PINKERTON DETECTIVE AGENCY.
BEEN SENT OVER HERE TO FIND OUT WHAT HE'S UP TO.
WHY? WHAT'S HE UP TO?

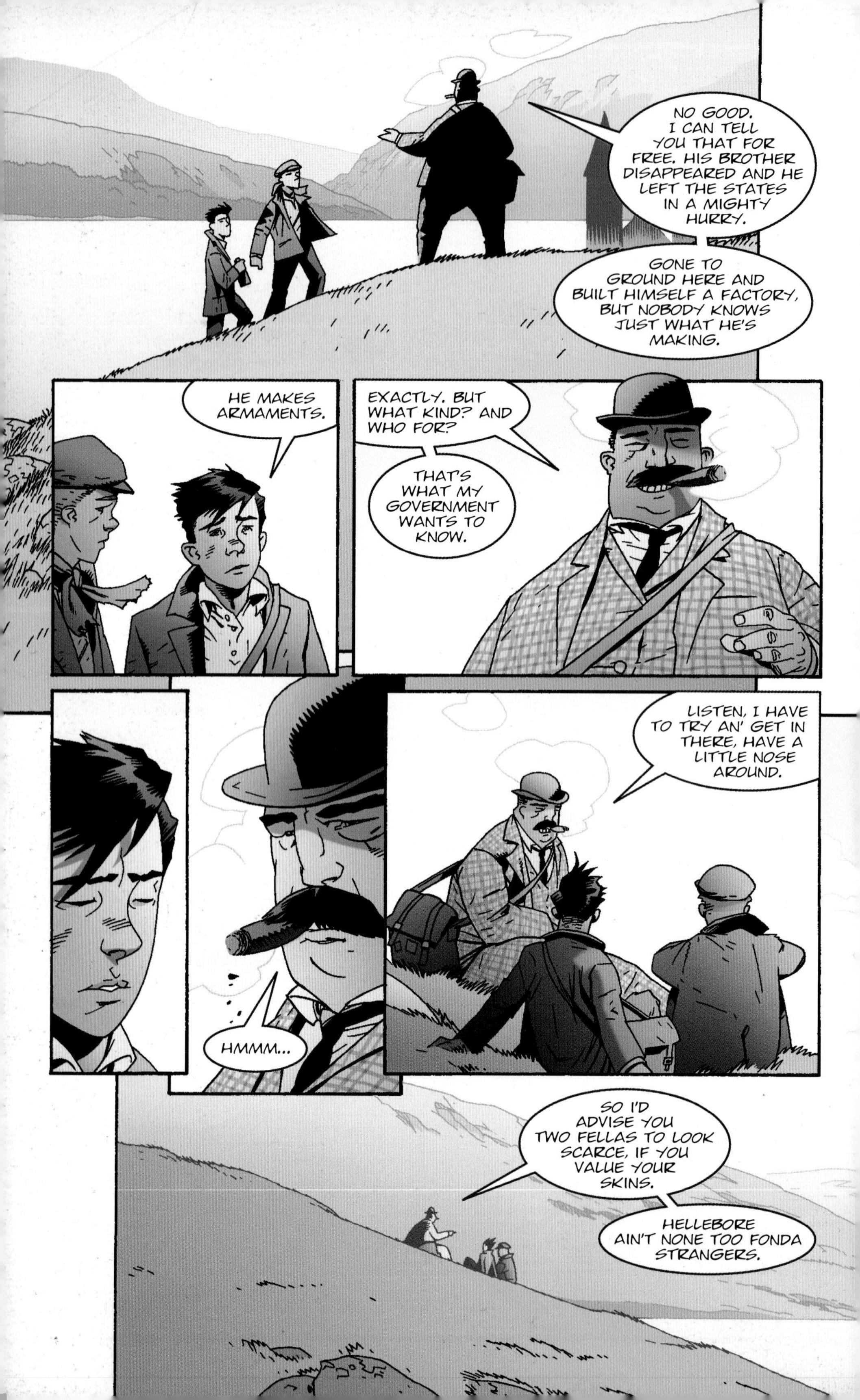
NO GOOD. I CAN TELL YOU THAT FOR FREE. HIS BROTHER DISAPPEARED AND HE LEFT THE STATES IN A MIGHTY HURRY.
GONE TO GROUND HERE AND BUILT HIMSELF A FACTORY, BUT NOBODY KNOWS JUST WHAT HE'S MAKING.
HE MAKES ARMAMENTS.
EXACTLY. BUT WHAT KIND? AND WHO FOR?
THAT'S WHAT MY GOVERNMENT WANTS TO KNOW.
HMMM...
LISTEN, I HAVE TO TRY AN' GET IN THERE, HAVE A LITTLE NOSE AROUND.
SO I'D ADVISE YOU TWO FELLAS TO LOOK SCARCE, IF YOU VALUE YOUR SKINS.
HELLEBORE AIN'T NONE TOO FONDA STRANGERS.

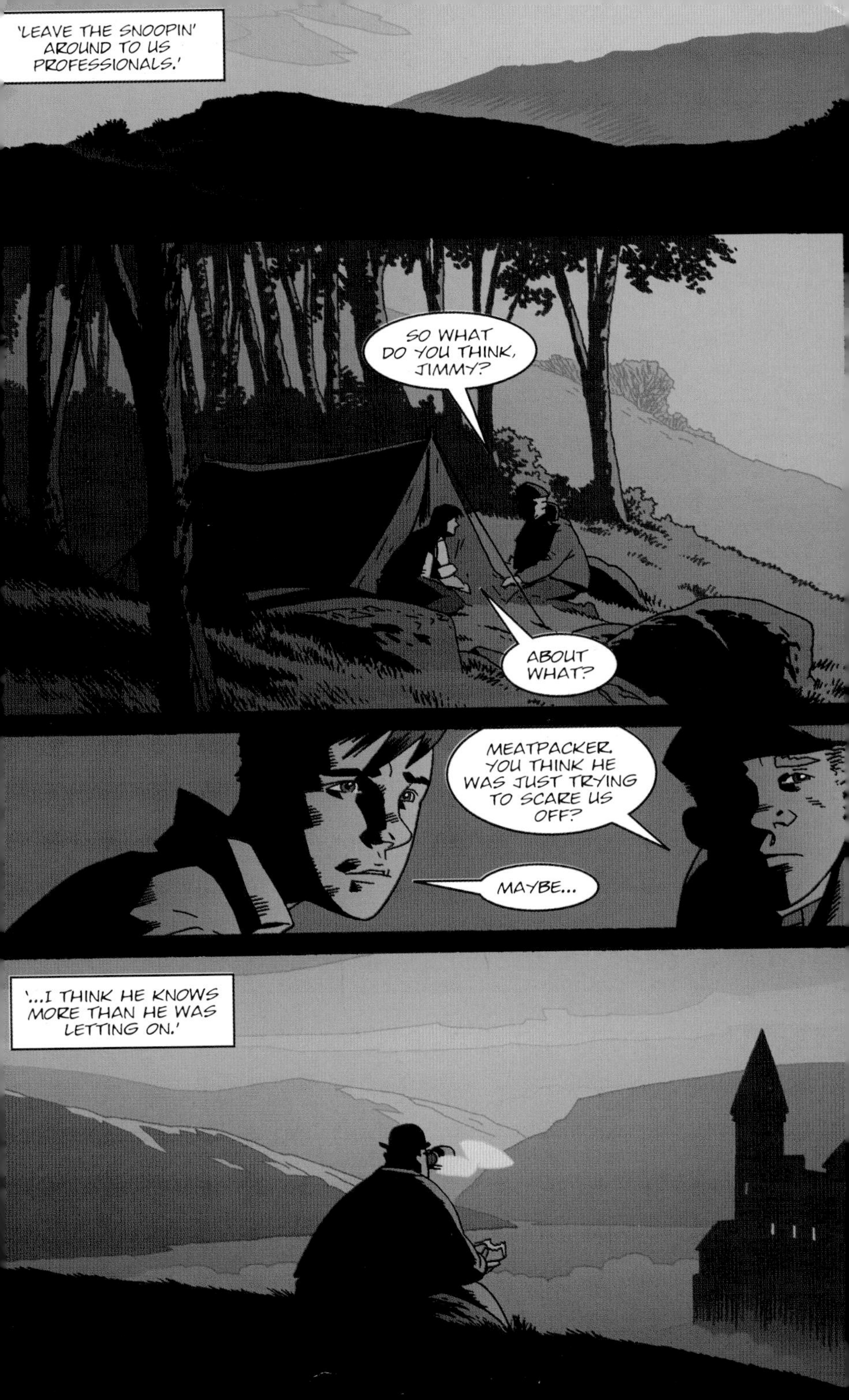
'LEAVE THE SNOOPIN' AROUND TO US PROFESSIONALS.'
SO WHAT DO YOU THINK, JIMMY?
ABOUT WHAT?
MEATPACKER. YOU THINK HE WAS JUST TRYING TO SCARE US OFF?
MAYBE...
'...I THINK HE KNOWS MORE THAN HE WAS LETTING ON.'

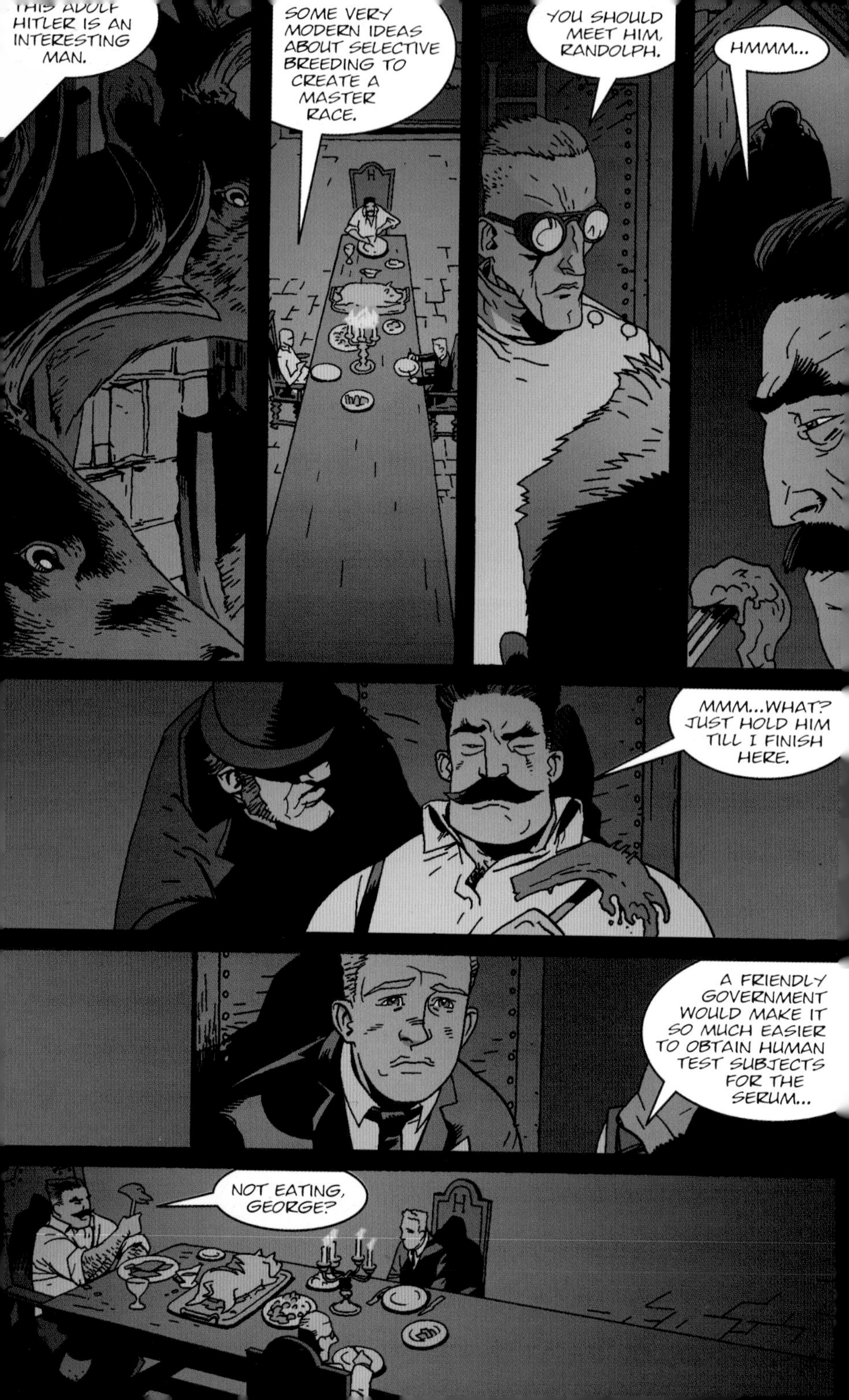
THIS ADOLF HITLER IS AN INTERESTING MAN.
SOME VERY MODERN IDEAS ABOUT SELECTIVE BREEDING TO CREATE A MASTER RACE.
YOU SHOULD MEET HIM, RANDOLPH.
HMMM...
MMM...WHAT? JUST HOLD HIM TILL I FINISH HERE.
A FRIENDLY GOVERNMENT WOULD MAKE IT SO MUCH EASIER TO OBTAIN HUMAN TEST SUBJECTS FOR THE SERUM...
NOT EATING, GEORGE?

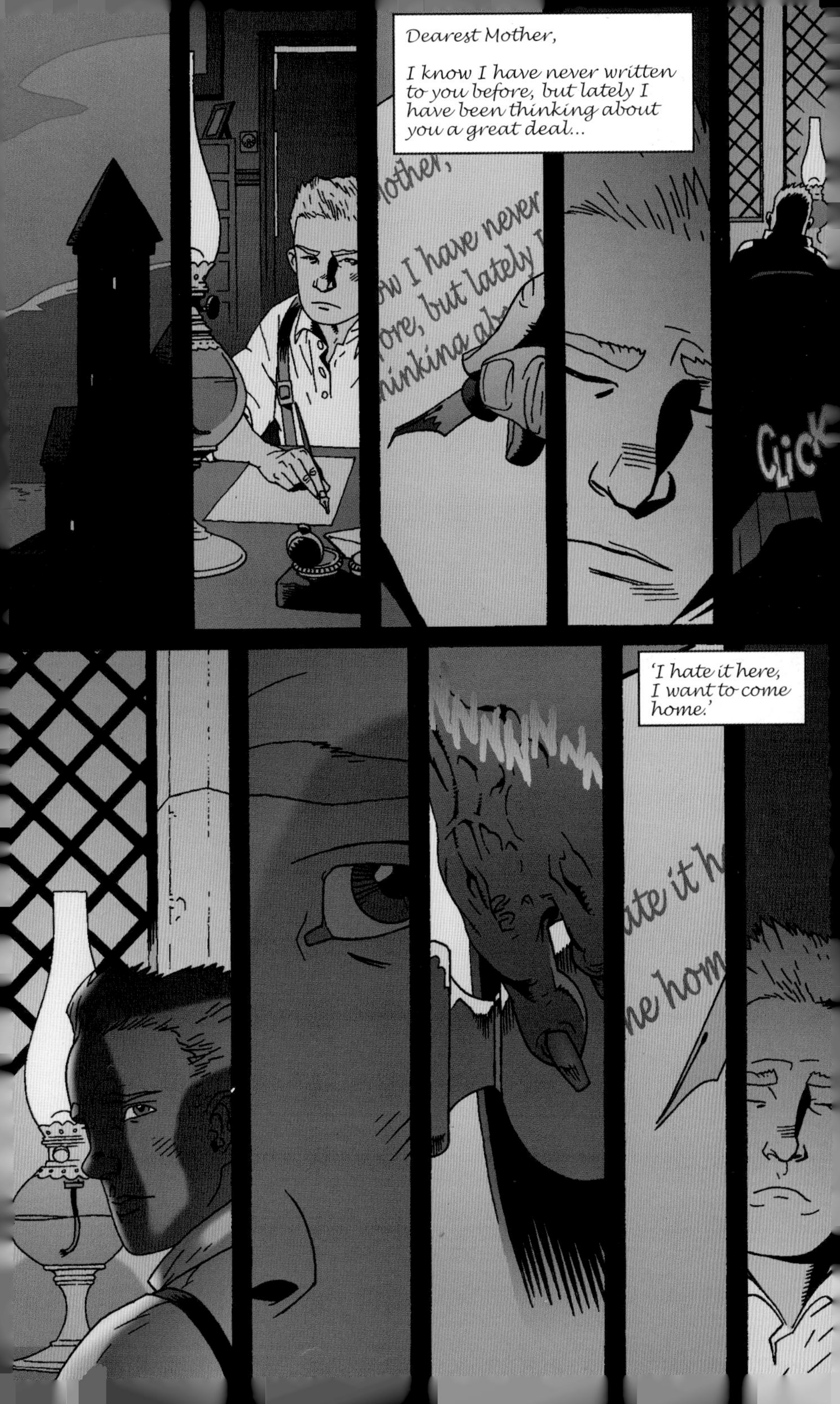
Dearest Mother,
I know I have never written to you before, but lately I have been thinking about you a great deal...
CLICK
'I hate it here, I want to come home.'

PART THREE

SILVERFIN

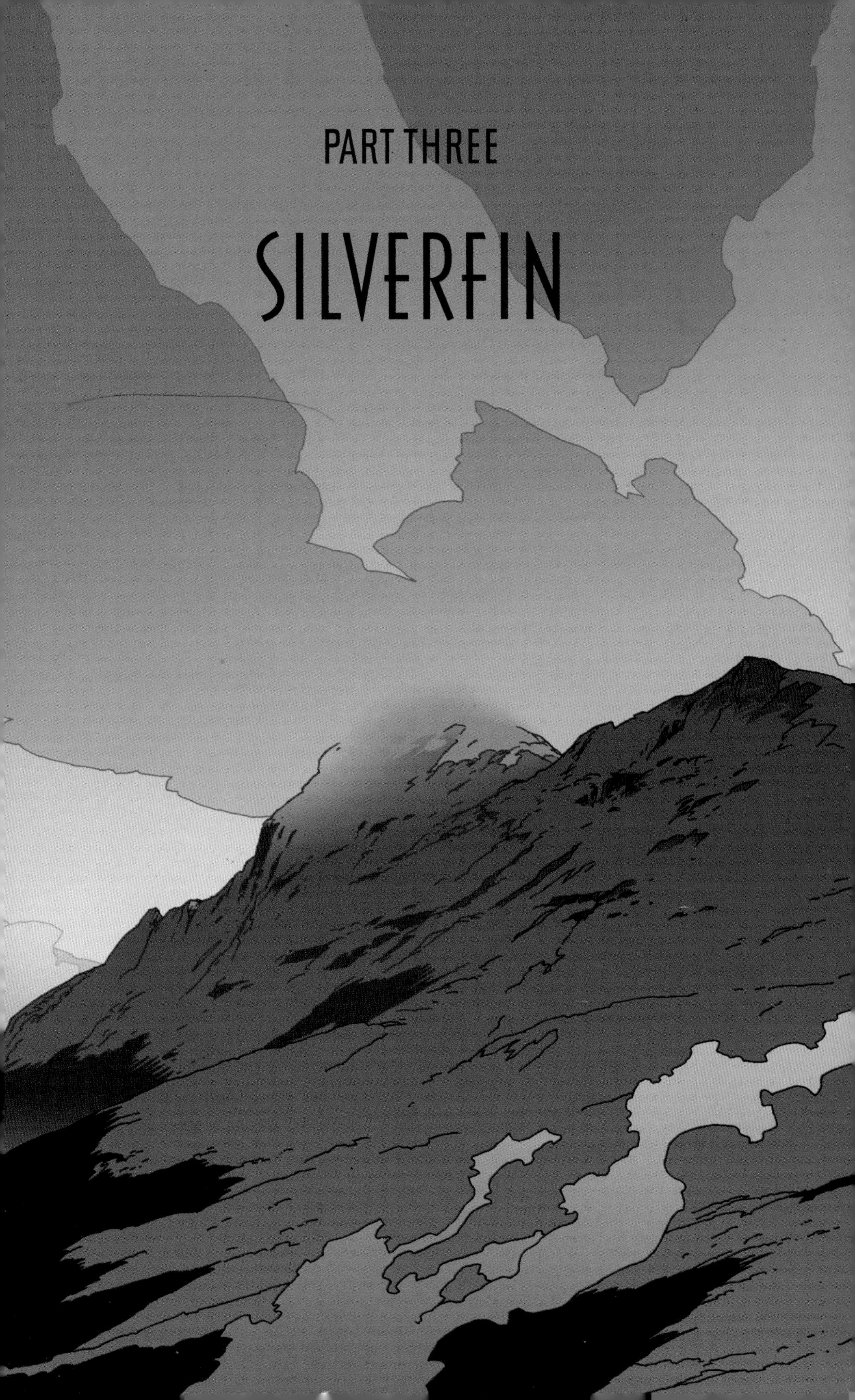

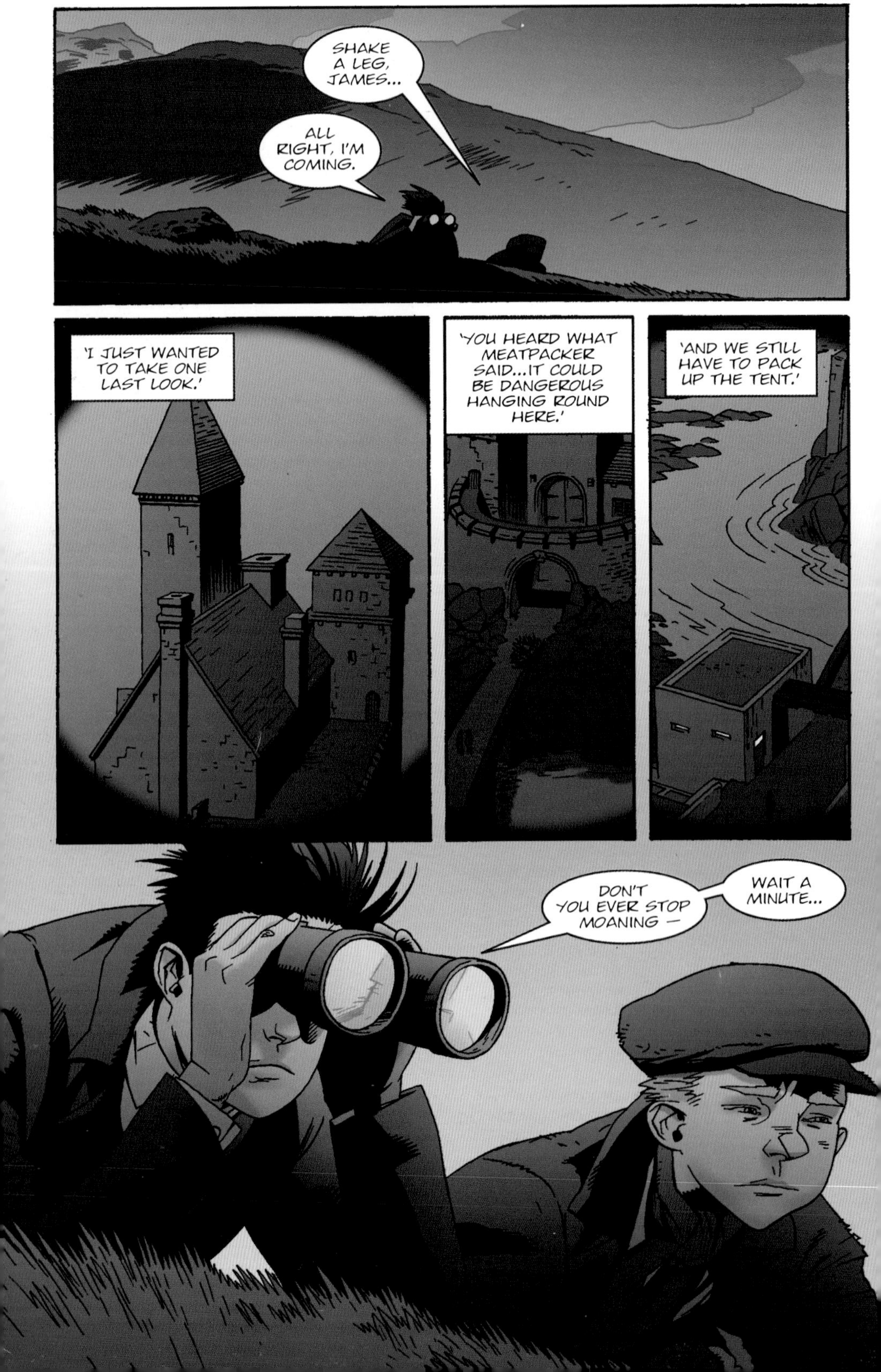
SHAKE A LEG, JAMES...
ALL RIGHT, I'M COMING.
'I JUST WANTED TO TAKE ONE LAST LOOK.'
'YOU HEARD WHAT MEATPACKER SAID...IT COULD BE DANGEROUS HANGING ROUND HERE.'
'AND WE STILL HAVE TO PACK UP THE TENT.'
DON'T YOU EVER STOP MOANING –
WAIT A MINUTE...

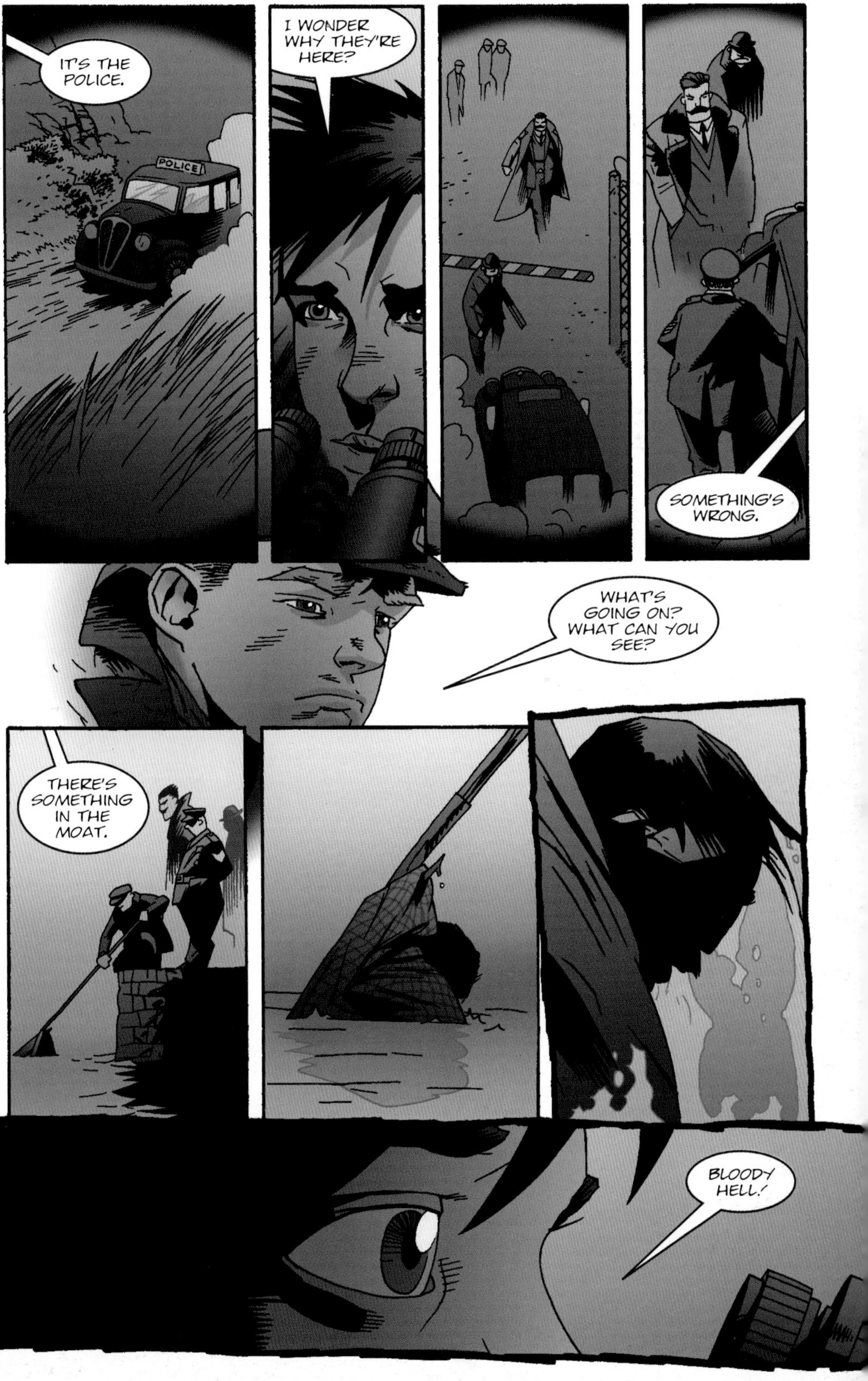
IT'S THE POLICE.
I WONDER WHY THEY'RE HERE?
SOMETHING'S WRONG.
WHAT'S GOING ON? WHAT CAN YOU SEE?
THERE'S SOMETHING IN THE MOAT.
POLICE
BLOODY HELL!

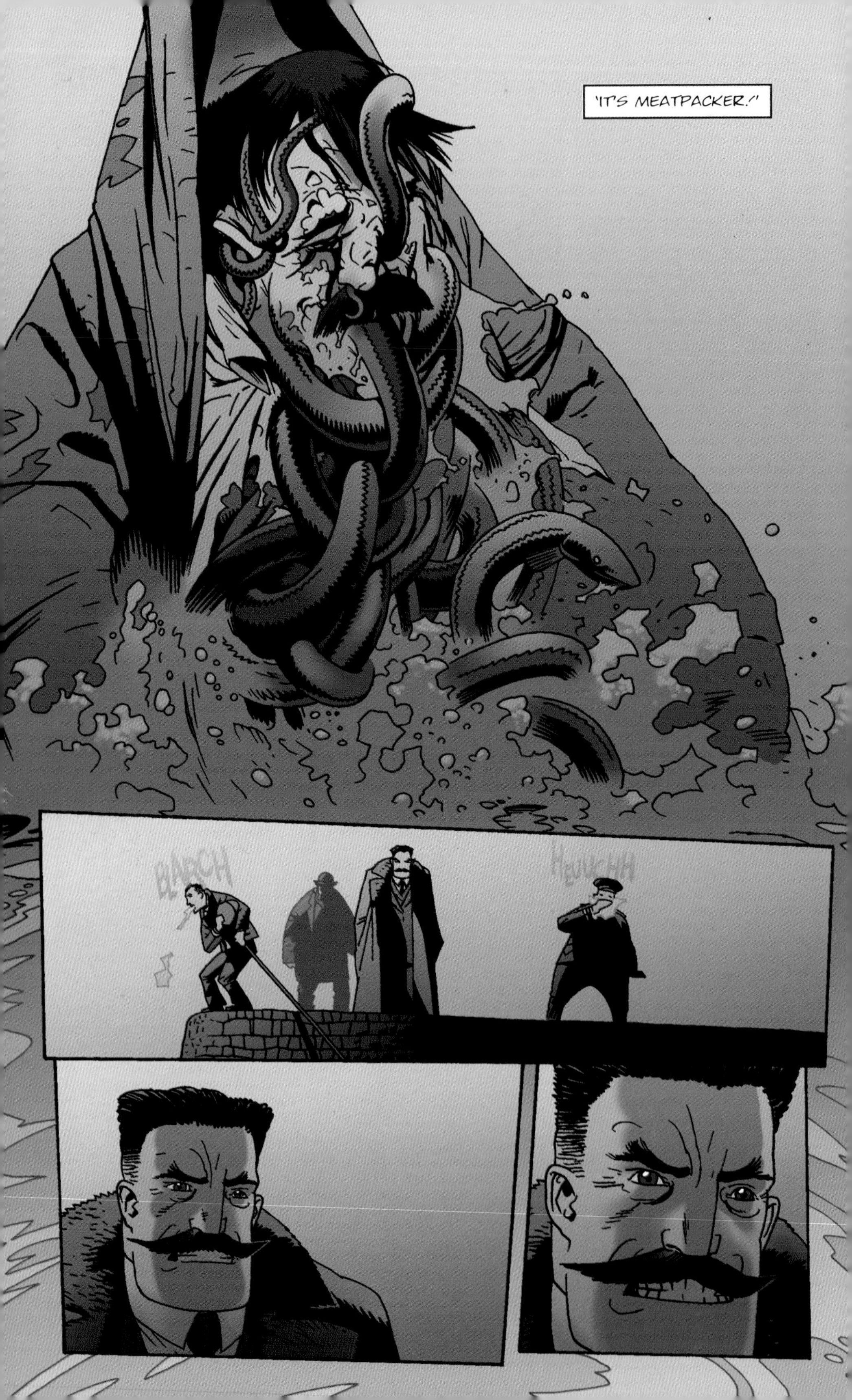
'IT'S MEATPACKER!'
BLARCH
HEUUCHH

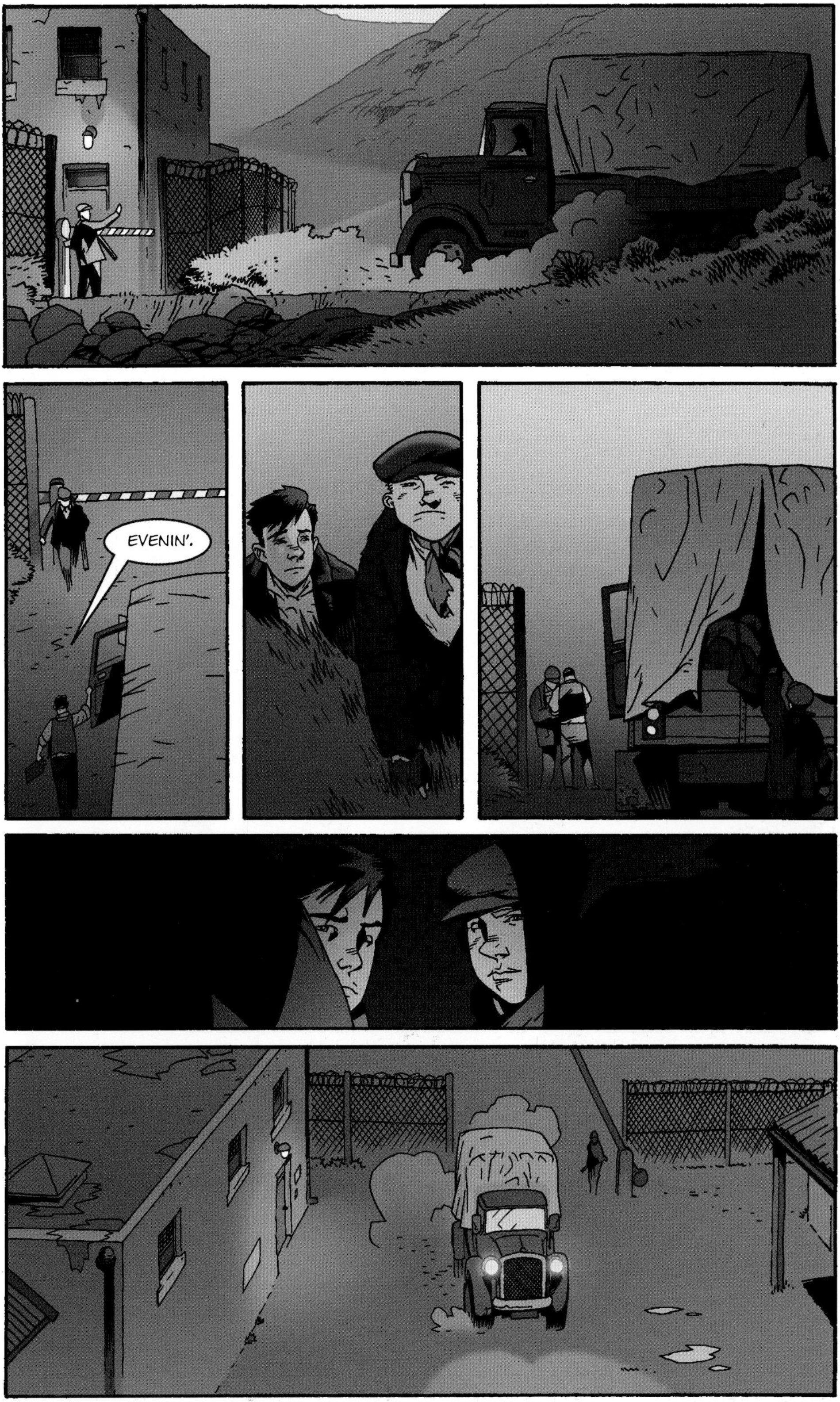
EVENIN'.

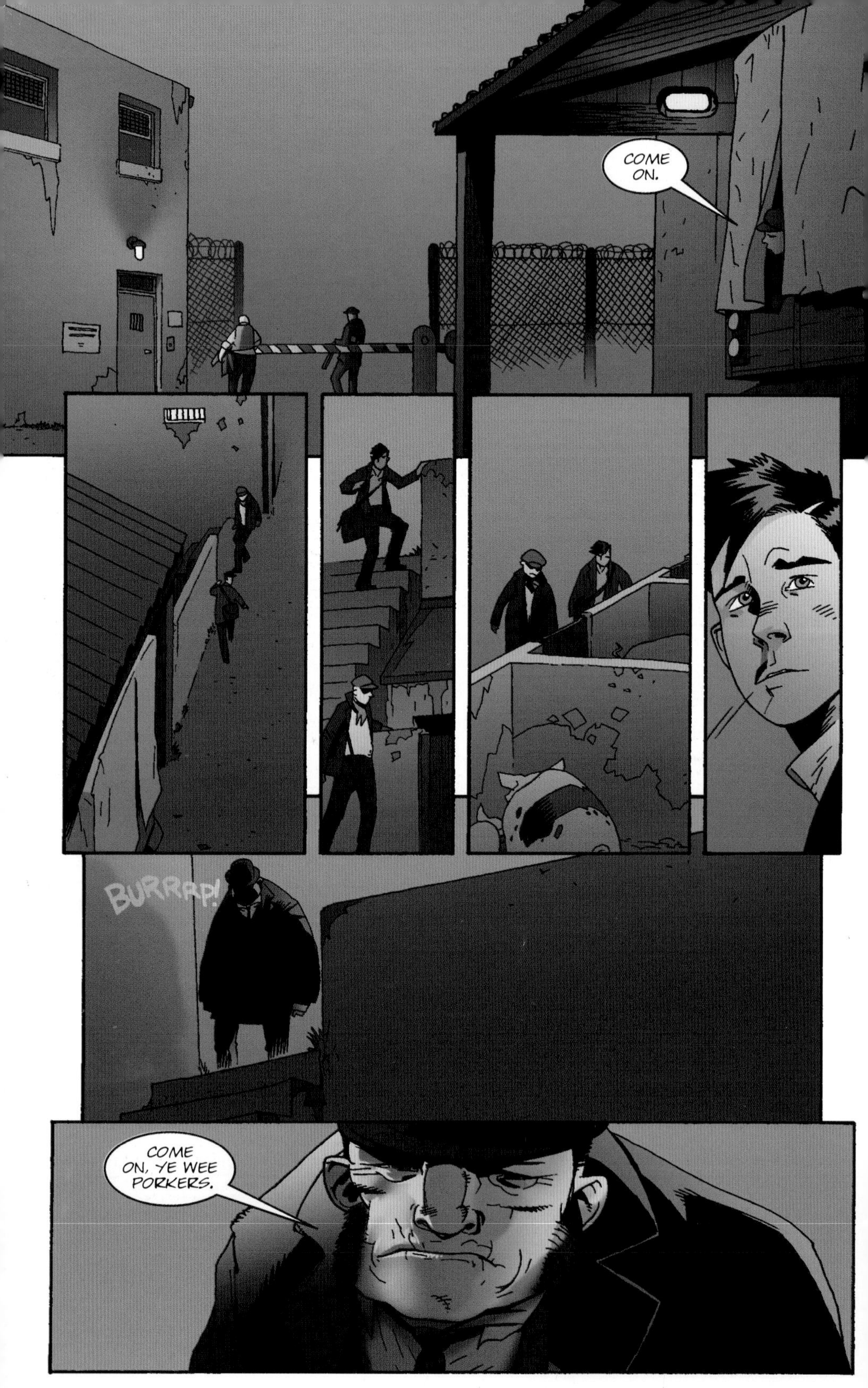
COME ON.
BURRRP!
COME ON, YE WEE PORKERS.

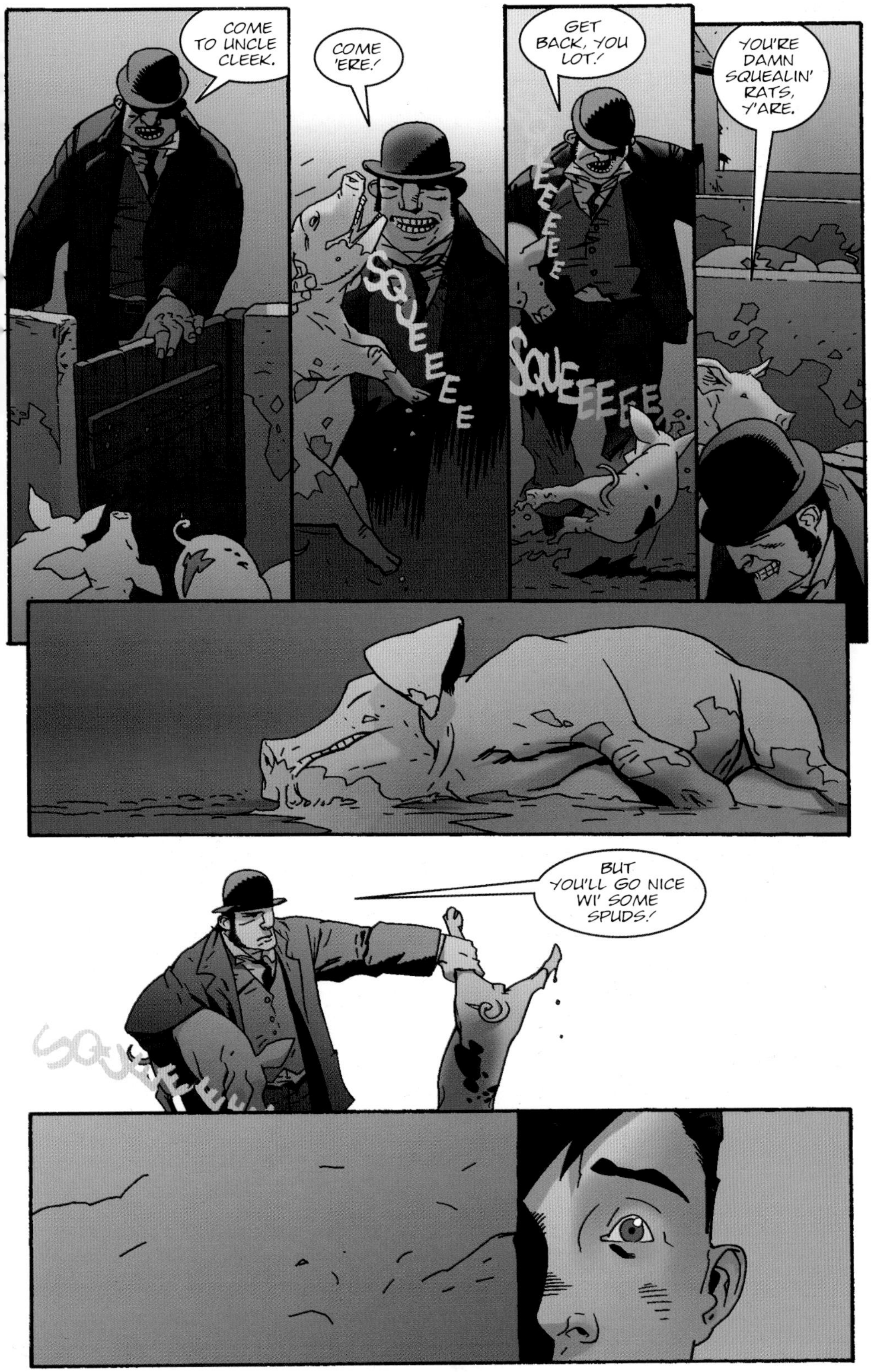
COME TO UNCLE CLEEK.
COME 'ERE!
SQUEEEE
GET BACK, YOU LOT!
EEEEE
SQUEEEEEE
YOU'RE DAMN SQUEALIN' RATS, Y'ARE.
BUT YOU'LL GO NICE WI' SOME SPUDS!

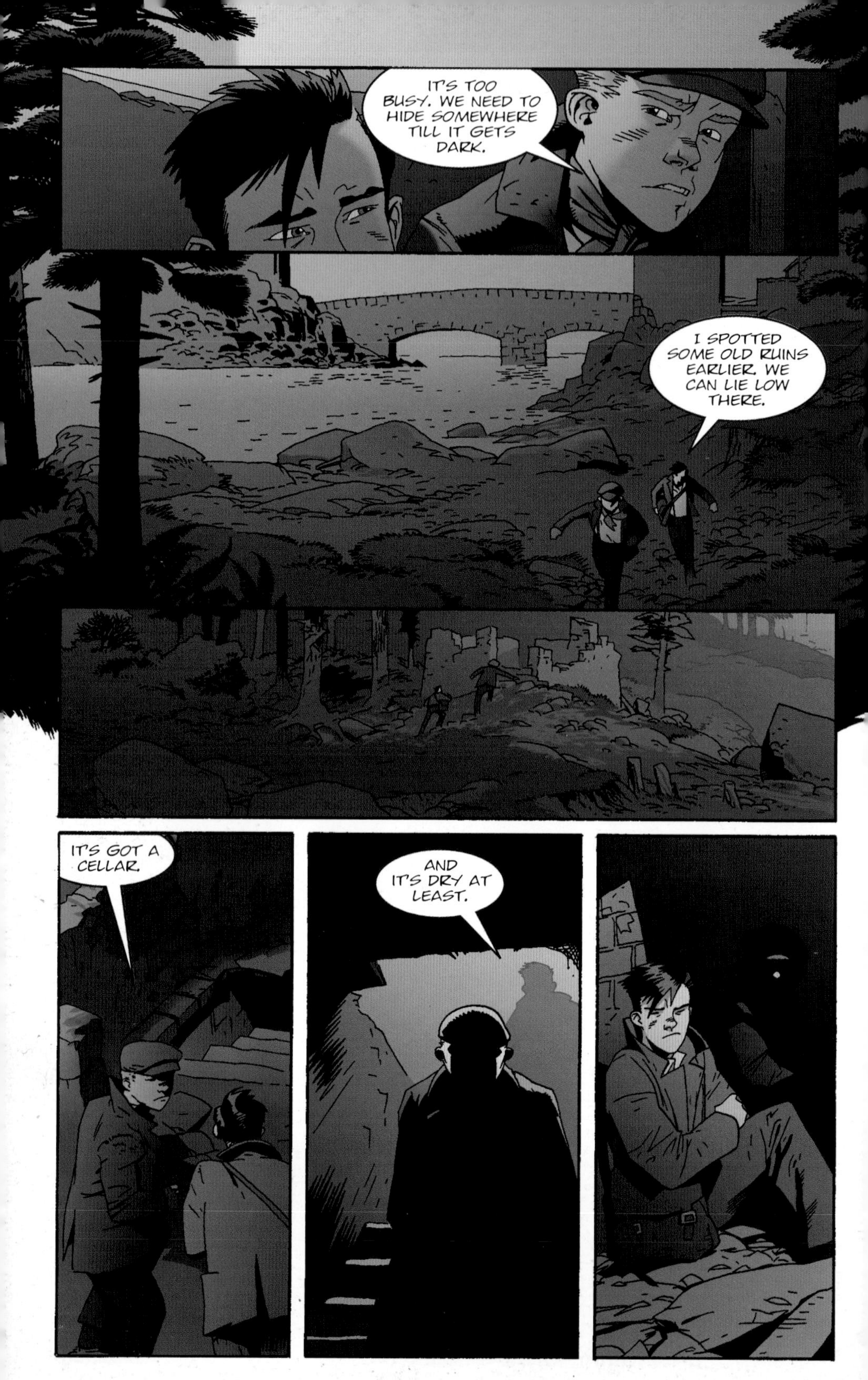
IT'S TOO BUSY. WE NEED TO HIDE SOMEWHERE TILL IT GETS DARK.
I SPOTTED SOME OLD RUINS EARLIER. WE CAN LIE LOW THERE.
IT'S GOT A CELLAR.
AND IT'S DRY AT LEAST.

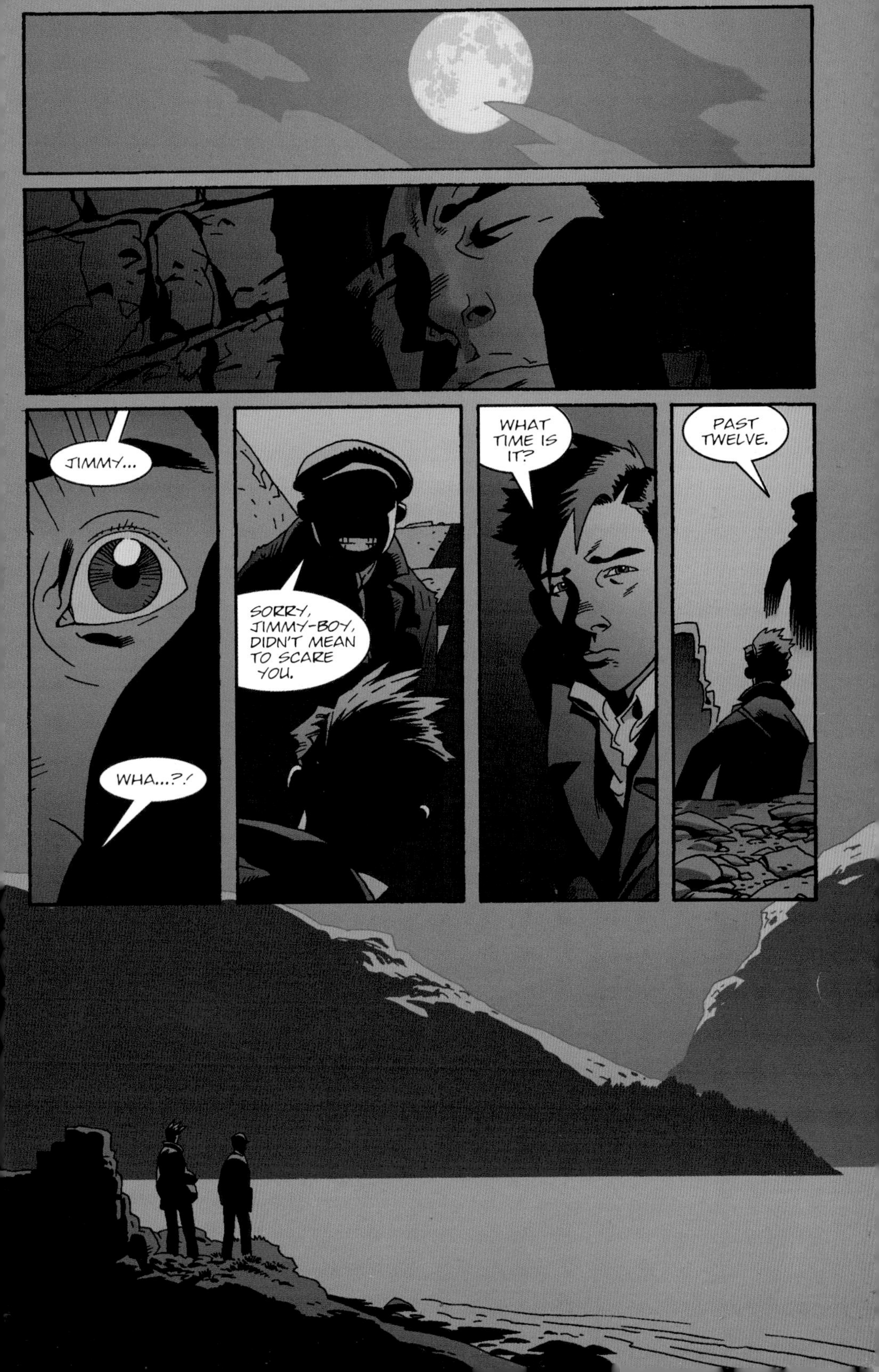
JIMMY...
WHA...?!
SORRY, JIMMY-BOY, DIDN'T MEAN TO SCARE YOU.
WHAT TIME IS IT?
PAST TWELVE.

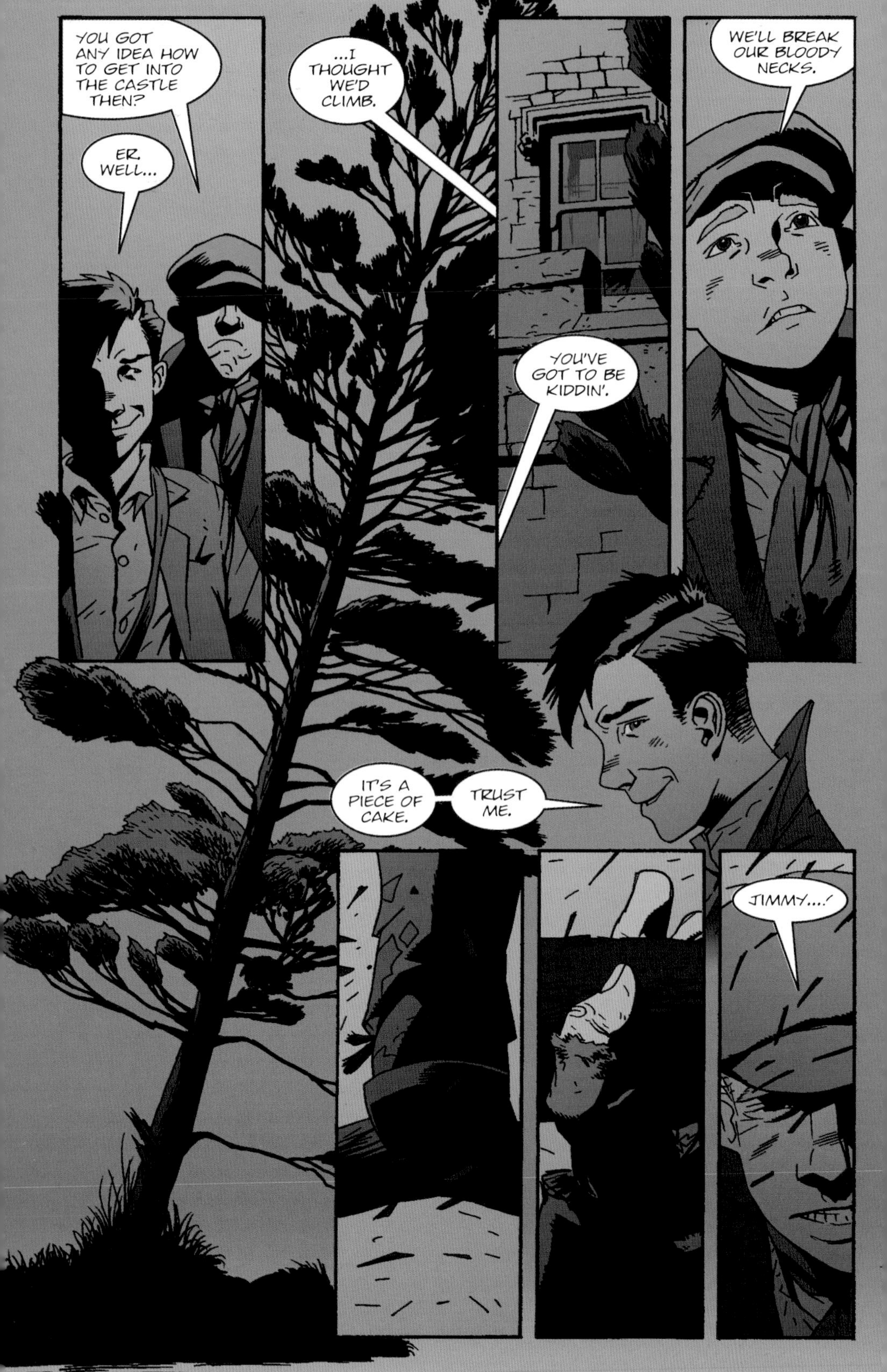
YOU GOT ANY IDEA HOW TO GET INTO THE CASTLE THEN?
ER. WELL...
...I THOUGHT WE'D CLIMB.
YOU'VE GOT TO BE KIDDIN'.
WE'LL BREAK OUR BLOODY NECKS.
IT'S A PIECE OF CAKE.
TRUST ME.
JIMMY....!

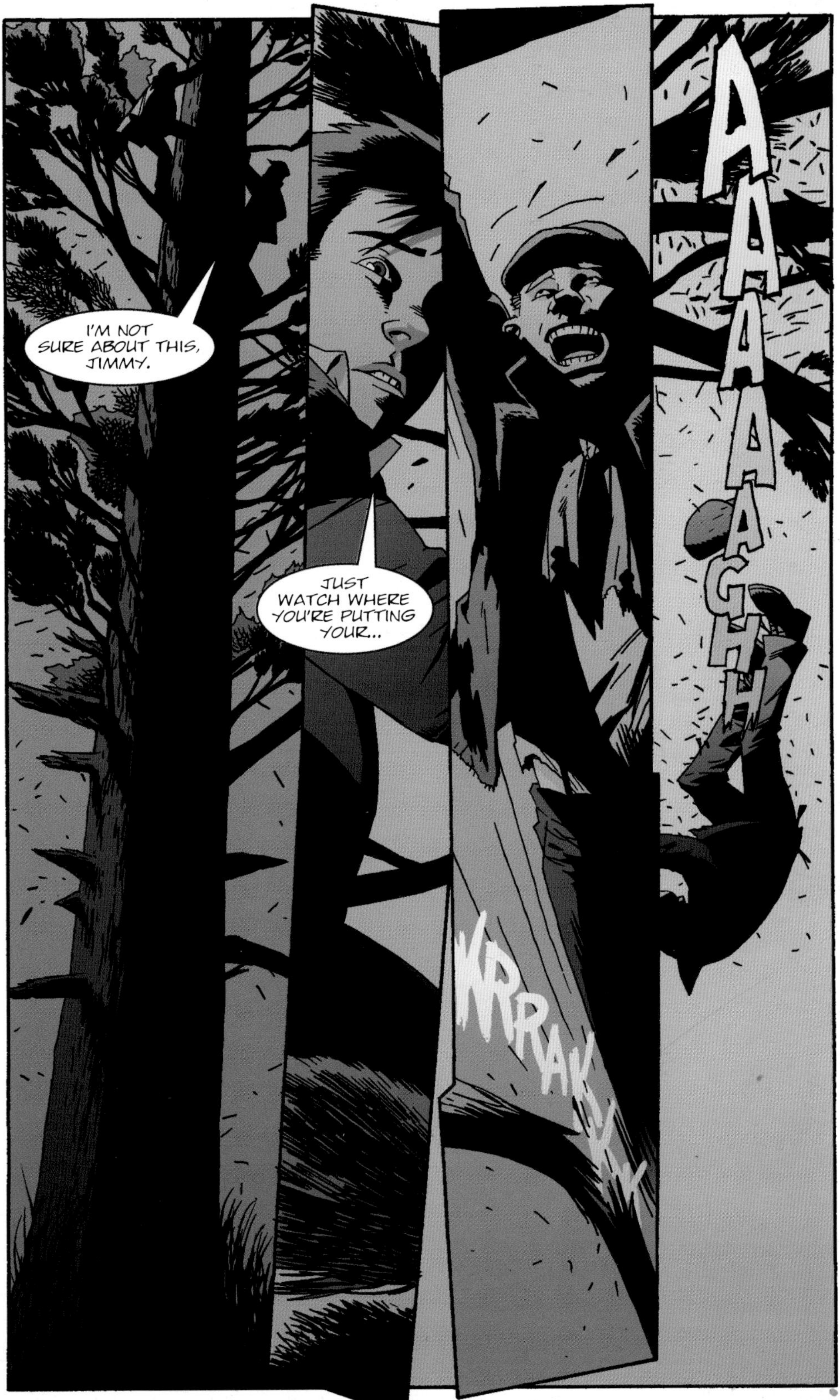

I'M NOT SURE ABOUT THIS, JIMMY.
JUST WATCH WHERE YOU'RE PUTTING YOUR...
AAAAAAAGH!
KRRAK

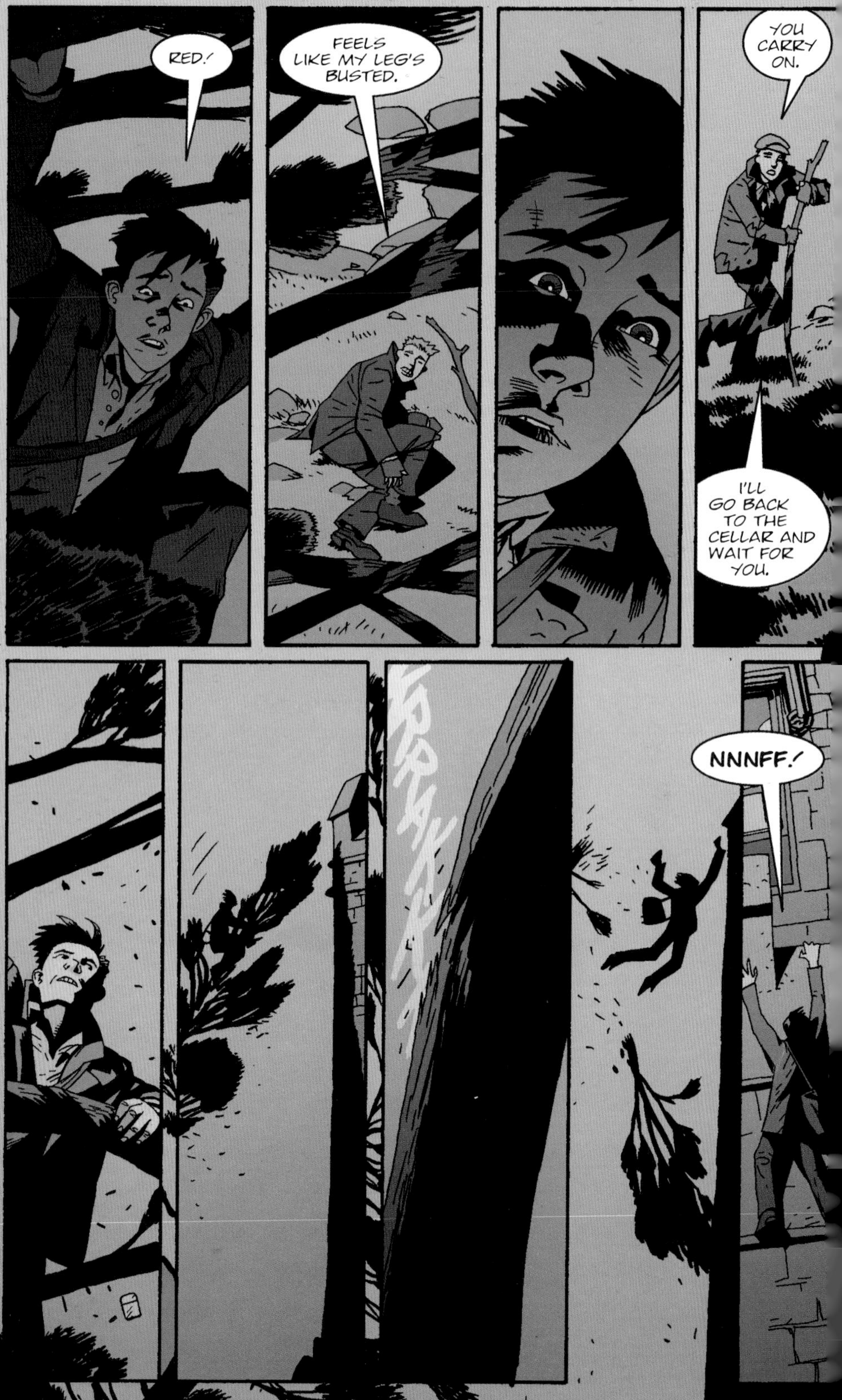
RED!
FEELS LIKE MY LEG'S BUSTED.
YOU CARRY ON.
I'LL GO BACK TO THE CELLAR AND WAIT FOR YOU.
NNNFF!

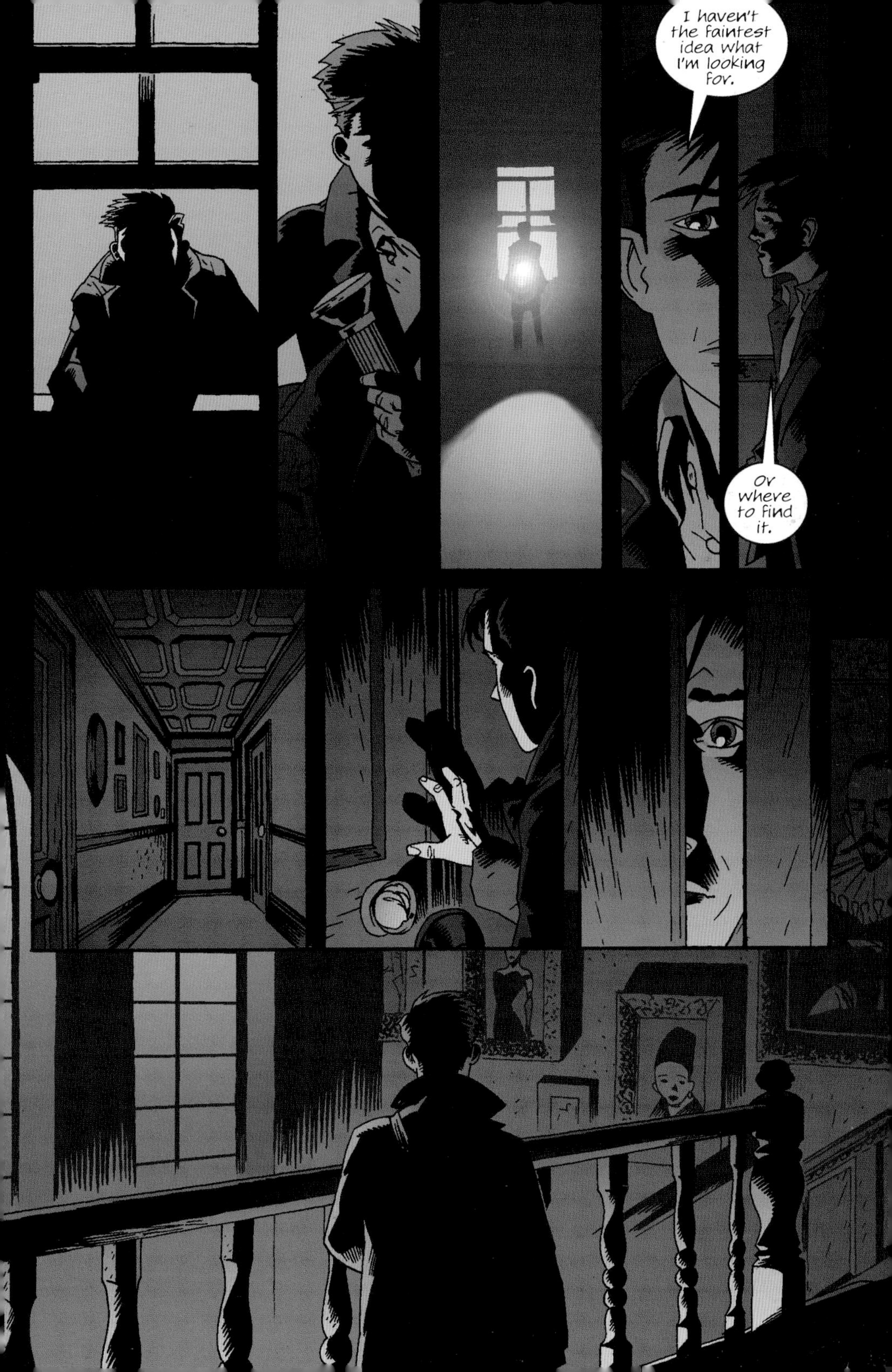
I haven't the faintest idea what I'm looking for.
Or where to find it.

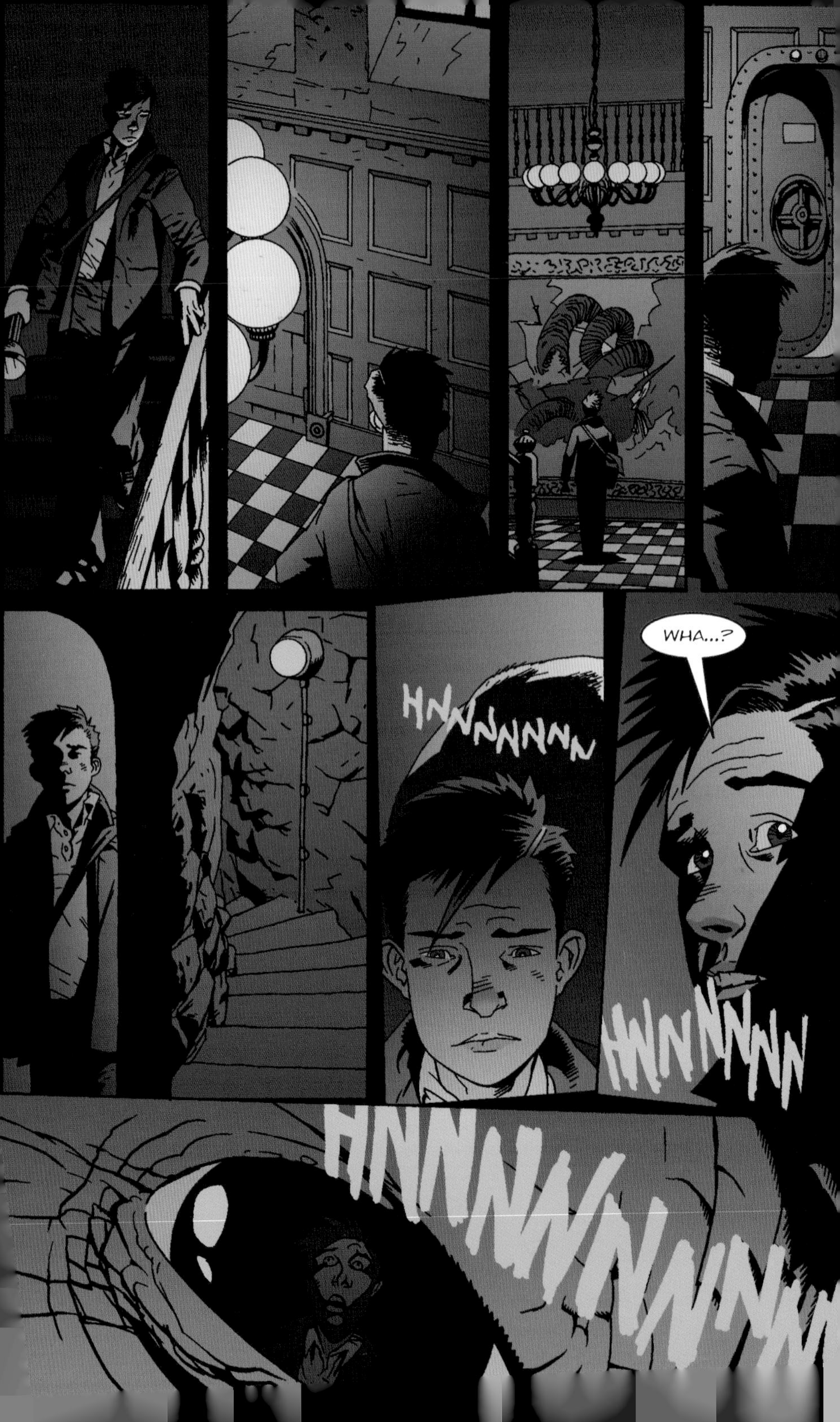
HNNNNNNNN
WHA...?
HNNNNNNN
HNNNNNNNNNNNNN

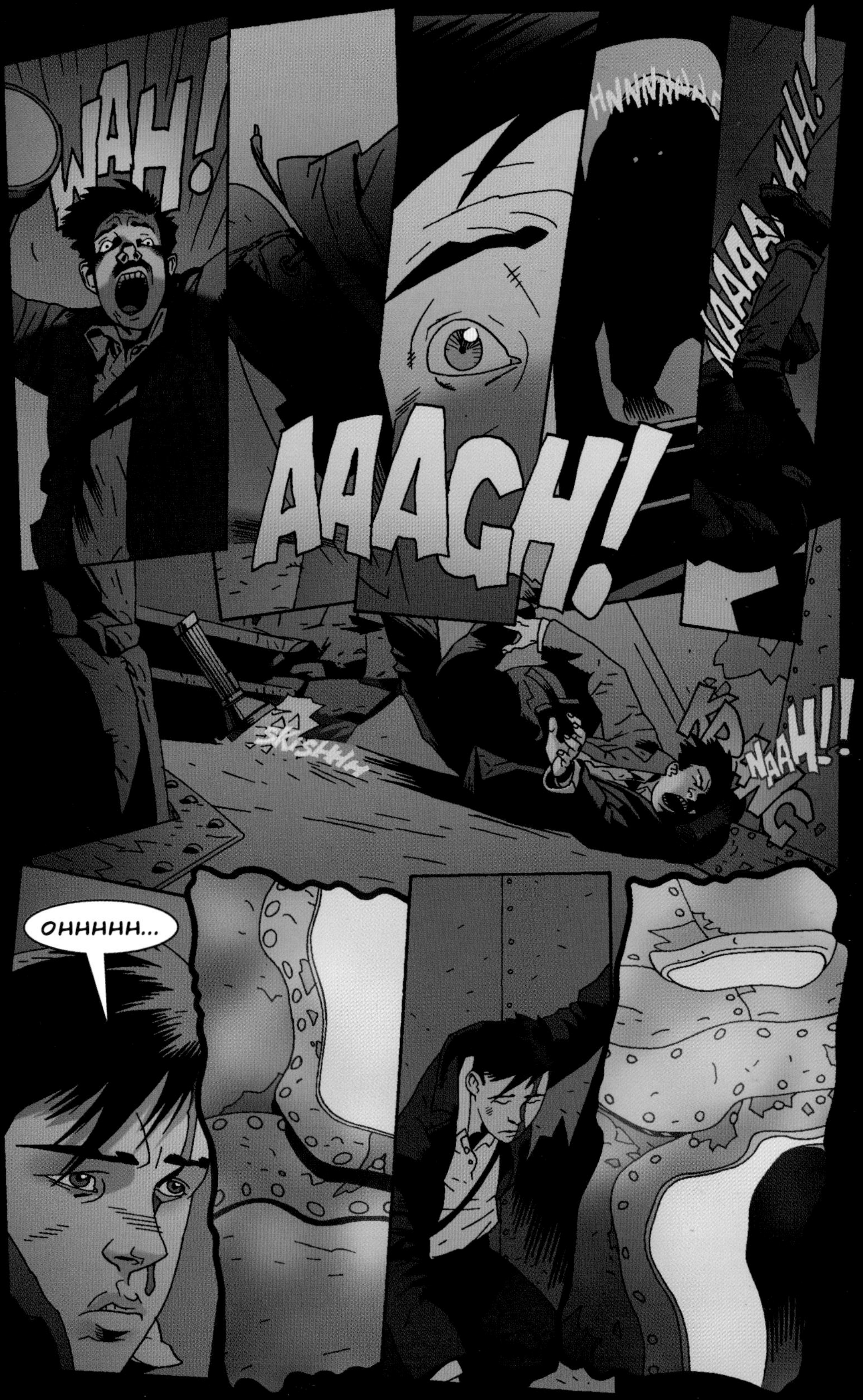
WAH!
AAACH!
SKISHHH
NAAH!!
OHHHHH...

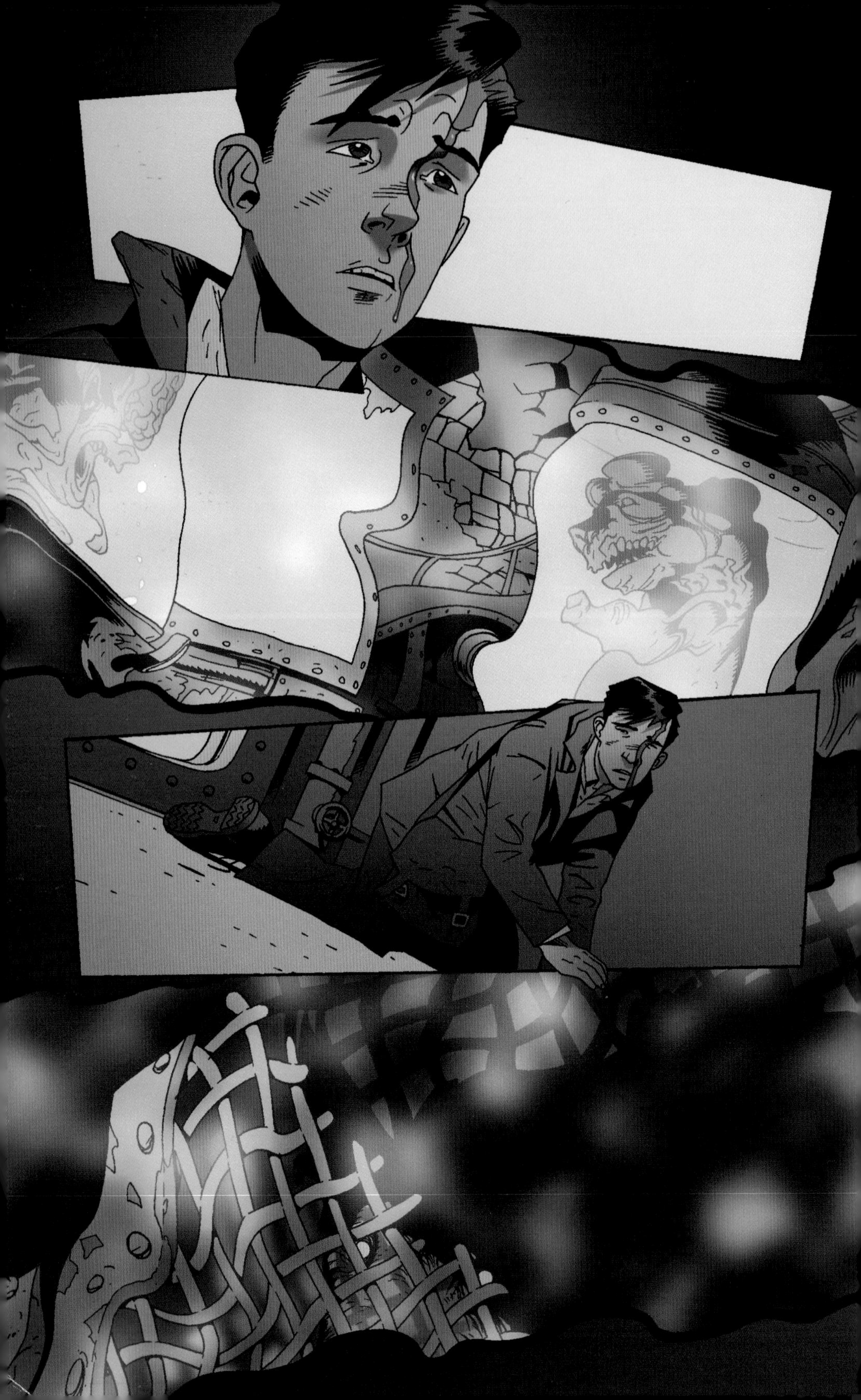

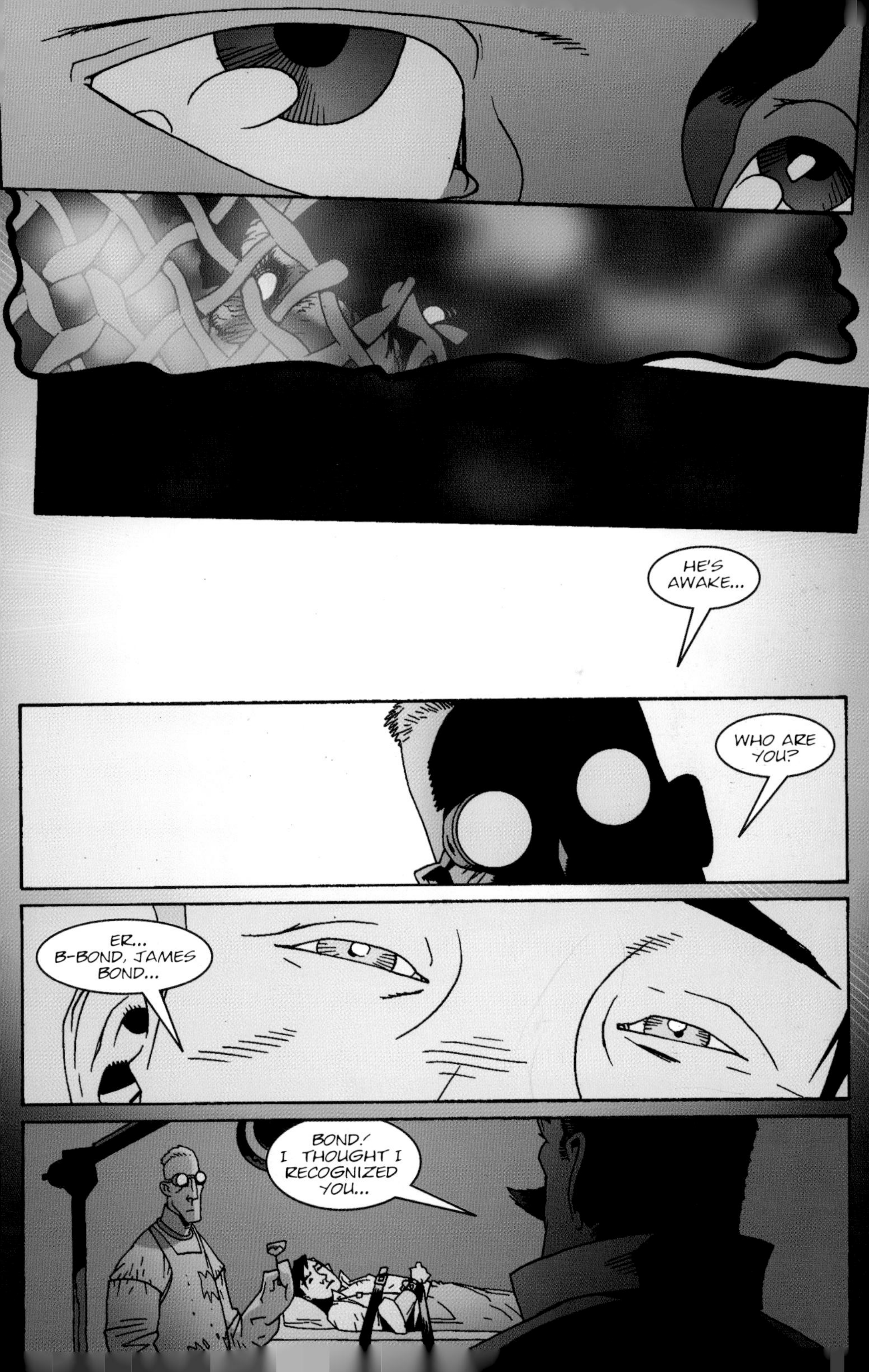
HE'S AWAKE...
WHO ARE YOU?
ER... B-BOND, JAMES BOND...
BOND! I THOUGHT I RECOGNIZED YOU...

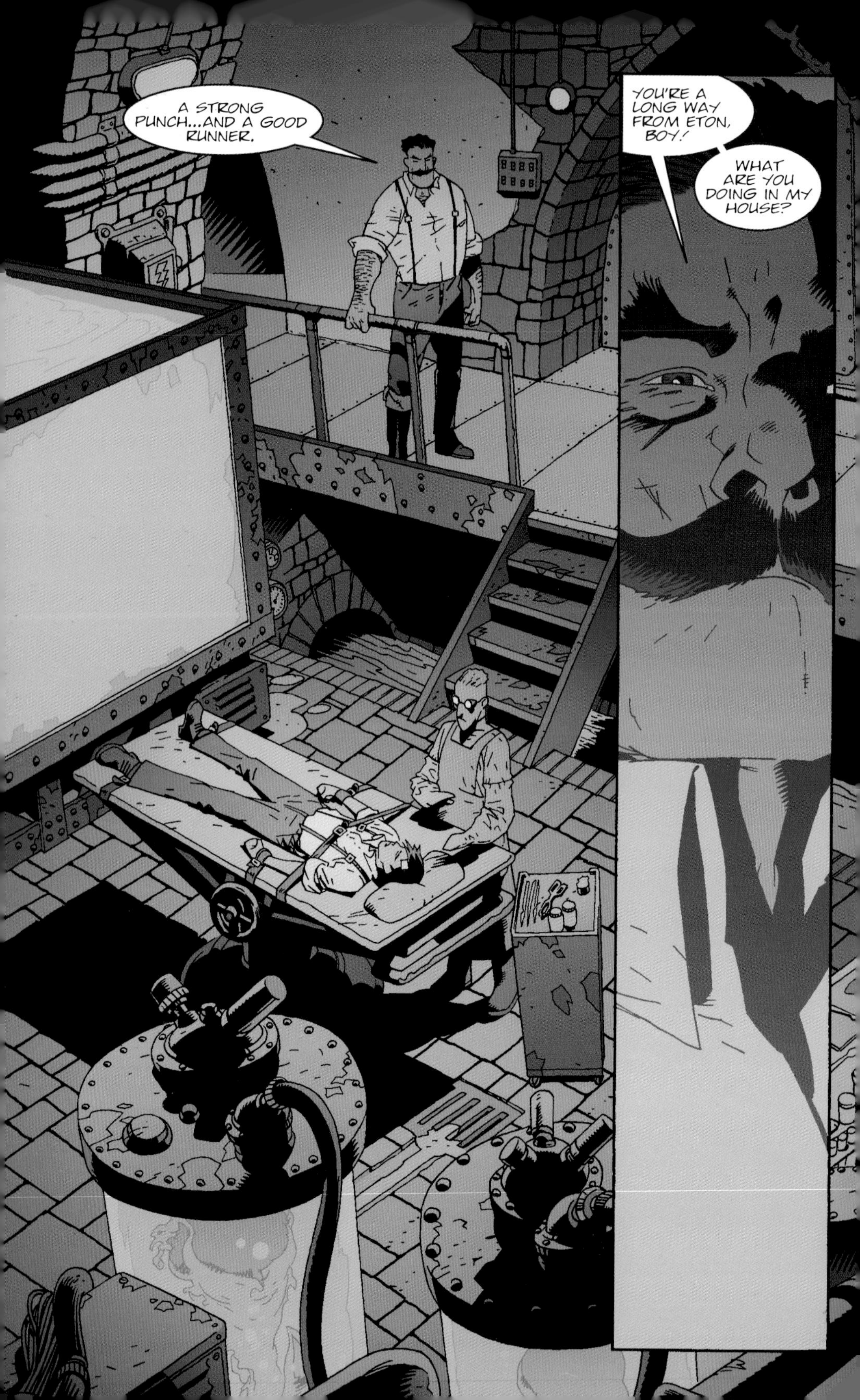
A STRONG PUNCH...AND A GOOD RUNNER.
YOU'RE A LONG WAY FROM ETON, BOY!
WHAT ARE YOU DOING IN MY HOUSE?

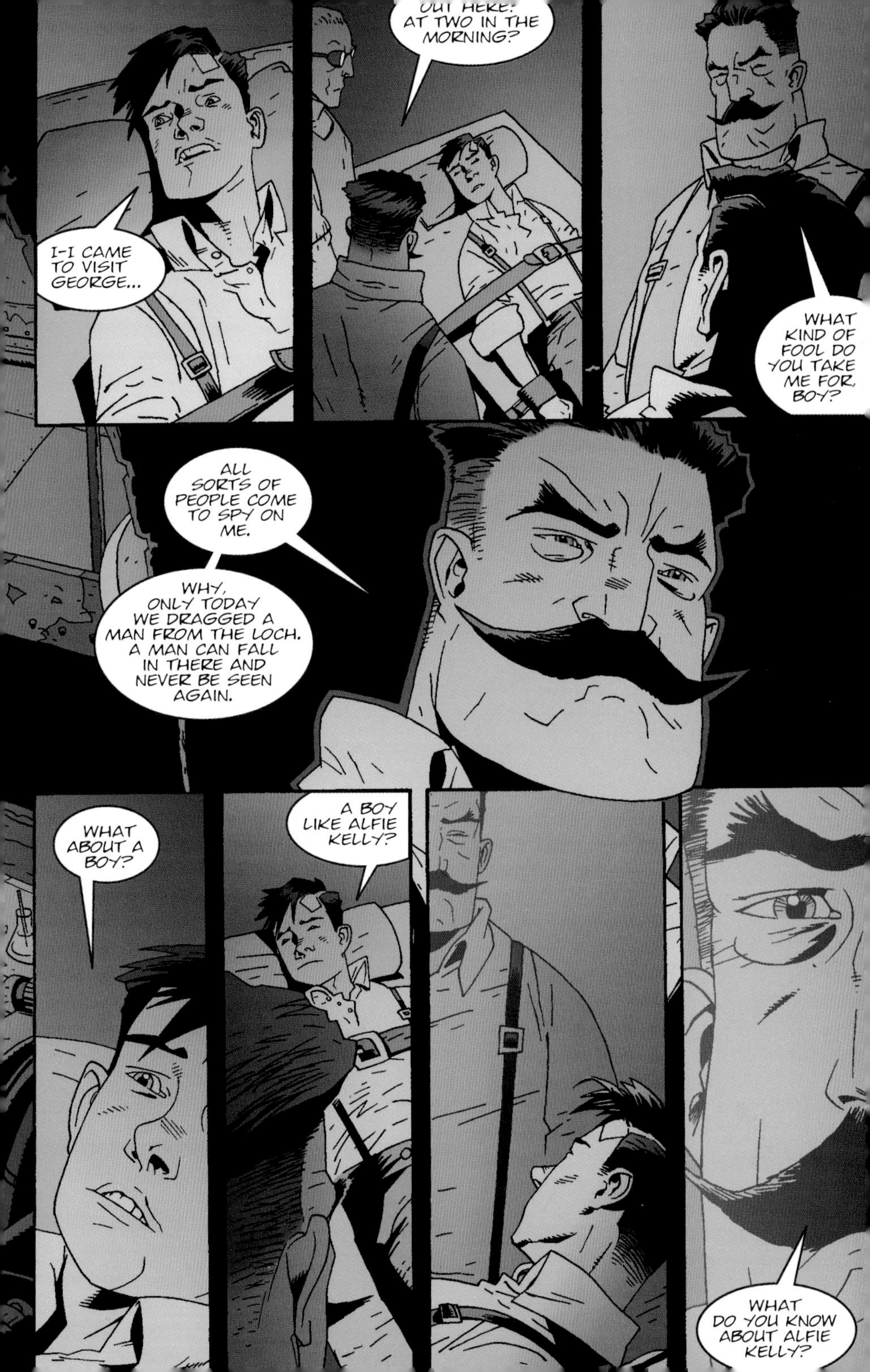
I-I CAME TO VISIT GEORGE...
OUT HERE? AT TWO IN THE MORNING?
WHAT KIND OF FOOL DO YOU TAKE ME FOR, BOY?
ALL SORTS OF PEOPLE COME TO SPY ON ME.
WHY, ONLY TODAY WE DRAGGED A MAN FROM THE LOCH. A MAN CAN FALL IN THERE AND NEVER BE SEEN AGAIN.
WHAT ABOUT A BOY?
A BOY LIKE ALFIE KELLY?
WHAT DO YOU KNOW ABOUT ALFIE KELLY?

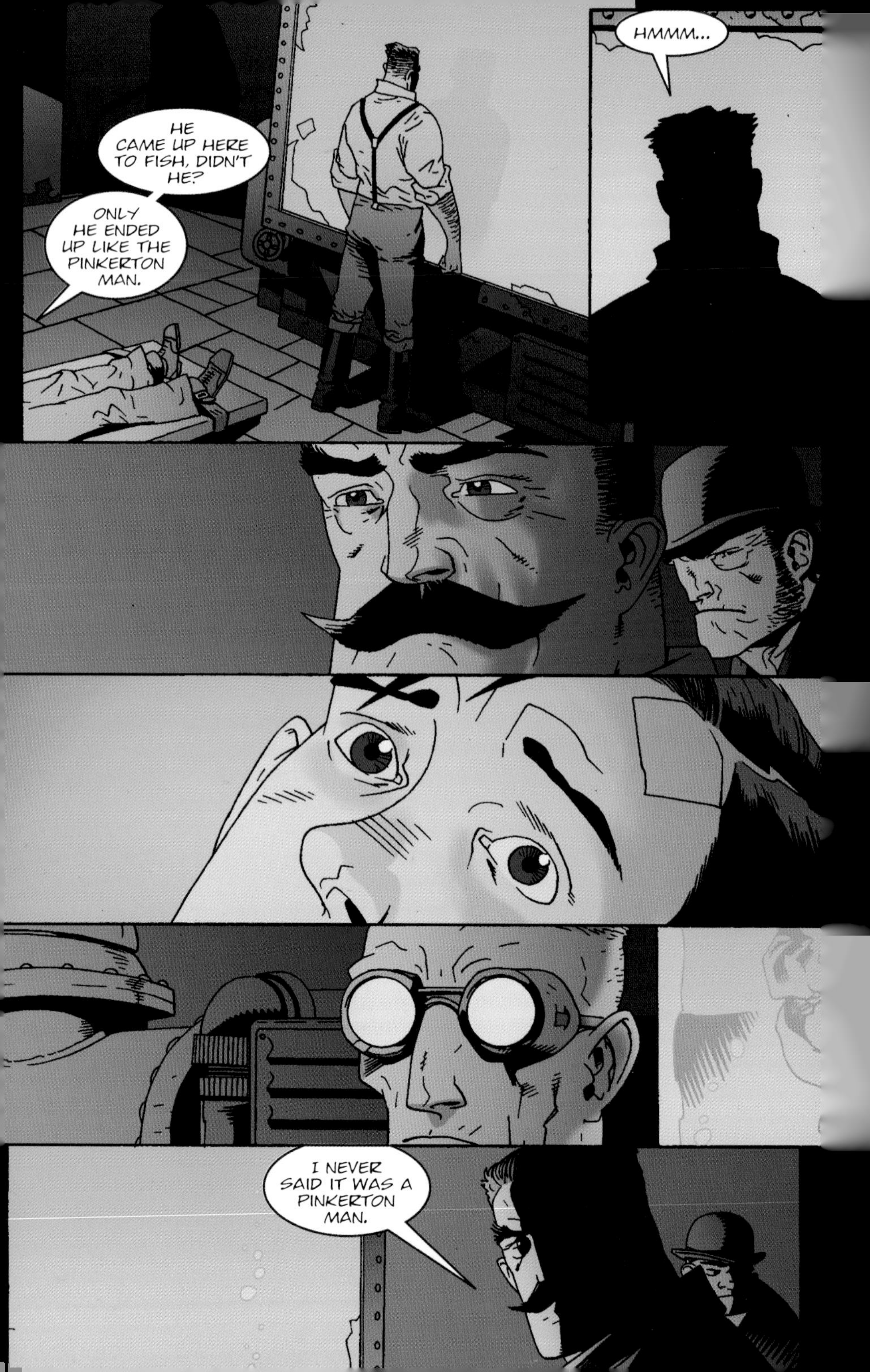
HE CAME UP HERE TO FISH, DIDN'T HE?
ONLY HE ENDED UP LIKE THE PINKERTON MAN.
HMMM...
I NEVER SAID IT WAS A PINKERTON MAN.

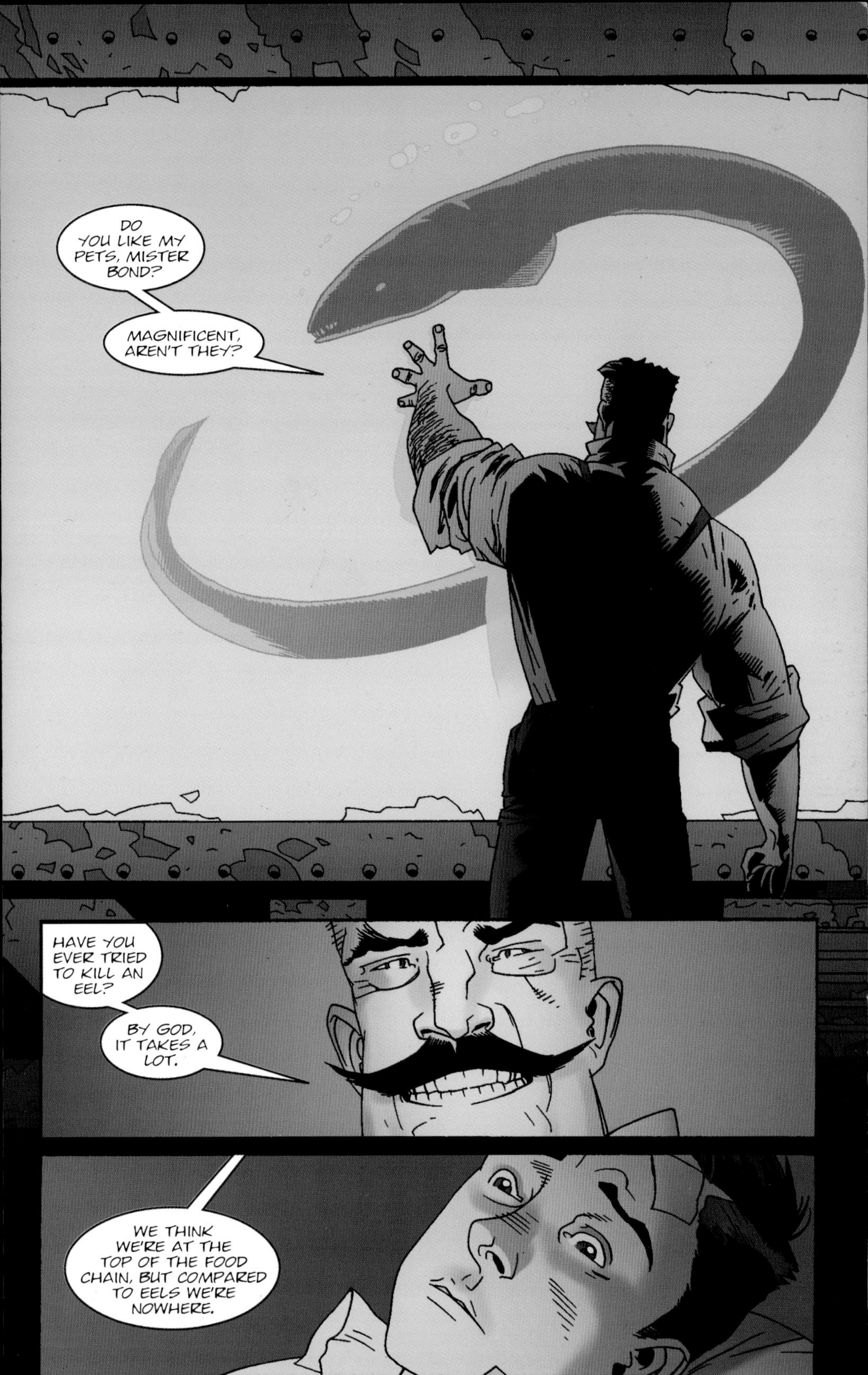
DO YOU LIKE MY PETS, MISTER BOND?
MAGNIFICENT, AREN'T THEY?
HAVE YOU EVER TRIED TO KILL AN EEL?
BY GOD, IT TAKES A LOT.
WE THINK WE'RE AT THE TOP OF THE FOOD CHAIN, BUT COMPARED TO EELS WE'RE NOWHERE.

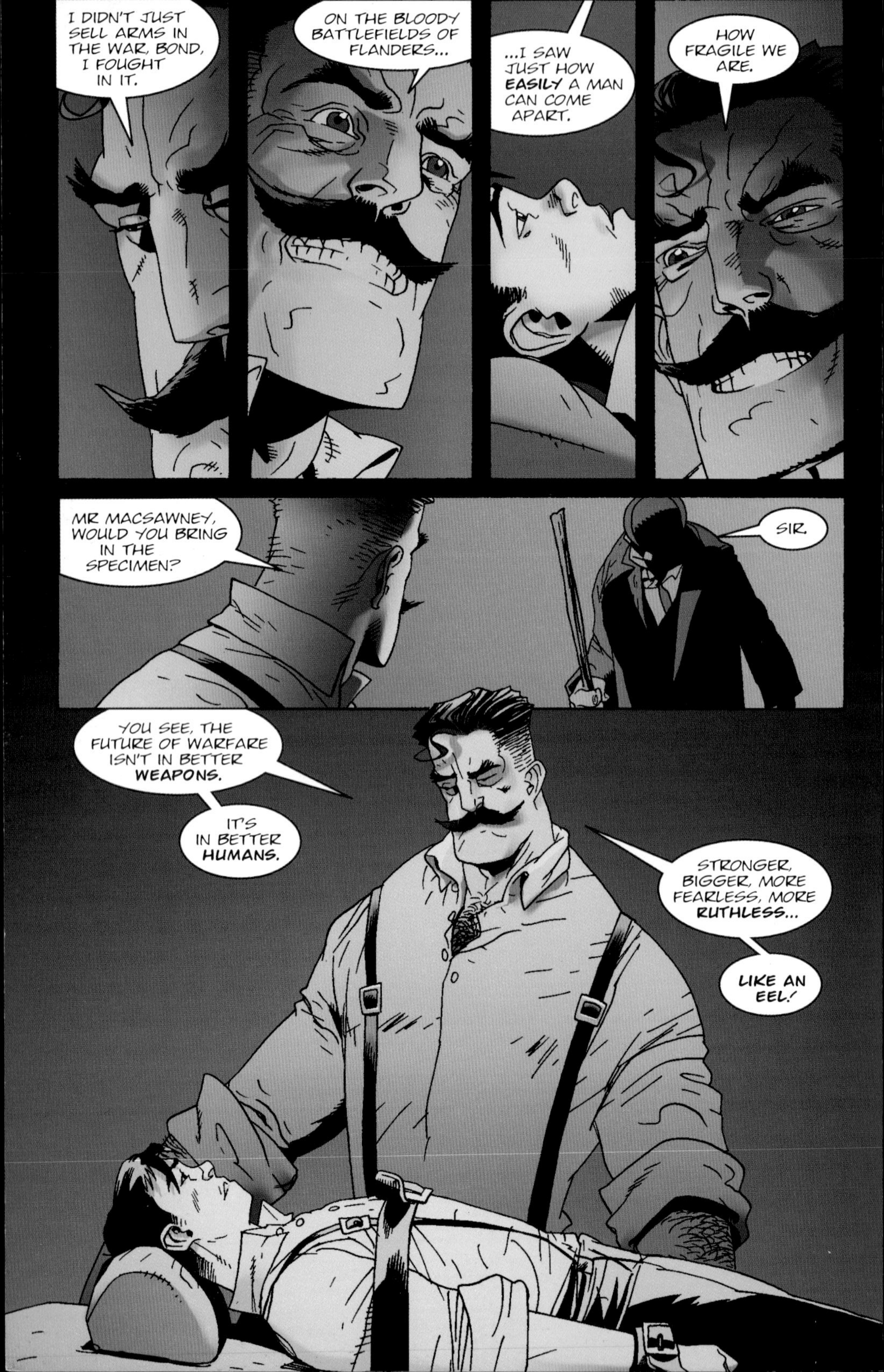

I DIDN'T JUST SELL ARMS IN THE WAR, BOND, I FOUGHT IN IT.
ON THE BLOODY BATTLEFIELDS OF FLANDERS...
...I SAW JUST HOW **EASILY** A MAN CAN COME APART.
HOW FRAGILE WE ARE.
MR MACSAWNEY, WOULD YOU BRING IN THE SPECIMEN?
SIR.
YOU SEE, THE FUTURE OF WARFARE ISN'T IN BETTER **WEAPONS.**
IT'S IN BETTER **HUMANS.**
STRONGER, BIGGER, MORE FEARLESS, MORE **RUTHLESS...**
LIKE AN EEL!

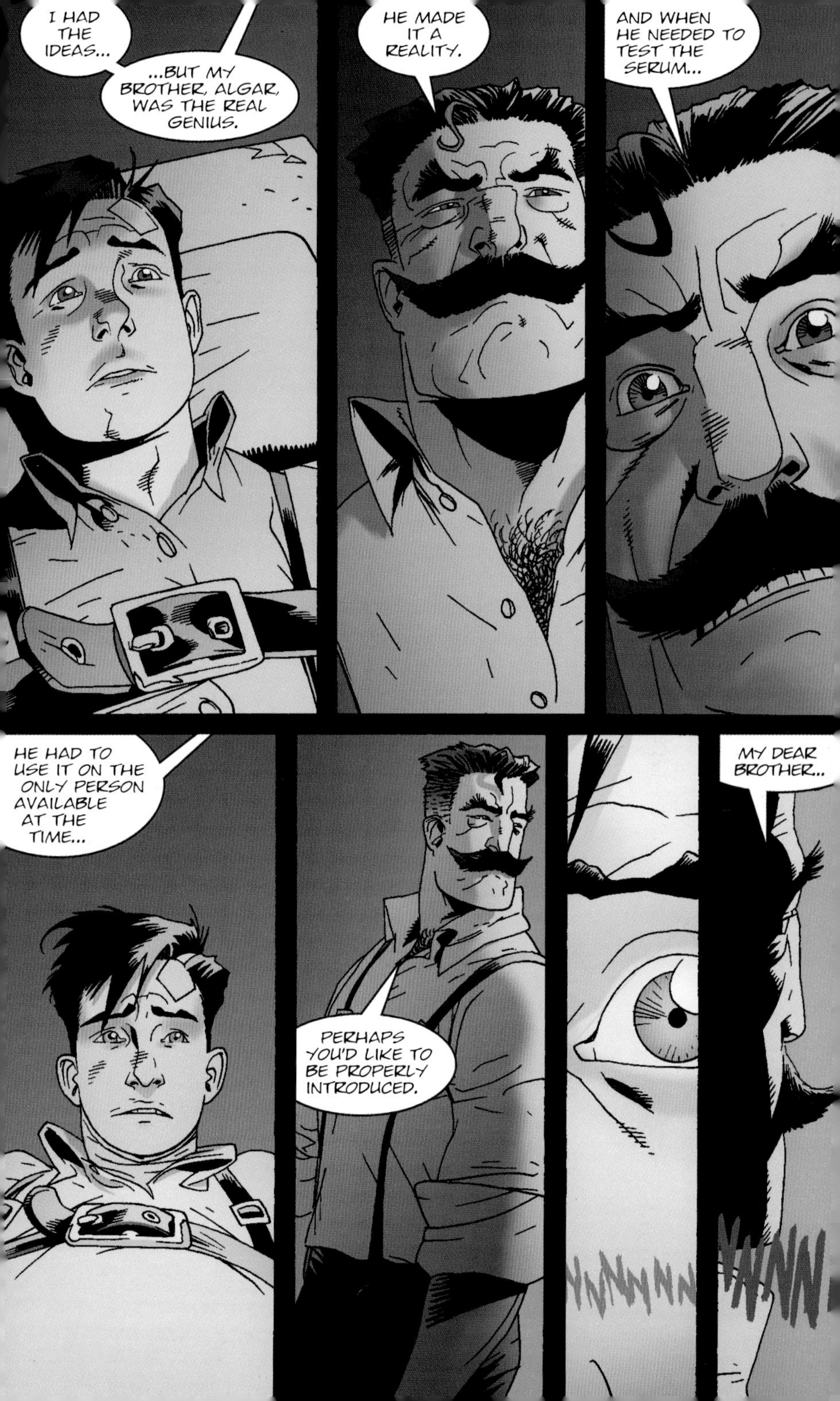
I HAD THE IDEAS...
...BUT MY BROTHER, ALGAR, WAS THE REAL GENIUS.
HE MADE IT A REALITY.
AND WHEN HE NEEDED TO TEST THE SERUM...
HE HAD TO USE IT ON THE ONLY PERSON AVAILABLE AT THE TIME...
PERHAPS YOU'D LIKE TO BE PROPERLY INTRODUCED.
MY DEAR BROTHER...

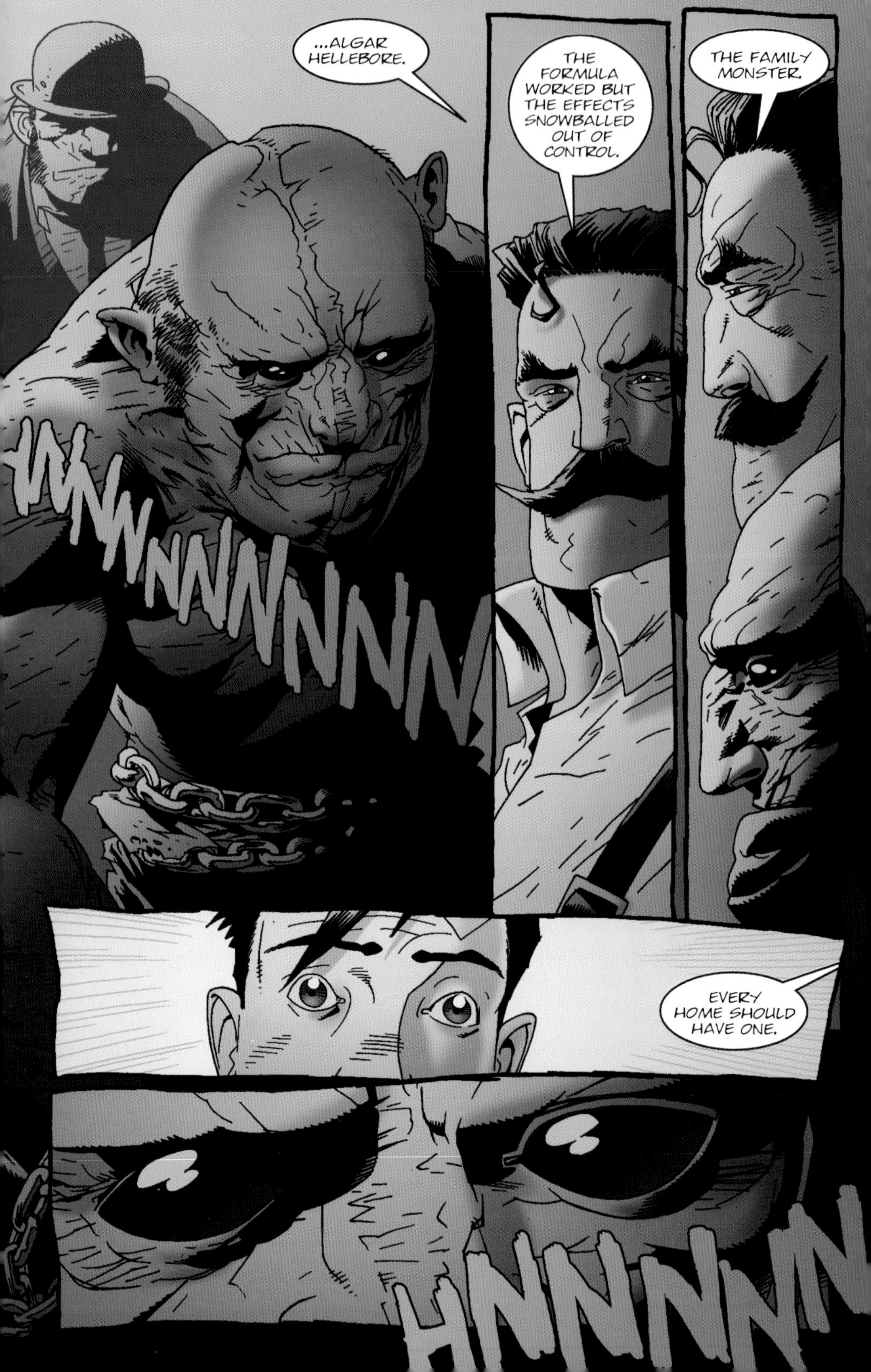
...ALGAR HELLEBORE.
THE FORMULA WORKED BUT THE EFFECTS SNOWBALLED OUT OF CONTROL.
THE FAMILY MONSTER.
MMMMMNNNNNNNNM
EVERY HOME SHOULD HAVE ONE.
HNNNNNN

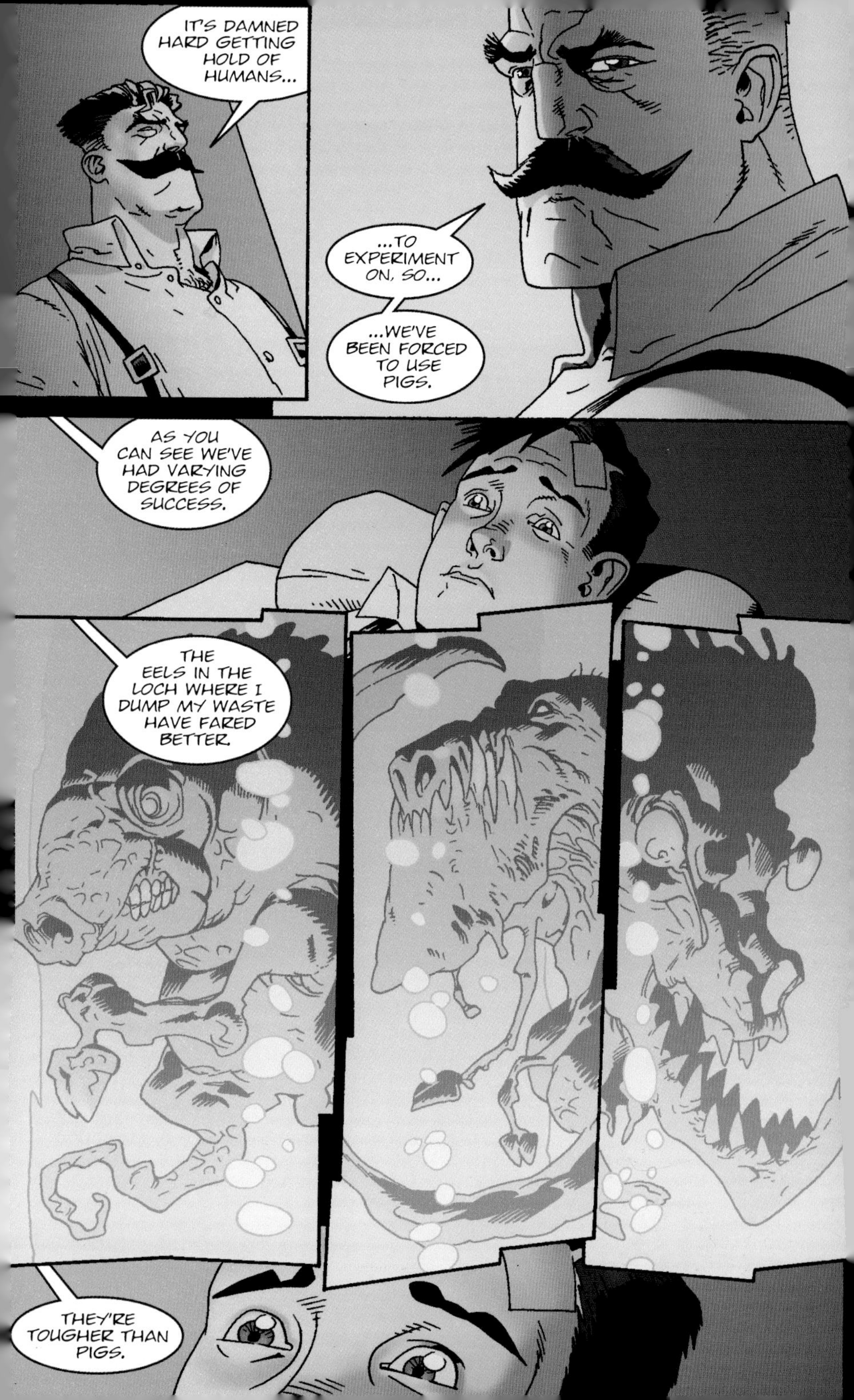
IT'S DAMNED HARD GETTING HOLD OF HUMANS...
...TO EXPERIMENT ON, SO...
...WE'VE BEEN FORCED TO USE PIGS.
AS YOU CAN SEE WE'VE HAD VARYING DEGREES OF SUCCESS.
THE EELS IN THE LOCH WHERE I DUMP MY WASTE HAVE FARED BETTER.
THEY'RE TOUGHER THAN PIGS.

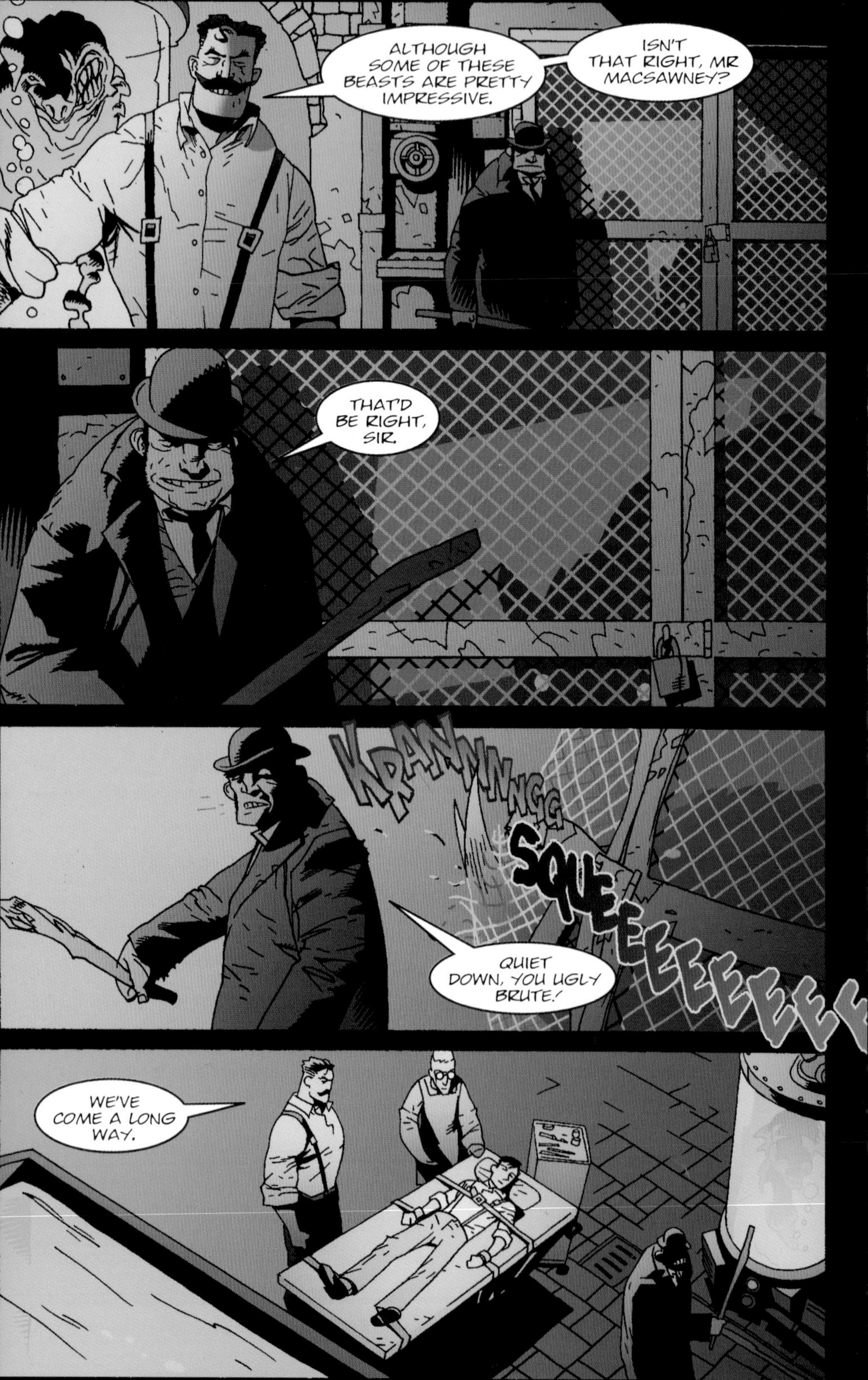
ALTHOUGH SOME OF THESE BEASTS ARE PRETTY IMPRESSIVE.
ISN'T THAT RIGHT, MR MACSAWNEY?
THAT'D BE RIGHT, SIR.
KRANNNNGG
SQUEEEEEEEEE
QUIET DOWN, YOU UGLY BRUTE!
WE'VE COME A LONG WAY.

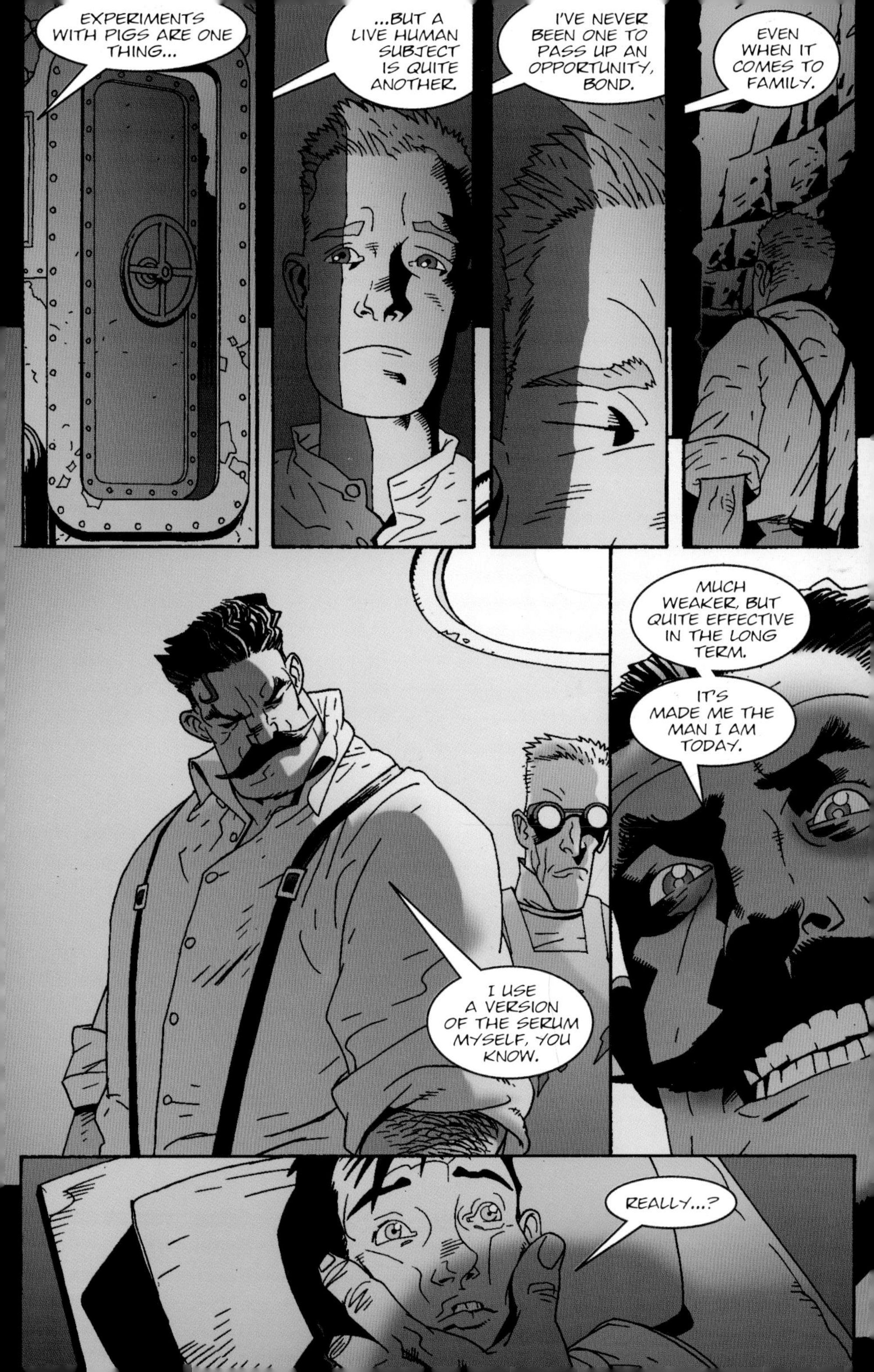
EXPERIMENTS WITH PIGS ARE ONE THING...
...BUT A LIVE HUMAN SUBJECT IS QUITE ANOTHER.
I'VE NEVER BEEN ONE TO PASS UP AN OPPORTUNITY, BOND.
EVEN WHEN IT COMES TO FAMILY.
I USE A VERSION OF THE SERUM MYSELF, YOU KNOW.
MUCH WEAKER, BUT QUITE EFFECTIVE IN THE LONG TERM.
IT'S MADE ME THE MAN I AM TODAY.
REALLY...?

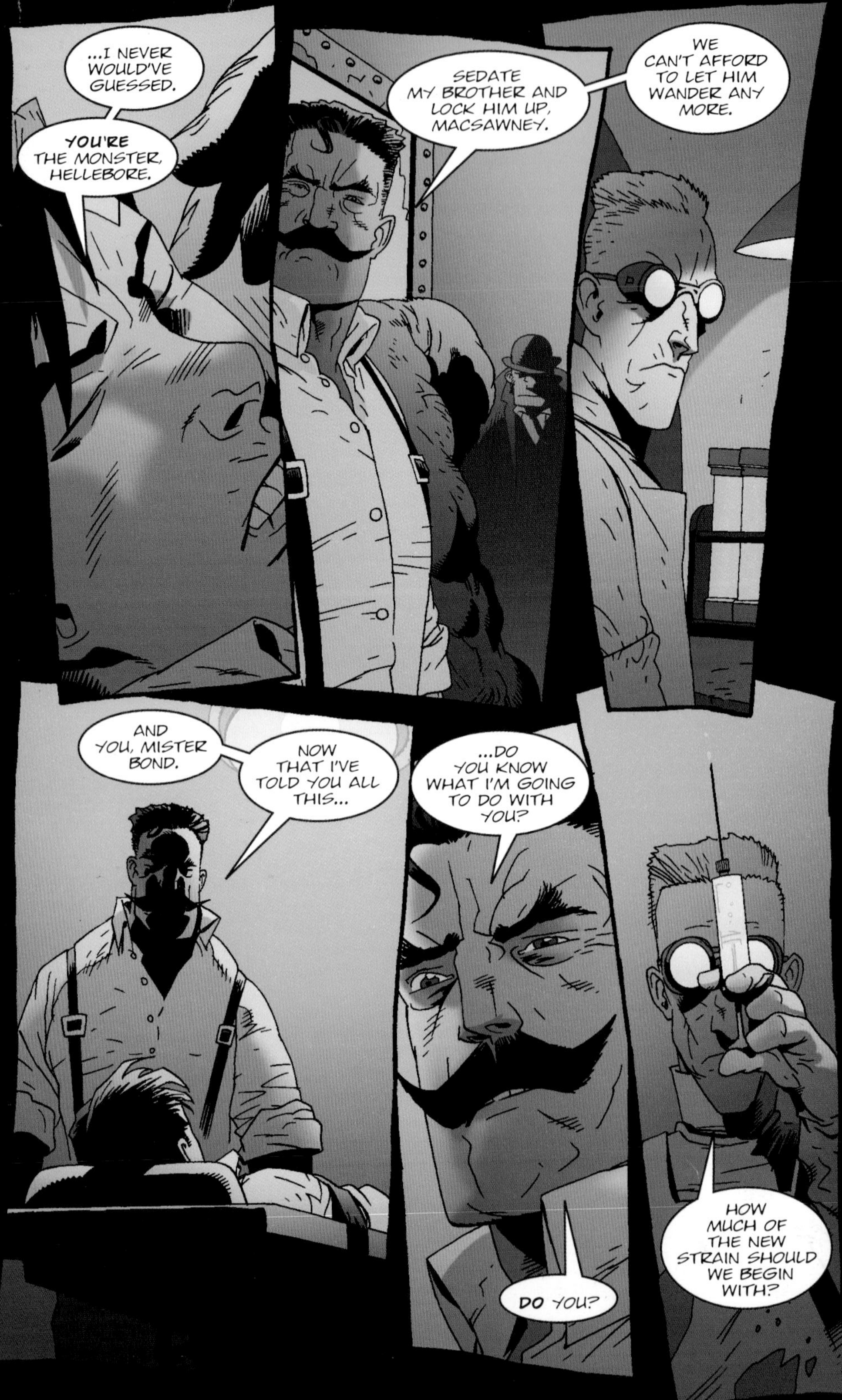
...I NEVER WOULD'VE GUESSED.
YOU'RE THE MONSTER, HELLEBORE.
SEDATE MY BROTHER AND LOCK HIM UP, MACSAWNEY.
WE CAN'T AFFORD TO LET HIM WANDER ANY MORE.
AND YOU, MISTER BOND.
NOW THAT I'VE TOLD YOU ALL THIS...
...DO YOU KNOW WHAT I'M GOING TO DO WITH YOU?
DO YOU?
HOW MUCH OF THE NEW STRAIN SHOULD WE BEGIN WITH?

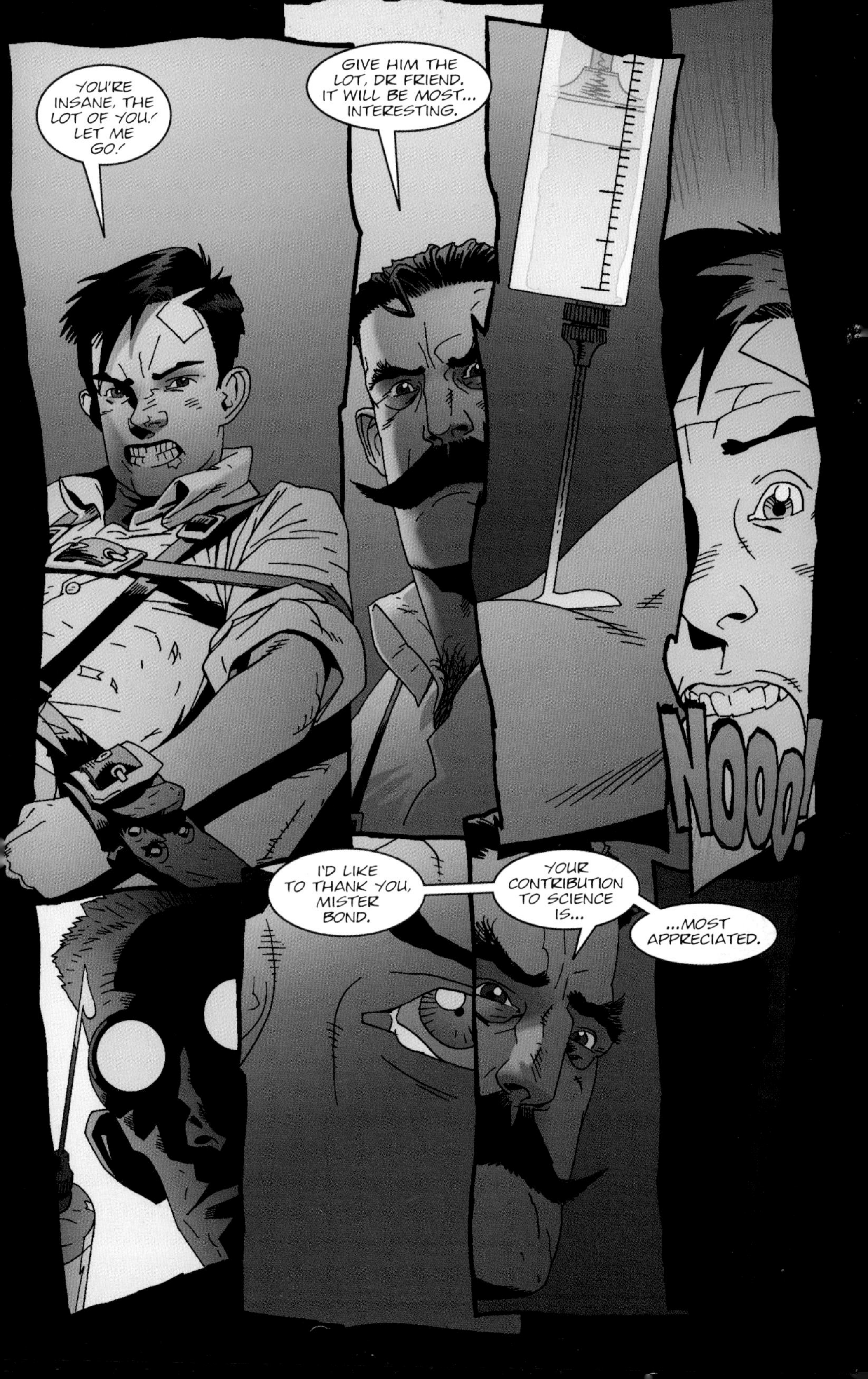
YOU'RE INSANE, THE LOT OF YOU! LET ME GO!
GIVE HIM THE LOT, DR FRIEND. IT WILL BE MOST... INTERESTING.
NOOO!
I'D LIKE TO THANK YOU, MISTER BOND.
YOUR CONTRIBUTION TO SCIENCE IS...
...MOST APPRECIATED.

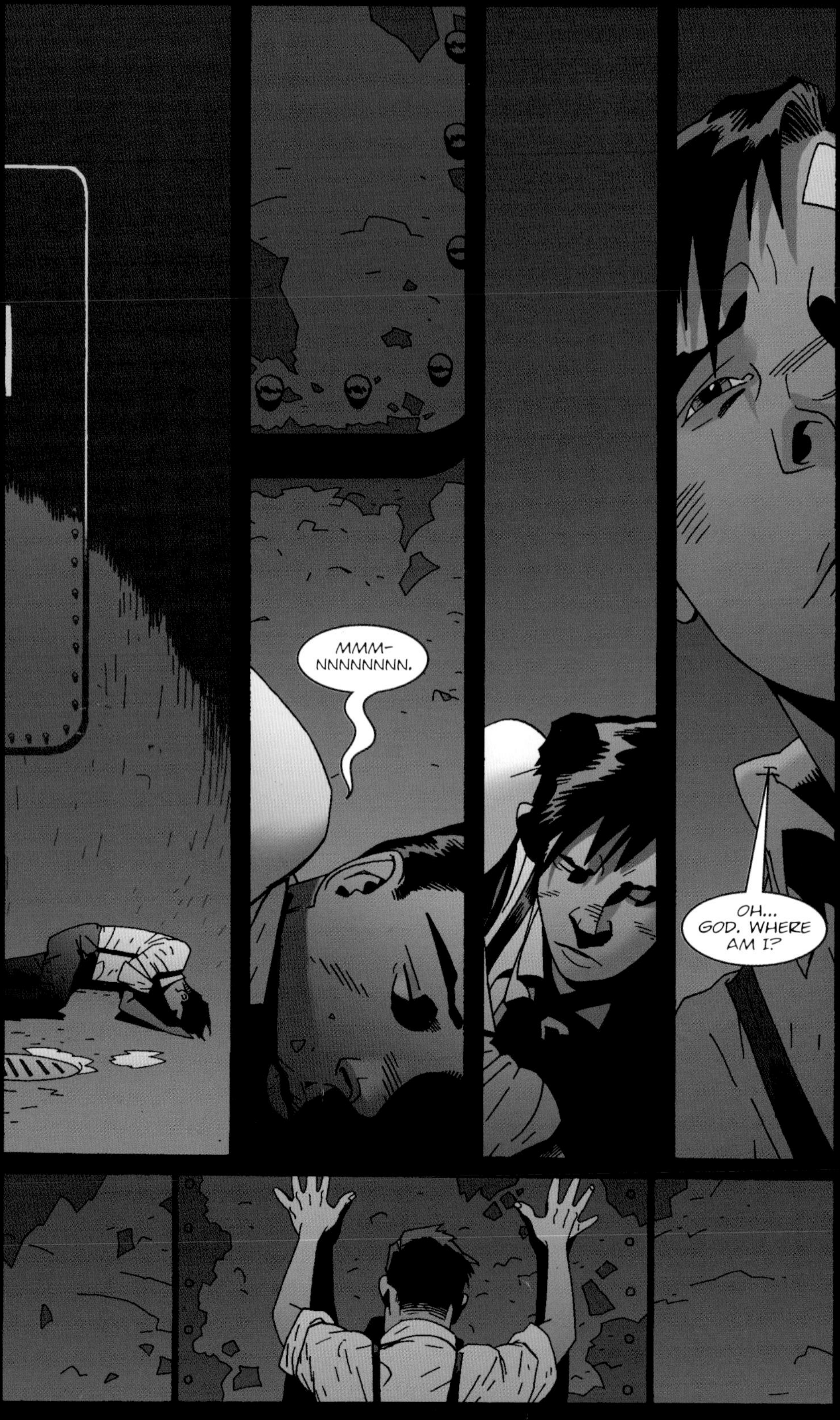
MMM-
NNNNNNNN.
OH...
GOD. WHERE
AM I?

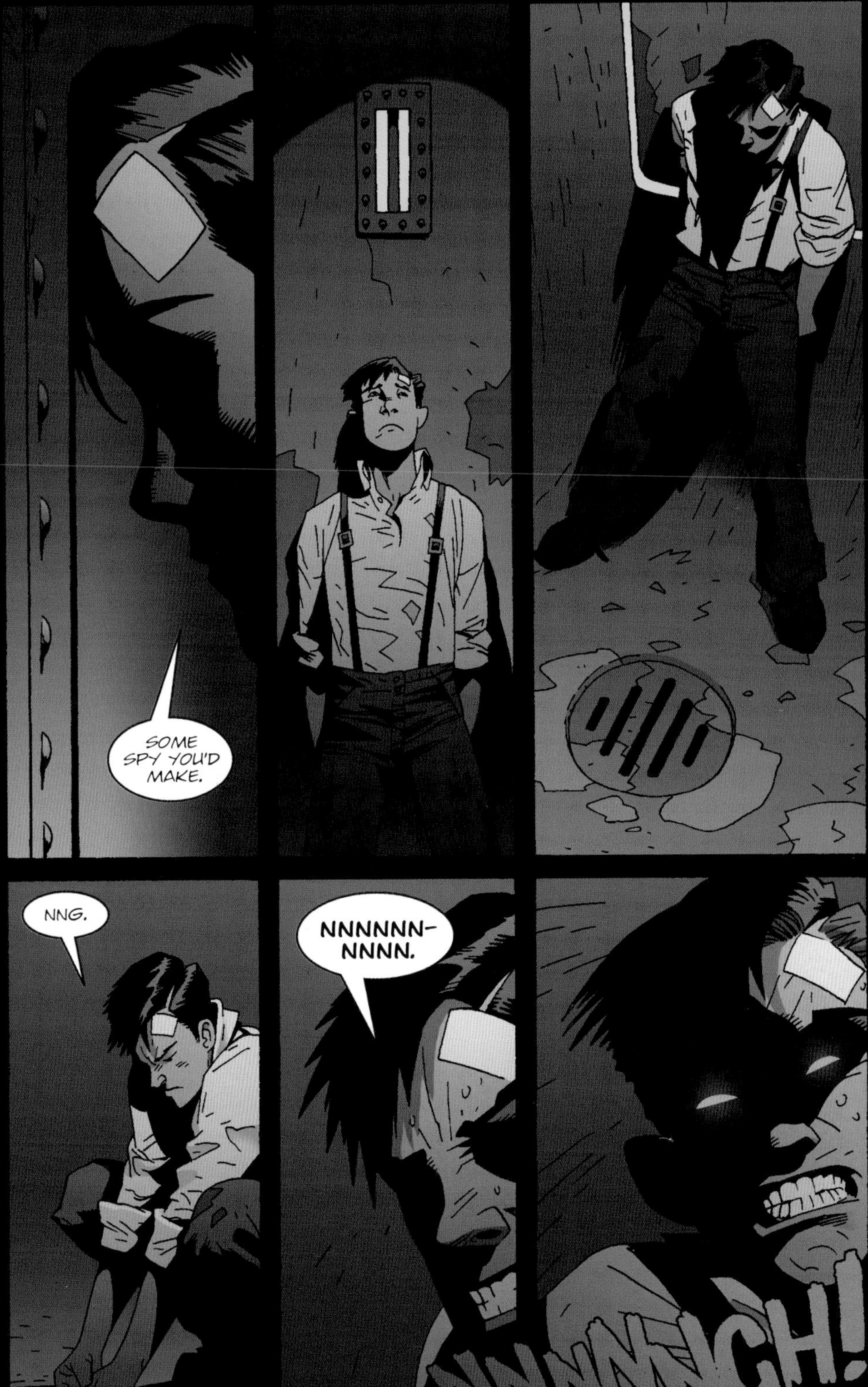
SOME SPY YOU'D MAKE.
NNG.
NNNNNN-NNNN.
NNNNNNCH!

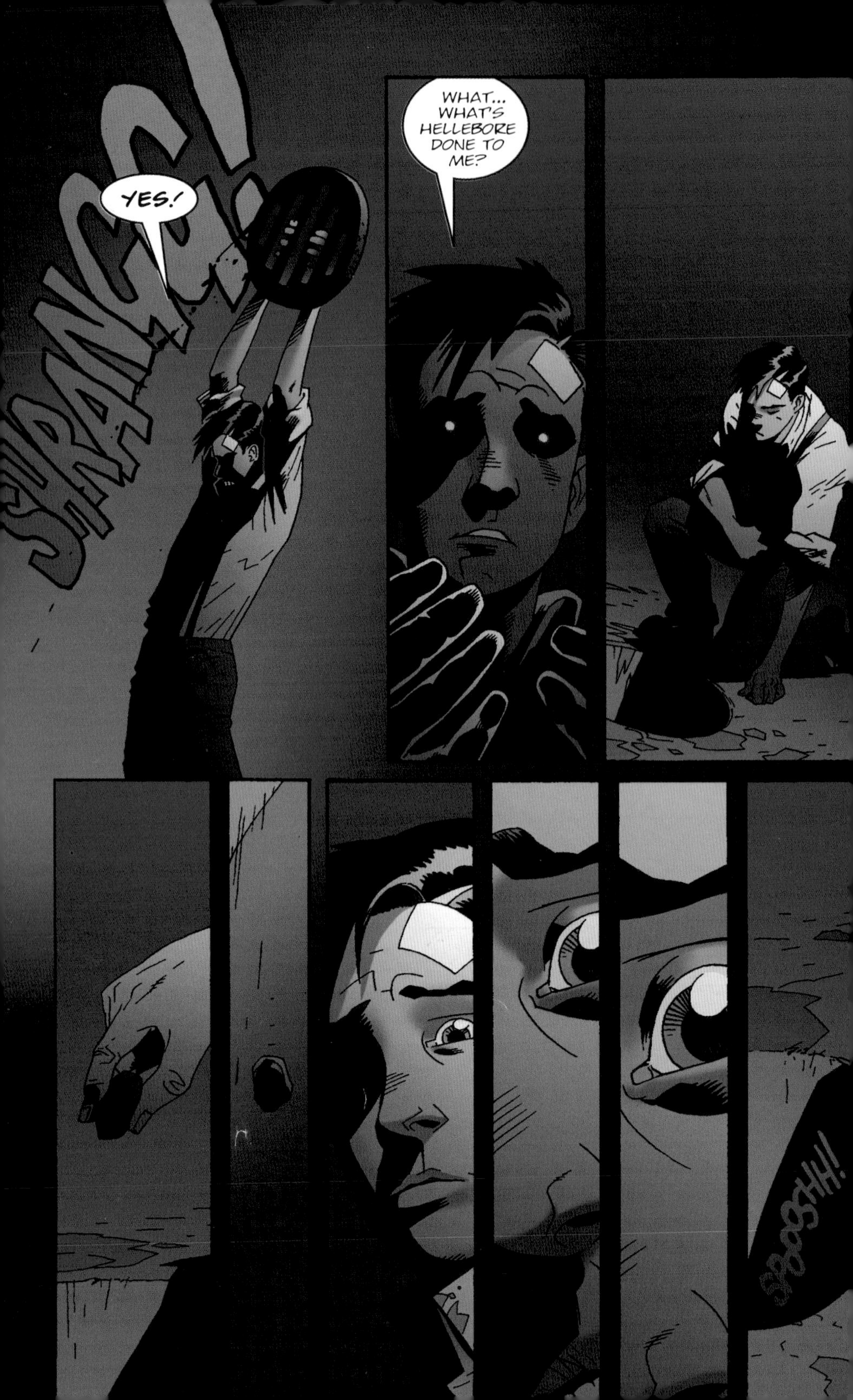
SHRANGG!
YES!
WHAT... WHAT'S HELLEBORE DONE TO ME?
SBOOSHH!

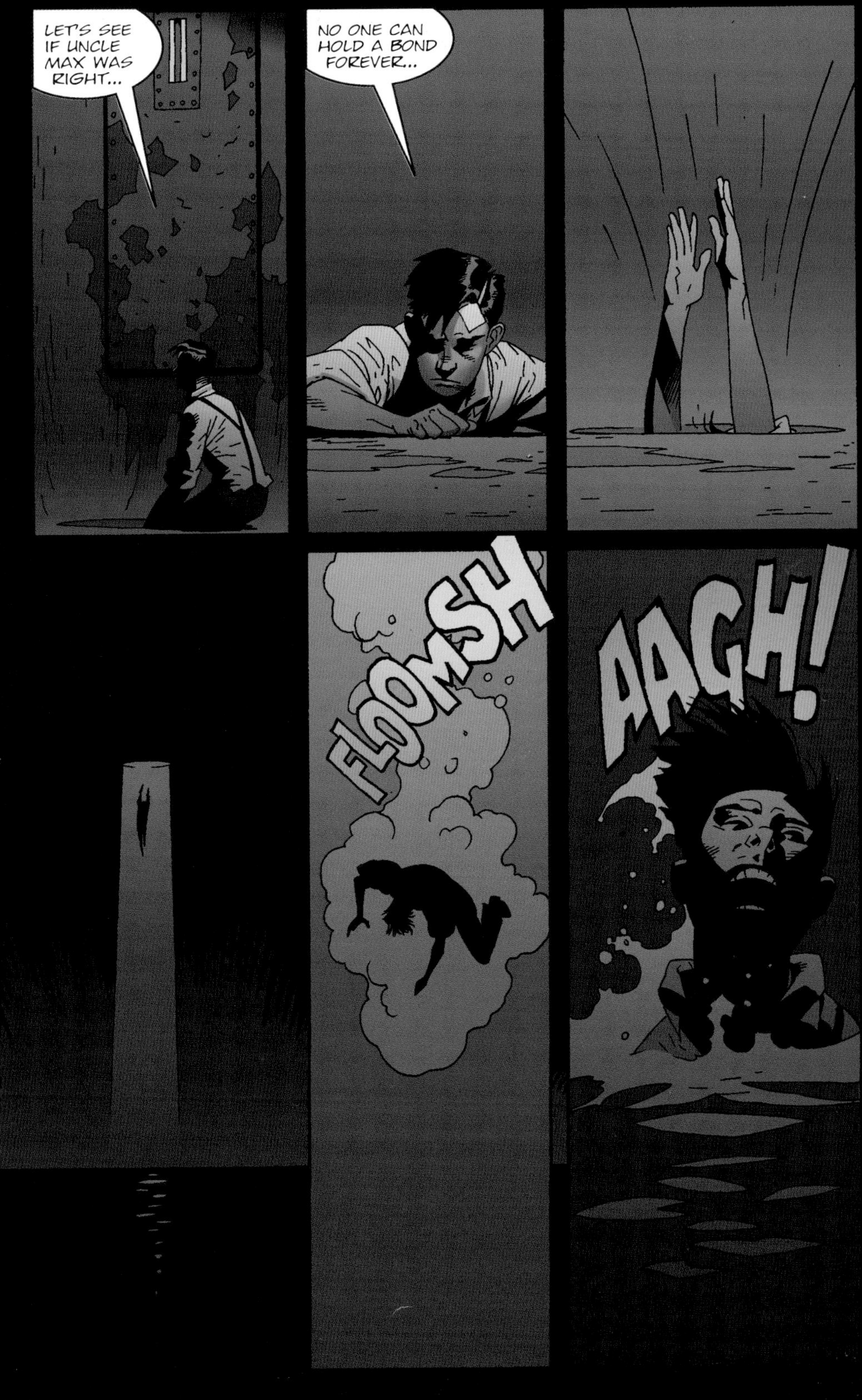
LET'S SEE IF UNCLE MAX WAS RIGHT...
NO ONE CAN HOLD A BOND FOREVER...
FLOOMSH
AAGH!

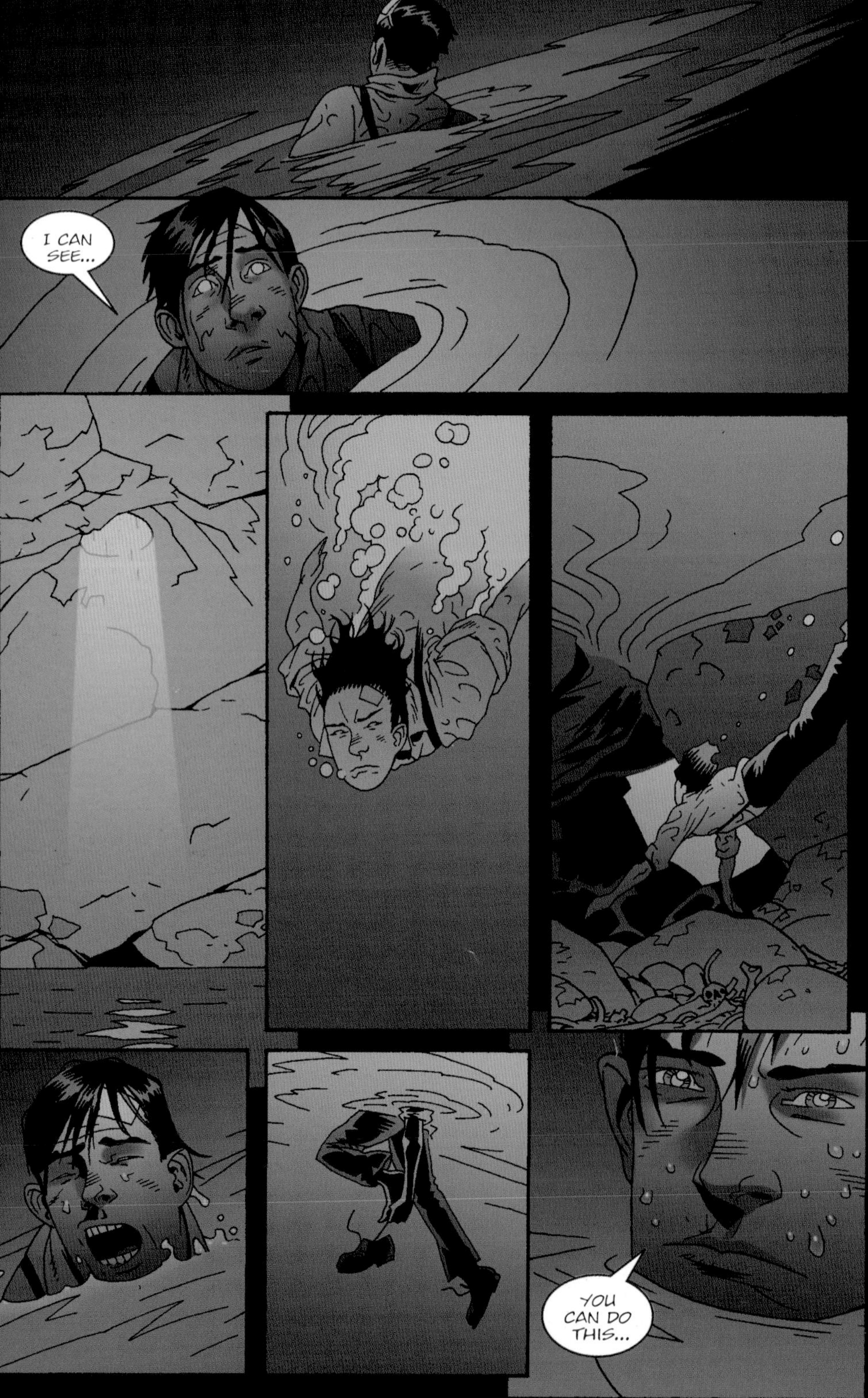
I CAN SEE...
YOU CAN DO THIS...

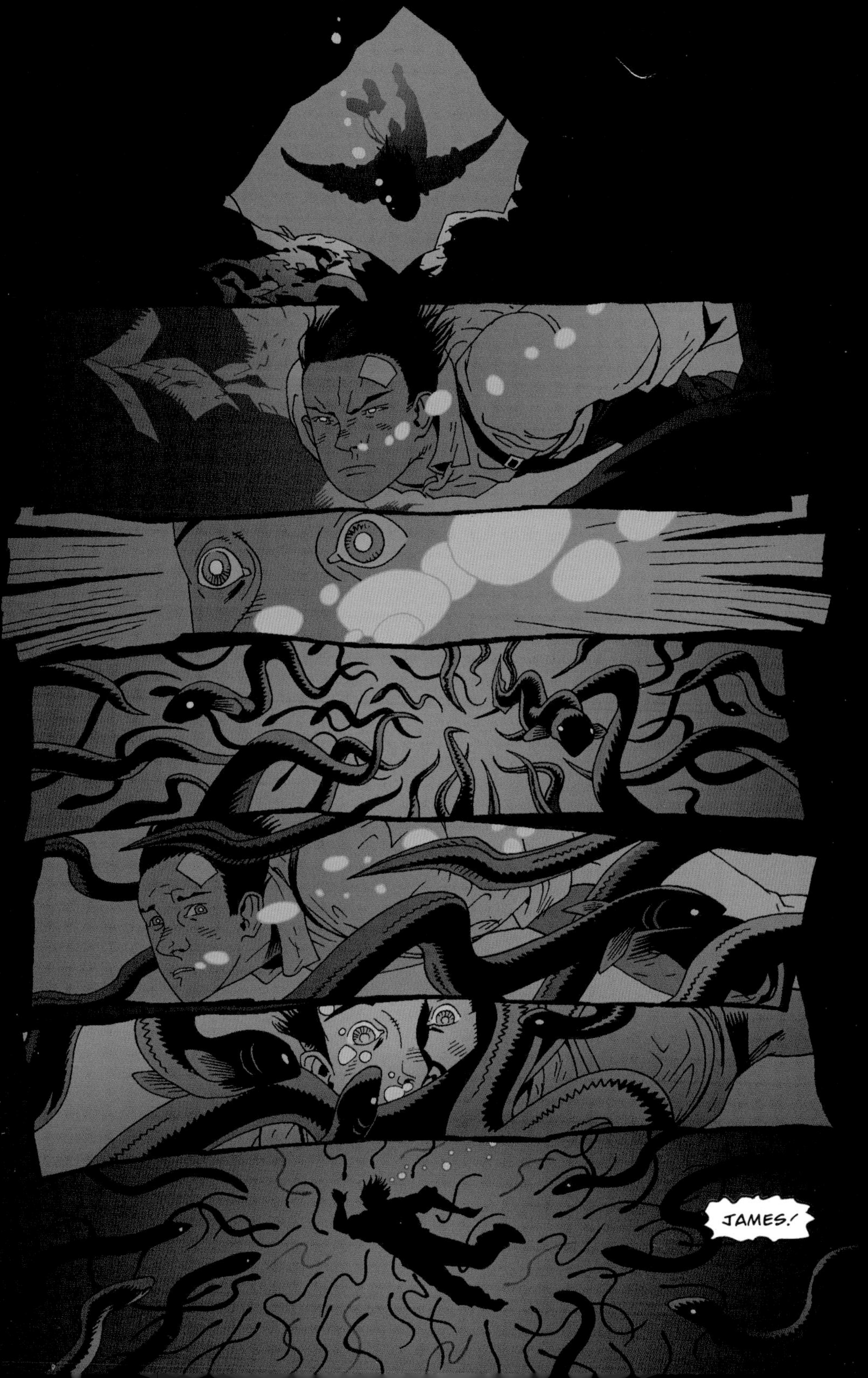
JAMES!

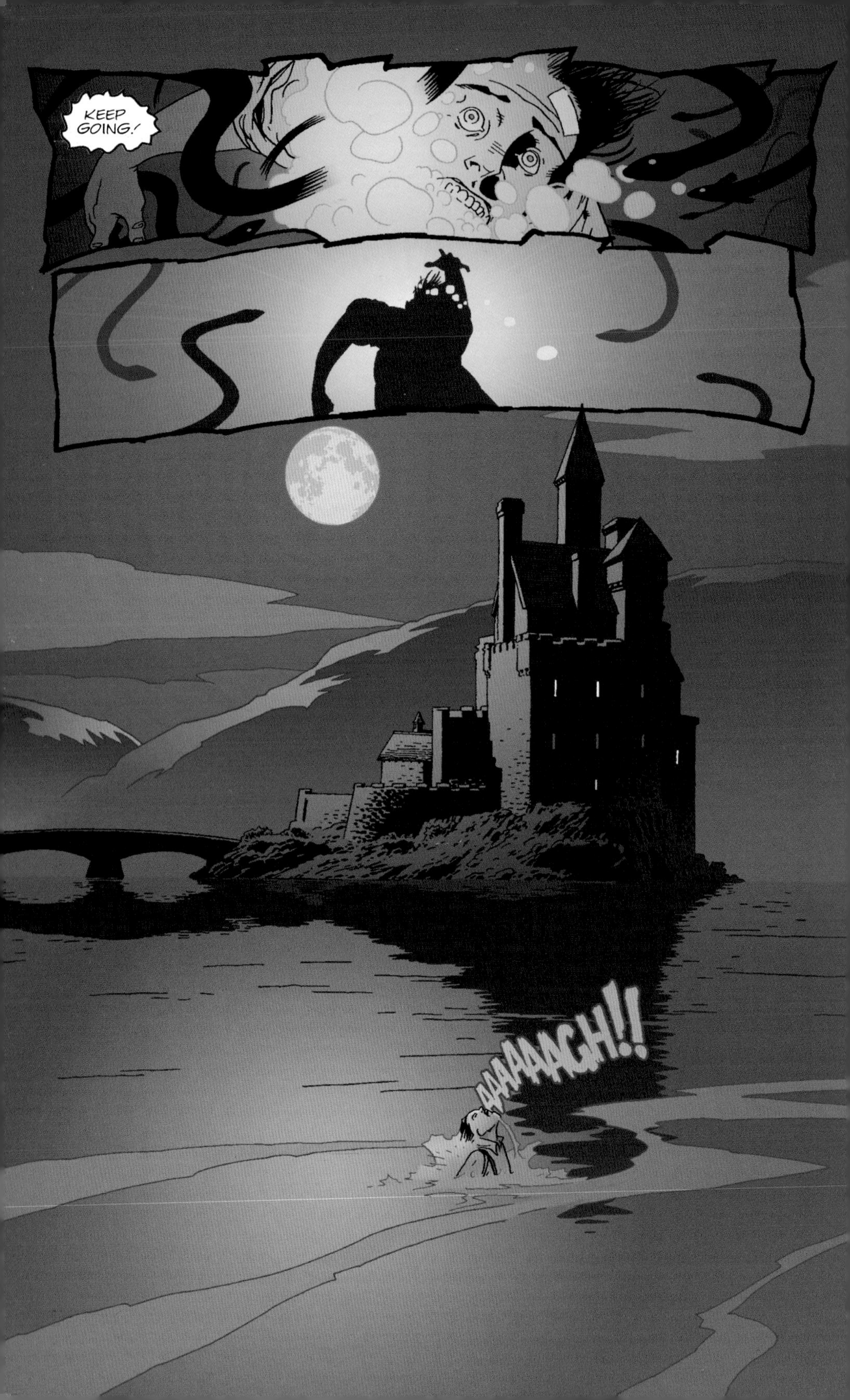
KEEP GOING!
AAAAAAGH!!

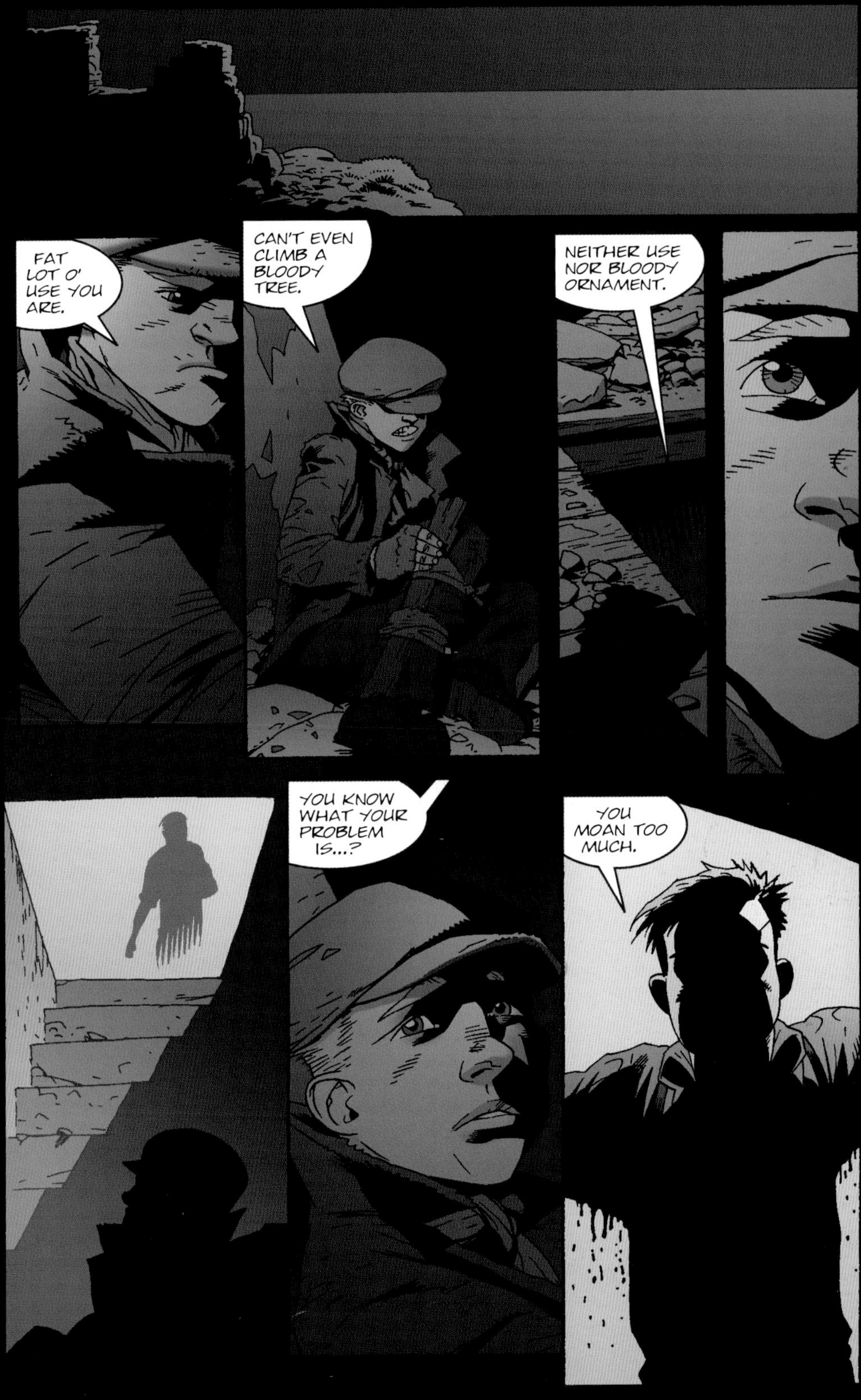
FAT LOT O' USE YOU ARE.
CAN'T EVEN CLIMB A BLOODY TREE.
NEITHER USE NOR BLOODY ORNAMENT.
YOU KNOW WHAT YOUR PROBLEM IS...?
YOU MOAN TOO MUCH.

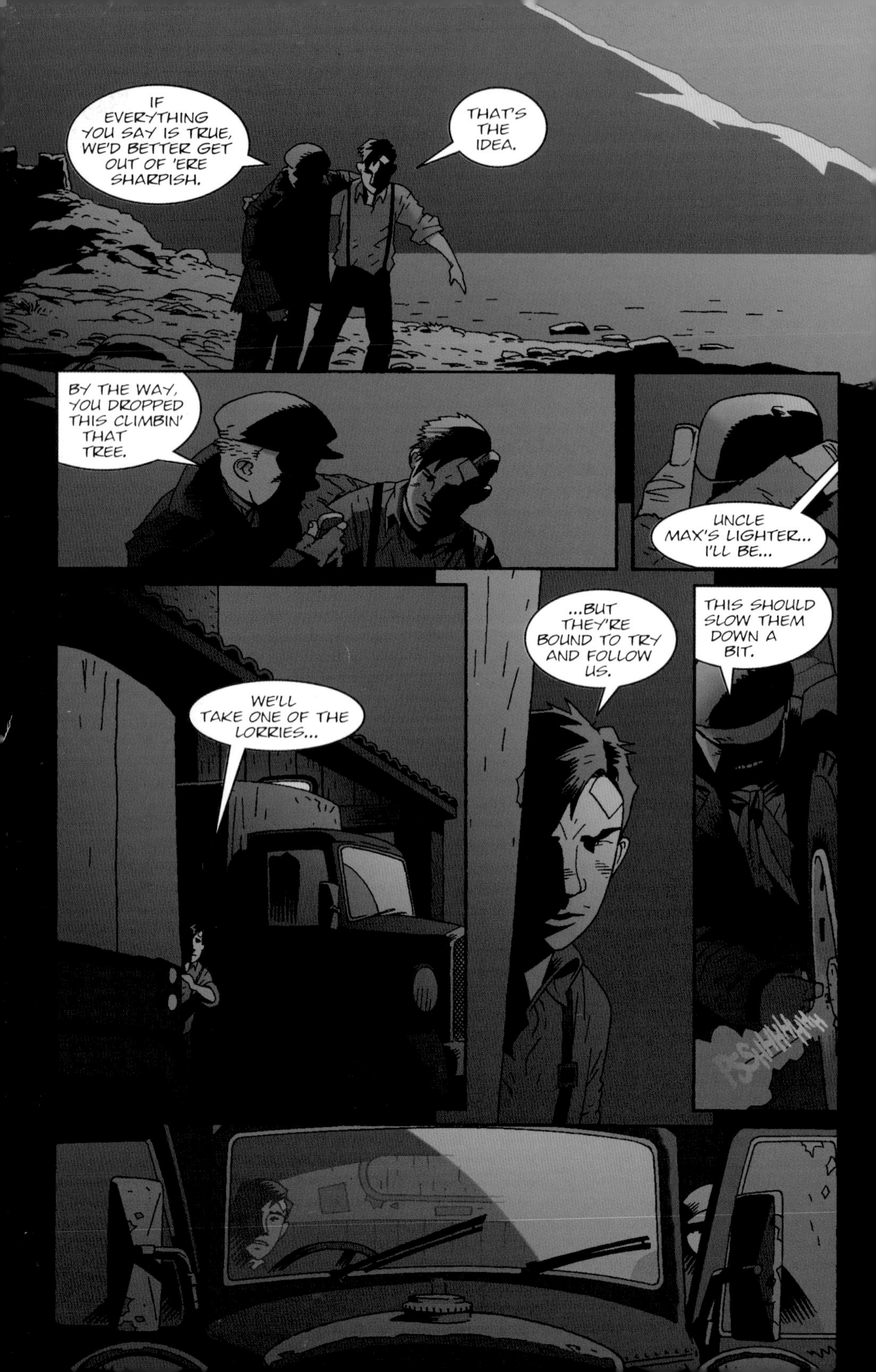
IF EVERYTHING YOU SAY IS TRUE, WE'D BETTER GET OUT OF 'ERE SHARPISH.
THAT'S THE IDEA.
BY THE WAY, YOU DROPPED THIS CLIMBIN' THAT TREE.
UNCLE MAX'S LIGHTER... I'LL BE...
WE'LL TAKE ONE OF THE LORRIES...
...BUT THEY'RE BOUND TO TRY AND FOLLOW US.
THIS SHOULD SLOW THEM DOWN A BIT.

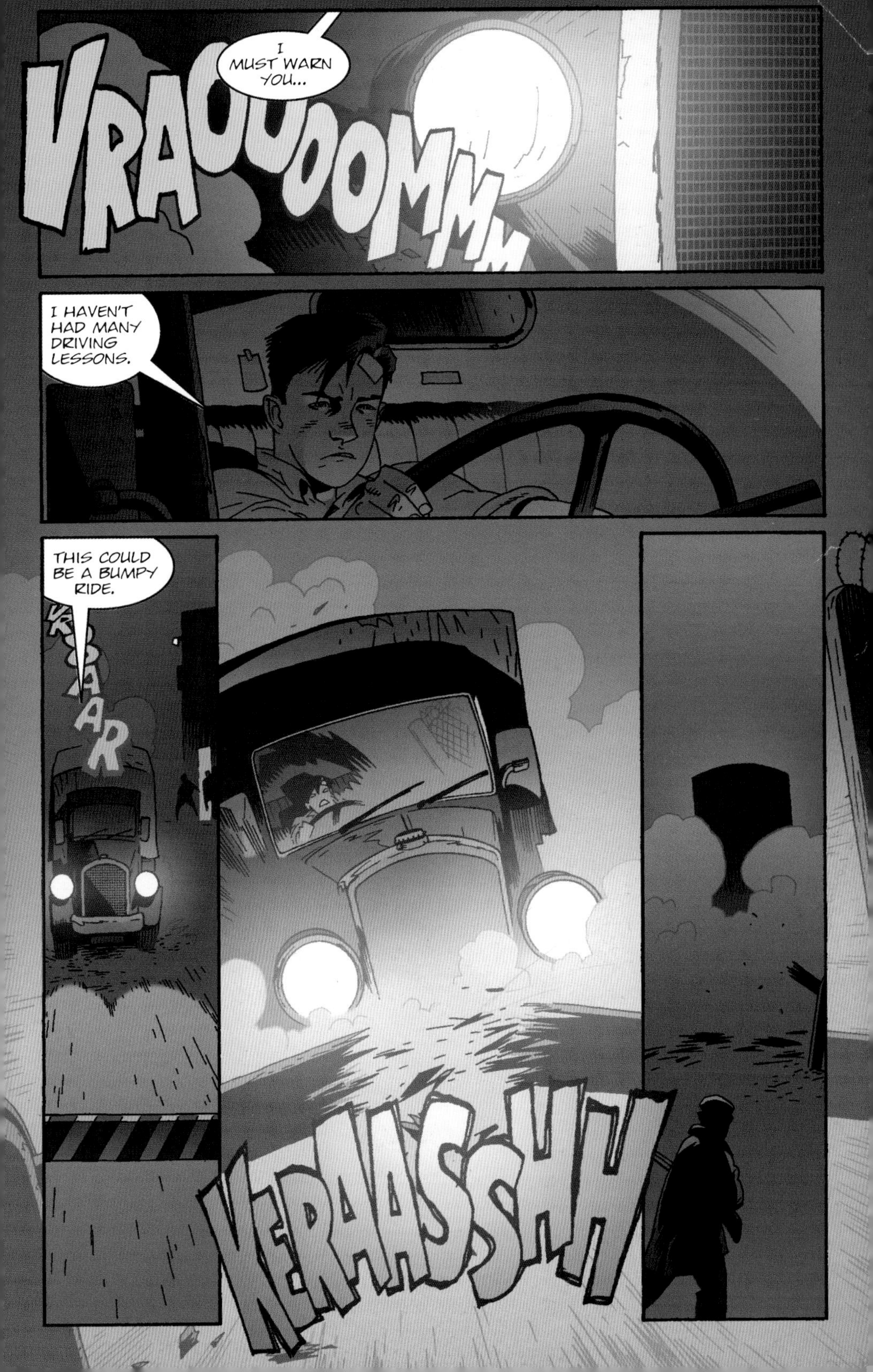
I MUST WARN YOU...
VRAOUOOMMMM
I HAVEN'T HAD MANY DRIVING LESSONS.
THIS COULD BE A BUMPY RIDE.
AR
KERAASSHH

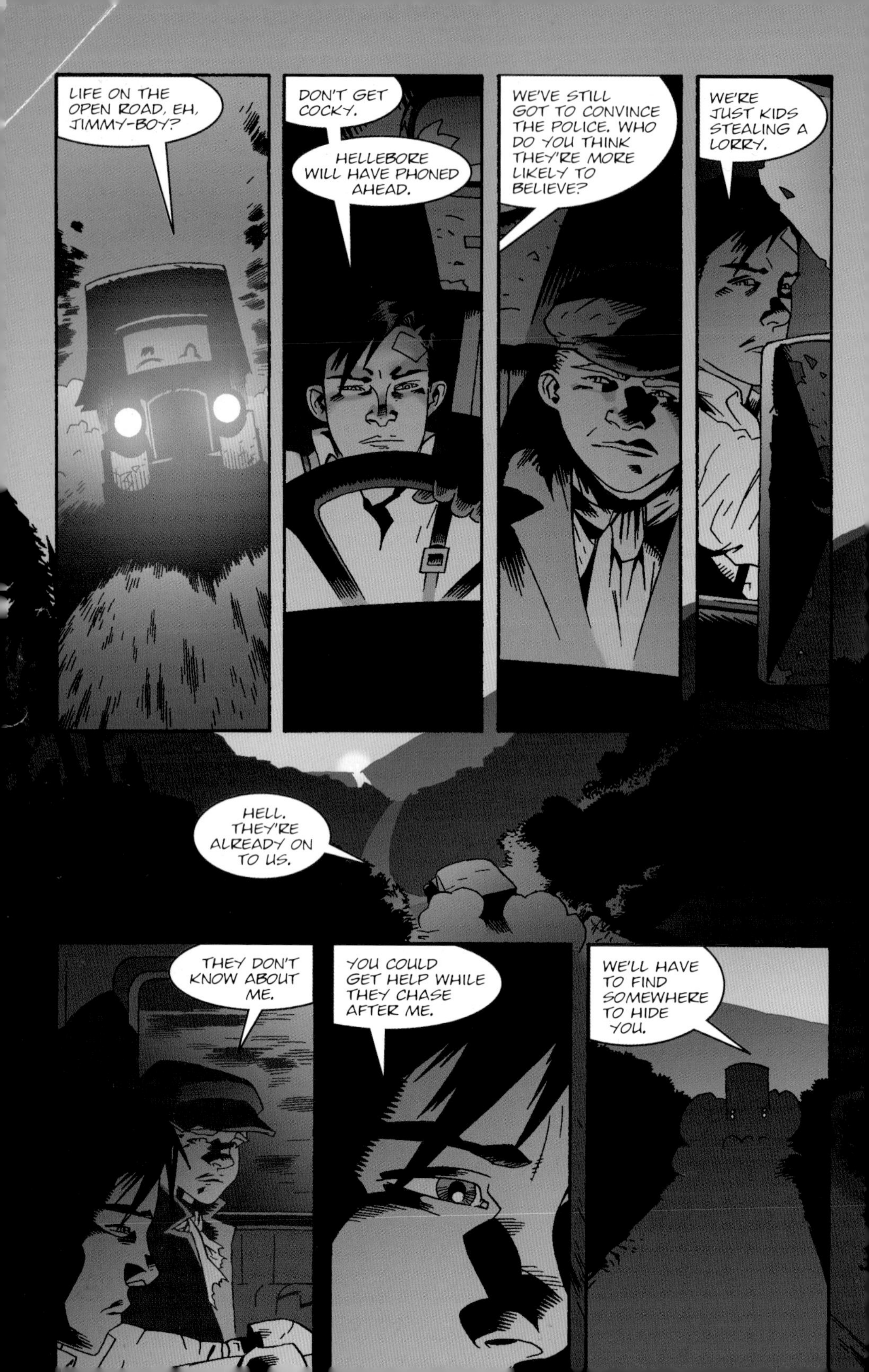
LIFE ON THE OPEN ROAD, EH, JIMMY-BOY?
DON'T GET COCKY.
HELLEBORE WILL HAVE PHONED AHEAD.
WE'VE STILL GOT TO CONVINCE THE POLICE. WHO DO YOU THINK THEY'RE MORE LIKELY TO BELIEVE?
WE'RE JUST KIDS STEALING A LORRY.
HELL. THEY'RE ALREADY ON TO US.
THEY DON'T KNOW ABOUT ME.
YOU COULD GET HELP WHILE THEY CHASE AFTER ME.
WE'LL HAVE TO FIND SOMEWHERE TO HIDE YOU.

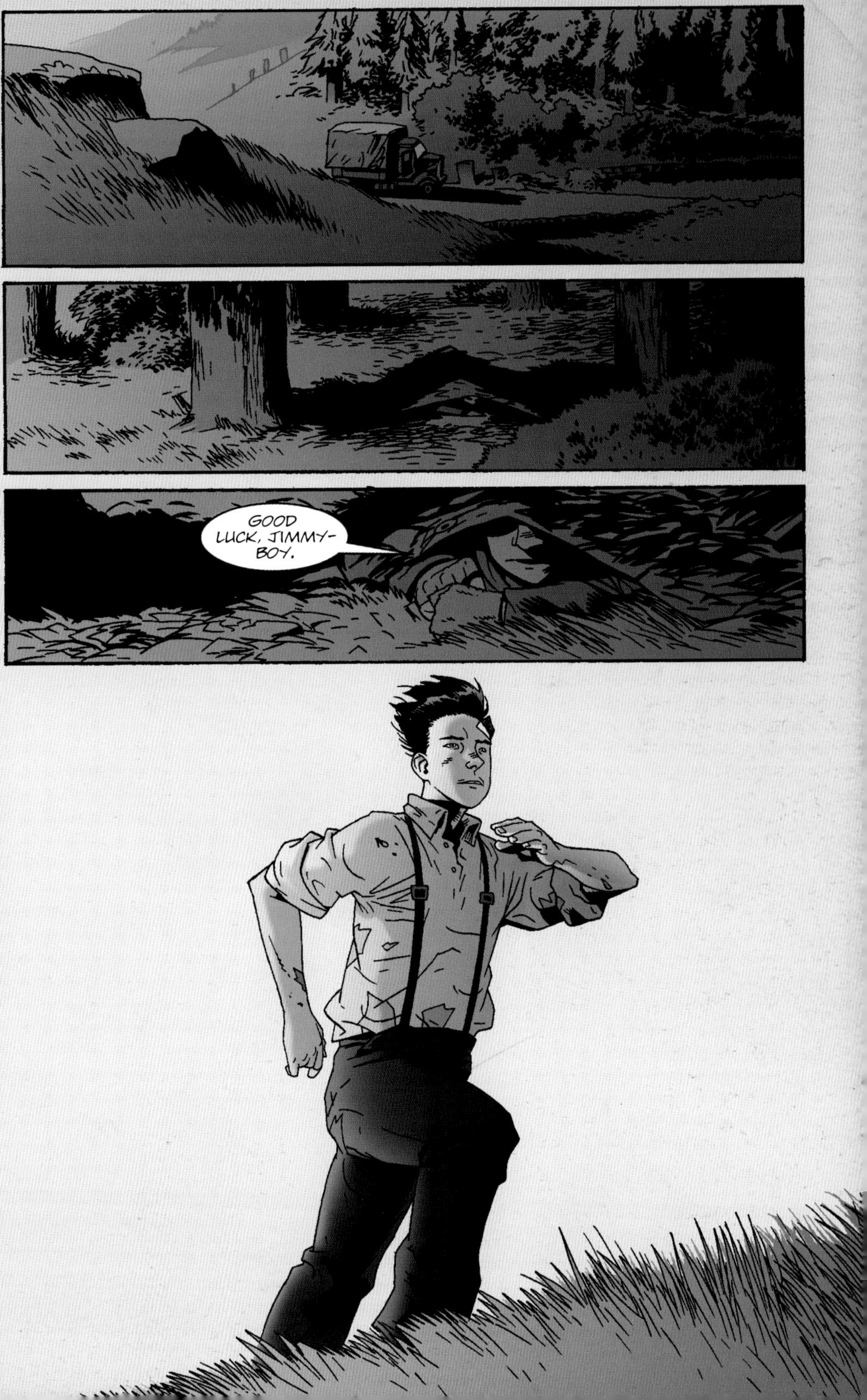
GOOD LUCK, JIMMY-BOY.

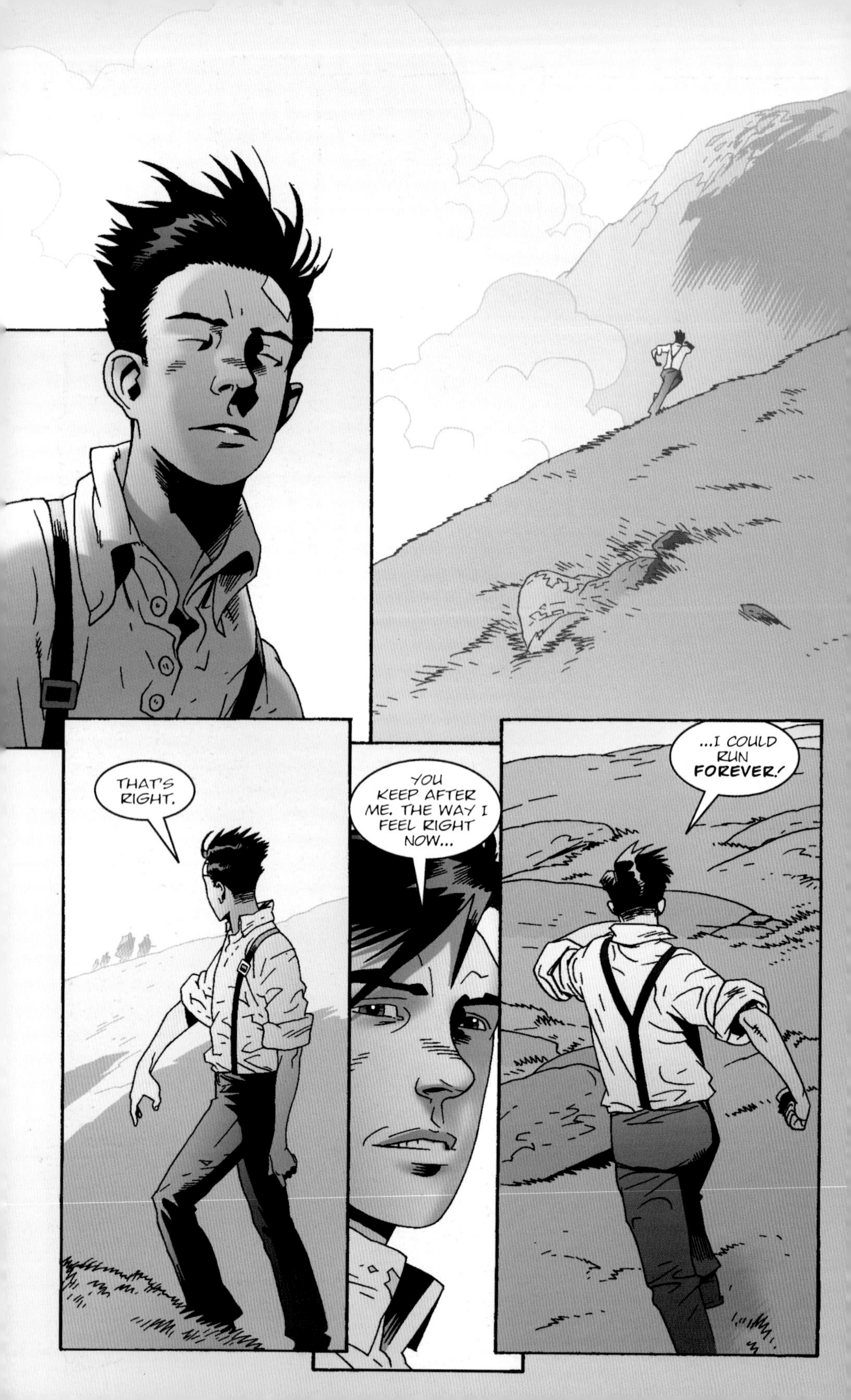
THAT'S RIGHT.
YOU KEEP AFTER ME. THE WAY I FEEL RIGHT NOW...
...I COULD RUN FOREVER!

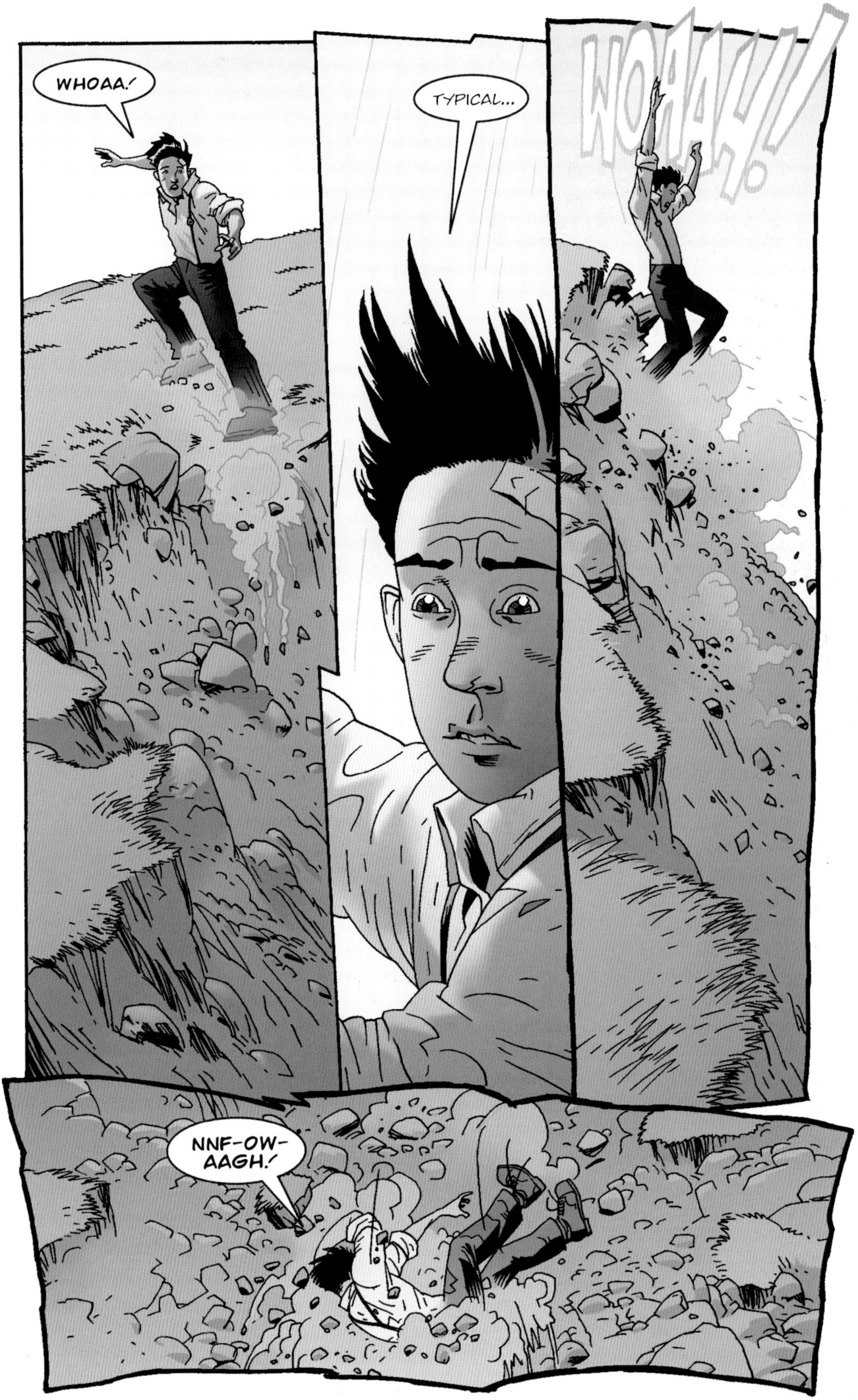
WHOAA!
TYPICAL...
WOAAH!!
NNF-OW-AAGH!

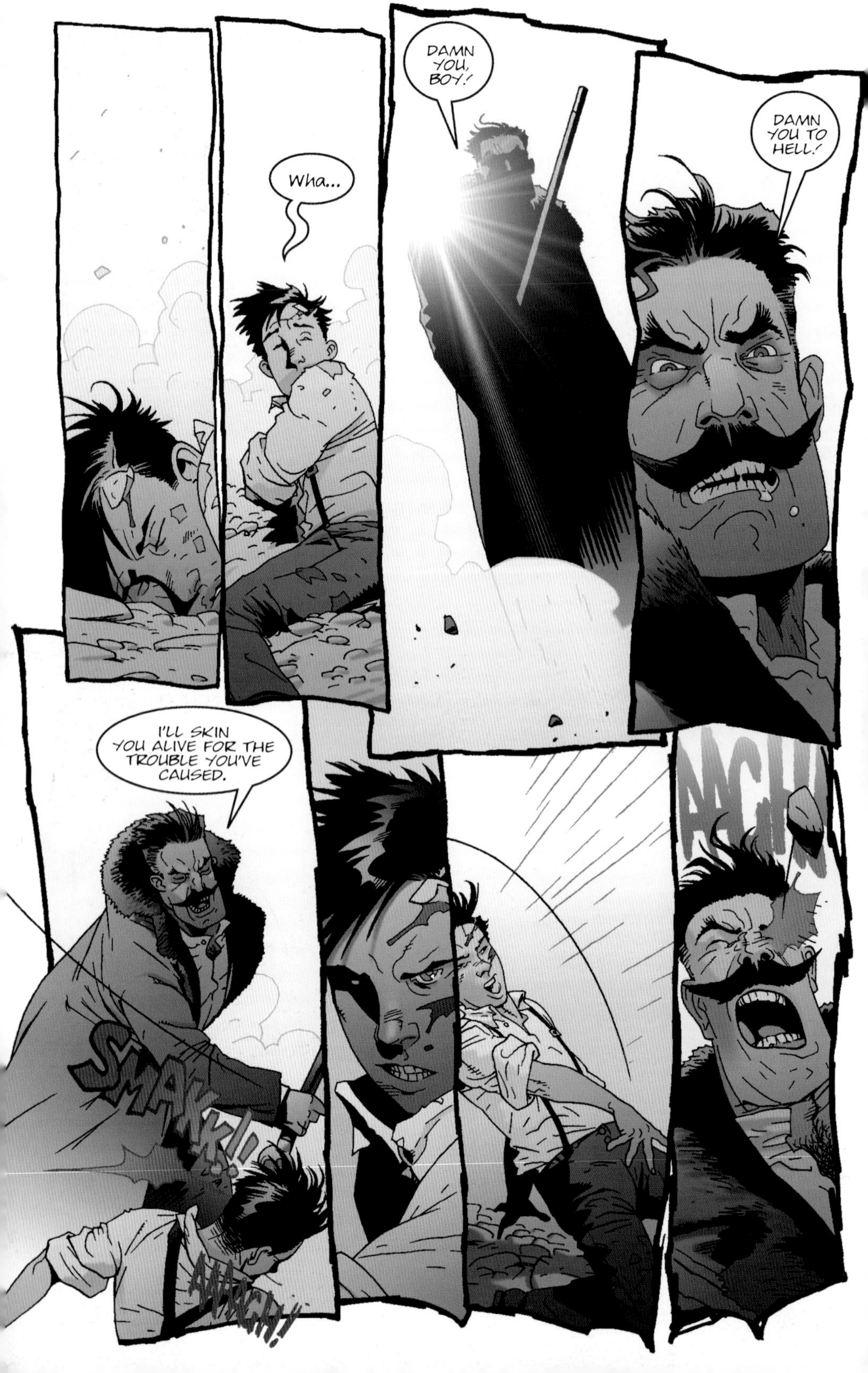
Wha...
DAMN YOU, BOY!
DAMN YOU TO HELL!
I'LL SKIN YOU ALIVE FOR THE TROUBLE YOU'VE CAUSED.
SMAK!!

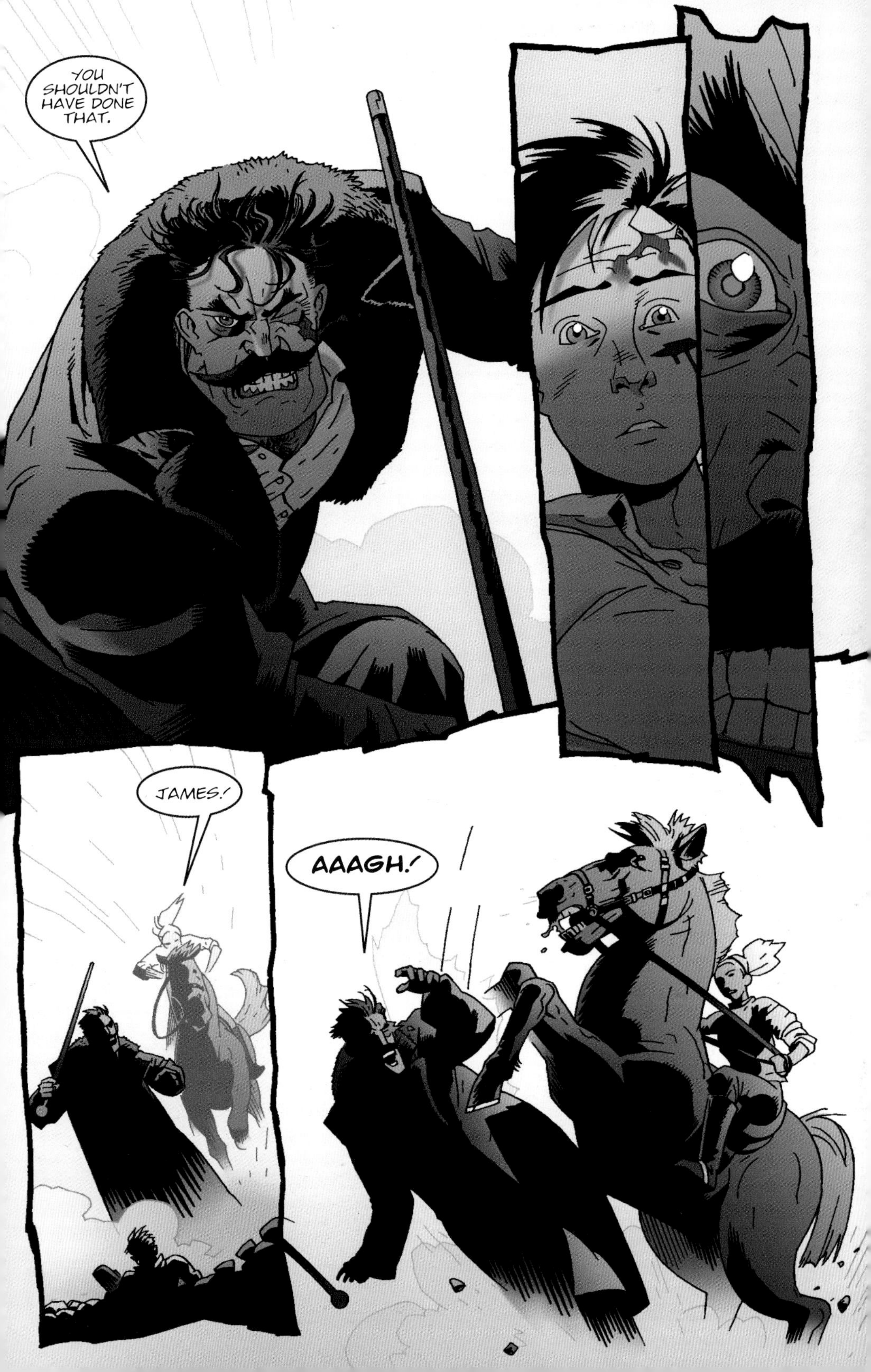
YOU SHOULDN'T HAVE DONE THAT.
JAMES.!
AAAGH.!

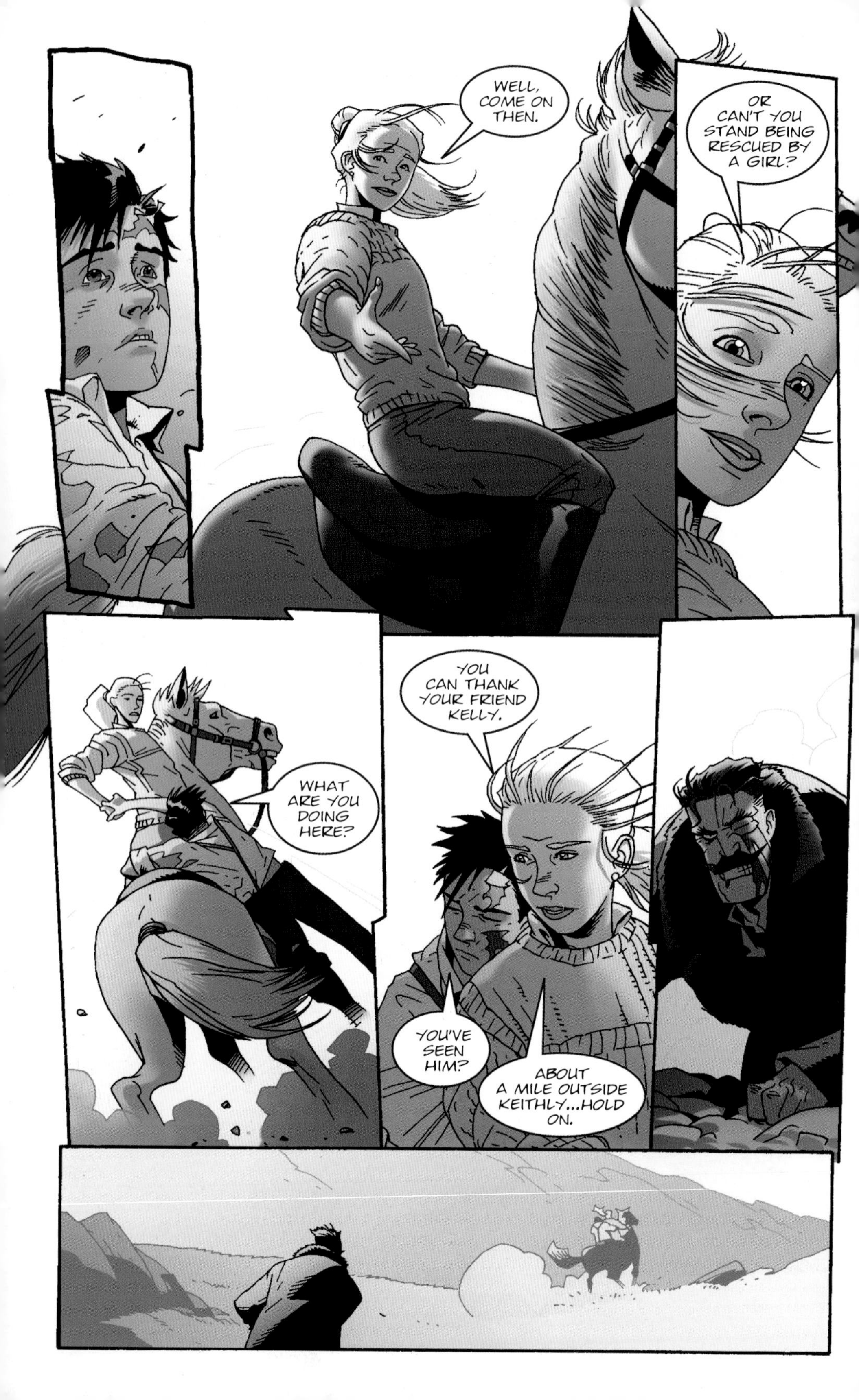
WELL, COME ON THEN.
OR CAN'T YOU STAND BEING RESCUED BY A GIRL?
WHAT ARE YOU DOING HERE?
YOU CAN THANK YOUR FRIEND KELLY.
YOU'VE SEEN HIM?
ABOUT A MILE OUTSIDE KEITHLY...HOLD ON.

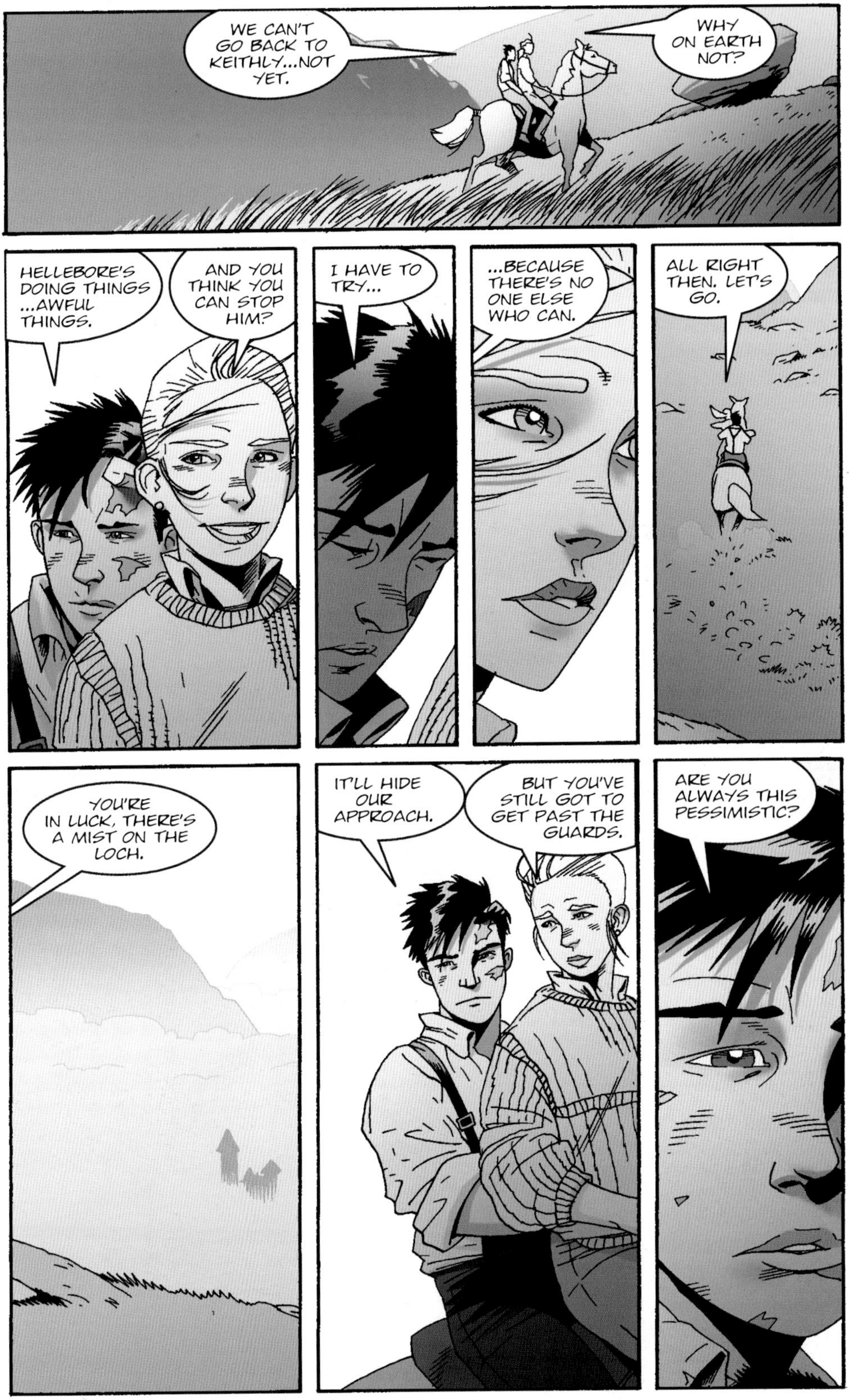
WE CAN'T GO BACK TO KEITHLY...NOT YET.
WHY ON EARTH NOT?
HELLEBORE'S DOING THINGS ...AWFUL THINGS.
AND YOU THINK YOU CAN STOP HIM?
I HAVE TO TRY...
...BECAUSE THERE'S NO ONE ELSE WHO CAN.
ALL RIGHT THEN. LET'S GO.
YOU'RE IN LUCK, THERE'S A MIST ON THE LOCH.
IT'LL HIDE OUR APPROACH.
BUT YOU'VE STILL GOT TO GET PAST THE GUARDS.
ARE YOU ALWAYS THIS PESSIMISTIC?

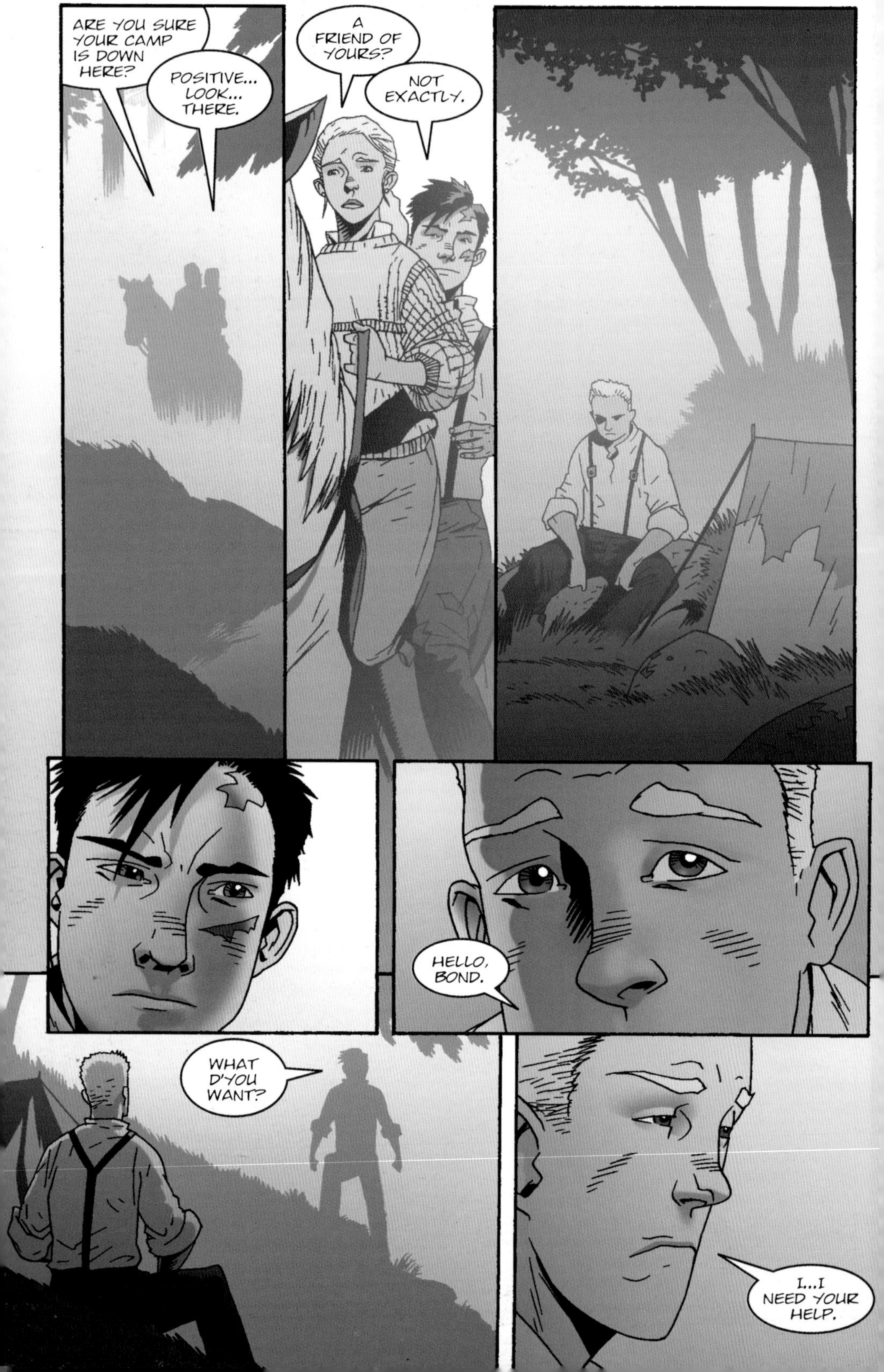
ARE YOU SURE YOUR CAMP IS DOWN HERE?
POSITIVE... LOOK... THERE.
A FRIEND OF YOURS?
NOT EXACTLY.
HELLO, BOND.
WHAT D'YOU WANT?
I...I NEED YOUR HELP.

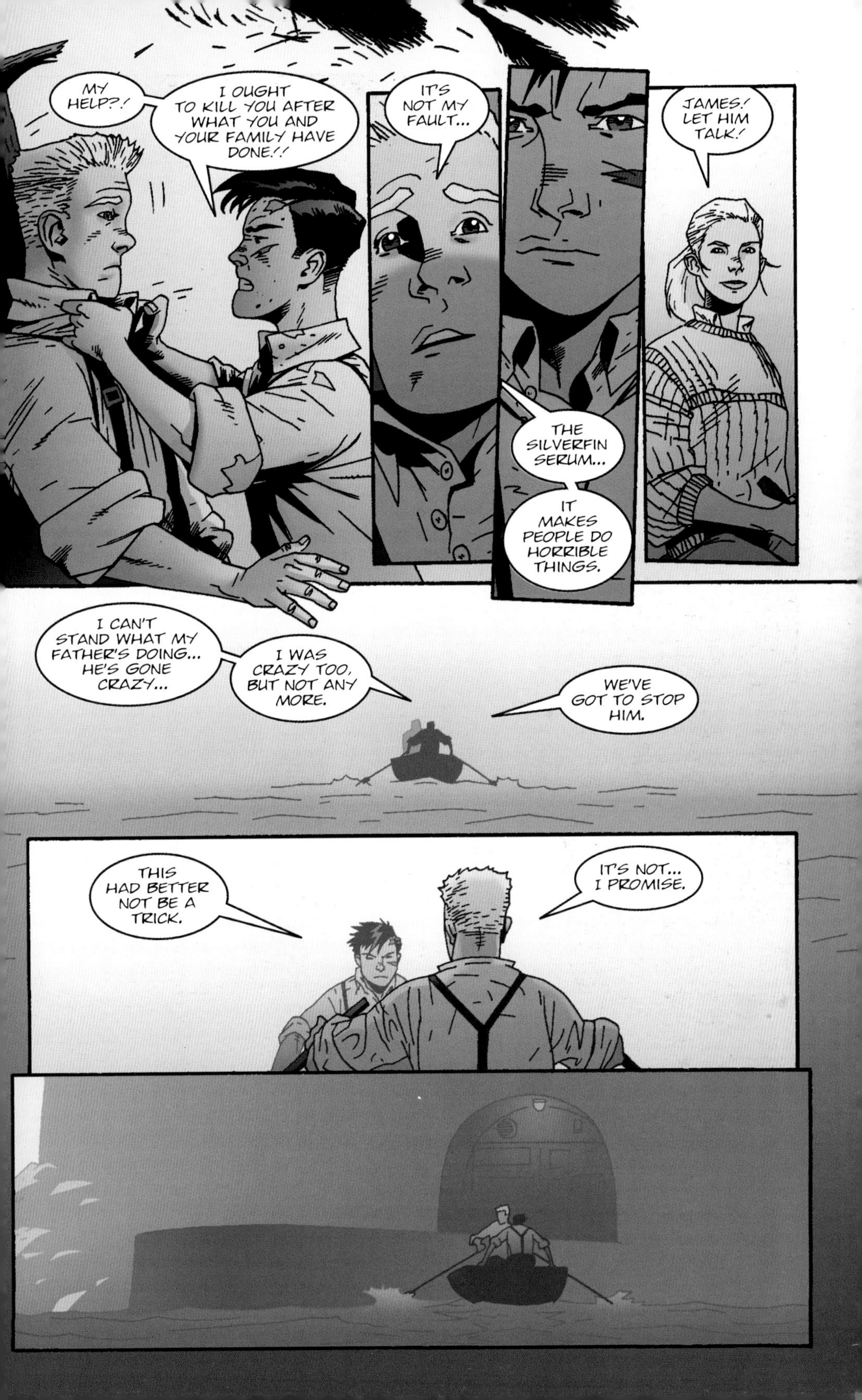
MY HELP?!
I OUGHT TO KILL YOU AFTER WHAT YOU AND YOUR FAMILY HAVE DONE!!
IT'S NOT MY FAULT...
THE SILVERFIN SERUM...
IT MAKES PEOPLE DO HORRIBLE THINGS.
JAMES! LET HIM TALK!
I CAN'T STAND WHAT MY FATHER'S DOING... HE'S GONE CRAZY...
I WAS CRAZY TOO, BUT NOT ANY MORE.
WE'VE GOT TO STOP HIM.
THIS HAD BETTER NOT BE A TRICK.
IT'S NOT... I PROMISE.

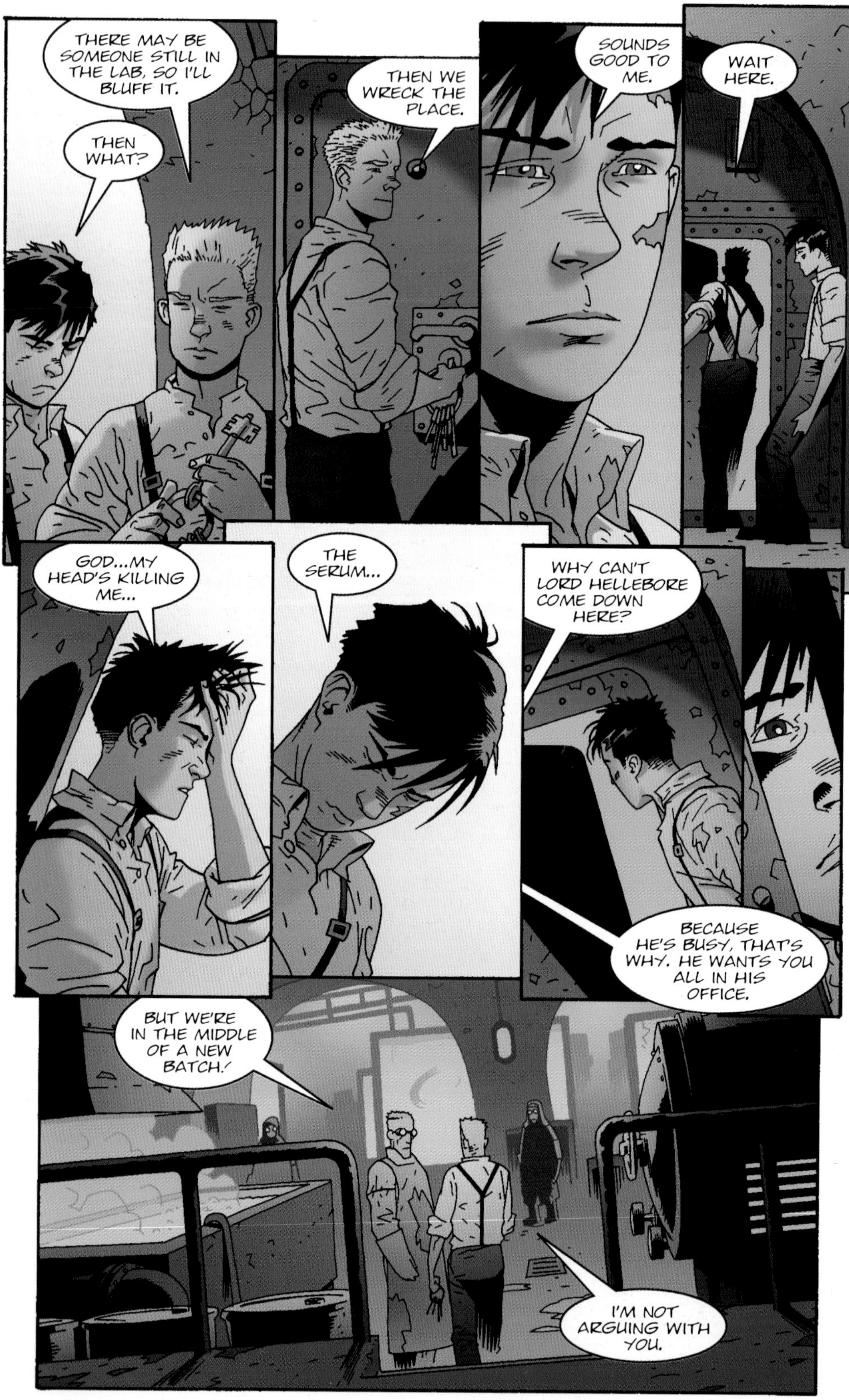
THERE MAY BE SOMEONE STILL IN THE LAB, SO I'LL BLUFF IT.
THEN WHAT?
THEN WE WRECK THE PLACE.
SOUNDS GOOD TO ME.
WAIT HERE.
GOD...MY HEAD'S KILLING ME...
THE SERUM...
WHY CAN'T LORD HELLEBORE COME DOWN HERE?
BECAUSE HE'S BUSY, THAT'S WHY. HE WANTS YOU ALL IN HIS OFFICE.
BUT WE'RE IN THE MIDDLE OF A NEW BATCH!
I'M NOT ARGUING WITH YOU.

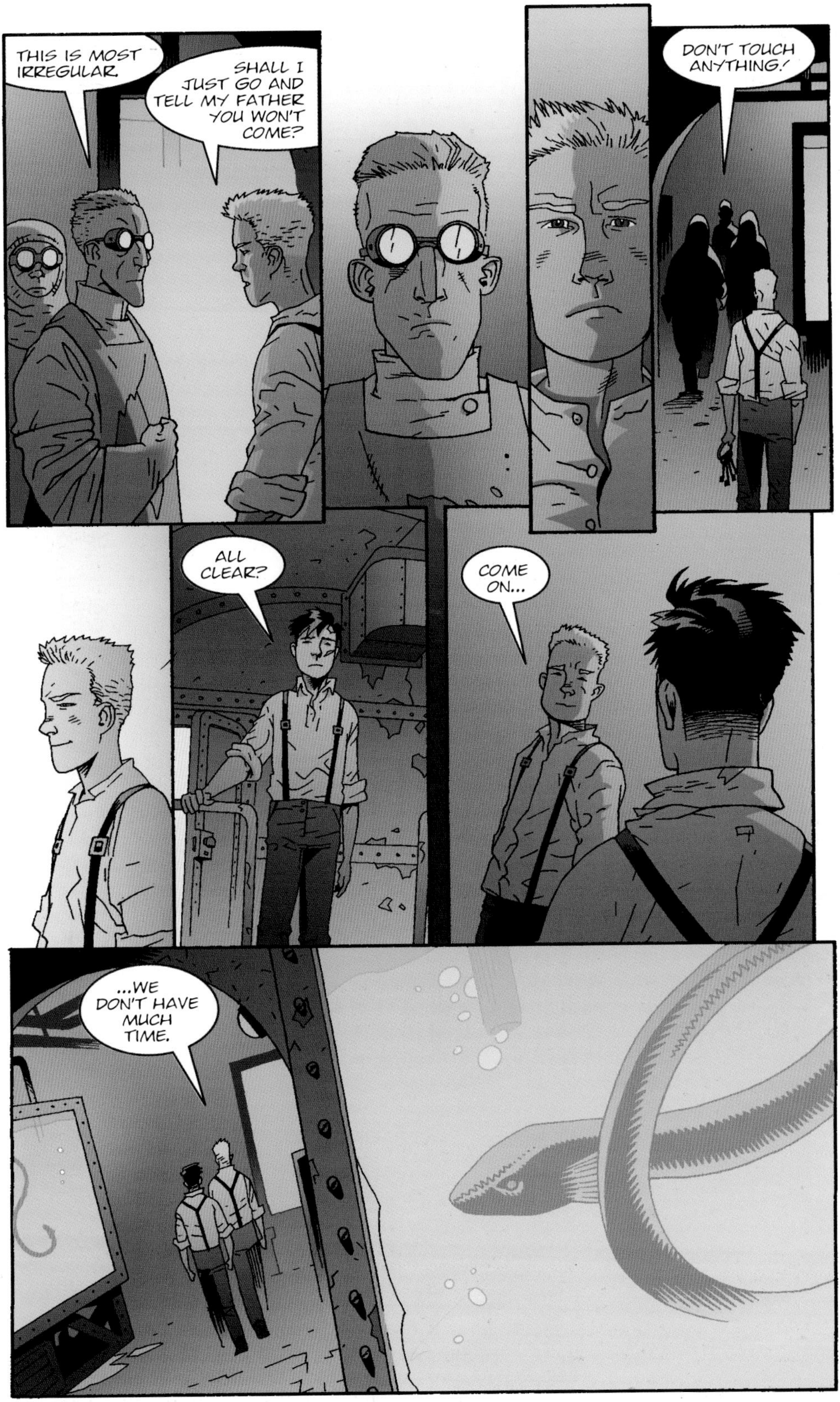

THIS IS MOST IRREGULAR.
SHALL I JUST GO AND TELL MY FATHER YOU WON'T COME?
DON'T TOUCH ANYTHING.!
ALL CLEAR?
COME ON...
...WE DON'T HAVE MUCH TIME.

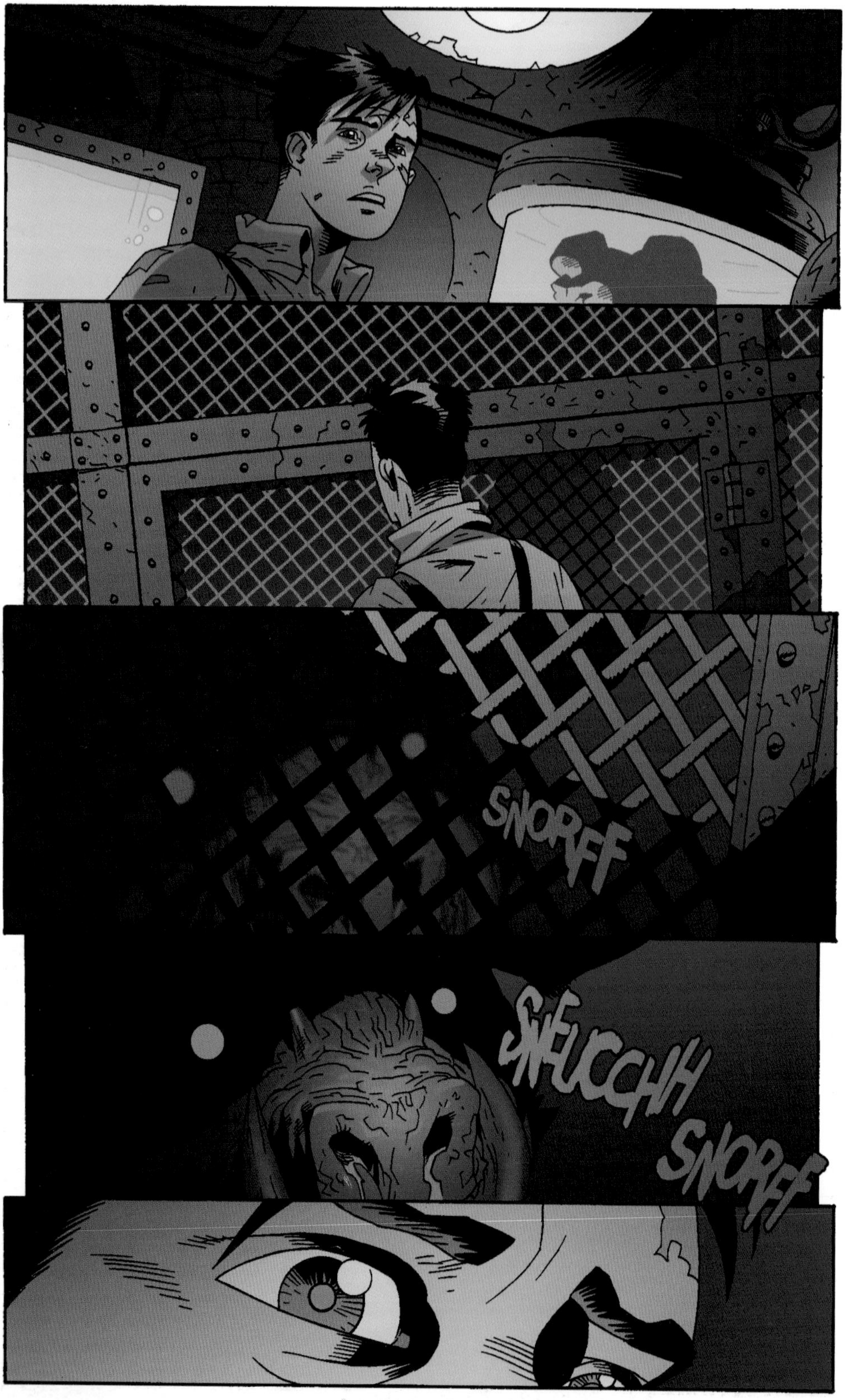
SNORFF
SNEUCCHH
SNORFF

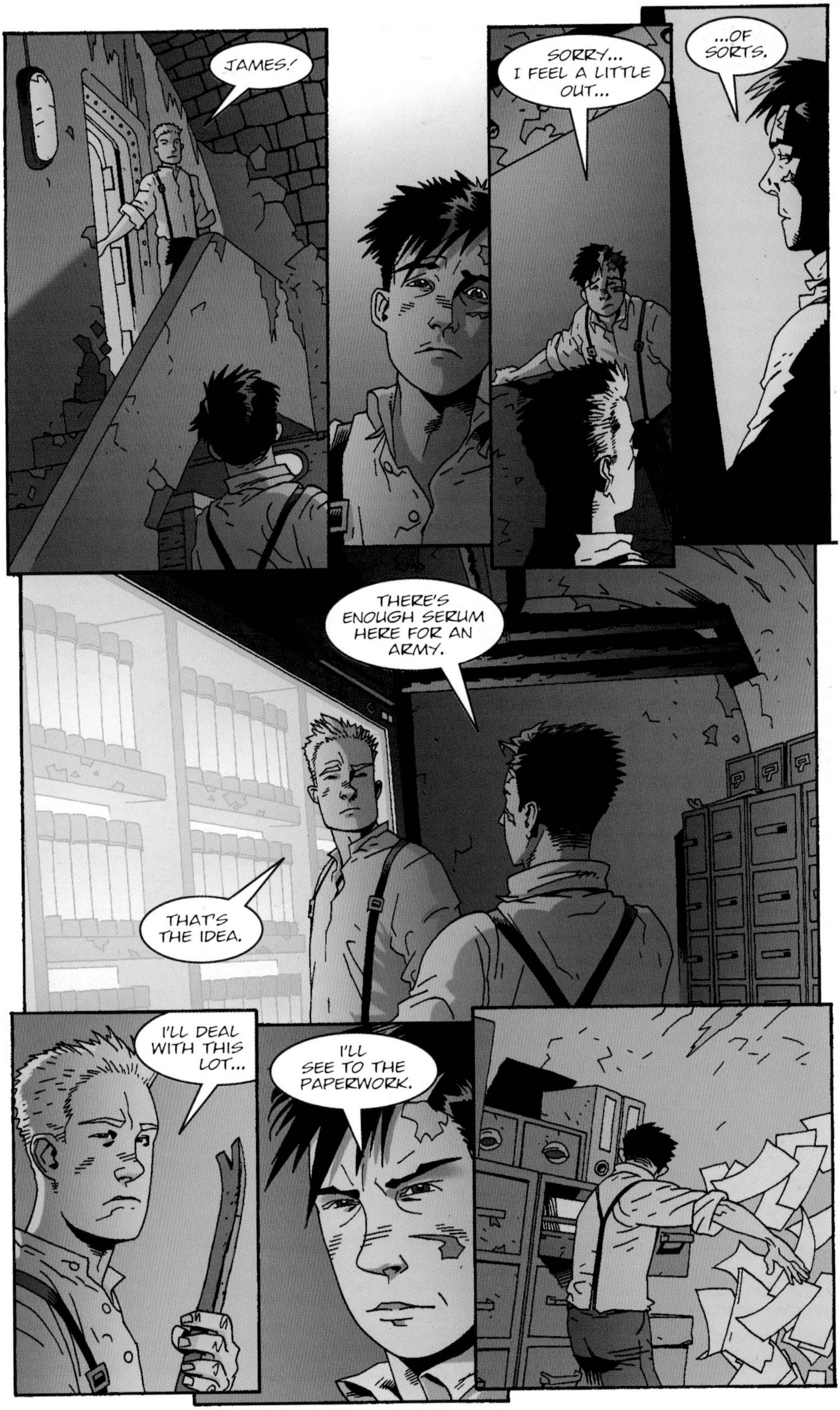
JAMES!
SORRY... I FEEL A LITTLE OUT...
...OF SORTS.
THERE'S ENOUGH SERUM HERE FOR AN ARMY.
THAT'S THE IDEA.
I'LL DEAL WITH THIS LOT...
I'LL SEE TO THE PAPERWORK.

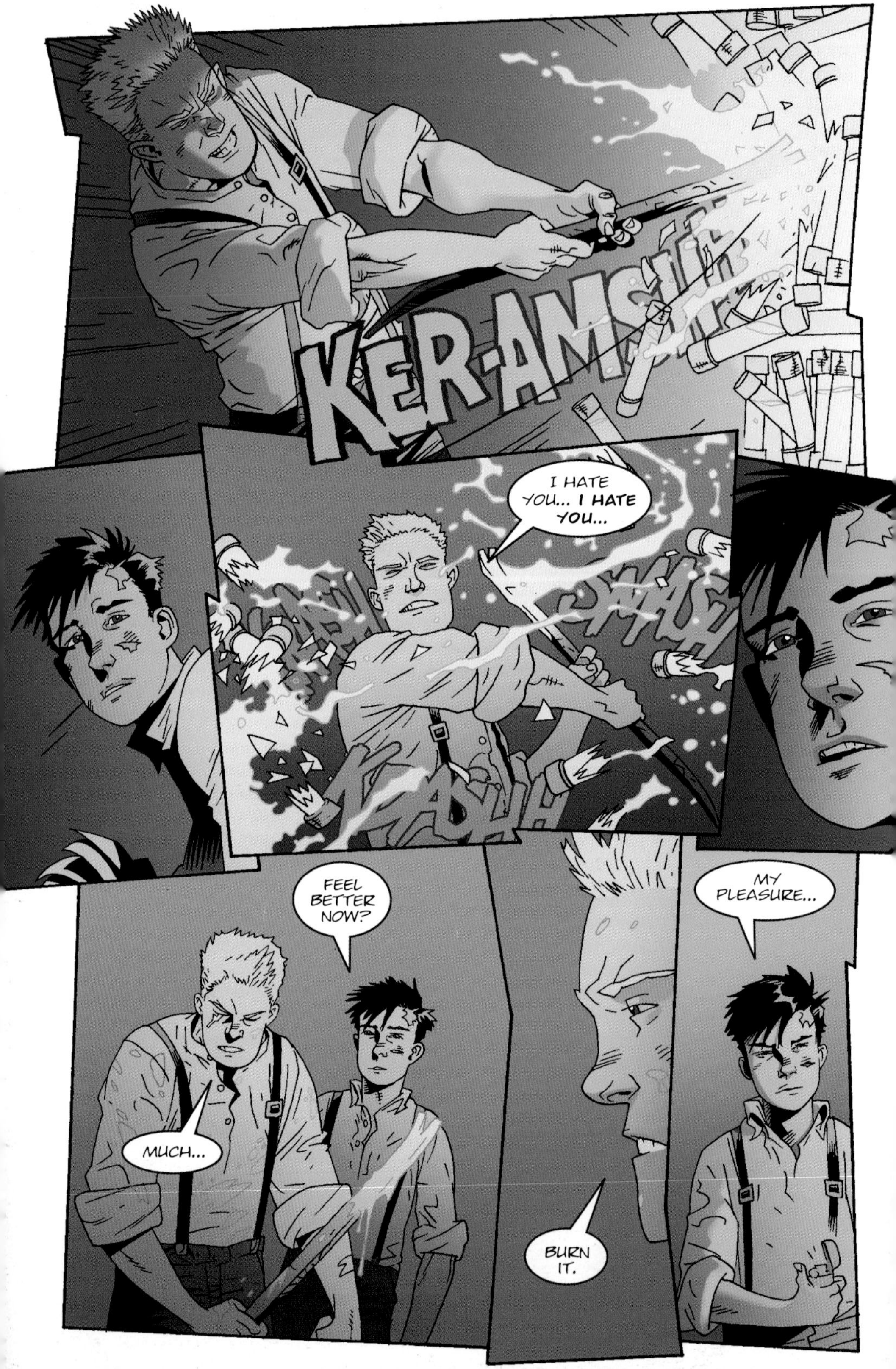
KER-AMSH
I HATE YOU... I HATE YOU...
FEEL BETTER NOW?
MUCH...
BURN IT.
MY PLEASURE...

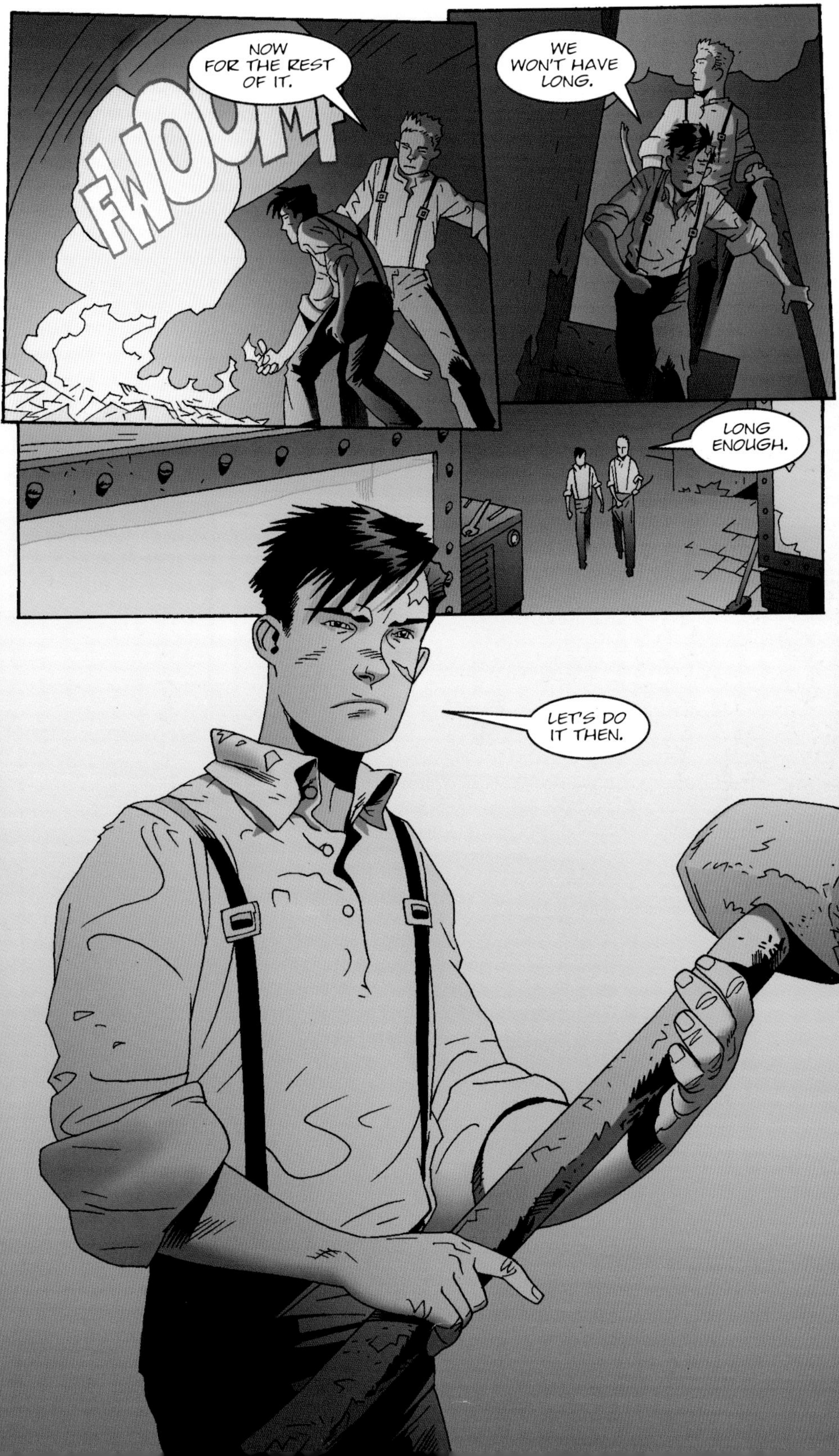
FWOOMP
NOW FOR THE REST OF IT.
WE WON'T HAVE LONG.
LONG ENOUGH.
LET'S DO IT THEN.

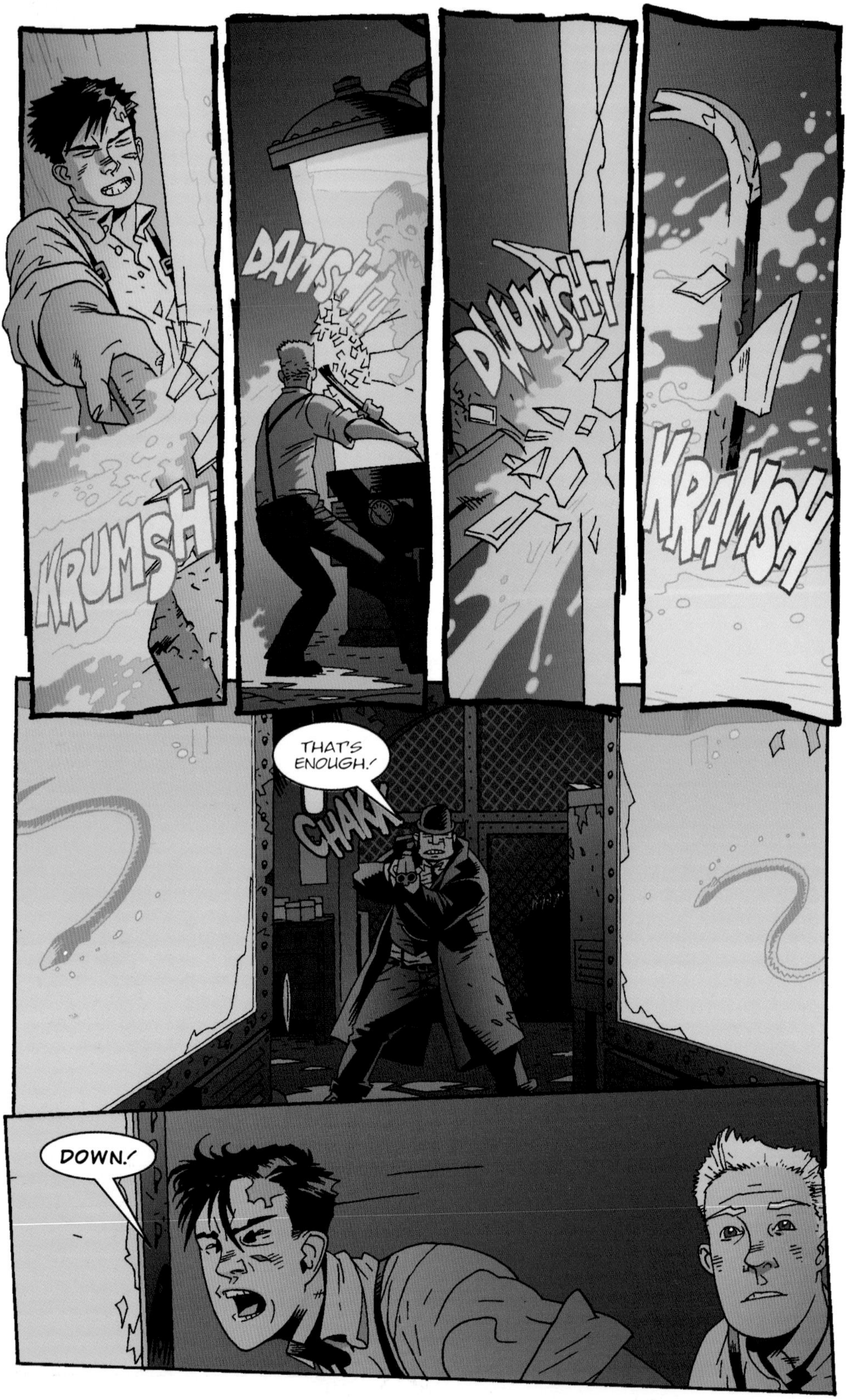
KRUMSH
DAMSHH
DWUMSHT
KRAMSH
THAT'S ENOUGH.!
CHAK
DOWN.!

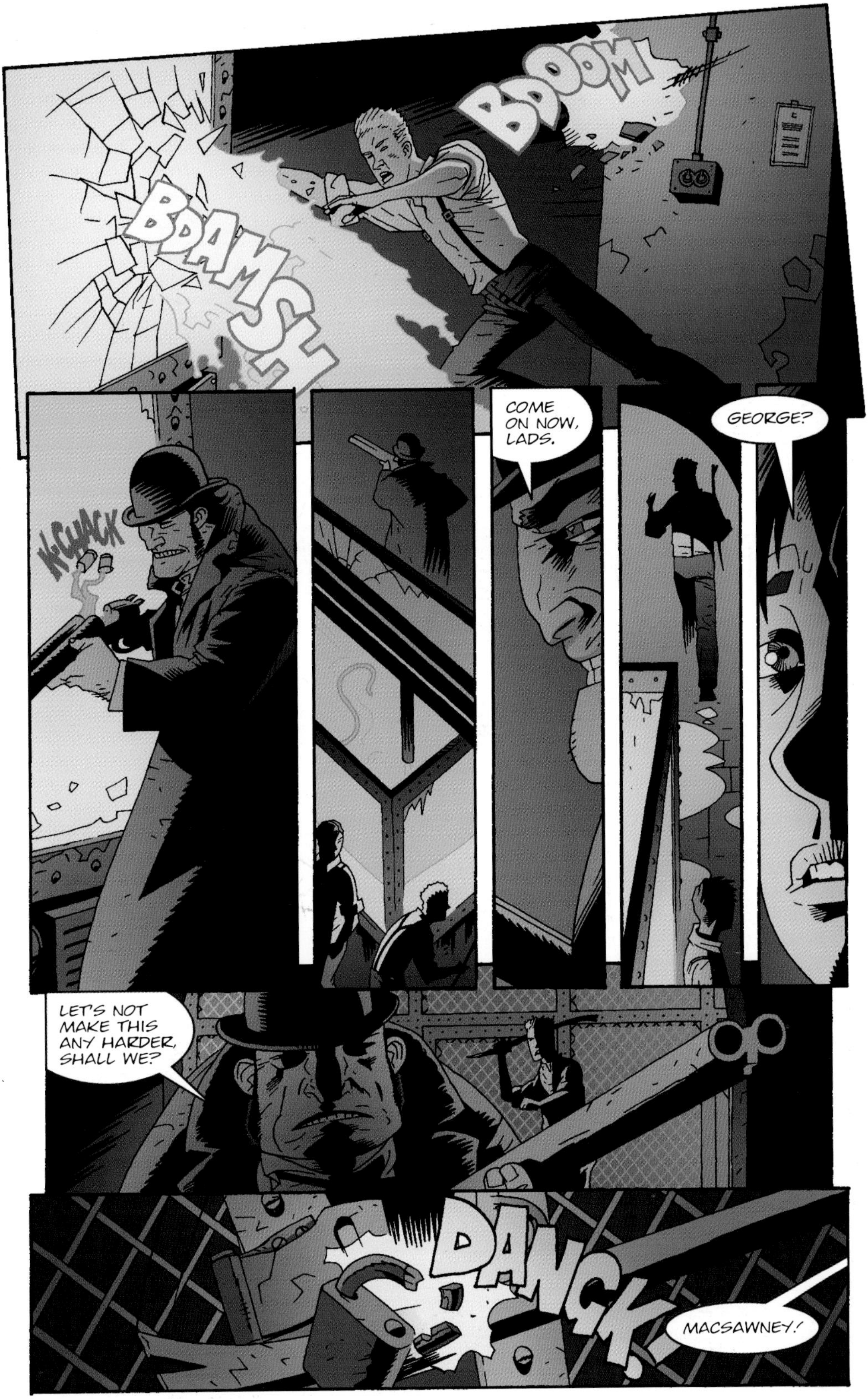
BOOM!
BDAMSH
K-CHACK
COME ON NOW, LADS.
GEORGE?
LET'S NOT MAKE THIS ANY HARDER, SHALL WE?
DANCK!
MACSAWNEY!

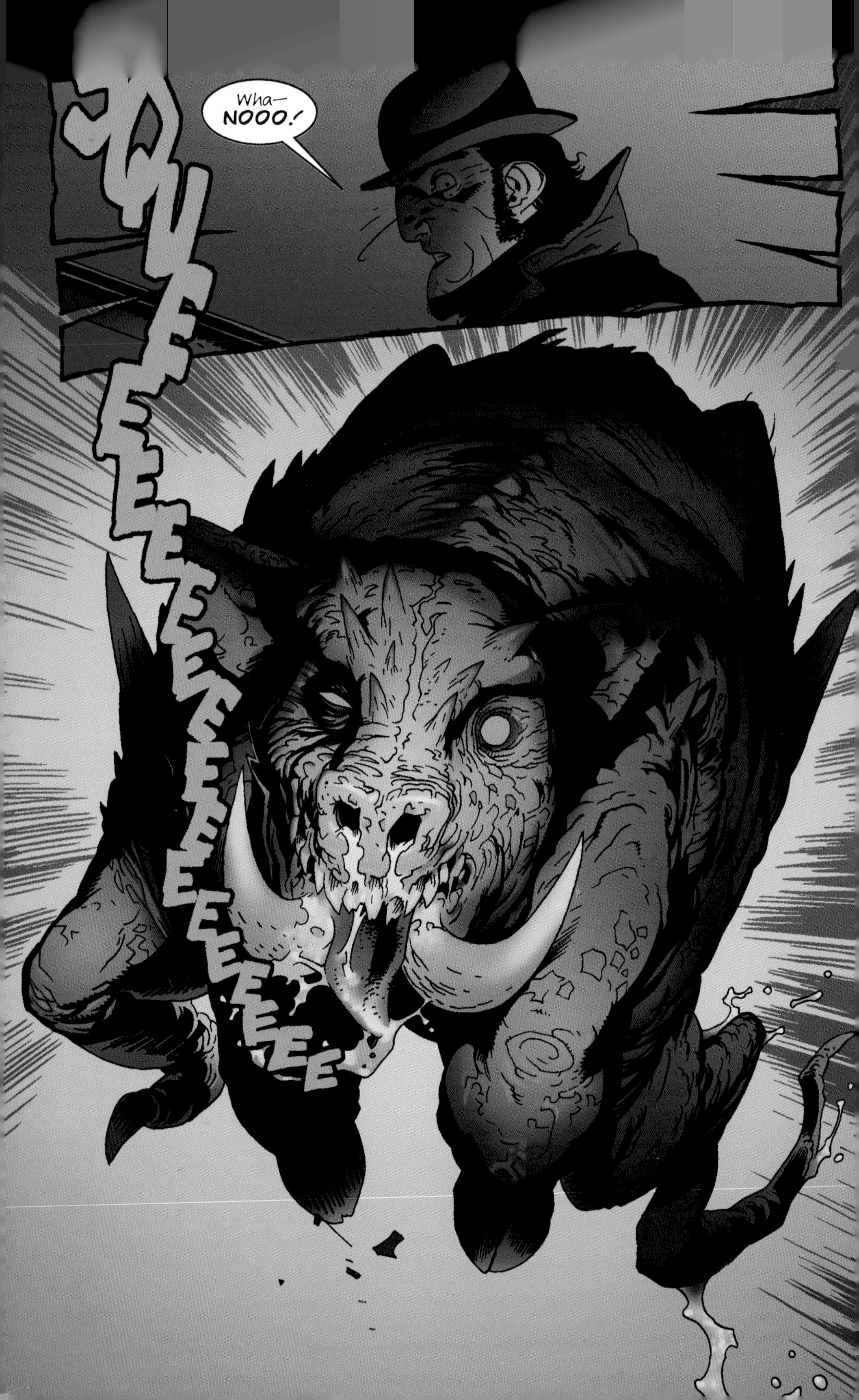
Wha—
NOOO!
SQUEEEEEEEEEEEEEEEE

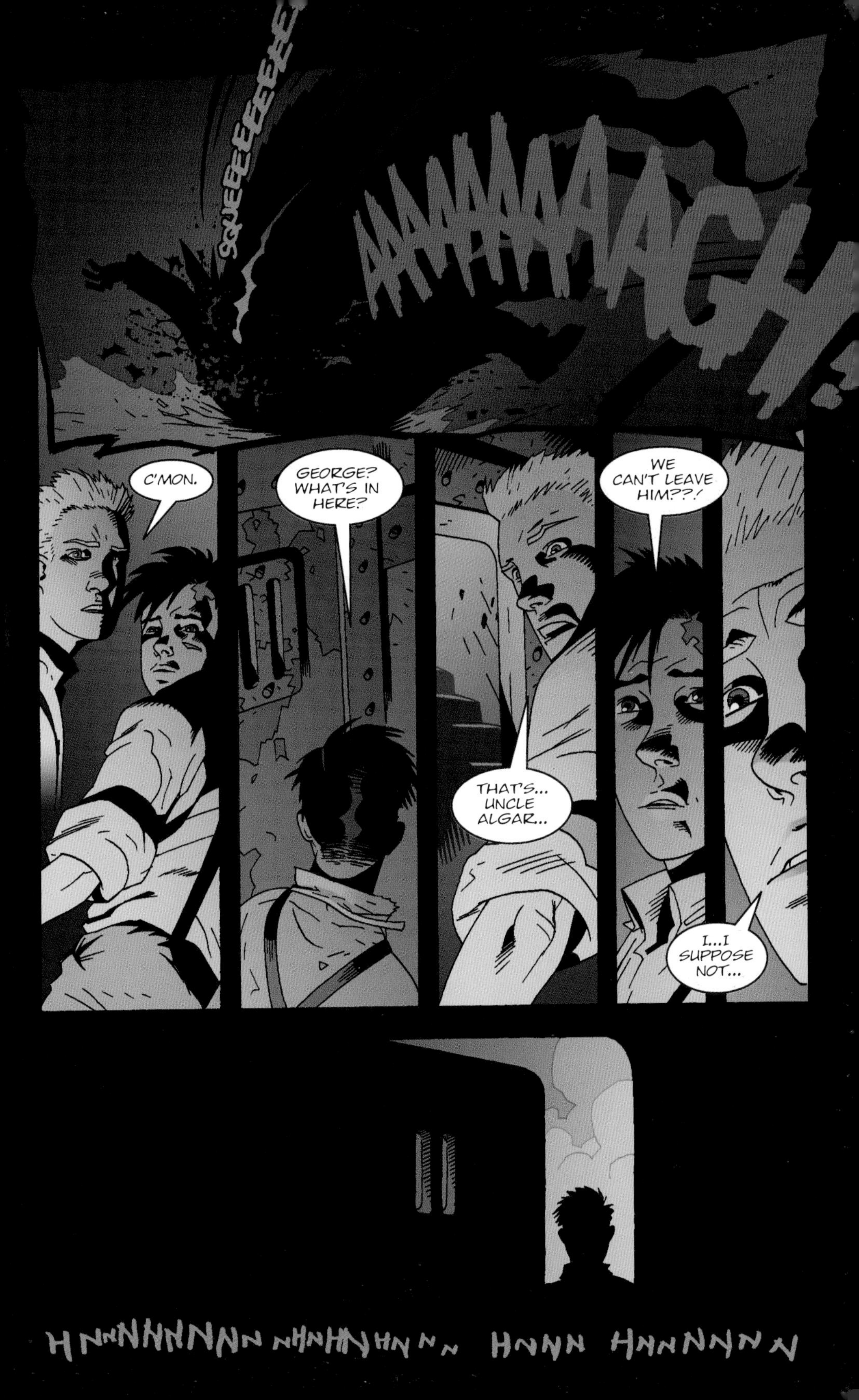
SQUEEEEEEEEE
AAAAAAAAAGH!
C'MON.
GEORGE? WHAT'S IN HERE?
THAT'S... UNCLE ALGAR...
WE CAN'T LEAVE HIM??!
I...I SUPPOSE NOT...
HNNNNNNNN NHNHNHN N N HNNN HNNNNNN

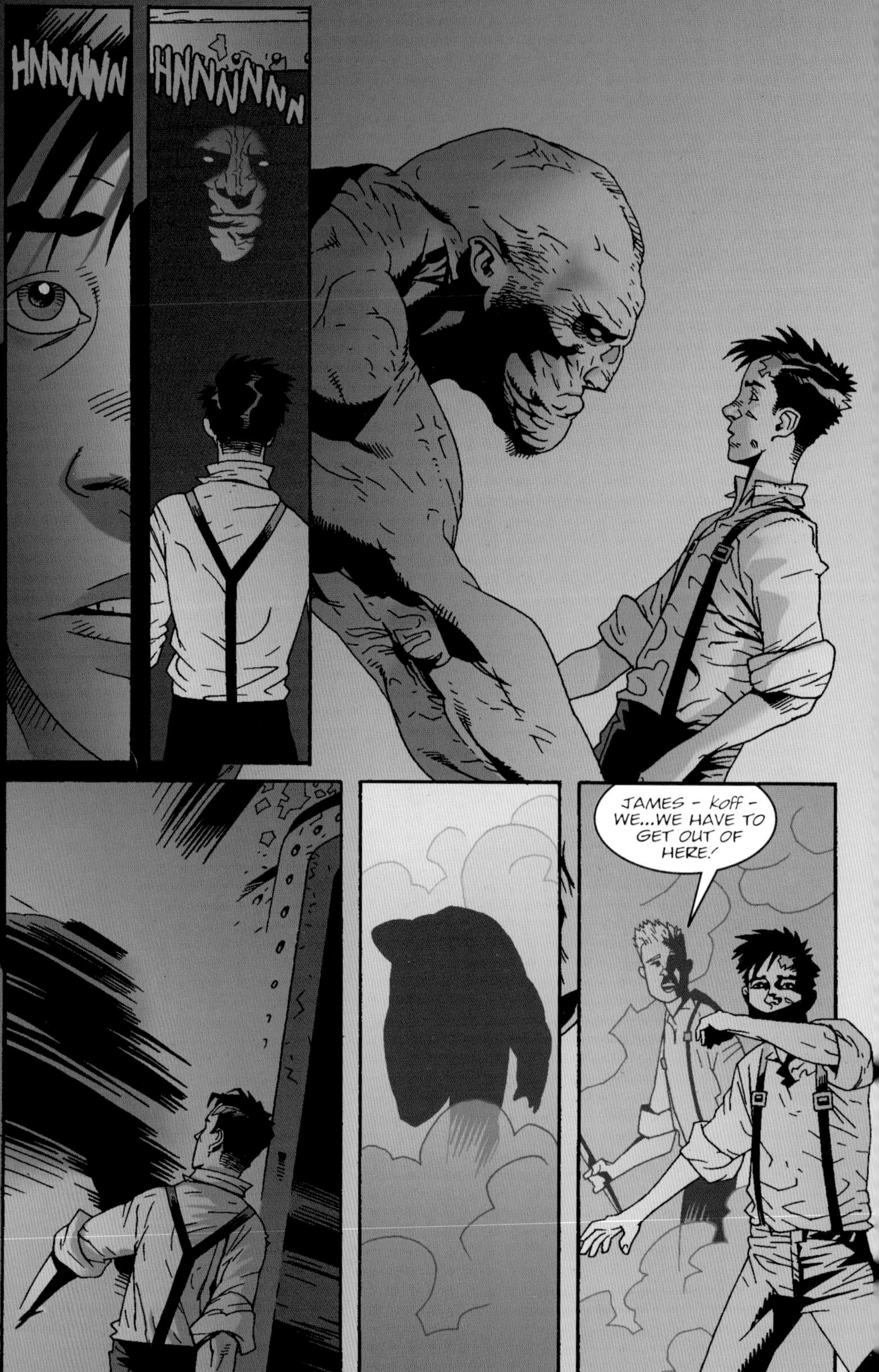
HNNAWN
HNNNNNN
JAMES - koff - WE...WE HAVE TO GET OUT OF HERE!

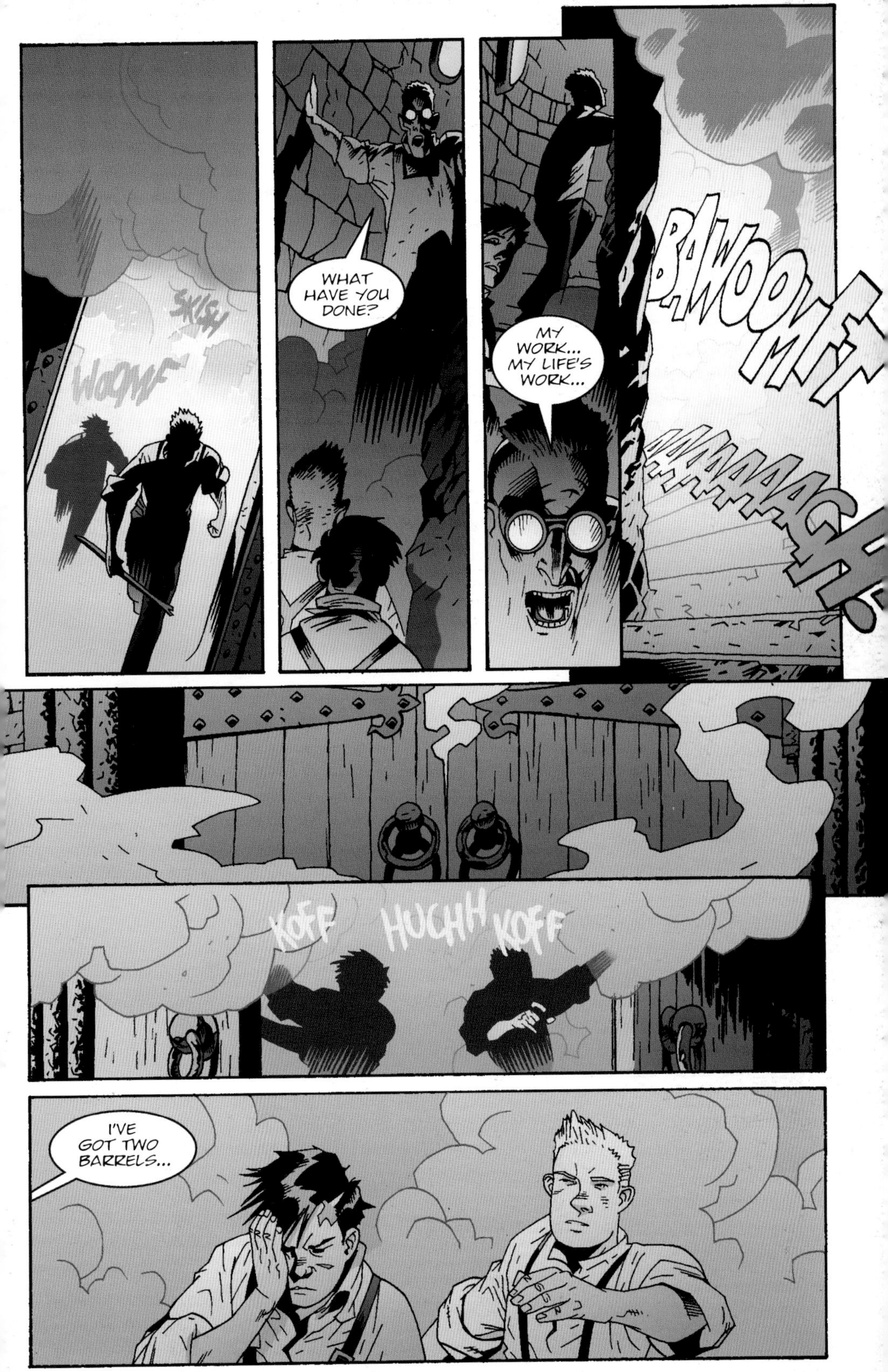
SKISH
WOOMF
WHAT HAVE YOU DONE?
MY WORK... MY LIFE'S WORK...
BAWOOMFT
NAAAAAAGH!
KOFF
HUCHH
KOFF
I'VE GOT TWO BARRELS...

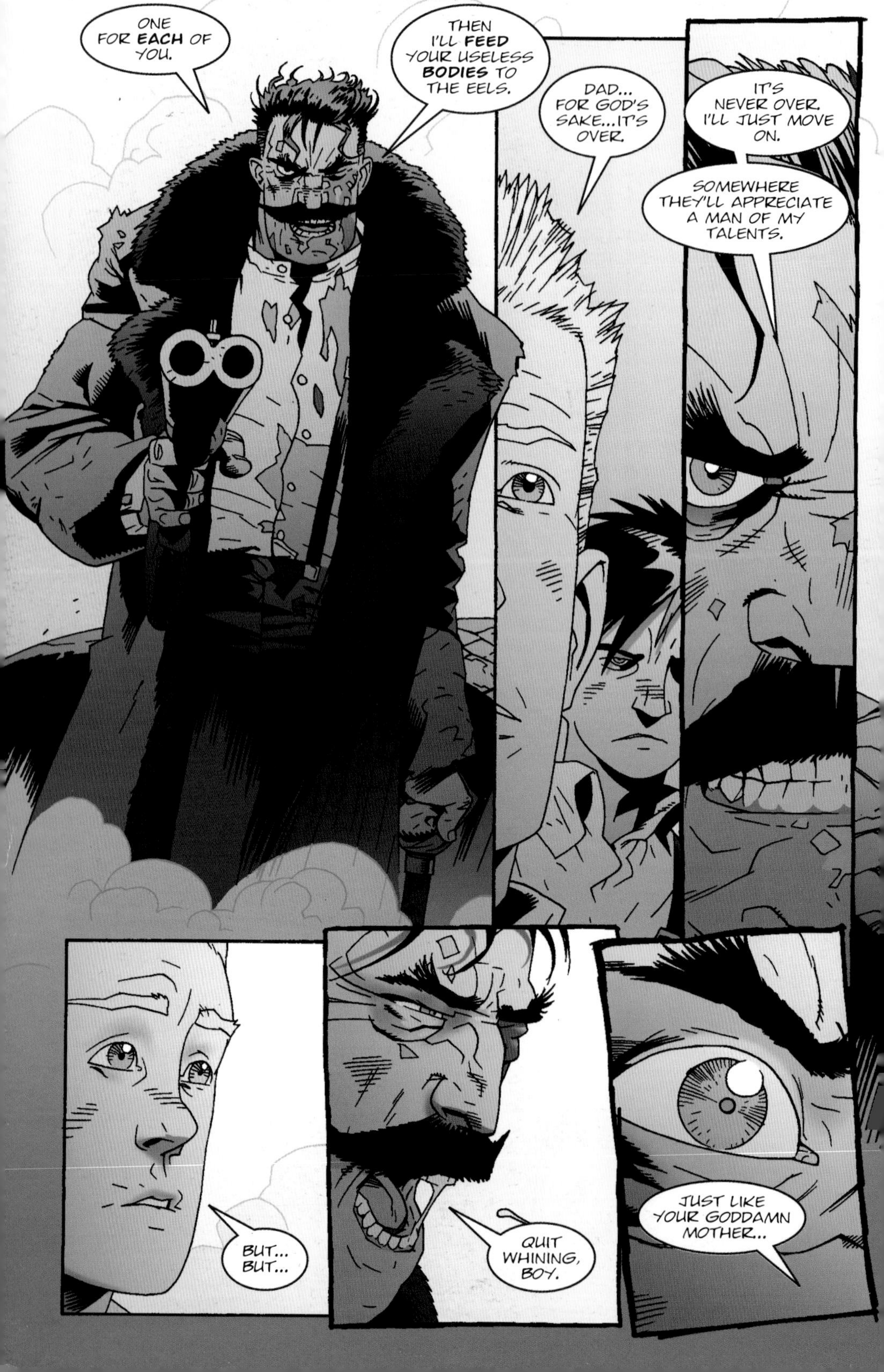
ONE FOR EACH OF YOU.
THEN I'LL FEED YOUR USELESS BODIES TO THE EELS.
DAD... FOR GOD'S SAKE...IT'S OVER.
IT'S NEVER OVER. I'LL JUST MOVE ON.
SOMEWHERE THEY'LL APPRECIATE A MAN OF MY TALENTS.
BUT... BUT...
QUIT WHINING, BOY.
JUST LIKE YOUR GODDAMN MOTHER...

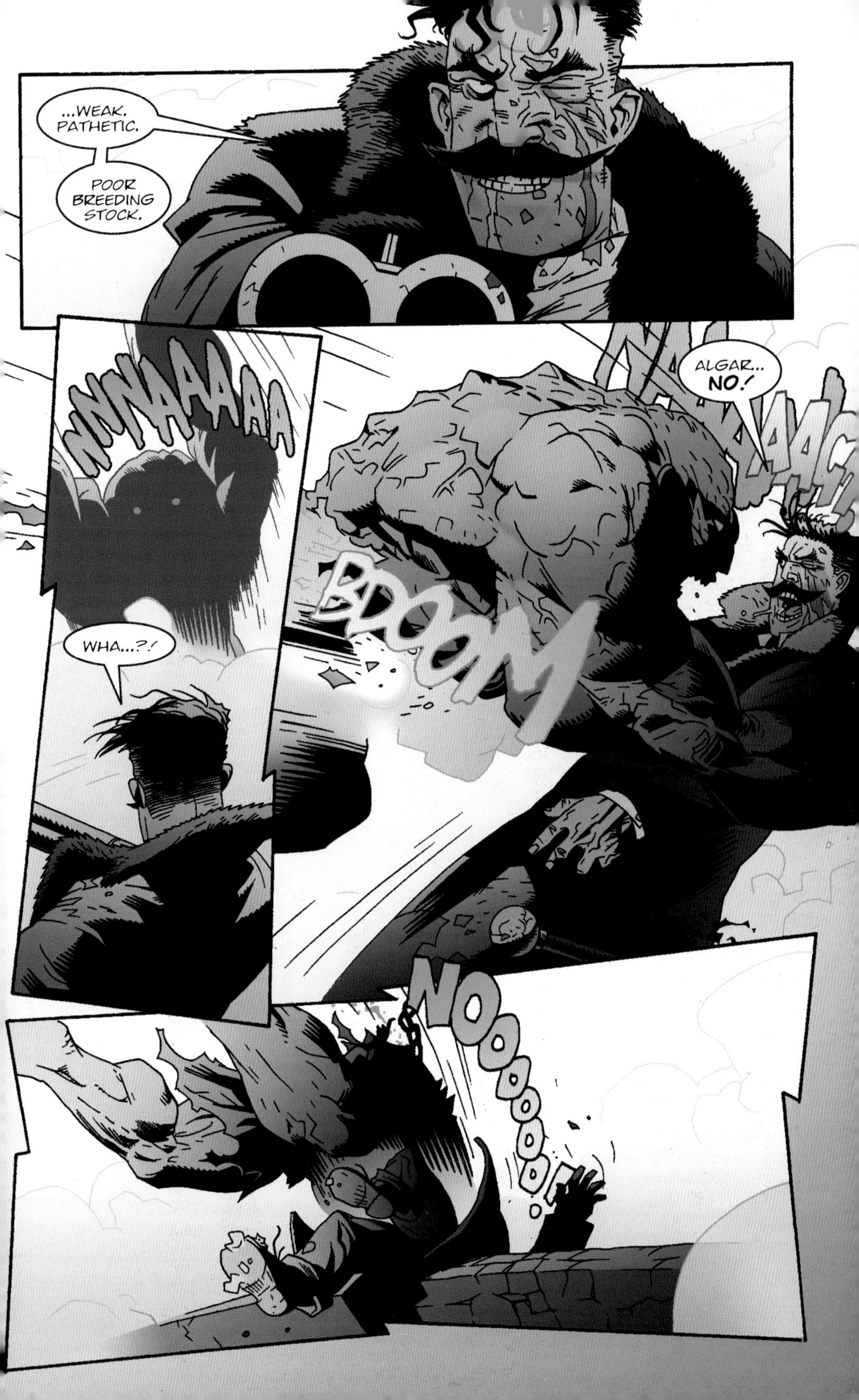
...WEAK. PATHETIC.
POOR BREEDING STOCK.
NNNAAAAAA
WHA...?!
ALGAR... NO!
BOOOM
NOOOOOOO!

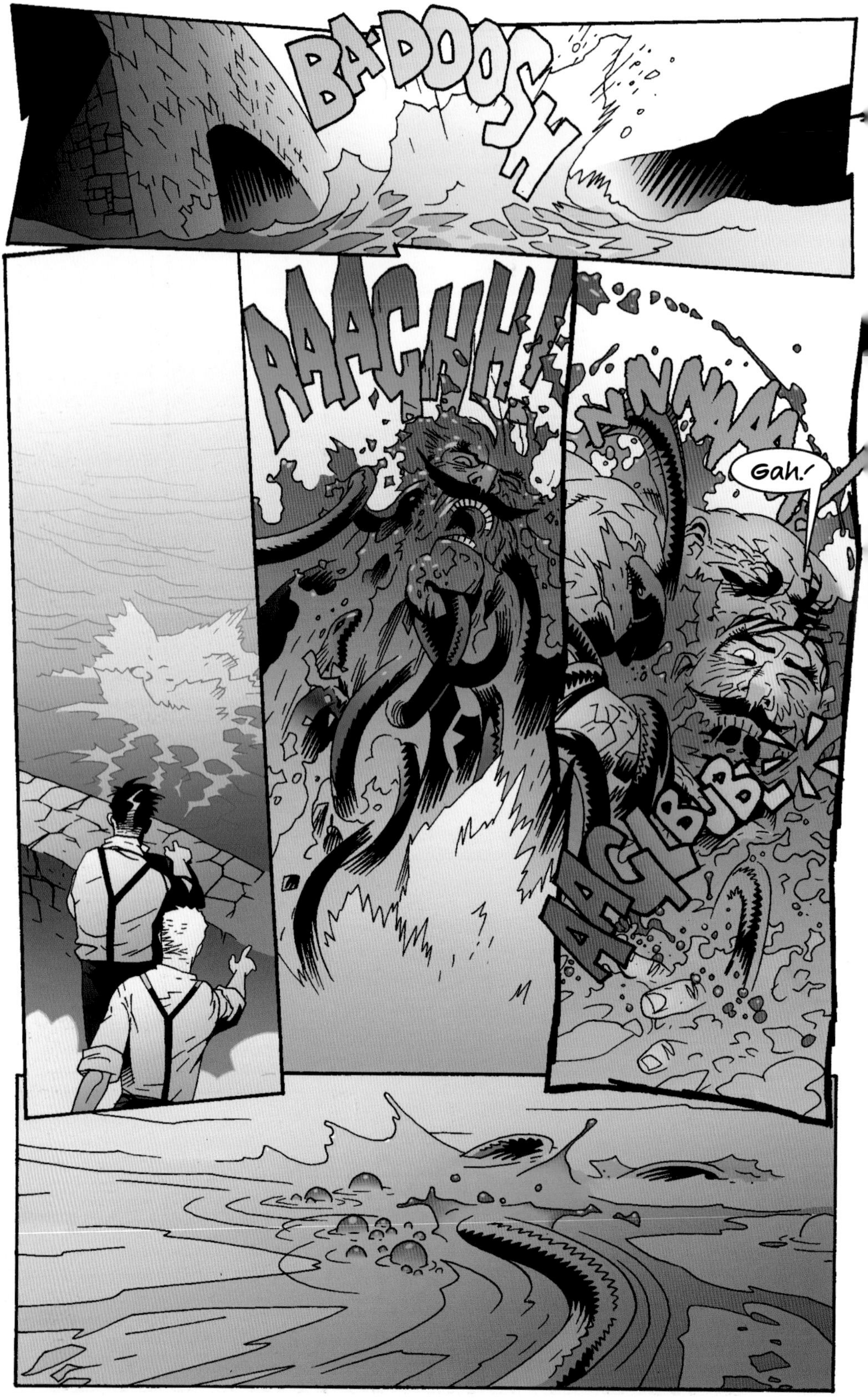
BA-DOOSH
AAAGHH!
NNNAAA
Gah!
AAGLBUB

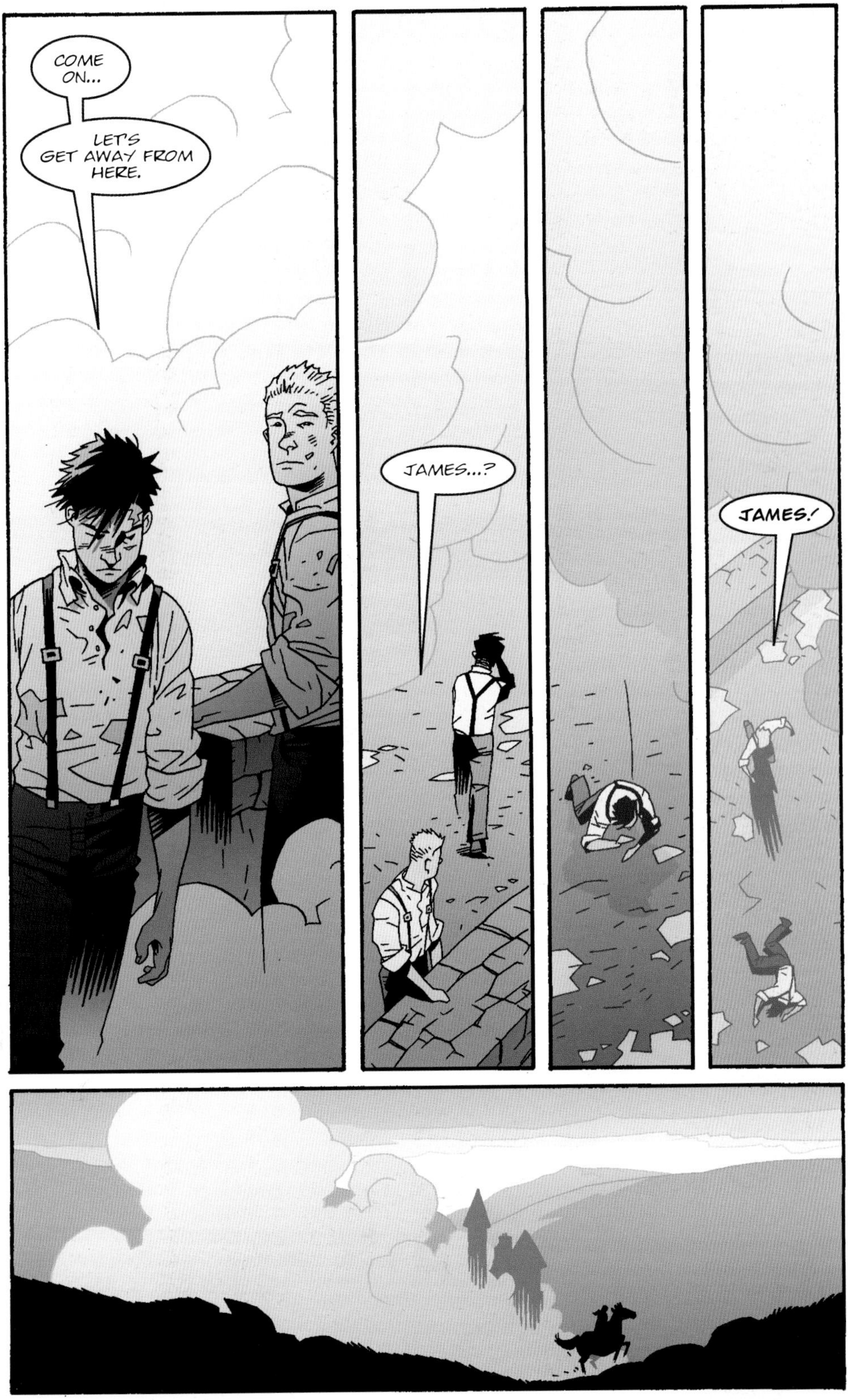
COME ON...
LET'S GET AWAY FROM HERE.
JAMES...?
JAMES!

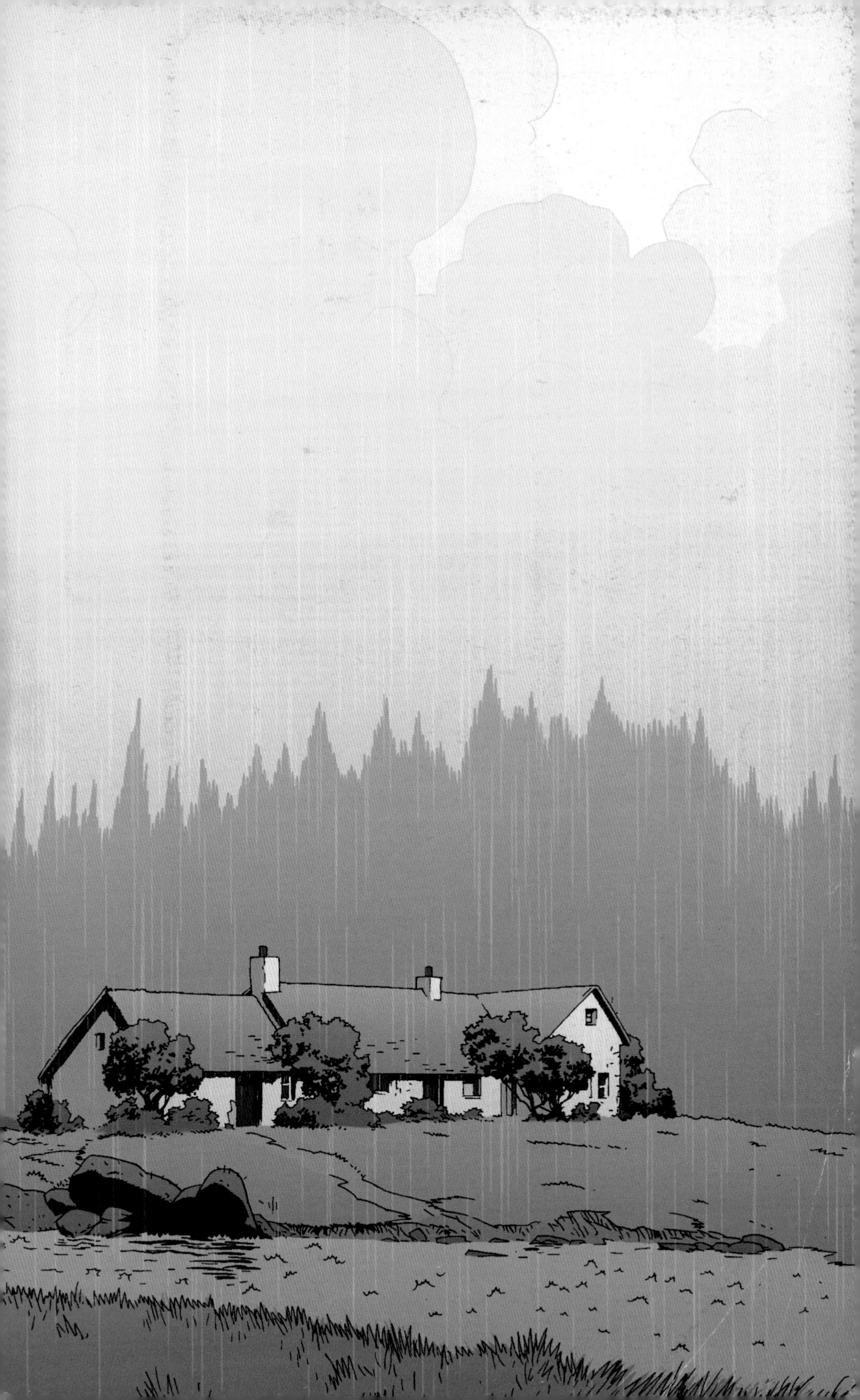

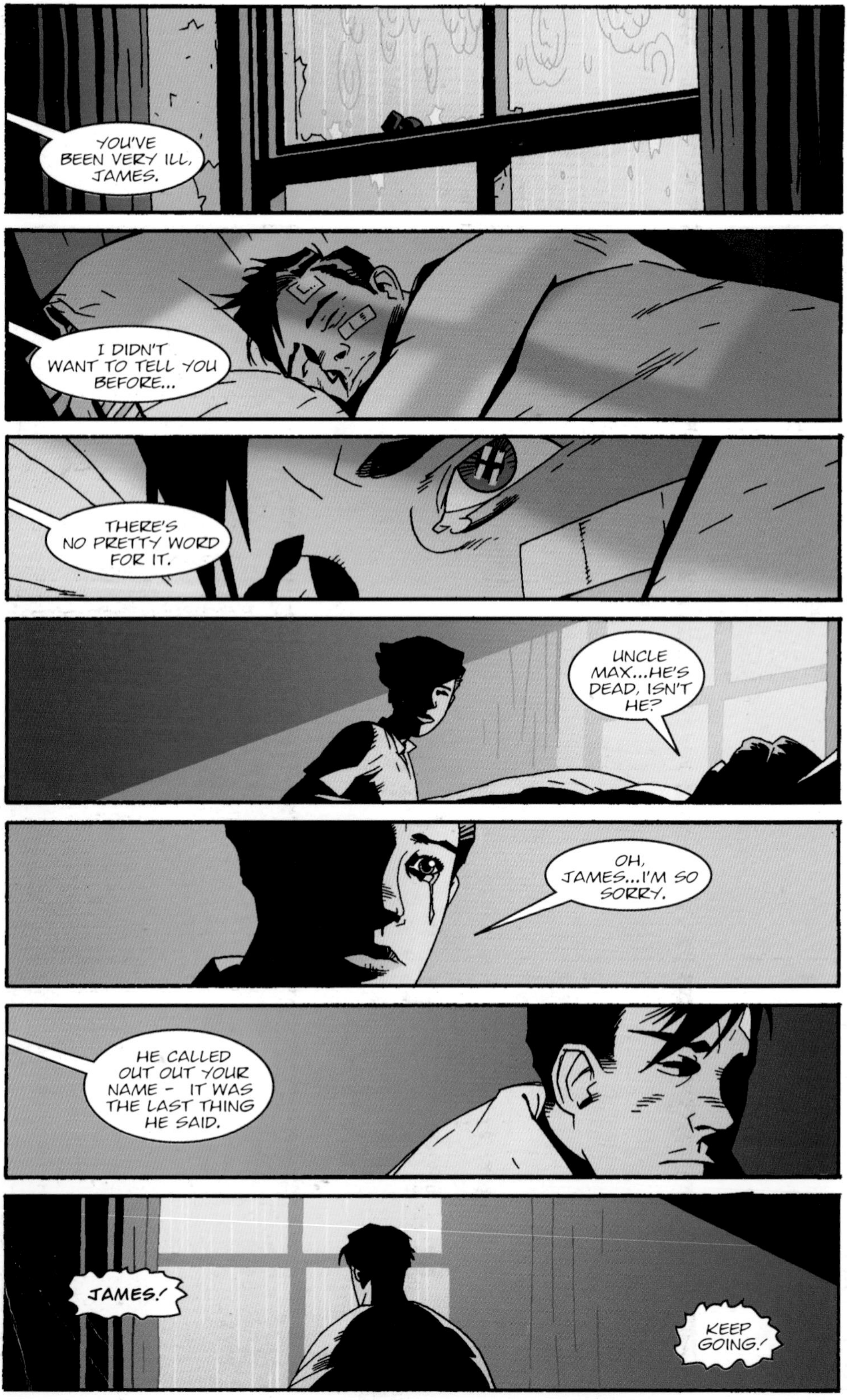
YOU'VE BEEN VERY ILL, JAMES.
I DIDN'T WANT TO TELL YOU BEFORE...
THERE'S NO PRETTY WORD FOR IT.
UNCLE MAX...HE'S DEAD, ISN'T HE?
OH, JAMES...I'M SO SORRY.
HE CALLED OUT OUT YOUR NAME - IT WAS THE LAST THING HE SAID.
JAMES!
KEEP GOING!

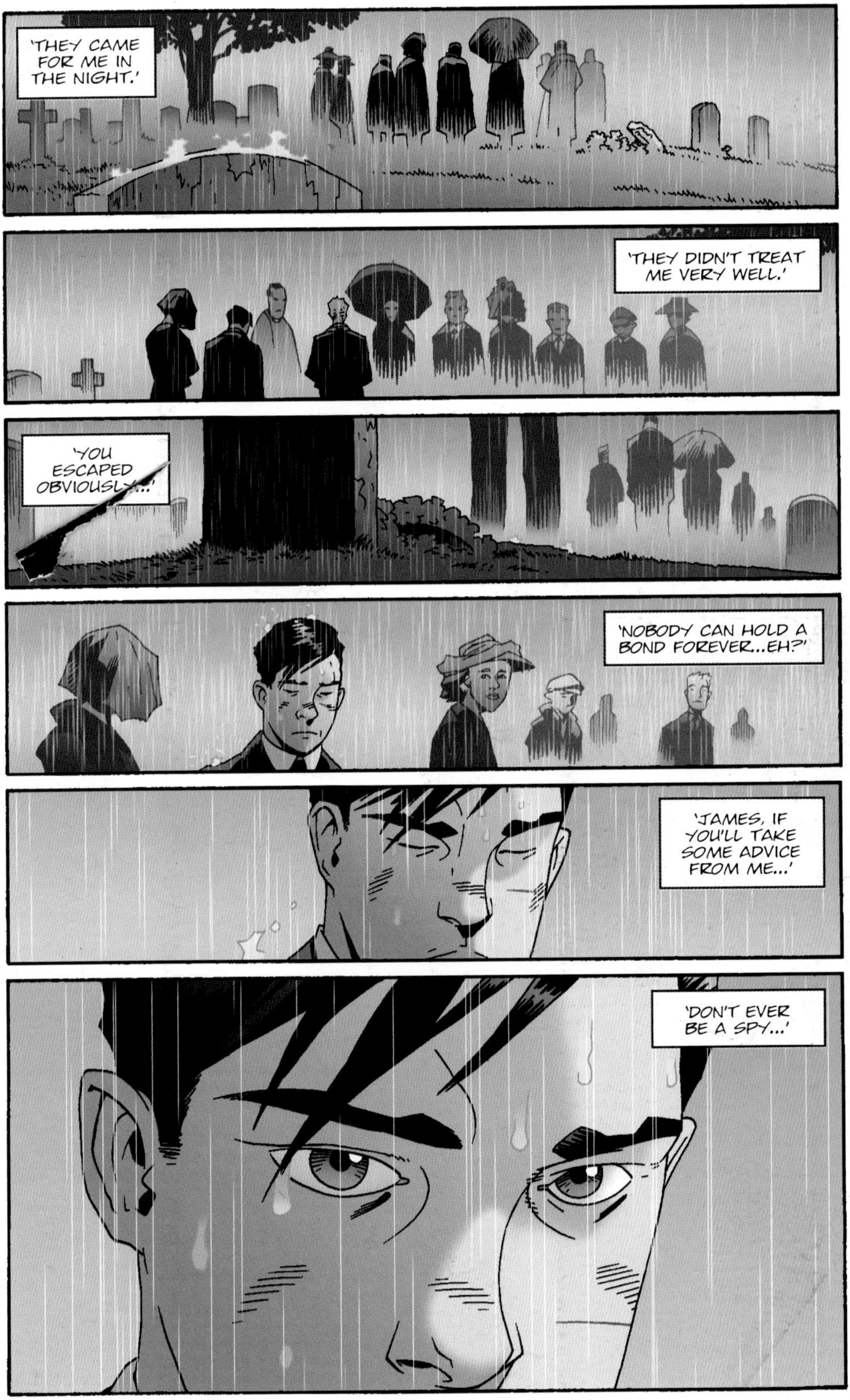
'THEY CAME FOR ME IN THE NIGHT.'
'THEY DIDN'T TREAT ME VERY WELL.'
'YOU ESCAPED OBVIOUSLY...'
'NOBODY CAN HOLD A BOND FOREVER...EH?'
'JAMES, IF YOU'LL TAKE SOME ADVICE FROM ME...'
'DON'T EVER BE A SPY...'

CHARLIE HIGSON is a well-known writer of screenplays and novels, as well as a performer and co-creator of *The Fast Show*.

KEV WALKER has been illustrating Young Bond since its debut in 2005. Since he began in 1988 he has worked for *2000 AD*, Games Workshop, DC Comics, Marvel Comics, *Dark Horse* and *Wizards of the Coast*.

PUFFIN BOOKS

Published by the Penguin Group: London, New York, Australia, Canada, India, Ireland, New Zealand and South Africa

Penguin Books Ltd, Registered Offices: 80 Strand, London WC2R 0RL, England

puffinbooks.com

First published 2008

1 3 5 7 9 10 8 6 4 2

Copyright © Ian Fleming Publications Ltd, 2008

Based on the original novel by Charlie Higson

Adapted by Kev Walker

Scripted by Charlie Higson and Kev Walker

Lettering by Annie Parkhouse

Printed in Italy by Graphicom, srl

ISBN: 978—0—141—32253—7